Loretta always wanted to be a writer. As a kid she filled pages of exercise books with stories to amuse her friends. Her father, who never wasted his time on fiction, didn't see much worth in this pastime and pushed her to pursue a 'sensible' career. She graduated from the University of Western Australia as a structural engineer and took her first job with a major West Australian engineering company.

For her bestselling novels *The Girl in Steel-Capped Boots*, *The Girl in the Hard Hat* and *The Girl in the Yellow Vest*, Loretta Hill drew upon her own outback engineering experiences of larrikins, red dust and steel-capped boots.

However, she is also the author of *The Maxwell Sisters* and *The Grass is Greener*, stories exploring family, sisters and best friends. Her ebook novellas are *Operation Valentine* and *One Little White Lie*, which was a number one bestseller on iTunes.

Loretta lives in Perth with her husband and four children.

Also by Loretta Hill

The Girl in Steel-Capped Boots
The Girl in the Hard Hat
The Girl in the Yellow Vest
The Maxwell Sisters
The Grass is Greener
One Little White Lie (ebook novella)
Operation Valentine (ebook novella)

LORETTA HILL

the Secret Vineyard

BANTAM

SYDNEY AUCKLAND TORONTO NEW YORK LONDON

A Bantam book
Published by Penguin Random House Australia Pty Ltd
Level 3, 100 Pacific Highway, North Sydney NSW 2060
www.penguin.com.au

Penguin
Random House
Australia

First published by Bantam in 2018

A catalogue record for this
book is available from the
National Library of Australia

ISBN 978 0 14378 143 1

Cover photography © Monica Lazar/Arcangel
Cover design by Louisa Maggio © Penguin Random House Australia Pty Ltd
Internal design and typesetting by Midland Typesetters, Australia
Printed in Australia by Griffin Press, an accredited ISO AS/NZS 14001:2004
Environmental Management System printer

Penguin Random House Australia uses papers that are natural, renewable
and recyclable products and made from wood grown in sustainable forests.
The logging and manufacturing processes are expected to conform to the
environmental regulations of the country of origin.

For my beautiful, courageous and cheeky scallywags,
Luke, James, Beth and Michael.
Love you to infinity.

Chapter 1

It's just another evening of horrors.

My older boys, Ryan and Alfie, are fighting over a plastic Ninja Turtle sword, screaming at the top of their lungs. I have burned our dinner, having been distracted by the 'you need to do your homework' argument. As I am extracting the black lasagne from the oven, my three-year-old, Charlie, pulls the flour I have been using for the béchamel sauce onto the floor. The paper packet explodes with a bang. A puff of white mist fills the room. As I swat the air, inhaling a lungful of flour, Alfie, who has been running in socked feet away from Ryan, slips in the white powder. I've always been secretly proud of my five-year-old's feline reflexes and quick thinking. This time, however, I am less than impressed when he grabs the kitchen blinds to break his fall. They certainly slow him down as they tear straight off the railing.

In the aftermath of this unspeakable disaster, there is a small, two-second silence, in which none of us can do anything but gape. Then Ryan, my eldest, aged seven, tentatively raises his chin.

'Are we in trouble?'

Now, I don't know what a good mother would do at this point but I can tell you what I did.

I left.

It was kind of the last straw in a very, *very* shit day.

Hands slightly shaking, I take off my oven mitts, walk out of the kitchen, go straight to my bedroom and shut the door. It's actually quite satisfying, slamming the door on your kids like that. I mean, they do it to me all the time. Why shouldn't I get a turn every now and then?

The shock of my abandonment doesn't take long to wear off.

'Mum!' yells Ryan. 'Since Alfie's pulled the blinds down, can I have the sword now?'

And then Alfie's protest. 'Noooo!!! *You can't!*'

'Mum! Muuuuummmmm!!!!'

I lean back against the door and shut my eyes, willing myself to just disappear. Where are those ruby slippers when you need them? Or even the *Starship Enterprise*. Beam me up, Scotty!

Ryan starts rattling the knob. 'MUUUMMMM! Can you hear me? What's the matter with you?' I slide to the floor. He tries to push the door open and I push back.

I don't know why I'm doing it. It's completely irrational. But this is the best I can do right now. The usual unanswerable questions go round and round in my head like a song on repeat.

Why are my children so naughty?

Do other mothers have days like this?

I think about those other mothers. I often see them conversing in the car park before school, their children already in the classroom while I beg Alfie to get out of the car.

What's their secret?

Seriously, somebody tell me the bloody secret. I can handle it. I have a university degree in Commerce. Every day, other adults trust me to handle their finances.

So what am I missing?

Apart from my bastard of an ex-husband.

Why do I feel like I'm falling through life, one bump at a time?

'Mum,' Ryan bangs his fist on the door again, springboarding me back to reality. 'Are you okay? Let me in.'

Charlie must be copying them because I can hear him giggling and thumping on my bedroom door as well. His older brothers are like gods to him. 'Mummy!' he is yelling, his tiny fist making a more muffled knock than theirs. Just picturing the delight on his little face elevates my mood a notch.

That's the thing about kids. They've got this built-in fail-safe mechanism to protect them from outright abandonment. I call it 'killer gorgeousness'. Succulent cheeks. Wide, trusting eyes. Skin as creamy and sweet as freshly whipped icing. Sometimes I look at Charlie and just want to devour him, with his curly mop of blond hair, cuddly little body and a smile that could liquefy rock. Shame about the naughty streak.

I put my forehead on my knees and wait. Maybe if I just sit here without responding they'll eventually get sick of thumping and walk away. Just as this rather stupid plan is solidifying in my brain, my good friend 'luck' gives me another dud surprise. A fourth voice.

'Grace! Grace! Are you there?'

My head flips up. The voice is muffled but clearly female. Someone is at our front door. *Shit.*

It's probably my neighbour, Mavis. Wouldn't be the first time she's popped round to check what the commotion is. Last time, I made a solemn promise to keep the noise down.

Embarrassment, hot as lava, rolls through me.

Not again.

Scrambling to my feet, I yank the bedroom door open and stride out, almost knocking Ryan and Alfie over in the process.

'Stop yelling,' I hiss as I whip past them. 'You'll get us all into trouble.' Thankfully, they shut their mouths and follow hot on my heels to the foyer, with Charlie eagerly bringing up the rear.

I plaster on the most unperturbed expression I can muster and open the front door. It isn't Mavis.

It's worse. It's my sister.

'Aunty Rachel!' Alfie and Ryan both squeal in delight.

Rachel is looking very stern. 'Grace, what's going on? I've been knocking for ages and all I can hear is the kids calling out for you and asking if you're okay. Are you?'

'Of course,' I say evenly. 'I'm fine. Couldn't be better.'

'She was just hiding,' adds Ryan offhandedly. 'She does that sometimes.'

'*I do not.*' My gaze swings to Rachel. 'I wasn't hiding.' I draw Ryan firmly into my side, hoping he'll interpret the tight squeeze I'm giving him as a signal to shut the fuck up.

He doesn't. 'Yes you were.'

Rachel is folding her arms, her left eyebrow is raised and she's tapping her right foot.

Damn.

'Okay, you got me.' My mouth twists. 'I was teaching Charlie how to play hide and seek.'

'But Charlie was with us.' Ryan frowns. 'And he already knows how to play hide and seek.'

This kid just won't cut me a break.

'*Ryan.*' I turn his shoulders so he's facing me. 'Sweet, responsible Ryan. Why don't you take your brothers to the games room? Aunty Rachel and I need to chat.'

'About what?' he enquires.

Silently, I rack my brain for something he will not want to talk about. 'The two times table.'

Ryan blanches. 'I'm outta here!'

He dashes off down the hall, but Alfie and Charlie remain annoyingly focused on Rachel. 'I wanna see you test Aunty Rachel,' Alfie says gleefully. 'Ryan always gets 'em wrong. Are you good at your times tables, Aunty Rachel?'

'Not really,' Rachel admits.

'Did you want to go home and practise first?' I ask with polite innocence.

Rachel, however, is having none of it. '*You,*' she jabs a

finger at me, 'are going to let me in. And *I* am going to stay as long as I want.'

Great.

Rachel is my younger sister but could easily have been the older one – the way she bosses me about, tells me what to do, implores me to get my life back on track, as if that's such an easy thing to do. Don't get me wrong, I love my sister despite her in-your-face tough love and her annoyingly perfect life. You know the stats. Great career, devoted husband, well-behaved children, size ten. I honestly can't work out why other women don't hate her. Maybe it's because she's a psychologist. She gets people. Honestly, it's uncanny. The one thing you can rely on with Rachel is that she'll always show up when you need her the most. Which is more often than I would like these days. I'm probably her top patient right now. Thank goodness she offers me her services for free. If I had to pay her I couldn't afford to eat.

I can tell she's thinking the same thing as she steps over the threshold into my very basic-looking foyer. I like to call my decor style 'minimalistic' with a touch of 'hard times'. It's really quite fashionable in this part of town.

Though I will admit, most people at least have a painting or a hall table in their foyer. My ex-husband has two hall tables in his foyer, which, by the way, is twice the size of mine. One of them has a gilded mirror hanging above it.

Why? you might ask.

I believe it's there to show me how bedraggled I look every time I drop the kids off, hair a mess, bags under my eyes, clothes worn and tired because I haven't been shopping since . . . well, forever.

But of course, I could be wrong.

The point is, I don't have a hall table in my foyer, or anything, really, unless you count the shoes and schoolbags tossed we-don't-give-a-shit style in one corner. This is why I tend to discourage visitors. I get judged enough in the school car park. I can't be absolutely certain what the other mums are saying, but I'm pretty sure it's something along the lines of:

'Why doesn't she ever volunteer in the school canteen?'

'Her kids are always late to school.'

'She never bakes!'

To be fair, I didn't bake before I had kids, either. Only back then it was socially acceptable and nobody noticed. Now people look at the store-bought cupcakes on my disposable plastic plate with such pity, I wonder why there aren't warning labels on the packaging: *May damage reputation and prompt concern from friends.*

Speaking of concern, my sister steps into the kitchen and her mouth drops open in shock. I have to admit, it's a bit of a slap in the face for me too.

'What happened in here?' Rachel demands.

'Er . . . Ninja Turtle war. I was just about to start cleaning it up when you arrived.'

'Do you want some help, Mum?' Alfie asks brightly. His big blue eyes sparkle as he scans the kitchen. All my boys' blue eyes glitter when they smile, but Alfie's the only one with a dimple, and it flashes gleefully as he studies the flour-covered floor, his toes literally curling in his socks. I know exactly what he's thinking. If I'd had a better day, I might have grinned. Cheeky devil. Instead, I hold out my hand.

'Take off those socks and give them to me right now. You are *not* helping.'

'Aw!' he groans, but complies.

'I'll just put a movie on for them,' I tell Rachel as she steps gingerly over the exploded packet of flour towards the broom cupboard. Her nose wrinkles. 'What is that smell?'

'Lasagne. I'm trying for a crispier finish,' I joke.

She spies the burned tray next to the sink then glances back at me. 'Pretty bloody crispy.'

I grin. 'You don't think it works? I was just about to offer you a piece to take home.'

'Don't you dare! Right after you put on that movie we'll order some pizza. My treat.'

'Pizza!!!' Alfie and Charlie cry in unison, drawing Ryan back into the room to see if the rumour is true.

'You don't need to do that,' I protest half-heartedly, already feeling both insanely grateful and completely inadequate.

She shudders. 'Yes I do.'

As she begins to sweep, I march the boys into the family room, which doesn't look much better than the kitchen. There are toys all over the floor. Games with small pieces are a nightmare. I'd really love to know how other mothers stop their kids mixing up all the bits. Our toy box (when it's full) is just a stir-fry of disjointed parts. The couch, a rather decrepit-looking blue thing, is covered in a blanket – a vain attempt to keep it clean. Alfie bounds into the room, launching himself from the coffee table onto the couch, throwing his legs up so he lands in the seated position.

'I want *Ninja Turtles*.' He does a karate chop to emphasise his point.

'*Transformers*!' Ryan counters.

'*Thomas*. Choo choo!' says Charlie.

I was hoping to skip the fight over the television but it doesn't look like I'm getting any free passes this evening. Five minutes later, I put on *Ninja Turtles*, having promised that *Transformers* will go on after dinner. Luckily, Charlie has lost interest in the argument and is busy playing with a wooden Thomas he found on the floor among the debris. Suddenly, the house is quiet.

I have reached the eye of the cyclone. It's a beautiful moment.

Relief fizzles off my skin as I softly pad out of the room. When I rejoin my sister she has almost finished sweeping up the flour. The room is starting to look less like a bomb site and more like our kitchen.

The vinyl floors are faded. The kitchen counter laminate is chipped in more places than not, and there's a lot less cupboard space than any mother of three boys would hope for, and yet it's my favourite room in the house. This is where I get all my morning hugs, all the after-school news, and where everyone's achievements, big or small, hang on our fridge for all to see. This is the room where we are a family. And that's all I want for my kids.

Love and security.

It is a goal that clashed with my ex-husband's desire for status, assets and friends in high places. I remember how over-joyed I was to find this cheap rental. Finally, a place I could afford, close to the school, close to work. It was so far removed from anything Jake would have chosen, and had I been better off financially maybe I wouldn't have chosen it either. But it was a safe harbour, and has been since that day.

The old white metal blinds, or what's left of them, lie in a heap on the floor. I sneeze from the dust as I gather them up and take them to the garage, where I dump them next to the other rusty heap of metal that usually functions as my car.

What am I going to tell the landlord?

It isn't the first time I've found myself wishing for a handyman about the house, or a husband who could pass as one. Biting my lip, I stoically put the thought aside. My chances of meeting someone, dating them, starting a relation-ship are slim to none. I'm not exactly a catch.

I have three children. Not one, not two, but *three* boys who suck the life out of me. What man would sign up for that?

No one.

'Have you ordered the pizza yet?' Rachel asks when I return to the kitchen.

'I wasn't sure what to get,' I say as I retrieve the menu from under a magnet on the fridge. 'Have you eaten?'

'No, I came straight from work.' She smiles. 'Ron has the kids.'

Ron has the kids.

I thought I'd left my loneliness in the garage but the minute she says this the ache in my chest intensifies. I know she means nothing by these words. She's simply informing me that her husband is caring for their children while she is here. No doubt he swung by after-school care on his way home from the office. Took the kids home and got them started on their homework. Perhaps even cooked their dinner, if Rachel hadn't already prepared something. So why am I teary? I mean, *really*. That's normal life for most people. They take turns.

The lump in my throat is so big it threatens to choke me. The simple art of 'turn taking' is a forgotten dream, so far beyond my grasp I can no longer see the mist of its evaporation.

'Are you okay?' Rachel stops sweeping.

'Fine, fine.'

'Every time you say that, I believe it less,' she chides. 'I swear, Grace, you could go blind and nobody would know until they saw you walk into a wall.'

I grimace. 'If I went blind, I'd definitely get one of those walking canes to make sure that didn't happen.'

'*Grace!*'

'*What?*'

'It's not a crime to ask for help.'

I pause for a moment before saying, 'You've got your own life.'

'Are you telling me to mind my own business?' she demands.

'I'm trying not to stress you out.' I get a garbage bag from the kitchen drawer and scrape the lasagne into it with a spatula.

'Well, you're not doing a very good job of it,' Rachel tuts. 'Working yourself to the bone, raising three kids on your own – one with ADHD and one still toilet-training. How's that going, by the way?'

I think about the accident Charlie had at the supermarket that afternoon. The one I slipped in on the way to the check-out.

'Swimmingly.' My mouth quirks at the private joke.

'Do you want to know what I think, Grace?'

'What?' I ask nonchalantly.

'You're the biggest bloody liar the world has ever seen.'

'I wouldn't say much of the world has seen me.' I shrug in amusement. 'I hardly ever get out.'

'Stop it.'

'Stop what?' I spread my hands innocently.

'Trying to laugh everything off. It's not going to work this time.'

'Honestly, Rachel, I have no idea what you're talking about.'

'You are not fine,' she says sternly. ·

'Wow! Thanks.'

'You're as overwhelmed as a virgin in a brothel.' She holds up a hand to cut me off. 'No brothel humour.'

I pout. 'That's really not fair. You know I don't tell dirty jokes. I'm much too dignified for that.'

Rachel doesn't even crack a smile at my quip. She puts her hands on her hips. 'You need to ask that bastard for more help.'

There is no need to ask which 'bastard' she is referring to. Of all the bastards that ever lived, my ex-husband takes the champion's trophy by a landslide. Honestly, he should be in the *Guinness Book of Records*. Maybe I'll nominate him next year. Do people get paid for that? I should really look into it.

'It doesn't bother me that Jake doesn't see the kids much.' I try to reassure Rachel. 'In fact, to be perfectly honest, I prefer it that way.' The less I see of my ex-husband and his new wife, the better.

'Not that sort of help.' Rachel shudders. 'The last thing I want that man to do is pass on his values to your children. I'm talking about money, Grace. Financial assistance. Something to take the pressure off you. It's not like he can't afford it.'

He can afford it all right. Jake is a merchant banker. A very successful merchant banker.

'Maybe if you didn't have to work so much . . .' Rachel trails off.

'He won't contribute more,' I respond matter-of-factly.

Two and a half years ago, Jake hired the best lawyers in town to strip me of all our worldly possessions. They also arranged that he would pay only the barest minimum in child support even though he earns twice as much as I do. It wasn't that I didn't protest. I did – long and loud. But it was all in vain. He was extremely well prepared for our separation and subsequent divorce; it was like he'd been mapping out the scenario for months – and he probably had. Jake is meticulous like that, especially when it comes to protecting his best interests. For me, it was more like being led blindfolded to the side of a cliff and then unceremoniously pushed off it.

I never saw it coming.

I was pregnant, for goodness sake. Charlie had been conceived not five months before Jake decided that my best friend Carrie was the better woman for him.

Carrie and I met in high school. Rachel used to say she was jealous of me. And I, of course, with my brilliant foresight, had ignored this warning, first and foremost because I just didn't believe her. Carrie is smart and pretty – she had a zillion boyfriends in high school, whereas I had just the one. Aaron Cottier. We broke up after he moved to America with his family. The long-distance relationship didn't work. They never do.

'Lots of boyfriends doesn't mean anything, except perhaps that you're less picky,' Rachel told me at the time. 'Trust me, I know an unhappy person when I see one.'

Perhaps that was the psychologist in her coming out. However, it turned out to be quite true. Carrie never found the right man until she snared my husband. Slyly, too, like a snake in a nest. She was so 'sweet' in my time of need. Helping out with the kids while I was in hospital recovering from extreme morning sickness. I was so grateful to her. It never occurred to me that she was helping herself to my husband as well.

Don't get me wrong, I can see why he found her more attractive. She wasn't fat as a rhino, a bubbling fountain of vomit that was tired all the time and completely uninterested in sex.

Not that I discovered them in bed together or anything. Nothing so dramatic. The end of our marriage was extremely civil. Jake came home one day, waited till the kids were in bed and we'd finished dinner, then, over a cup of tea, told me he didn't love me anymore.

Just like that.

There were a number of reasons, and he scattered them before me like random cards from a deck of well-meaning break-up lines.

'You don't fulfil me emotionally.'

'You and I are actually two different people.'

'We have different paths in life.'

He didn't even mention Carrie, at first.

I didn't know what to do. I didn't know what to say. I thought we were fine. I mean, of course, there were a few red flags and bumps in the road but I thought that's all they were. Bumps.

Not insurmountable mountain ranges.

We weren't one of those couples who fight for years before deciding to call it off. Our problem was that we never spoke about how we really felt.

In hindsight, I can see that after we had Ryan and Alfie, he started spending less and less time at home. Withdrawing from our family. At the time, I thought that was just what happened when you had kids.

Men withdraw.

Women do more.

Isn't that the way of the world? It certainly seemed that way among my female friends. They were never short of complaints about their husbands' lack of interest in the domestic side of things.

What I didn't get back then was that their husbands were avoiding *housework*.

Which is very different to avoiding *the home*.

I remember trying to pull him back and pin him down. I nagged him about working all the time. I nagged him about not paying attention to his kids. I nagged him about going out too much with colleagues on the weekend. And I guess, yes, unwittingly I made things worse. The harder I clung to him, the more he tried to shake me off.

'You're always all about the kids,' he would say. 'There's no real time for us when I'm at home. I might as well go back to work.'

I did try to be a better wife. I tried to carve out time for us, but it must have been too late. He was never particularly interested in my efforts. And I was resentful that he didn't reciprocate by making time for the kids.

When I became pregnant with Charlie, insanely, I was over the moon. I thought, *there*, that's proof our marriage is solid. Who has another baby when their marriage is on the rocks?

I never in a million years imagined that he would ask me for a divorce while I was carrying his child.

But that's Jake for you.

Apparently, my pregnancy was actually the catalyst for his affair. The straw that broke the camel's back, if you will.

You see, there's a simple truth about Jake that I didn't realise till much too late. Jake's top priority is Jake. If you want to be in a relationship with him, he must be your top priority too.

No exceptions.

To be honest, I don't think Jake chose Carrie to spite me or to cause me extra pain. He chose her because she happened to be the first cab at the taxi rank – his one-way ticket out of the 'trap' he thought he was in. I'm sure if she had refused he would have waited five minutes and picked up the next ride that came through.

Carrie's choice, on the other hand, wasn't random or convenient. It was considered.

She was my best friend.

My best friend.

My rock. I told her everything. More so, in fact, than Rachel, who wanted to give me advice all the time.

Carrie knew Jake and I were having problems.

She knew I was desperate to connect with him.

Yet she got into bed with him anyway.

'It's not how you think it is, Grace,' she said when I demanded an explanation for her betrayal. 'When we first started talking, it was all about you. I was trying to help him see that he should stay with you. I tried everything to convince him.'

'Even sleeping with him, apparently,' I flung at her.

She flinched briefly but then seemed to straighten her shoulders, bolstering her courage. 'It didn't happen like that, Grace. It was more that I grew to understand him.' Her face hardened with purpose. 'He doesn't want you, Grace. He doesn't love you. And you can't make him.'

'So what?' I demanded. 'That gives you the right to just waltz in and take over? You of all people – my *best* friend.'

'You can't choose who you love,' she said in a quiet, forlorn tone, like she was being driven by a higher power.

That's bullshit.

It's the excuse people give for hurting others, relieving themselves of any blame when they choose to be selfish.

You *do* choose who you love. People do it every day. Mothers choose to love their children even when they annoy the living daylights out of them. Brothers choose to stick up for each other even when they're outnumbered ten to one. And husbands *choose* to be faithful even when a younger, prettier version of their wife enters their social sphere.

It's not fate, people, it's choice!

Frankly, Carrie and Jake deserve each other. Cut from the same cloth as far as I'm concerned. I no longer resent them being together. What I do resent is the legacy they have left me with.

If possible, Jake is a far worse father in divorce than he was in marriage. He sees the boys under sufferance, one weekend a fortnight, but most of the time he cancels or only takes them for the Saturday. Jake likes the idea of being a family man, and the kudos it brings him among his peers: *Three strapping boys! What an achievement.* But, like most of his 'achievements', he prefers to hang them on a wall for people to admire rather than interact with them. His usual reason for cancelling is work. I know from experience that merchant banking does require long hours – it was the cause of many arguments throughout our marriage. But seeing his unreliability progress since the divorce has been heartbreaking for our children.

'Well?'

I look up and realise Rachel is still staring at me, waiting for an explanation about Jake's lack of financial help.

'I've asked him,' I sigh. 'He says he will pay what he's legally required to and not a cent more.'

Rachel snorts. 'What about all Alfie's medical bills? Speech therapy and the OT he's been seeing? He can't possibly expect you to fork out for all that yourself.'

I grit my teeth. 'I have broached the issue.'

'And?'

I nervously lick my lips. 'Jake believes that Alfie doesn't have ADHD or any other disorder. He says I'm either making it up as an excuse or it's all in my mind. Alfie's bad behaviour and poor school results are due to me being a bad mother.'

Rachel's jaw drops. 'This guy just gets better and better.'

I nod glumly.

'*Grace,*' Rachel examines me sharply. 'You don't believe you're a bad mother, do you?'

I spread my hands helplessly. 'I don't know. It's not that cut and dried, you know? I do my best, of course, but sometimes I wonder if because I work almost full-time hours . . .'

'Enough.' She shakes her head. 'We' – she does a quick finger flip between my chest and hers – 'are taking him to court. You need to gather up all your medical evidence. We can serve this guy with a court order.'

It seems like a lot of work, and I already have so much on my plate. Maybe with a lot of hard work, persistence and a lengthy court battle we could get Jake to relent, but I'm so tired.

So bloody tired.

'Why not?' I smile cynically at Rachel. 'I've been wondering what I'm going to do with all my free time. Sleep is so overrated.'

Her mouth twists. 'Stay here. I'll make you a cup of tea and order the pizza.'

She returns a few minutes later with two steaming mugs. I take a grateful sip. Tea always seems to make the world a little lighter.

'Tell me what you're thinking right now.' Rachel breaks the silence.

I know she wants to hear my thoughts on her plan to get our day in court, but I'm just not there. My mind is a whirl of disjointed images and latent anger. Not so much at Jake as at myself.

'I was wondering how I could have been so wrong about him,' I admit finally.

I mean, I was the one who fell for Jake in the first place. I thought he was the most wonderful man in the world. He had everything going for him: looks, charm, big plans for life. It was a short courtship. He was ever so charming, and all my friends liked him. Jake is very charismatic. He was going places, and he made you want you to be part of that. Until, of course, you became the obstacle standing in his way.

'And then, of course, there's Carrie,' I add forcefully. 'I was just as wrong about her.'

'Carrie has always been a selfish bitch.' Rachel flips a hand dismissively. 'I never liked her. The trouble with you is that you're always making excuses for people, like there's a reason they are the way they are.'

'Well, isn't there?' I say uncertainly. 'You're the psychologist.'

'Excuses aren't free passes,' Rachel reminds me flatly. 'At some point a person needs to start taking responsibility for their actions.'

'Yes, but maybe there was something I could have done differently.'

'No!' She grabs my hands. 'You are not to blame for what they did, Grace. Promise me you believe that.'

I look away, biting my lip and remembering the fog of incredulity that clouded the journey towards divorce. For a time there, I honestly believed it was a nightmare, and that at some point I was going to wake up.

Surely I hadn't fallen in love with the most stone-hearted man on the planet? I'm no genius, but honestly, wouldn't any rational person have been more aware?

I thought of all those women I'd pitied in the past, whose marriages had fallen apart for one reason or another. Those women who I'd had the gall to patronise or think I was superior to. After all, that sort of thing would never happen to me. I wouldn't let it. Not without a fight. Not when I had two kids to consider, and another on the way. I had no idea that it wouldn't be up to me. You can't force someone to love you. You can't force someone to be a decent human being if they don't want to be. So there I was, cast adrift and floating away on a current I had absolutely no control over.

'Sometimes,' I say quietly, 'I feel like it was because I wasn't good enough.'

'Good enough?' I can hear the fury vibrating in Rachel's voice as she repeats my words.

'Good enough to be faithful to,' I explain.

'Grace,' Rachel says slowly and succinctly, 'this happened to you, not because of you. It is not your fault. You were a victim. And if I ever hear you say something like that again, I might have to slap you.'

I raise an eyebrow and remove my hands from hers. 'Is this a new type of therapy you're using? Because it doesn't sound very professional to me.'

'Ha de ha ha!' She rolls her eyes. 'I'm serious. Honestly, you should be looking to the future. Is there a new man in your life?'

I choke on my tea, then grab a tissue to wipe the dribble from my chin. 'Are you for real?'

'What?' Rachel spreads her hands. 'You're a beautiful, intelligent woman. Any man would be lucky to have you.'

'Thanks,' I laugh. 'But even if that were true, you're forgetting about my copious amounts of baggage.'

'The boys? They're adorable.'

'Oh yes,' I moan, 'in photographs!'

'You make too much of it.'

'*Rachel*,' I say, with all the patience of the older sister I'm supposed to be. 'You know that perfect, self-sacrificing, wholly devoted romantic love you see in movies? It doesn't actually exist. Most people enter into relationships for what they can get out of them, not what they can put in. I am far better off on my own. At least I can control that. I can rely on that.'

Rachel gasps, hand over her mouth. 'You don't believe in love anymore.'

'Is it that obvious?'

'You think if you let someone else into your life, they're just going to let you down.'

I shrug. 'It makes sense, doesn't it? I mean, a single mum with three boys? I can't see anyone signing up for that long term.'

Rachel sighs. 'You've been through a lot, and I can see where this attitude is coming from, but the last time I checked, my sister never ran away from a challenge.'

I don't have a chance to defend myself because at that moment my mobile phone rings. I can see the caller ID flashing. It's a name that hasn't come up in a while.

Carrie.

Anger assails me.

I hope Jake isn't getting *her* to call to cancel his weekend with the kids. Without thinking, I snatch the phone up and press Accept.

'What do *you* want?' I growl, unable to soften my tone under Rachel's watchful gaze.

As it turns out, I am exactly right about Carrie's reason for calling. Kind of.

She sounds teary.

'There's no easy way to say this, Grace. It's Jake. He's . . . dead.'

Chapter 2

It's a strange thing to receive the news that a man you used to love is dead.

It isn't grief that hits me first, but rather a numbing kind of shock. I mean, of course I didn't want him to die. No one deserves to go like that – so young and so randomly. Despite everything, I feel for Carrie in a detached kind of way.

But just because Jake is dead doesn't suddenly make him a saint. So when feeling starts to return to my body, the first emotion to wade in is anger. Like – *shit*, he's done it again.

He's left me. Again.

And he's done it to the kids again as well.

I am devastated for them. He was their dad. Even if he wasn't a very good dad, he was still their dad, and any chance he had to redeem himself is now gone. Any chance they had to get to know him is gone.

And then there's me.

Just me.

All on my own.

No emergency number.

No back-up plan.

To be honest, that part is more crushing than all the rest. After I get off the phone to Carrie, I can barely speak. Rachel has to painstakingly draw the story out of me as my words tumble over each other.

'It was an aneurism – in the brain . . . So weird. He was fine yesterday. Completely fine . . . Then after dinner . . . a headache – went to bed early . . . This morning . . . never woke up.'

Rachel calls her husband and stays the night. We don't tell the kids. I am still too shell-shocked to put two sentences together and I don't want to tell them in that state.

The next day, I don't go into work, though I do send Ryan and Alfie to school. It's Friday. Rachel begs me to let her take the kids for the weekend.

'They can play with their cousins, have a break from the humdrum, while you take some time out.'

Rachel has two daughters, Tanya and Zoe, who have never really got on with my boys, for obvious reasons, but I find myself saying yes. I do need some time out. I think it might help settle my racing mind.

But after I've waved them off, the house seems unnaturally quiet. Being there by myself with nothing but my demons for company is rather suffocating, and so before too long I find myself in the car, driving. On automatic pilot, I somehow end up at the coast. I'm not surprised. The beach has always been my favourite place on earth. It's like looking at infinity or having a conversation with God. I leave my car and stand in the sand. My sandals are off and I'm digging my toes in deep, letting my gaze stretch to a horizon that has no beginning and no end. The sun sets against it, sending warm pink fingers of light streaking across an endless blue sky. Waves crash and fizz like the emotions in my chest. The wind whips my hair and it jumps wildly, strands spreading across my face.

I have to tell the boys.

The funeral is next week. I can't put it off indefinitely.

I sit down in the sand, letting the grains sift through my fingers. A song from a nearby cafe filters over to me. I know it. It's one of those big hits everybody's playing to death right now, though I can't remember the name of the singer. I'm not good with artist names and album titles. Nor do I follow the lives of the rich and famous. I have enough trouble keeping up with my own drama.

I don't know why, but for some reason the lyrics stick with me.

Loving gets harder the harder you love
And takes you on journeys you'd never think of
But when you're wasting away in darkest despair
Hard love is the one who will pull you from there.

The song has a strong, throaty beat and a tone that resonates in my bones. The singer is amazing. I grasp for his name but it doesn't come to me. The song has lifted my mood, though. I know what it's trying to tell me: when the going gets tough, the tough keep loving. I return to my car.

The next morning I call Rachel and say that I want to tell the boys about Jake that afternoon.

'Do you want me to be there when you tell them?' Rachel asks.

'I don't know.' I frown. 'What do you think? What's the best way to do it? How do I soften the blow? Is that even possible?'

'Be open and honest,' Rachel tells me. 'Encourage them to express how they feel and give them extra love and affection.'

The day passes slowly. I do a heap of laundry and drink several cups of tea. I watch the clock in the kitchen as I sip chamomile, wishing the hands would move faster, or slower, depending on which direction my thoughts are skittering. At some point, I go out to the shop and buy five chocolate bars. One for each of us, including Rachel.

I know, a little silly, and they probably won't help, but I feel like I can't turn up unprepared or empty-handed for a talk like this.

Around five o'clock, there's a knock at the door and I can hear a lot of noise outside.

'When Mum opens the door pretend you're a monster, okay?' Ryan is instructing everyone.

Sure enough, as I swing open the door I'm greeted by a ruckus of scary growling noises and hands held up like claws. Rachel is standing at the back of the group, an apologetic shrug on her shoulders.

'Honey, we're home,' she grins. 'Come on, boys, we can't stand outside forever. Pick up your backpacks and let's go in.'

Ryan immediately turns it into a game. He swings his bag over his shoulder. 'Soldier,' he says to Alfie. 'You grab the rest of the supplies and meet me back at base. I have a feeling we're going to be attacked tonight.'

Alfie snaps to attention. 'Copy that, Sergeant.'

'Move out!' Ryan shouts.

'Moo out!' mimics Charlie.

The squadron race down the hall completely immersed in their own imaginary world. I meet Rachel's eyes and she silently puts her arms around me. 'Oh, sweetie, I wish . . .' She trails off and we hug for a while. When she finally pulls back, her mouth is turned down in a frown, her gaze steady and searching.

Uh-oh.

I know that face.

It's not a good face.

'What?' I rasp.

'Maybe we should call Mum.'

This suggestion shakes off my self-pity quicker than manure being dumped out of a wheelbarrow. I step out of her reach, gesturing emphatically and saying adamantly, '*No way.*'

'Why not?'

I look at her, aghast. 'I can think of a million reasons why not! I'm surprised you would even ask that question.'

'You need help more than ever. I mean, last week was bad, but it looks like good times from today's perspective.'

I take a deep breath. 'What are you saying? You can't help me anymore?'

'No,' she says quickly, 'of course not. But . . .' she pauses. 'I can't be here for you full-time.'

I smirk. 'Neither can Mum.'

'That's not true,' Rachel says quickly. 'She's changed.'

'Alcoholics don't change,' I spit. 'They just get better at covering their tracks. Honestly, Rachel, this is the worst possible time to bring Mum back into my life. *The worst!*'

'I know there's a lot of unresolved issues.' Rachel nods. 'Trust me, *I know*. But she's been sober for four years now, that's gotta count for something.'

'How can you know that for certain? She could just be making it up to appease you. She's been lying to us for years.'

So many broken promises lie in Francine Middleton's wake. My mother is the consummate actor. Honestly, I don't know why Hollywood hasn't snapped her up.

'It's different this time,' Rachel tries again.

'It's always different *this time*,' I sigh in exasperation.

'I've seen her,' Rachel insists. 'If you did too, you'd know she's telling the truth.'

Unlike me, Rachel has been in contact with our mother over the last couple of years, and they've started building a relationship again. Francine has made several attempts to contact me too, but I haven't made myself as easy to catch.

'I can't risk it,' I insist. 'Particularly not now.'

The kids come marching back into the foyer – well, Charlie and Ryan are marching, Alfie is doing combat rolls on the side while his older brother keeps yelling at him to get back in line. Trying to keep a lid on Alfie's energy is hard, even for his siblings.

Charlie is pulling a blue cart that's supposed to be full of wooden blocks. The blocks have probably been tipped out all over the floor somewhere. *Yay!* Our cordless phone is resting on a small cushion in the centre of the cart.

'We've brought you a communication device,' Ryan announces as they come to a halt in front of us. He tilts his head to one side, a hopeful expression much like that of a stray puppy sweetening his features. 'Maybe you'd like to order pizza.'

As my eyes rove over his sunny countenance, his cheeks dusted with freckles and his smile revealing a missing front tooth, a fist tightens around my heart. I'm not doing my boys any favours by waiting. I have to do this right now. I hear myself say, 'All soldiers report to the master bedroom.'

My room is the cosiest in the house, mainly because of its size, rather than the decor. There are a couple of large beige throws on my bed that we can wrap around each other if we get cold. Despite spring having arrived, the winter chill still creeps into the evening. I sit down and pull Charlie onto my lap. Ryan and Alfie bound onto the bed, Ryan on my left, Alfie on my right. Rachel sits down too, but a slight distance away.

'Boys, something has happened.'

'What, Mummy?' Alfie demands. He is kicking his legs like he's sitting on the side of a swimming pool.

I take a deep breath. 'It's your father. He . . . he died yesterday.'

It sounds so harsh, but I know they won't understand the phrase 'passed away' and I don't want to be ambiguous.

'What?' The word isn't an exclamation. Ryan sounds confused, more than anything. I don't blame him. He falters. 'H-how?'

'He had some bleeding in his brain.'

'Why? Did someone hit him?'

'No, nothing like that. It was just one of those things.'

'For real?' asks Alfie. His tone is surprised. 'Has he got any health points?' He's referring to the *Lego Stars Wars* game he plays on Jake's old Xbox.

'Unfortunately not,' I say quietly.

'So he's not coming back to life?' Ryan whispers. His glasses are fogging up. His lower lip is trembling.

'No.'

'Will we ever see his face again?'

'If you want to.' I suck in a breath, not entirely sure of the right thing to say, but wanting to be as open and honest as possible. 'You can see him one last time at the funeral.'

'When is that?'

Seeing that I'm fighting tears, Rachel quickly jumps in. 'It's next week, on Wednesday.' I had almost forgotten she was there.

Ryan begins to cry. Alfie's legs stop kicking. Charlie wriggles off my lap and turns around, grabbing my knees in his little hands.

'Biscuit time?' he says, looking up, wide-eyed and hopeful.

'Actually, I've got something better.' I reach around and grab the plastic bag I dumped earlier on the side of the bed. The chocolate bars spill out.

There is no immediate pounce for the goods. Alfie is stroking my arm from elbow to wrist again and again and again. He often does that when he is upset. His occupational therapist says he's a very sensory kid and loves the feel of textures. His school teachers would agree. Instead of listening to instructions he often learns by touch, running his hands over everything in his immediate surrounds and impulsively putting things in his mouth. In winter, he catches every bug in town and passes it on to the rest of us. If nothing else, at least my kids are pretty resilient when it comes to illness.

My other arm is feeling damp from Ryan's tears, and I'm starting to feel quite sick.

Too sick to eat chocolate.

I glance across at Rachel, who looks as heartbroken as I feel. 'It was a dumb idea,' I say helplessly. 'The chocolate.'

Despite popular belief, it doesn't fix everything.

Rachel shakes her head and moves closer. 'In this case, no idea is a dumb idea.' She puts her arms around us.

With her movement on the bed the chocolate bars fall on the floor. Charlie picks them all up. 'Open! Open!' he demands.

I open one bar for him.

'Mum,' Ryan hiccups, 'you're not going to die too, are you? Will your brain start to bleed one day?'

'No, no. Definitely not,' I assure him. 'There's no history of that in my family. Besides, I've got too much to do to be dying.'

Ryan looks up at me in relief. 'Are you sure?' He rubs his foggy lenses, trying to clear them. 'You're quite old.'

I'm thirty-five, but I nod at him solemnly. 'And haggard too, I suppose.'

Ryan's face lightens somewhat. 'No, Mummy. You're the most beautiful lady in the world. You've got the bestest face I've ever seen. Hasn't she, Aunty Rachel?'

A lump the size of a golf ball lodges in my throat.

'Absolutely,' says my sister.

'Hubba hubba,' agrees Alfie.

'Kiss, kiss,' says Charlie, climbing onto my lap. His face is covered in chocolate. In fact, he looks like he's having a blast.

I laugh and comply. 'Kiss, kiss.' His cheek, soft as butter, melts against my lips as I wrap my arms around his squirming body. Everyone else joins in the hug. We fall back on the bed and start a tickling match. There are no winners, but there's an extraordinary amount of laughter on what is one of the saddest days of my life.

I decide then and there that come hell or high water, I am going to give these kids the best childhood anyone could ever have.

Chapter 3

Sydney Morning Hearsay
26 August 2017

Fans fear Beauchene's 'No Holding Back' world tour will be cancelled

With singer/songwriter Michel Beauchene still out of touch, fans fear the tour will be cancelled. Beauchene's agent, Nicholas Cooper, and record label Sony have been inundated with questions regarding the star's health but nothing conclusive has been revealed. His 'No Holding Back' world tour is due to commence in November. Tickets went on sale in January.

Beauchene has not been seen publicly for almost six months, following his car accident in Sydney's Potts Point. Since his release from hospital after a three-month stay in a private burns unit at Royal North Shore, Australia's number one musical artist has withdrawn from the public eye, living very privately at his Bondi mansion. Few visitors and only a handful of medical staff have been permitted through the gates.

His Twitter and Facebook accounts have all but stagnated and there have been no further updates to his website. Fans are starting to get worried, particularly as Beauchene has been known to manage his own social media and has always been very responsive online.

'Many of us have purchased tickets to his "No Holding Back" world tour,' a fan told *Sydney Morning Hearsay*. 'We are worried he's not going to be well enough to perform.'

Some extra-keen Beauchene followers camped out in his street last week, hoping to catch a glimpse of the singer. 'We just want to know if he's okay,' they claim.

Perhaps next week they will finally get the answers they are looking for. Beauchene is scheduled to make an appearance on Channel Nine's *60 Minutes* for his first interview since the accident.

Given the secrecy surrounding the musician's car accident and his subsequent recovery, it's not surprising that there are a lot of questions the public want answers to.

The accident did not involve any other vehicles. Michel was driving and his brother, Claude, was a passenger. Allegedly, Michel's silver Porsche Carrera ran headfirst into the back wall of Beats Nightclub in Sydney's Potts Point after the car failed to make a left turn. An ambulance was called to the scene by an onlooker who at the time did not realise the identity of the driver. It was reported that the engine of the car exploded and Michel pulled both himself and his brother out of the car. Both suffered severe burns.

The Beauchene family have so far refused to comment on how the accident occurred or give any details about the extent of Michel's and Claude's injuries.

Nicholas Cooper has stated repeatedly that Michel has given him no instructions to cancel the shows. 'Michel is at the top of his game right now,' says Cooper. 'His last album, *Hard Love*, stayed at number one in Australia for five consecutive weeks and is charting in the top ten in the US right now.

He signed his first movie deal before the accident and was voted Australia's sexiest man by *Who* magazine. He is not going to let you down.'

Australia has to ask, though, how will Beauchene's burns injuries affect his career? Are things really as rosy as Cooper claims, given that Beauchene will not step outside?

Tune in to *60 Minutes*, Sunday next week, to find out.

Chapter 4

To be perfectly honest, I didn't expect to be invited to the reading of Jake's will. After he married Carrie, I pretty much ruled out the possibility of any financial inheritance for my boys. However, a few days after the funeral, I find myself sitting next to my ex-best friend in the plush executive office of Jake's lawyer.

Carrie's perfectly manicured fingernails pluck in agitation at the threading on the top of her armrest. Her eyes dart suspiciously between me and the man sitting at the desk in front of us. One long, bare, beautifully waxed and moisturised leg is crossed over the other. She is dressed to the nines in a white dress and three-inch heels, looking like a modern bride waiting in a registry office. I'm wearing black slacks that are at least ten years old, because my legs are neither hairless nor moisturised. I've made some effort at class with a smart knee-length, grey, belted coat with huge black buttons. It is by far one of the newest things I own and, to its credit, can dress up almost anything. This is why, even though it's stiflingly hot in the office, I haven't taken it off. All I'm wearing underneath is a black skivvy that has seen more of the world than my pants have. And even I'm too competitive to sit next to Carrie in that.

'Thanks for joining me, ladies,' says Gerard, who's been Jake's lawyer for the last ten years. 'Won't be a moment.' I remember meeting Gerard when Jake made his first will, with me. We'd been married a year and had just bought our first house. You know, the one he ripped out from under me during our divorce. As my familiar friend, anger, begins emerging from her cave I have to remind myself that Jake is dead.

Dead.

He can no longer pay for the problems he dealt me.

There isn't any point dreaming up revenge scenarios, as inconceivable as they may be. You know the type of fantasy I'm talking about, right? I win lotto, buy Jake's bank, sack him and offer the job to his handsomest rival, who also happens to be madly in love with me. Ahh, that was one of my favourites, but . . . no more.

I still can't believe Jake is gone.

It's completely surreal.

Gerard hasn't changed much – maybe a little balder, a little fatter. He appears impartial, but I know he holds more of Jake's secrets than both his wives combined. The will Jake and I so painstakingly put together has long since been replaced. Yet now, as my eyes flicker in Carrie's direction again, I can't help wondering if some of my wishes were retained without her knowledge.

Jake liked to keep his cards close to his chest when it came to business, and even closer when it came to his love-life. A smile of satisfaction curls my mouth.

Surprise, Carrie!

Gerard stands up holding two documents. He hands one to each of us. My eyes glance at the cover sheet. It's a copy of Jake's last will and testament. Carrie immediately flips hers open, scanning the words like they are military orders, direct from the prime minister.

'I'm not going to be so formal as to read it to you both,' Gerard smiles. 'It's not very long and quite simple in its entirety. He's left the vast majority of his assets to Carrie, obviously, but there has been some provision made for the children.'

A genuine ripple of both surprise and delight whips through me. I open the document. Is it possible that Jake actually spared some thought for me and the boys after strategically dumping us to start a new life? I hadn't credited him with any sense of obligation at all.

It's so good to be wrong for once.

'You will find,' Gerard says to Carrie as she frantically turns pages, looking for that unexpected clause, 'that your late husband, rather than allocating a portion of the estate to his children, has allocated them a property.'

'A property?' Carrie glances up, aghast. Her voice quavers. 'Which property?'

'The property in Yallingup.'

For a moment Carrie looks nonplussed. I have long since stopped reading my copy of the will to watch her. This is far more entertaining.

'I don't understand,' Carrie snaps. 'Jake doesn't have a property in Yallingup.'

'He most certainly does,' Gerard smiles benignly.

'What sort of property?' She sits forward in her chair.

'I believe,' Gerard winces, 'and this is going on memory – it's been a long time since I discussed this will with your late husband – that it's a vineyard.'

A vineyard?

I sink back into my chair in amazement, the will dropping into my lap.

'A vineyard,' Carrie repeats faintly.

'Yes,' Gerard nods. 'Jake makes a modest amount every year by leasing the majority of the land to grape growers. It's well tended. Which is more than I can say for the house.'

'A house?' Carrie squeaks. 'You mean, like a holiday home?'

I can almost see her eyes ringing up dollar signs like a Looney Tunes cartoon character. Yallingup is, after all, a top destination for Perth city dwellers wanting a taste of the quiet life for the weekend. Best beaches, best food and wine, a mere three hours' drive out of the big smoke.

Oh Jake. You naughty boy!

I briefly wonder if there is a third woman out there, living in that house. Perhaps he keeps her just for the holidays when he's in a good mood? Otherwise, why wouldn't Carrie know about his holiday home in Yallingup? Gerard squashes this theory with a scratch of his chin.

'It's a rundown old place. Highly unlikely that it's even liveable. It's been unoccupied for twenty years.'

There's a pensive silence before Carrie throws up her hands. 'This makes absolutely no sense. I can't fathom what Jake would want with a vineyard, or why he would buy one without consulting me first.'

'Well –' Gerard begins, but she cuts him off.

'In any event, as his wife,' she throws a pointed look at me, 'don't I have a right, by law, to at least half of any property that was purchased during our marriage? Even if it wasn't purchased in my name?'

Oh crap. She has a point there. I hope she isn't going to contest the will.

I sigh. Who am I kidding?

Of course she's going to contest it.

'Er . . . actually,' Gerard interrupts our staring contest, 'this particular property ownership pre-dates your marriage to Jake. In fact, the estate known as,' his eyes flick down to his own copy of the will, 'Gum Leaf Grove, was acquired before Jake was even married to Grace.'

It's my turn to be shocked. 'What?'

'I remember he owned it when I met him for the first time,' Gerard adds.

My mind races. *Jake had a secret vineyard he never told me about!*

Where did he even get the money to buy it? Before we were married, his career was still in its infancy. In fact, he didn't really come into his own until after I fell pregnant with Alfie.

Carrie blusters, uncrossing and recrossing her legs. 'This is ridiculous.' She addresses Gerard, not me. 'You don't happen to know why Jake never mentioned purchasing this property, do you?'

'Actually,' Gerard clears his throat, 'Jake didn't buy this property. He inherited it.'

I blink. 'From who?'

'His parents.'

That makes sense.

I never met Jake's parents. Apparently they both died just before he started university, ages before he met me. It was a car accident that killed them both. Jake didn't like to talk about it, or about them. The most he said was that they weren't a very close family. I didn't judge. I'd been estranged from my own mother for at least seven years by the time we met.

My father died of cancer when I was seventeen. He was a lovely man, the very foundation of our family. When he was alive, life was the best it ever was for me. I miss him so much.

After he died, Mum kind of lost her way.

And I get that part.

He was the love of her life, and she had left her family in America to be with him. She had few friends in Australia. Mum, even when not on the booze, was a rather . . . opinionated person, and I guess not very approachable. She never lost her high-pitched New York accent, and it would sometimes come off as rather condescending, so people tended to avoid her. To be honest, her isolation hadn't really bothered her that much until Dad checked out. She depended on him to be her everything, and when he was gone, her world just fell apart.

Like I said, I get that part, but what I can't understand is how she forgot she had two teenage girls who needed her more than ever.

When Mum turned to alcohol, Rachel and I had to fend for ourselves. I deferred university for a couple of years to get Rachel through high school. I worked full-time at Coles while our mother snuck in and out of our family home like the shifty roommate you're always chasing for rent money.

Sure, she had her good days. Times when she would cry and apologise and promise her heart out that she wasn't drinking anymore. And for a week it would be wonderful, almost like she'd come back to us. We'd come home to hot meals and cookies fresh from the oven. She'd shower praise on her beautiful, intelligent girls, hug us and kiss us and beg for our forgiveness. The first couple of times she did this I was moved. But I soon learned it was nothing more than an ever-repeating cycle.

Sobriety never lasted more than a fortnight. During the low points, our mother became loud and aggressive. She didn't hit us, but man, she could be mean. Other times, she'd be zombie-like, death on legs. Sometimes she'd stay in bed all day, refusing to move. I don't know which type of bender I preferred.

When Rachel finished high school, Francine took that as a sign that her responsibilities as a parent were finally over. One morning we found a note from her in the kitchen. She said she'd gone to Melbourne to find herself. Our family home reminded her too much of Dad, and she needed to get away.

Funnily enough, her abandonment was almost a relief. We finally had stability. We both moved out and went to university, supporting ourselves with part-time jobs and Austudy. It wasn't the perfect life, but it was a damn sight better than it had been.

'So basically, the property, or the proceeds of the sale of the property, is left in trust to you, Grace, until your youngest boy turns eighteen.' Gerard's voice jolts me back to the present. I can't believe what I'm hearing. Are my boys really getting a trust fund?

At the end of the meeting I leave the room in a dazed state. Carrie stalks past me furiously, tossing her hair over her shoulder as she gets into the lift and closing the door before I can step in. I'm not upset about this. She did everything she could to convince Gerard that the Yallingup property couldn't possibly be left to the boys. To Gerard's credit, he didn't back down.

My kids are going to inherit the property, or the money from the sale of it. I just have to make that choice.

I step out into the street and pause for a moment. Rachel has Charlie till two, after which we both have to pick up our other kids from school. I have a free hour.

I can't remember the last time I had proper coffee in a real cafe, and now seems like a good time to revisit the experience. I really need some time to think.

I walk a block before I discover a charming-looking teahouse. The smell of hot drinks, savoury pastries and cake wafts out from the kitchen, drawing me in. It's not long before I'm sitting on a wooden bench scooping the froth off my cappuccino.

A bubble of excitement wells in me. It's been a long time since I've had any good news. If I sell the property I might be able to put the proceeds into a managed fund. All Alfie's therapy could be paid for, I could send the kids to a better school. I might even be able to work part-time, and be around for them more. We could live in a better house, the kids could have their own rooms. Ryan could have those guitar lessons he's been bothering me about. I'd have money to hire a babysitter every now and then. I might even get a life.

My brain overflows.

But then there's the other option.

We could keep the property and use the money the grape growers pay as a supplement. Gerard said it wasn't much, maybe eight thousand a year. But sinking that money into the boys' education and health expenses would go a long way. Plus, we'd have a holiday home!

Well, a holiday shack, or a gorgeous piece of country to pitch a tent on, at any rate.

The urge to see the place is suddenly undeniable.

I sip my coffee, enjoying both the aroma and the feel of the warm, soothing liquid slipping down my throat.

The September school holidays start in a couple of weeks. Maybe we could go down then and check it out, and look for a suitable real estate agent in case we decide to sell it.

I've already booked one week's leave during that time, after much begging and pleading with my boss, Adrian. 'It's really not a good time to take leave, Grace,' he said. 'Management is doing a huge staffing review over the next month or so, to decide which departments are most essential to the firm.'

I know this is not good news, and if I had any choice I would probably heed his warning. A number of the mothers at school have lost their part-time jobs due to the recent economic downturn. But what am I supposed to do? I can't put three kids in holiday camp for two weeks. It's too expensive. Besides, the kids have been through so much lately. I want to be present for them these holidays, especially because they won't be having their usual time with their dad. Despite the risks, this is the best thing to do.

I wrap my fingers carefully around my steaming mug.

There's another reason I want to see the place for myself.

It was Jake's secret vineyard.

Jake, who kept secrets and lied to me during our marriage.

I would like to know what he was hiding.

I would like to know very much.

Chapter 5

Sydney Morning Hearsay
9 September 2017

Where is Michel Beauchene?

Despite heightened expectations from fans, singer/songwriter Michel Beauchene did not turn up for his tell-all interview with Channel Nine's *60 Minutes*. In fact, there have been reports that Beauchene mysteriously left his Bondi residence sometime between Friday and Wednesday last week. It is uncertain how he managed to do this, given the number of reporters surveying his home. His disappearance is being regarded by police as planned rather than suspicious, given his complaint to them ten days ago: 'If you do not get the media off my back I'll be forced to move out.'

Katie Beasley, his housekeeper of seven years, revealed that she also received an email from Michel announcing his intention to stay away for 'a while' several days after his absence was noted. He advised her to take some time off. How much, he did not specify. Katie is selling her story to *Women's Weekly* for their November issue.

When questioned about Michel's whereabouts, the Beauchene family were typically silent, with only his sister, Adele Beauchene, making one cryptic remark to *Hearsay* reporters: 'Can't you guys take a hint?'

As concern for the star's safety grows, media personnel have staked out Adele's home in Sydney's outer suburbs, where she lives with her husband and two kids. Although Michel was not spotted coming or going from this residence, *Hearsay* journalists reported being verbally abused by his sister, who told them to 'get the fuck' off her property. It is thought that her recent aggression is only a cover for deep-seated pain.

Michel's brother is still in hospital and his mother, who has dementia, resides in a home. As the rest of the Beauchene family lives in France, Michel has no one to turn to. Fans have been madly reaching out to him on Twitter and many of their pleas can be found under the hashtag #Michelcomelivewithme.

Doctors from Royal North Shore Hospital have expressed concern that Beauchene is out of contact. While Royal North Shore will not release the specifics of Michel's injuries, local specialist Dr Kenneth Woolworth offers his opinions.

'Recovery from severe burns is a slow process and can take many years, particularly with regard to the psychological damage that many patients suffer. PTSD is not uncommon.'

It is unclear why Michel Beauchene has felt the need to suddenly withdraw from the public eye. However, if he is indeed suffering post-traumatic stress, it is vital that he returns to the care of his psychologist.

If you would like to join the drive to find Michel Beauchene, get online and sign the petition, TalkToUsMichel.com.

Fellow artist Alexis Lovejoy offers this chilling thought: 'Michel Beauchene is such a rare talent, one of Australia's best. This disappearance is more than just a stunt. It's a cry for help.'

Chapter 6

Rachel is worried. But then, when isn't she?

'Are you sure you should go down there on your own with three kids? What if the house is completely unliveable?'

'Then we'll pitch a tent.'

'You hate camping.'

'The boys will love it though.'

'What if you can't get the tent up?'

'Wow, thanks for the vote of confidence.'

Rachel ignores this statement. 'Maybe I should come with you?'

'You have your own family to take care of,' I argue. 'Besides, I thought you couldn't get time off for the school holidays.'

'That's true,' Rachel agrees reluctantly. 'Ron has taken off a few days instead, but I could push the issue. Say it was a family emergency or something.'

'You're being ridiculous,' I scoff with a confidence that's completely fake. 'What's the worst that could happen?'

Charlie gets bitten by a snake.

A kangaroo eats our food.

The engine falls out of the car. In terms of probability this one has the highest rating.

I firmly switch off my imagination.

'We'll be fine!'

The truth is, I'm not really the outdoorsy type. The idea of going on a road trip with three children (one still in nappies) without the creature comforts of home is a little scary. Okay, a lot scary. But I simply must see this property, and I can't keep relying on Rachel all the time. She's been helping me out so much lately. I know I'm running her ragged, between taking care of me and looking after her own family as well. Then there's the issue of my mother, which she mentioned again last week. I can't help thinking that Rachel wouldn't keep bringing her up unless she was feeling overwhelmed.

It's different for Rachel, though. She and Mum actually talk.

After many years of silence, Mum contacted us both. Apparently she was living in Melbourne, working in a green-grocer's. Somewhere along the line she had sobered up and 'turned over a new leaf'.

'Would you have it in your heart to meet with me if I flew over to see you?' she asked slowly over the phone, her American accent made thicker somehow by the huskiness of her voice.

I couldn't believe she was asking this of me after all this time. I thought I'd never see her again. To be honest, my gut reaction was suspicion.

'Why do you want to see me now?' I demanded after a long pause. There didn't seem to be a logical explanation. Wouldn't it be easier to hit someone up for money in Melbourne, rather than flying all the way to Perth?

She took a deep breath. 'I think it's time we put your father's death behind us.'

'O-kay.'

'I know losing your father was hard on you girls. It was equally hard on me. We lost each other as a family. I really think it's worth getting that back, don't you? Becoming close again.'

I choked. 'We lost each other? Mum, you abandoned us! You got repeatedly drunk and then you took off. You haven't given me or Rachel a second thought for years.'

She sniffed as though she was about to cry. 'People deal with grief in different ways. Besides, you and Rachel were too caught up in school and your friends to give your mother a second thought.'

'*What?*'

'Honestly, I felt completely redundant. I knew I had to take myself out of the situation. I know you might find this hard to believe, but all I've thought of since I left is you and Rachel.'

I found this pill a little difficult to swallow.

Did she honestly think I would just forgive and forget without an apology? Where's the 'I'm sorry, I only cared about myself'? The 'Hey, I shouldn't have started drinking'? Her remorse was so noticeably absent it was laughable. In fact, she seemed to blame me for her actions.

I don't know how many times I longed for my mother to wake up. Stop drinking. Love me. Care about me. *Want* to get better.

Be sorry.

Each time that wish went unfulfilled, I learned to stop wishing and start accepting what she really was.

'What do you want, Mum?' My voice was contemptuous.

'I want to be a family again,' she said in a rush. 'I realise that you might not . . .' her voice trembled, 'might not be ready . . .'

Damn right I wasn't ready.

'. . . to do that just yet. But I want to say, if there is anything I . . . that I –'

'There's nothing,' I cut her off. How could we be a family again when I'd seen firsthand how little she loved me?

At the time, I also had two children. I had just found out I was pregnant with Charlie and I could feel Jake starting to slip away from me. The kids had never met their grandmother.

I never spoke about her – I didn't have anything good to say. The last thing I wanted was for her to use her long-lost grandchildren to aid her recovery from alcoholism.

I just didn't trust her.

Nor was I in a position to seek advice or solace from Jake.

For months he had been making me feel like I wasn't good enough. Like I was the anchor holding his life back. The thought of saying, 'So, hey, my alcoholic mother wants to be part of our lives' just seemed to add weight to everything he'd said. Francine Middleton was the dirty family secret that Jake would never want aired. Bringing her into the foreground would only fan the flames of his contempt. I stupidly believed I could still save our marriage. So I told my mother, in no uncertain terms, that it was too late. Far too late for her to be part of my family.

But Rachel didn't do that. She invited our mother to meet her husband and her kids.

I couldn't believe it. I was shocked, and even felt a little betrayed.

For years, I, not Francine, was Rachel's mum. And now my sister was letting this woman back into her life. This woman who had hurt us and abandoned us, moved halfway across the country and not contacted us for years. But it wasn't up to me.

A few months later, Francine flew over to meet Rachel and her family. Rachel said it was hard and awkward, but once they got through that first meeting they made a date for another. And after Francine flew back to Melbourne she called Rachel regularly.

I'm not sure exactly what happened after that, because that was when my own life fell apart.

The affair.

The divorce.

I was too busy with present-day problems to let the past creep in as well.

Rachel and I haven't spoken about my relationship with Mum until now. And for the first time, I find myself wondering about Francine. Does she ask Rachel about me? How much does she know? Has Rachel told her about Carrie and Jake? What does she think?

You're not honestly looking for your mother's advice now, are you? After all these years?

The first day of the school holidays seems to arrive quicker than I expected. Despite all Rachel's protests, I'm hitting the road to Yallingup. This is the first windfall I've had in a long time and I'm going to make the most of it.

There's a tent and four sleeping bags in the boot of my old Holden sedan, just in case the accommodation doesn't hold up. I've filled the car with petrol and made sure all the tyres are pumped up, though, in hindsight, this is the least of the car's problems. I bought the vehicle when it was just five years old, in my pre-Jake days. It surpassed him in reliability but now I feel like it too is on its last legs – or wheels.

There's just enough room left in the boot for our luggage. The kids each packed a backpack last night. I check the bags to see what they've put in. According to Ryan the essential items for a five-day trip are Pokémon trading cards, one cap, two books and a drink bottle – half full. I spend the next hour taking toys out of bags and replacing them with clothes and toiletries. I also pack a small bag for myself. After that, I'm pooped, and we haven't even started our journey yet.

I walk into the lounge room, where the boys are on the floor playing 'traffic' with a crate of Matchbox cars and a series of ramps made out of my favourite books.

Sigh.

With an effort, I ignore the damage to my much-loved keepsakes and clap my hands. Time to train some good husbands.

'Okay, boys. Mummy needs some help. I want you to carry your bags out to the car.'

Nobody moves.

'Boys,' I say sternly. 'Get your bags. There are no servants in this house.'

Ryan looks up at me thoughtfully. 'Then maybe we should get some.'

I look at him in consternation before I realise he is actually serious.

'No, Ryan, we should not *get some*.'

His face screws up. 'Why not?'

'Because even if servants were available for hire in Australia, I would not be able to afford one.'

Ryan's eyes light up. 'I could. I'm *rrrrrrich*.' He draws out the final word triumphantly. 'I've still got all my birthday money. I could lend you some.'

Prior to the 'good husband' program I ran a 'smart spending' workshop with the boys, followed by a course in 'accumulating funds for a rainy day'. Must be the accountant in me. That, and the fact that I'm flat broke. Of course, Ryan's life savings only amount to fifteen dollars.

'Hmmmm,' I stall. 'Thanks for the offer. I'll let you know if I get desperate. In the meantime, get your bag.'

'Fine,' he shrugs.

I prod Charlie, who is lying over the armrest of the couch, chubby legs dangling off the side. 'Come on, no sleeping on the job.'

Alfie requires slightly more encouragement, but it isn't long before we have the car fully packed, the traffic game tidied up and three kids on the back seat.

The fun isn't over yet, though. I've been driving for about fifteen minutes when Alfie pipes up from the middle seat, 'Are we there yet, Mummy?'

I knew he'd be the first to ask. ADHD does not beget patience. I glance at him in exasperation via the rear-view mirror. He's biting on his fingers.

'Alfie, please take your hands out of your mouth,' I say, even though I know they'll be back in there within minutes. 'And no, we aren't there yet. Remember I told you, Daddy's old house is very far away.'

'But we *are* very far away from home,' says Alfie. We haven't even left the outer suburbs of Perth yet.

'Far, far away,' says Charlie.

'It's going to be much longer,' Ryan tells them knowledgeably. 'We have to get to the country, where there are only farms with lots of cows and sheep.'

'Mooooo,' says Charlie. 'Moo.'

'How many seconds, Mummy?' demands Alfie, whose hands are back in his mouth.

'It's too many, Alfie,' I try to say patiently. 'We're going to be driving for a least another three hours.'

'How many seconds is that?'

I do a quick mental calculation. Alfie always wants to know how long everything will take in seconds. It's the only measure of time he can quantify, I guess. 'Ten thousand, eight hundred seconds.'

'*Ten thousand!*' There is loud moaning and groaning from the back as Alfie rolls around in his seat, knocking Charlie and Ryan. 'That's too much.'

'Hey.' Ryan shoves him back.

'No worry, Alfie,' Charlie pats him sympathetically. 'I count. One, two, three, five, ten, one, two, three, five, ten.'

'Muuuum!!!!' Alfie whines. 'He's getting it all wrong.'

'One, two, three, five, ten.'

'Charlie, thank you,' I say over my shoulder. 'You're doing very good counting but I think that's enough for now.'

'I can count,' says Charlie proudly, looking at his brothers as though they're imbeciles.

Alfie groans and is silent for a moment. Just when I think I might get a reprieve he suddenly sits up straight.

'So here's the deal.' His eyes sparkle deviously. 'I'll drive.'

I laugh as the mental image of us tearing up the freeway with Alfie at the wheel, half hanging out the window, flashes into my head. 'No, you will not.'

'Aw!'

The drive to Bunbury is peppered with conversation of much the same variety. Attempted negotiations, sibling rivalry and the occasional game of I Spy, in which Alfie always cheats. How does one cheat at I Spy? Alfie finds a way.

'Mum, Alfie changed his answer again,' Ryan whines. 'I know it was S for sky. But he says he was looking at a sheep.'

'I *was* looking at a sheep.'

'How is a sheep above us?' Ryan demands, citing earlier clues. 'How is a sheep blue?'

'I never said it was blue,' Alfie argues.

'*Muuummm!*'

'Okay, okay, this game is officially over,' I announce as I pull off the road at a public rest stop. There are picnic tables here, as well as a pop-up cafe and a large outdoor restroom that is not gender specific. This long row of toilet cubicles is sheltered only by a tin roof suspended half a metre above the stalls. Opposite, sporting its own high tin roof, is an open-air trough with as many taps as there are cubicles.

'Okay, who needs to go?'

Silly question. We've been driving for two hours.

We hurry over to the line leading up to the toilet block. It's lunchtime, so there are quite a few people waiting, including one of the most gorgeous men I've seen in a while. Tall, blond, broad shouldered. He's wearing dark sunnies so I can't see his eyes, but his jaw is square and chiselled and his lips are shaped in a sumptuous curve.

In any event, he's definitely my type. *Well*, my type back when I was single, pre-babies and likely to get a second glance. This guy doesn't even turn around when we join the line. Not that I blame him. If I heard a bunch of rowdy brats and their harried mother coming up behind me, I'd probably keep my head down too. He's dressed with surprising smartness for a country pit stop. A pale blue shirt with a fine check print, beige slacks and brown leather lace-ups, good enough to wear in an office. Must be coming to the region on business.

Reluctantly, I tear my gaze from his chiselled profile and turn to Ryan, who is tugging on my sleeve and dancing from one foot to the other.

'I don't think I can hold it. I'm so busting.'

'I'm sorry, Ryan, you'll have to try. Won't be much longer,' I promise, glancing nervously up the queue.

As the line moves up, Alfie starts spinning on the spot with his arms out, making what I can only assume are helicopter noises. 'Clear for take-off.'

I grab his arm to stop him spinning into an old lady who is standing behind us and looking annoyed. 'I don't think so.' I drag him forward to our new place in the queue. 'For goodness sake, just stand still.'

I know saying this to a kid with ADHD is like asking an emu to please fly away, but I can't help it. It's a reflex action born of frustration.

I keep my hand on Alfie's arm and he starts tap dancing, which thankfully he is doing on the spot for the moment.

'Oooh,' Ryan starts jiggling again too. 'I don't know if I'm going to make it.'

Thank goodness Charlie seems content to just stand there sucking his thumb. He's wearing a pull-up, so it doesn't actually matter if he has an accident.

Then a masculine voice cuts through my scattered thoughts. 'Why don't you guys go before me?'

I look up in surprise and gratitude to see that the handsome man I'd been eyeing off earlier has reached the front of the line. He's flipped his sunglasses onto his head and his green eyes twinkle at me. For a second I forget the kids and inhale deeply.

He's beautiful.

As in perfect.

Like a David Jones catalogue cut-out, with that slightly shy but earnest-looking smile.

Somehow I find my voice. 'Are . . . are you sure?'

'Yeah. I can, er . . . afford to wait a bit longer.' He tips his chin. 'You and the kids go.'

Ryan replies before I do. 'You're a legend!' Clutching his privates, he runs straight into a cubicle that has just been vacated and slams the door behind him. There's an audible sigh from within.

'Thanks. I really appreciate it,' I say, feeling my skin go pink with embarrassment.

Two more doors open and Mr Handsome gestures once again for us to take them.

'Thanks.' I send Alfie down to the one at the far end.

'Wait out here when you're done,' I say.

'Okay, Mummy.'

Charlie and I have to go in together. He'll need help, and I don't really trust him not to wander off while I'm in a toilet by myself. We take the door directly in front of the queue.

The cubicles are quite big. I assist Charlie first, pulling down his shorts and pull-up, which is, thankfully, dry, and seating him upon the toilet.

He obediently pees and I give him an encouraging thumbs up. 'Well done.'

He smiles up at me, his cherubic face the very picture of pride, and then he hops off and I pull up his shorts. Just as I start congratulating myself on another toileting success story, Charlie starts talking.

He can be a real chatterbox when he wants to be, and as I take my own turn on the toilet he decides to give a running commentary. As in, a blow-by-blow account that echoes off the high tin roof, audible to all the people in the line outside.

'You going to pull down your pants now, Mummy?'

'Yes,' I whisper.

'You got jocks on, Mummy. Pink jocks. Are those flowers,

Mummy? You like flowers on your jocks. Blue flowers, Mummy.'

'Yes, ssshh,' I hiss.

'Mummy, have you got a hole in your jocks?'

'No!' He sits down on the filthy floor to look at me thoughtfully, then disagrees.

'Yes you do.'

'Charlie, get off the floor. It's not clean.' I place my hand over the small hole in my knickers, which is just under the waistband and not really that big at all. I told you earlier that I needed to go shopping. It's just a little more urgent than I implied. So shoot me.

'Mummy, why you not sit on the seat when you wee? Why you stand up like that? You teach me, Mummy?'

'Yes. Definitely,' I hiss. 'Now get off the floor.'

He stands up and starts running his hands across the equally dirty walls, which have smudge marks on them. I cringe.

'Charlie,' I squirm, unable to move because I'm mid-flow, '*don't touch the walls.*'

'You gotta lot of wee, Mummy. It just keeps coming and coming.'

Tell me about it.

Finally, my body completes its job. I wipe myself and practically yank up my jeans.

'Well done, Mummy.' Charlie nods approvingly and then gives me a thumbs up, too. 'Well done.'

With a face as hot as an overcooked ham, I pull open our cubicle door, praying that Mr Handsome isn't still out there.

But of course he is.

He let that cranky old lady in line behind us go before him as well and he's still waiting, right there, outside my cubicle. His eyebrows are up and his lips curled in unmistakable amusement.

Honestly, I want to die.

God, please strike me down now. I've lived my life. This world doesn't need me anymore.

But God lets me live.

I tug Charlie over to the water trough to wash our hands. Mr Handsome walks quietly past us into the cubicle.

As we finish washing our hands I look up and notice the other people in the line smirking. A couple of ladies are covering their mouths with their hands, looking at the ground with studied concentration.

Great.

Just great.

'Come on, Charlie.' I take his hand and try to walk off with some dignity. 'It's time for lunch.'

Chapter 7

As soon as I turn the car off the main highway onto Rickety Twigg Road, I feel the worries I've lugged all the way from Perth drop away. The countryside is green and blooming. Spring has definitely arrived. There are wildflowers every-where, in white, purple and pink. They are gorgeous, even though I'm sure some must be weeds, due to the randomness of their plantation. Tall gum trees arch like a tent over the road. Sunshine dapples the dashboard through the shadow of their leaves.

It's vineyards galore out here, I can see fields of them rolling over gentle green hills. It's the low season, so the vines have been trimmed back to their stubs and the trestles are bare. But all that means to me is full cellars and a heap of wine to taste . . . *if* I didn't have three boys in tow, of course. I don't imagine I'll have the chance to cruise the cellar door scene while we're here. The boys would be bored senseless. Their whingeing would drive me and everyone else crazy if I took them along. And after my embarrassing incident at the pit stop just outside Bunbury, I'm reluctant to build on my reputation as the woman with the hole in her knickers.

Nonetheless, we can certainly check out the local berry farm, and the cheese and chocolate factory. The latter might require a few visits, just to make sure we get to try everything. I hear they've got a great park out the back, and they sell Simmo's ice-cream. Imagining all the flavours makes my mouth water. I'm sure the boys won't have a problem with that sort of tasting.

A sense of excitement begins to fill my chest. This is going to be a good trip. It's exactly what we all need.

I can feel it.

The first winery we pass is called 'Oak Hills'. It looks huge and well-tended. I can see five stars embossed under its name. Guess James Halliday has given it his stamp of approval.

'We're nearly there,' I announce without thinking, and then instantly hear a belt unclick, causing my blood pressure to go through the roof. Swearing under my breath, I glance up at the rear-view mirror.

Alfie's nose is pressed against the window, his body half over the top of Ryan, who is trying to shove him off.

'Alfie!' I yell. 'Get back in your seat!'

'But you said we're nearly there,' he complains.

'Emphasis on *nearly*.' I roll the word severely off my tongue. 'Put your belt back on *right now*.'

'Okay, okay,' he huffs, but complies, and I breathe a sigh of relief. I swear that kid is going to be the death of me – if he doesn't do himself in first.

The property is located somewhere on Rickety Twigg Road. The problem is, other than the winery we just passed, none of the properties on the road seem to be well marked.

I pull over onto the gravelly shoulder. The boys push their noses against the windows and look at the horses in the paddock in front of us. I study my map. There are only two wineries on Rickety Twigg Road. 'Oak Hills', which we have just passed, and 'Tawny Brooks', right at the far end. I've marked Gum Leaf Grove as somewhere roughly between. The house, I know from Gerard, is set back from the road, behind the leased vineyard. So I suppose I'm looking for a dirt track. I fold up the map and re-start the car.

'Aw!' Alfie and Ryan protest. 'We thought we were going to get out and pat the horses.'

'Pat the horsie,' approves Charlie. 'I pat the horsie too?'

'They're too far away,' I say. 'Besides, Mummy is more worried about finding a place for us to sleep tonight.'

'Aw!'

That word is used so often in my household, I sometimes feel I should notify Oxford or Macquarie so they can add it to the dictionary.

Aw /awwww!/ *Interjection, Colloquial* 1. An expression conveying dissatisfaction with a parent or guardian.

2. You're mean.

3. You're really, really mean.

4. You should really let us have our way.

I drive slowly. Luckily, there are no other cars on the road, so I can take my time looking for clues. Another wire fence appears, marking the end of the last paddock, and an area of overgrown land covered in native shrubbery and white lilies comes into view. The vegetation extends quite far back from the road, so I can't see if there is a vineyard behind it. I squint like an old woman over my steering wheel. 'Okay, boys, look for a –'

Then I see it.

An unmarked red gravel dirt track leading into the bushes. I put my foot on the brake just in time.

'This is it!' I exclaim and make the turn. My old bomb bumps and jolts as the wheels roll off lovely smooth tar onto unkempt red pebbles.

'Are you sure?' asks Ryan.

'No,' I grin.

'*Mu-uumm.*'

We drive for about a kilometre into the bush before the trees clear and I suck in a breath.

It's gorgeous.

The vineyard stretches either side of the road and over the hills beyond. The bare stubs stand like soldiers waiting for instructions. The trestles are laid out in rows and then cut into blocks by more gravelly dirt tracks. The vines are not green, but the roses at the end of each row are in full bloom and their scent fills the air. A group of bright blue birds take off from their perch on a nearby trestle and swoop our car as we pass, as if to say, 'Come to disturb the peace, have you?'

We keep going and as we crest the hill, the house comes into view.

And what a house it is.

The lower level is made of stone and is clearly the older section of the establishment. The upper rooms seem to have been added a little later, and are all timber. A verandah sweeps around three sides of the building. Don't get me wrong, it's not in good nick. There are boards missing and a section of gutter that's kind of just hanging there. Weeds grow thickly around and through the cobbled path leading up to the front door. The stone walls, particularly under the broken gutter, are stained and slightly moss-ridden. And yet . . . my foot lifts a little off the accelerator. The car chokes and slows as I stare, mesmerised.

You know when you meet someone so unbelievably charismatic you can't help but stop and listen to them? They might not be particularly good looking, or even a polished speaker. It's just something in the way they relate to you. They seem to know exactly what you're thinking, because they've already been through it. Well, that's how I feel about this house.

It knows stuff about me that I'm not even aware of.

And I need to find out what that stuff is.

I'm so wrapped in wonder, I don't notice the ute parked out

the front of the house till I draw up alongside it. Dismay pricks at me as I wind down my window to take a better look.

Damn.

Is this someone else's property?

Do I have the wrong house?

As though hearing my questions, the awful peeling front door opens and the house spits out a tall, wiry man. Mid-thirties, gangly of gait, his long brown hair tied in a ponytail at the nape of his neck, he freezes rather comically when he sees me. One foot hovers above the unkempt cobbles before he turns and goes straight back into the house. The door makes a decided click as he shuts it.

'Who's that, Mum?' Ryan enquires.

'I have absolutely no idea,' I say, then add, 'You guys wait here. I'll be right back.'

I kill the engine and get out of the car, then walk up the path and knock on the front door.

'Hello?'

No answer.

'Hello, I know you're in there.'

The door is flung open and I find myself once again confronted by the strange man.

'Madame?' His haughty French accent is accompanied by raised eyebrows over a long, ostentatious nose. 'How may I assist you?'

'Er . . .' I am momentarily taken aback by his excessive formality. 'I'm looking for Gum Leaf Grove. This wouldn't happen to be the homestead, would it?'

'It is, madame.' The man frowns, and then adds almost smugly, 'But I'm sorry to say that this is private property and, as such, if you wish to visit you must secure the permission of the owner first.'

'Well,' I smile just as smugly, 'good thing I am the owner . . . Or mother of the owners, I should say.' I gesture to my car, where two of my sons are half hanging out the windows, waving madly. 'Would you kindly let us into our house?'

The French man splutters. 'Your house? This cannot be. No one has seen the owner in years, and I do believe he is a man. Mr Jake, er, Beeman, or Bowman.'

I scoff. 'Yes, well, Jake was always rather self-absorbed. He never told anyone about this place. Not even his wife.'

'And you are?'

'His wife,' I respond, then screw up my face. 'Ex-wife. Grace Middleton.'

I hold out my hand and we shake, though his manner doesn't thaw.

'I still do not understand,' he says. 'Does Mr Beeman –'

'Bowman,' I correct.

'Mr Bowman. Does he know you are here?'

I tilt my head. 'Depends on whether you believe in the afterlife.'

He looks startled. 'Are you a believer?'

'Yes,' I say, my eyes narrowing as though peering through the branches of some weird forest we've accidentally wandered into. 'But that's not the point.'

'And the point is?' he prompts.

'Jake is dead. He passed away about a month ago, and left the house and the vineyard to our three sons. I am the trustee.'

'Is that so?' he responds, but remains where he is, clutching the side of the open door. A long pause stretches between us. He clearly doesn't want me to enter the house.

I sigh and then put my hand in my pocket and pull out the keys. 'If you don't let me into my house, I can let myself in.'

'Madame.' His long fingers flutter to his chest as though he is vaguely affronted. 'I would not be so presumptuous. Of course, if you have keys it is not for me to let you in or keep you out. It is just that I am not used to seeing anyone here, and one can't be too careful with vandals, you know.'

As if on cue, Ryan yells from the car, 'Muu-uum! What's taking so long? Can we get out of the car now?'

'Sure,' I say over my shoulder. 'Come on over.'

'Yay!!!'

The man at the door blanches as they come racing up the path and push past him, racing straight into the house with no care at all for his personal space. Sometimes it's kind of handy having kids. When he meets my gaze again, he steps back in resignation and I walk past him into the large entrance hall. The kids have already disappeared into the rooms beyond, and I can hear the echo of their screams and exclamations.

'Don't touch anything!' I call, doubtful they'll pay much heed.

I glance about. It actually isn't too bad. A little dark and musty, but it *is* an old house, and hasn't been lived in for twenty years.

I turn back to the man at the door. 'So, who are you and why are you here guarding Jake's house from vandals?'

The man's whole face seems to light up. 'I, madame, am Antoine Beauchene. Do not let my humble appearance deceive you.' The way he pushes out his chest doesn't deceive me at all. 'I am the son of Gaston Beauchene, whose great-grandfather founded Beauchene Wines in France, boasting the finest vineyards in all of Bordeaux and, indeed, the world. If you like, I can source you a bottle of our sauternes. You will not taste better.'

Is it just me or is he stalling?

'Thank you,' I say dryly. 'But that still doesn't explain why you are here. Or why you have "Oak Hills" written on your shirt.'

I have just noticed the white embroidered logo on his black polo shirt. It's my turn to raise my eyebrows.

His expression sours somewhat and he flicks the emblem with a long finger. 'This pains you, yes? It pains me too. That I, Antoine Beauchene, must sink below my calling as a winemaker to trudge about behind these amateurs, selling their substandard wine in their modern untried cellars, but I am powerless to leave.'

I blink. 'Why?'

'Australian women.' He shakes his head, a hand to his heart. 'They are both my weakness and my greatest love.'

I choke. 'Sorry?'

'It is not for you to apologise, madame. You cannot help the beauty, the temptation, the allure, that your sex uses to trap me so completely.'

A giggle escapes my lips. I can't help it. He's just too over the top.

'Ah, you laugh. Many do. But it is an affliction I cannot cure, despite having sampled many of the delights on offer in this town.' His hand makes a sweeping motion before he continues with a sigh. 'And so I remain here, by the side of my best friend, Jack Franklin, and his wife, the owners of Oak Hills, and generously offer my expert advice.' He frowns slightly. 'They don't always follow it, but that, madame, is a subject for another day.' His gaze suddenly focuses rather intently on me. 'Tell me, madame. Do you believe in second chances at love?'

For a moment, I am so astounded I can't speak. Am I hallucinating or is this guy actually coming on to me? The way his eyebrows are wiggling seems to confirm it.

It is perhaps a blessing that at this precise moment my boys return to the entrance hall.

'Is this where we're staying tonight, Mum?'

'Probably,' I say, choosing to answer Ryan's question rather than Antoine's.

'Awesome.' He darts through a doorway on our right and Alfie and Charlie try to keep up.

'You're staying here?' Antoine's voice seems uncharacteristically loud all of a sudden. 'Right here in this house? Tonight?' His eyes are darting up the staircase. I follow his gaze.

'Er . . . depends,' I say. 'What's the bathroom like?'

I move towards the wooden staircase, which appears to have a few steps missing. He quickly blocks my path.

'Oh, you don't want to go up there, madame. Very unsafe.' His hands flutter about his chest. 'Besides, there is a perfectly serviceable bathroom downstairs.'

'Serviceable, you say?' I enquire doubtfully. 'How serviceable?'

'It's through here.' He indicates the doorway opposite the one the boys went through.

I go in. The room is large, unfurnished and dirty but there is a stone fireplace on one side that gives majesty to an otherwise drab space. The carpet is gross, and peeling in one corner. Before I follow Antoine across the room, I pull it back further and am delighted to see solid wooden floorboards beneath.

Fabulous!

I drop the heavy mat and a plume of dust rises as it hits the timber. With a cough, I quickly follow Antoine into the adjoining bathroom. There's mould on the ceiling and lots of black spots on the mirror but, surprisingly, the actual amenities seem useable, and the room is quite spacious. The tiles are straight out of the seventies and chipping in places, but they seem clean enough. I turn on the tap over the cream enamel washbasin that was probably once white. The water runs crystal clear.

'Wow.' My eyes widen. 'I was expecting much worse. Does the toilet flush?'

I give it a go and laugh delightedly when it performs exactly as it should. 'Score.'

Antoine clears his throat. 'The grape growers who lease the vineyard have been allowed to maintain the water tank and pump, just so we have a bathroom facility when we are on the property. It's part of the agreement with Mr Bowman. We also pay for any electricity usage on the premises.'

My eyes narrow. 'So you're a grape grower then.'

'No.' Antoine shudders, then squares his shoulders. 'I mean, yes. That is one of my many roles at Oak Hills. One of my many unwanted roles in life.'

'So that's why you're here,' I clarify again, finger to palm. 'In our house. You're having a bathroom break between checking on the vines.'

'You're so very smart, madame.' Antoine inclines his head. 'It seems to me that I have no need to explain anything to you before you work it all out.'

With these words, he exits the room, clearly expecting me to follow him. I do so, not sure if he's being deliberately vague. This man, as far as I am concerned, hasn't shifted from my initial assessment, which is 'strange'.

'So,' he says loudly when we return to the foot of the stairs, 'wouldn't you rather go to a cosy B&B or a hotel? There are so many to choose from in these parts.'

'And no doubt all booked out over the school holidays,' I say.

Even if I could afford them.

'Nonsense,' he scoffed. 'Not if you have the right contacts – of which I have many. Would you like me to arrange something for you?'

'No,' I immediately decline. 'We always intended to rough it. In fact, we've brought tents.'

I walk across the entrance hall into the other room to see what the boys are doing.

The same dirty carpet covers the floor. On the chipped wall hangs a large, badly damaged oil painting in a gilded frame that is no longer very gold. The kids have dragged back the heavy, worse-for-wear curtains over the large window and let in some light. The glass pane is cracked and the frame riddled with cobwebs. All three boys have their arms out and are flying aeroplane-style through the dust particles illuminated by the sunlight streaming into the room. I cough at the sight of all that dust and cover my nose.

'Boys,' I whine. 'Really?'

'This house is awesome,' says Alfie. 'I've never seen snow before.'

'It's not snow,' I groan as the planes zoom out of the room. 'Don't go upstairs,' I call. 'It's not safe. How old is this house?' I ask Antoine.

He nods knowingly. 'Romantic, is it not? It used to be a coach inn, in the 1860s, for travellers journeying between Perth and the Bussell family home, Wallcliffe House.'

I look up in surprise. 'Bussell?' I repeat. 'You mean, the Bussells of Busselton?' I name the popular historical town just thirty kilometres east of Yallingup.

Antoine smiles. 'This was one of their properties, back when horses were the main mode of transportation. After that it was a dairy farm for more than five decades. I believe the second storey was added in the seventies when the new owners decided to turn the place into a bed and breakfast.'

A bed and breakfast.

For a second, just a second, I think about the possibilities. If I rip out the carpet, get rid of the painting, patch the walls and repaint, this room could actually be really nice. The glass in the window would have to be replaced, of course, and the curtains too. But the room itself is big and airy with high ceilings. It has such a great feel. The old stone fireplace, identical to the one in the other room, also gives it real character. I walk over to lay a hand on the mantel.

Who am I kidding?

Me? Grace Middleton? Running a bed and breakfast in the south-west?

Why not invite Ryan Gosling to be my business partner/ lover and make it a full-blown fantasy?

'So,' Antoine interrupts my pleasant daydream, 'these tents you speak of, you intend to pitch them outside?'

He seems to have this burning need to know exactly where I'll be sleeping tonight.

'Staying in the house seems safer. And with an operational bathroom, much more convenient.'

'But it's so dirty in the house,' he protests. 'You deserve better, madame.'

'The entrance hall is quite all right, and about the size of our tent.' I shrug. 'We can put down sleeping bags there.'

'But what about –' He breaks off, seeming to think better of what he was about to say.

I frown. 'What about what?'

'It is not my place to say, madame.'

I cross my arms in exasperation. 'It is your place now you've brought it up.'

'Well,' his hands flick up, 'of course, if you press me, then I must tell you. But honestly, I am surprised you haven't heard about it from someone else.'

'Heard about what?'

'The ghost,' he announces. 'This house, madame, is very, very haunted.'

Chapter 8

'*The what?*' I laugh.

Honestly, what does this man want? Gold medal for the world's freakiest first impression?

'The Ghost of Gum Leaf Grove,' he repeats, quite calmly. 'It lives here.'

I roll my eyes. 'You're kidding, right?'

Sure, I believe in life after death, good and evil, heaven and hell, and living a good life in order to go to the right place. But ghosts, as far as I'm concerned, don't have a role in my spiritual journey – nor do I want them to.

'You mock me.' Antoine puffs out his chest. 'But there have been reports of strange things happening here. Legends of tragedy in this house. Unresolved family business turned supernatural!' He widens his eyes on this last phrase, rolling the word on his tongue in the exaggerated fashion commonly employed by seventeenth-century soothsayers. Puh-lease!

'I'll take my chances,' I say confidently.

To be honest, it's not the evil spirit that worries me. It's the 'unresolved family business' that's got my mind ticking over. What has my wicked ex-husband left behind? Angry relatives holding a grudge? Bad blood between neighbours? This place has been deserted for over twenty years. Something terrible must have happened here for his family to just abandon it.

Antoine mistakes my silent contemplation for second thoughts.

'You cannot brush this off.' He shakes his finger at me. 'This ghost is after revenge.'

I shrug. 'But not on me, surely. I haven't done anything to it.'

'You're trespassing on its property.'

'This place belongs to my sons.' I fold my arms. 'And nobody else.'

'It won't care about that.'

'Then I'll just have to make it care,' I say, and then add with a cheeky grin, 'I can be pretty scary myself, you know.'

Antoine eyes me, clearly annoyed that I haven't fully grasped the ramifications of his point. But frankly, I'm a little over his opinion. I gesture towards the door and say with studied politeness, 'Well, thanks for giving me the tour and the local history. I think I can manage from here.'

'But, madame –'

I walk out of the room, hoping he will follow me. To my surprise, I emerge into the entrance hall to find Alfie, Ryan and Charlie crouching by the doorway. Have they been eavesdropping?

My eyes narrow. 'What are you lot up to?'

'We chasing the mouse.' Charlie beams at me.

Revulsion instantly replaces suspicion and I shudder. '*Great*. More good news.'

'It ran out the front door,' Ryan tells me. 'We were going to catch it and keep it as a pet.'

'And name him Mickey,' Alfie remarks wistfully.

'Come on,' says Ryan. 'Let's see if we can find another one.'

God forbid!

The three boys disappear into the rear of the house again.

'There, you see,' Antoine appears in the doorway of the room I have just left. 'This place is riddled with all kinds of pestilence, best to just leave.'

'I would rather the mice in here than the snakes out there,' I say with a firm smile.

'I can see, madame, that you don't believe me.'

'Really? What gave it away?'

He ignores my withering stare. 'Don't you see that your attitude only makes things worse?'

'How so?'

'You are a challenge!' he exclaims dramatically. 'Ghosts like nothing more than to convert nonbelievers. It is empowering to them, it is –'

Holding up my palm I cut him off. 'Antoine, I have three kids. I'm already used to things going bump in the night. I can handle it.' I move over to the front door and touch my hand to the knob. 'Now, if you don't mind, I have a lot of work to do to make this place habitable for the night.'

'Just for tonight?' he prompts. This is the last straw for me.

'Why are you so concerned about us staying here? It can't really just be about the ghost.'

Antoine sniffs. 'You have not heard the stories I have heard. The tales that –'

'We'll be fine, Antoine,' I interrupt sternly. 'Ghost or otherwise.'

'Very well,' he says with a stiff spine, his chin tipped up. 'Don't say I didn't warn you.' When I continue to stare at him, he sniffs again and struts over the threshold. '*Au revoir.*'

I watch him walk down the weedy path, then shut the door firmly behind him. Phew! That guy was starting to give me the creeps. Leaning back against the wall, I breathe in the sudden quiet of the old home. The only thing I can hear is the gentle tweeting of a bird in a tree outside.

Hang on a minute.

That really is *all* I can hear.

My heart flutters with that feeling that comes just before panic.

Oh shit!

'Boys!' I lift my voice and walk hurriedly into the rear of the house. The musty smell of unaired history hits me. I scan a large space that seems to be the dining and kitchen area. The dining room is bare of furniture, but relatively presentable. The kitchen, however, is a shambles. Most cupboards are missing their doors, though the hinges remain. The countertop is swollen with water damage around the sink. Scratch and burn marks stain the rest of it.

I open a large cupboard to make sure the boys aren't hiding in it. No boys, but some old brooms, buckets and mops that will come in handy later. There are two classic 1960s stoves and oven units next to the cupboard. You know the type, with the four coils on top and the large dials on the headboard at the back. They are painted a soothing aqua. Well, it would be soothing if the colour didn't have fifty years' worth of rust and grime worked into it. There are also three missing boys, who are probably off setting the house on fire, to keep my mind from relaxing.

'Boys!' I call again.

As I reach the other side of the dining room I catch their excited voices coming from the rooms beyond, and breathe a sigh of relief. I exit into a hallway where there are four rooms to choose from. A laundry (not much better than the kitchen), a large storeroom (housing shelves covered in junk), a second bathroom (best left undescribed) and, finally, a room that appears to be an office.

I say office because there's a desk in the centre of the room, though no chair. A dented filing cabinet sits in one corner, a rusty framed seascape print hanging on the wall above it. Old foolscap files litter the floor, and there's a box of loose pictures on the desk. This last item is what my kids are poring over.

'Mum, we found pictures of Dad,' says Ryan.

'Lots and lots of 'em,' says Charlie, who is enjoying the sensation of lifting the photos and letting them flutter out of his fingers back into the box, or onto the desk or the floor.

'Are you sure it's Dad?' Alfie's face is all screwed up. 'It doesn't look like him.'

'I'm sure,' says Ryan. He passes me a photograph. 'That's Dad, isn't it?'

I take the photograph. For some reason my gut twists at this younger, happier version of my ex-husband. He looks to be in his late teens – a shy, uncertain looking boy, a far cry from the man I knew. I realise I've never seen any pictures of Jake at this age or younger. I know nothing about his life before he moved to Perth. Unease tiptoes behind me once again.

I study the photo more closely. It's clearly a family party shot. There are people milling about in the background. Jake is standing with two adults I can only assume are his parents: a petite lady with short curly blonde hair, in a lace-trimmed blouse, and an older, balder version of Jake, in a white long-sleeved shirt and knit navy vest. They are both holding drinks. Mr Bowman is beaming with pride. Mrs Bowman has a more reserved expression, but she looks happy enough. There is nothing sinister about the photo. And yet, I get the odd impression that it's staged.

'Well?' Ryan prompts me, and I realise I haven't answered him. 'Is it him?'

'Yes,' I say slowly, my thumb on the central figure. 'That's your father.'

I look down at Ryan, who I suddenly realise is starting to tear up. 'Oh, honey.' I put an arm around him. 'What's wrong?'

'I want to show Dad what we found,' he says quietly. 'I want to call him up and tell him.'

I bite my lip. 'But you can't.'

Alfie taps Ryan on the head. 'Just tell him in your brain,' he says, with wisdom beyond his years. 'That's what I do.'

'Me too,' says Charlie with a grin. I'm almost certain he has no idea what we're talking about.

'That's a very good idea, Alfie,' I say solemnly. 'Your father can absolutely still hear you when you talk to him in your brain.' Then, to distract Ryan, I show him the picture again and point to the other people in it.

'These are your father's parents.'

'Our grandparents?' Ryan looks up at me earnestly.

'Yes.' I feel a pang of regret.

My kids have never known their grandparents. Not on my side or on Jake's. This is, in fact, the first time they've ever laid eyes on anyone from the previous generation.

'Where are they?' Ryan pushes his glasses up his nose. 'Can we go see them?'

'I'm sorry, Ryan,' I say. 'They both died, quite a long time ago. Before you were born.'

'Oh.' Ryan's face falls.

Alfie and Charlie are less interested in looking at the photos and more into playing with them. Alfie has begun using them to construct a house of cards, and Charlie is pushing piles onto the floor and watching them flutter into the dust.

'Charlie, no.' I quickly try to gather them all up. These may not be my memories, but they still feel precious. And who knows, the boys may want them when they are older. As Charlie runs out of the room I find myself studying each one.

There are some pictures of Jake and his family, but a lot of them are also of the house, set up as a bed and breakfast.

There's a picture of the dining room in all its glory. Three jarrah tables, fully seated with house guests. They've all raised their glasses to the photographer and are shouting something festive. Jake's mother is in the background, standing behind an immaculate kitchen counter, a tea towel slung over one shoulder. She looks . . . worried.

Another photo shows the front room with the fireplace fully stoked, the burning hearth casting a warm glow over the soft, tree-green couches, covered in throws and floral cushions. There are a couple of ottomans too, along with bookshelves and a coffee table overloaded with magazines and empty coffee cups. What an amazing room! The focal point of the picture, however, is two women. Jake's mother has her arms around another woman of similar age, stature and features. Cousins? Sisters? Whatever the case, for once her smile is radiant.

The rest of the photos are mostly of the house. And I have to say, my first instinct was correct. This place was gorgeous in its heyday. A true testament to country hospitality.

Majestic.

Warm.

Inviting.

So un-Jake.

I think of his interior design preferences – shiny and cold, modern and progressive. Always competing to keep up with the Joneses. It's hard to imagine that these were his roots.

What happened?

I mean, he told me there was a car accident, but it feels like there was more to it than that.

Unresolved family business.

And a ghost?

'Stop it,' I say out loud, throwing the photographs back in the box a little too roughly. 'You're not going there.'

Glancing at my watch, I realise it's nearly three o'clock. I'm wasting time. The boys have long since lost interest in the office, and indeed the house. I walk back through the dilapidated building and out onto the porch. The boys are playing cricket in the front yard. I stand on the porch watching them, and grin at their happy faces. They've never had this much space before. Back home, their cricket set is strictly a park-only toy. I watch Ryan hit the ball with a triumphant *thwack* and Alfie and Charlie groan as it goes flying off into the vineyard.

'Get it later,' I say. 'We need supplies. How about a drive into town?'

'Awww!' comes the response, like clockwork.

I don't blame them. The last thing I want to do is get back in the car, but I need cleaning products, and food for tomorrow.

'Don't be like that,' I say. 'We'll have an early dinner in town, too. How about it?'

Their cherubic faces turn to me as one. 'Pizza?'

'Why not?' It's fast becoming a staple.

As far as town centres go, Yallingup is not that big. There aren't really any shops, as such. Nowhere you can pick up more than a paper and a litre of milk, that is. So we drive further afield to Dunsborough, a coastal town on the shores of Dunn Bay, to stock up on groceries. A lot of Perth city folk enjoy Dunsborough as an easy holiday destination. In fact, I came here for school leavers' week after I finished high school. It's actually the last good memory I have of my childhood. The last time I remember not having a care in the world. I thought I was bulletproof back then. All I could see before me was opportunity.

Only a couple of weeks after that trip, my father was diagnosed with lung cancer. He died a few months later, leaving my family fractured and lost.

I shake off these morbid thoughts as I drive into the town centre. If I continue in this vein I'll start comparing that loss to this one. But Jake's death is very different. I'm no longer a defenceless child wanting my mum to come to my rescue. This time I am the mum, and there's no way I'm letting my kids down.

Dunsborough contains a few restaurants and cafes, a fantastic bakery, and a Coles conveniently situated in the centre of town. I pull in to the main shopping centre car park and kill the engine. 'Everybody out.'

There's mad clicking of belts and suddenly we're in the street. I grab the back of Alfie's shirt just as he's about to bolt in front of a car. 'Careful!'

Shopping with three boys is no picnic. In fact, I only do it when I'm in the mood for masochistic punishment of a violent nature. Today, however, we're on holiday and I feel quite upbeat despite one near-death experience already.

All in all, the boys are well behaved till we reach the check-out, where they immediately start lobbying for chocolates and lollies. I'm feeling generous, so I allow them to throw three lollipops onto the conveyor belt beside an array of cleaning products and sponges, and breakfast and lunch for tomorrow.

As we exit Coles, I notice a real estate agent across the street. Fletchers. The name is blazoned in blue and gold over the entrance, and the slogan 'We know what a home should be' is written beneath in cursive script.

Might be an idea to check them out, organise a consult or something? After all, I have to decide whether to sell Gum Leaf Grove. I look over at the boys. They are all quiet now, their mouths stuffed with lollipops. Seems like a good time. We dump the shopping in the car and cross the street.

As we draw closer to the building, I see the usual property photographs on display in the window with 'SOLD' stickers stuck across half of them. The double doors automatically open as our feet hit the welcome mat and we walk into a small reception area with a front desk flanked by two pot plants.

'Hello,' says the woman at the desk. She's got frizzy red hair, and acrylic nails to match. Her smile is as bright as her make-up.

'We've got lollipops,' says Charlie, as though this is the specific reason we've entered the building.

'So I see,' she nods enthusiastically. 'How jealous am I!'

'You can get 'em at Coles,' Ryan tells her helpfully. 'Except for the cola-flavoured ones. They're all out.'

Alfie pushes the top of the silver bell on the counter and I catch his hand just as he's about to do it again.

'Any chance you have an agent free for a quick chat?' I enquire.

'Absolutely,' the receptionist nods. 'Would you mind taking a seat over there? I'll see if our sales manager can talk to you.'

I hustle the boys over to some chairs by the window and we sit, momentarily. Alfie gets up after five seconds to do a lap of the room, picking up brochures from the coffee table, running his hands over another board filled with property listings. There's a framed family photograph right beside it, again with the words 'We know what a home should be' written beneath it. I stand up to grab Alfie's jiggling shoulders, and also to examine the photograph more closely. At a guess, I would have to say this picture is of the Fletchers. It's a portrait of a bearded man in his late forties – his arm is around his wife, a brunette of similar age – and they are standing behind a young man in his teens. He is a good-looking boy with dark hair and a pearly white smile. Quite the picture-perfect family for a family-run business. No wonder they've incorporated it into their advertising.

'We meet again.' There is a loose, masculine drawl behind me. I spin around in shock, involuntarily tucking some hair behind my ear. As if that's going to make a difference to my 'just blown in by the wind' appearance. My heart rate jumps to two beats per second and my palms start sweating.

'Er. Hi.'

It's the good-looking guy from the Bunbury toilet stop.

The one who knows exactly what my knickers look like.

That my bladder can hold a lot of urine.

And that I can do it standing up.

Damn! His hotness has not subsided one iota.

Did I have to run into him *again* today? I mean, why today? Why not tomorrow, when at least I wouldn't be wearing my ratty old T-shirt and jeans, which are now even dirtier after traipsing through the dust back at Gum Leaf Grove. Not that I think he took much notice of what I was wearing before. It's doubtful he even remembers my outfit, though he clearly remembers me.

He remembers me.

Now that's saying something, isn't it?

I mean, you wouldn't remember someone unless you kind of thought you might like to see them again. Would you?

Idiot! The six people in the line behind him would remember *you.*

And not because they want to see you again. Quite the opposite, in fact.

I realise my mind is running away like a six-horse chariot, so I yank on the reins and abruptly stick out my hand.

'I'm Grace. This is . . . certainly a coincidence.' I force myself to smile and meet his eyes. I like that I have to look up to do so. He's a nice height for a man. Just tall enough to lay my head on his manly shoulder when I'm in need of comfort.

Comfort?

Jake's death must have rattled me more than I thought.

My face grows hot as he takes my hand in his. 'I'm Scott.' His shake is firm and warm and his smile crinkles the skin around his laughing green eyes.

As I ponder this insignificant fact, Ryan covers for me as only a seven-year-old can. 'I would've wet my pants today if it weren't for you,' he says.

Scott clears his throat. 'Glad I could be of assistance.'

'So you married then?' Alfie suddenly stops pacing and steps in close. 'Got any kids our age?'

I gasp. '*Alfie*, your questions are too personal.' I shoot an apologetic glance at Scott. 'You don't have to answer that.'

'That's okay,' Scott laughs. 'I'm not married and I don't have any kids.'

'What about a girlfriend?' asks Alfie. 'Got one of those?'

Scott seems amused. I hope he doesn't think I've put my son up to this. 'No girlfriend.'

I find myself jumping down on my rising hope at his response. So what if he's single? I'm not on his radar. I'm not even on his planet. Get real!

'*I* have a girlfriend,' Alfie tells Scott smugly.

This statement is enough to cause my thoughts to snap off and my gaze to swing from Scott to Alfie in about a millisecond. 'What did you say?'

'I have a girlfriend.' He shrugs as though it's such a nothing, he almost forgot about it.

'Since when?'

'I don't know.'

'How did that happen?'

Alfie pouts. 'She started it. I just wanted a bite of her icy pole. Now she thinks we're in love.'

'I know exactly where you're coming from, mate,' Scott nods sympathetically. 'Women! Right?'

'She's not a woman.' Alfie snorts as though he's an imbecile. 'She's only five, like me. She has another boyfriend called Caleb but I don't mind because he doesn't like icy poles.'

As I realise in shock that my son is dating a tramp, he abruptly leaves the conversation and starts jumping over imaginary logs.

'Well, I don't seem to have much credibility with him,' Scott muses, and I return his smile. Just for a second, it feels like we're sharing a moment.

'Hopefully I do with you, though,' he adds seriously, his gaze never wavering from mine.

I can feel my face heating up again. 'Er . . . *with me?*'

'I assume you're here about a property to buy or sell?' His eyes twinkle as though he knows exactly where my thoughts have wandered off to.

'Er . . . um. Yeah . . .' I cough and bluster, trying to get the words out, but embarrassment is closing up my throat.

'I assure you,' he smiles again, 'I'm very good at my job. Fletchers is also one of the best agencies you can work with. We handle half the property market in the south-west. You'll be in good hands with me.'

Good hands?

Okay, buddy, I'm onto you! I resolve not to let any more innuendo, purposeful or otherwise, get to me. This is not the place or the time or the universe. I'm a single mum with varicose veins, stretch marks and limited free time. Let's get back to the real world.

'Perfect,' I agree, lifting my chin. 'I'm actually here to get some advice about a property my boys recently inherited in the area.'

'I see,' he nods. 'Whereabouts is it?'

'It's in Yallingup. The estate is called Gum Leaf Grove.'

His eyes light up in recognition. 'I know the one. Perhaps you'd like to come through to my office so we can sit and talk about this further?'

Ryan nudges me. 'Is this going to take long?' he asks. 'I'm bored, and Charlie is eating the magazines.'

I glance over at the coffee table, where sure enough, Charlie is sucking on the corner of *House and Garden* while simultaneously flicking through *Real Estate Monthly*. He still enjoys tasting everything he plays with.

'Charlie, please stop that.' I snatch *House and Garden* off him, wipe it on my top and replace it in the pile. Now I can add 'makes good spit sponge' to my previous list of attributes.

'Sorry,' I wince apologetically at Scott. 'The kids are getting to the end of their tether, I'll have to wrap this up quickly. Can I just ask you a couple of questions before I go?'

'Sure,' he replies.

'I'm really just curious about the property's market value and the ease with which you think it will sell. Not that,' I add hastily, 'I'm a hundred per cent certain I do want to sell it. I guess your answer will help me decide.'

'Well, as a local,' he says thoughtfully, 'I know a little about Gum Leaf Grove. Correct me if I'm wrong.' He ticks the points off on his fingers, 'There's about ten hectares, a home built by the Bussells – I think part of it is heritage listed, so you can't knock it down. There's also a leased vineyard.'

'Something like that.'

'I can do a valuation but I'll have to come out and inspect the property first. In terms of selling it, I'm pretty confident I could get a buyer fairly quickly, if you wanted to put it on the market. I mean,' he spread his hands, 'business has been slowing down lately, but Gum Leaf Grove is rather special. It's been sitting there for twenty years. I'm sure there are a number of people who have been waiting for it to be put up for sale. I could find out who they are.'

'Sounds good.' I nod. 'When are you free?'

'My schedule is pretty open on Tuesday.'

'Perfect.'

'Morning or afternoon?'

'Afternoon,' I say, determined to be more organised when I next see him. 'Perhaps around one o'clock?' There is no way I'm meeting this guy for the third time in a row looking like this.

Like what? my annoying inner voice demands. *Like you've got three boys and no life? Hard to cover that up with make-up, sweetheart.*

As if on cue, Alfie pipes up. 'Can we go now? I think it's time for pizza.'

'Absolutely,' I say. 'We'll see you on Tuesday, Scott.'

'Yes, you will,' he agrees.

We're about to leave when the double doors slide open and two men walk in – one looking close to retirement age, the other more middle-aged. It takes me a few seconds to recognise the older man from the photograph in reception. Firstly, because he no longer has a beard, and secondly because he's got at least two extra decades on him. But it's definitely the *Mr Fletcher* of Fletchers. The second man looks related to him, but doesn't seem to be the son in the photo, unless he's had a nose reconstruction. They both smile widely at us, but the older man addresses his sales manager. 'Hello, Scott, what have we here?'

'The new owners of Gum Leaf Grove, Bob,' Scott informs him.

Bob's jovial expression seems to freeze. 'New owners,' he repeats, seeming shocked. 'I didn't realise Jake was selling. I think I would have noticed if that property went on the market.'

'Me too,' his colleague agrees.

I decide to tread cautiously, not wanting to upset them. 'You guys . . . er . . . know Jake?'

Bob clears his throat. He seems a little embarrassed by the question, as though I've caught him out or something. 'I used to – when he was younger. I confess, I haven't spoken to Jake since he moved to Perth. He and my son Edmund were best friends throughout their school years. Edmund passed away when he was fifteen. It was a terrible loss for us all. He died in a surfing accident at Margaret River.'

The ghost!

A young boy perhaps, whose life was cut tragically short, tries to make contact with the best friend he left behind. I grit my teeth, forcing the speculation out of my mind like a toddler spitting peas. Stop it. Stop it. Stop it. I make myself speak again.

'So the photograph in the foyer . . .'

Bob's eyes flicker in surprise. 'Taken just months before.'

'I'm so sorry.'

I wonder how much more of Jake's hidden past I'm going to discover in the south-west. He never mentioned a childhood best friend. Though I guess by the time I came on the scene he probably thought it was irrelevant.

'I'm Sean.' Bob's colleague holds out his hand to me. 'Edmund's cousin. I also knew Jake. How do you know him?'

'He used to be my husband.'

'Oh.' Sean raises his eyebrows. 'I don't suppose you know how he is?'

I bite my lip. 'I'm sorry to be the one to have to tell you all. Jake recently passed away.'

Bob gasps.

I explain my connection to Jake, and the inheritance. Bob and Sean shake their heads, offering their condolences, which I can see are genuine.

'When young people die, it is a heavy, heavy blow,' Bob concludes. A dark cloud seems to descend on his brow. 'The world changes.' He makes a visible effort to rouse himself from the melancholy mood that seems to have overtaken him. 'So, selling Gum Leaf Grove, are you?'

'Another family business bites the dust,' Scott murmurs with a sideways glance at Sean.

'There aren't many of them left in town,' Bob agrees. 'It's a shame.'

Sean puts a hand on his uncle's shoulder and tells me, 'Fletchers have run Fletchers for the past three generations. So my uncle's a little biased about keeping business in the family.'

'And I'm getting old, too,' Bob groans. 'I'll be happy to pass the reins to you when I retire.' He turns his attention to my sons.

'So these are Jake's boys, are they?'

'Ryan, Alfie and Charlie,' I rattle off, gesturing to them each in turn.

'We're having pizza for dinner,' Alfie tells him.

He raises his eyebrows. 'Lucky you. And how old might you be, little man?'

'I'm not that little, I'm five and a half.'

Bob feigns shock. 'That old! My goodness, I'm sorry for mistaking you for someone younger. You look just like your father when he was your age, you know that?'

'Who do I look like?' Ryan demands, pushing himself forward and puffing out his chest.

I expect Bob to say me, because a lot of people do, but he doesn't.

'You have your grandmother's eyes,' he reveals, to my surprise.

'I've never met my grandparents,' says Ryan.

'Yes, I know,' Bob says sadly, and then abruptly turns to me. 'If you're looking for a good pizza place, I recommend the one next to the tavern on the other side of town. What's it called, Scott?'

'Ricardos,' Scott fills in for him. 'The Supreme is sensational.'

'Do they do Hawaiian?' asks Alfie sternly. 'Because we only like Hawaiian.'

'I believe they do.' Scott nods.

I take this as my cue to leave. 'See you later, Scott. Nice to meet you, Bob, Sean.'

'Same,' says Sean warmly, but his uncle just nods without smiling. I can't help feeling that 'nice' isn't really the word he would use to describe our chance encounter.

Chapter 9

We finish dinner just after five o'clock. I now have about two and a half hours of daylight left to clean a space in the Bussells' old house for us to sleep on. I still think the entrance hall is our best bet. The area already has all the jarrah floorboards exposed, so there's no stinky carpet to sleep on, no rickety old furniture to move out of the way. The only problem is, while the space is as big as our four-man tent, the boys will probably step on each other in the night to get to the toilet.

I decide to try ripping up the carpet in the large bedroom with the adjoining ensuite. It's not easy. Although it has torn away from its fixtures at the edges, it's heavy and smells like used socks and dog saliva. Luckily, unlike its neighbour, the room has no dust-riddled curtain. The railing is there, but the curtain itself must have been taken down ages ago.

It takes the combined effort of myself and my boys to roll up the carpet, and that's with a lot of screaming involved.

'No, Alfie! Don't let it go yet!'

'Charlie, wrong way!'

'Ryan, less chatting, more pushing!'

By the time we've rolled it up and dragged it out into the

entrance hall, I am exhausted, and I haven't even started cleaning the floor yet.

It takes about three sweeps and three mops. The first bucket of water is so black I momentarily consider bottling it and selling it online as ink. The boys have fun removing all the cobwebs in the room with the brooms, and then washing both sides of the window and, haphazardly, some of the wall beside it. Water splashes everywhere and the kids get soaked to the skin, but the glass and frame do look remarkably better, and they have a lot of fun doing it.

'Let's do the next one!' says Charlie.

'No, no,' I protest. 'Outside, all of you. Play and dry off.'

As they grab the cricket bat I turn back to the room and mop up the excess water.

Standing back with my hands on my hips, I realise it's a beautiful space. High ceilings, lovely ornate cornices and a large double awning window, beautifully framed in the same jarrah as the floor, with a generous wooden sill. I don't try to open the window because there's no flyscreen, though I do think one could easily be fitted.

Sure, if you were renovating this place, my inner voice makes haste to remind me. *But you're not. Are you?*

I turn my mind away from this pointed question and look at the view instead. Vineyard for miles, green hills on the horizon and the sun low, pink and orange fingers of light streaking across a violet sky.

Wow!

Sunset from my bedroom window every night.

I could get used to that.

But I can't afford to move here and renovate this place. It needs money to make it liveable, not just a good clean.

I eye the uncovered window again. Even though there's clearly no one for miles, I'm sure as soon as the sun rises tomorrow our bedroom will be flooded with light. I don't fancy waking at 5 am, so I get our tent out of the car, double it over and hang it from the empty railing above the window.

With the boys still busy outside, I walk across the hall into the room with the heavy curtains. Compared to the room we've just cleaned, it's a den of depression. If I'm going to sell this place as a renovator's dream, perhaps it would be best to strip this room down as well, just to give buyers an idea of how great the place could look with a little effort. I immediately decide to give it a go tomorrow, though I know the boys won't be pleased to be rolling up carpet again. My gaze wanders over to the damaged oil painting. It's definitely an eyesore, and should be easy enough for me to take down now and toss outside. I should probably start making a pile of junk. The painting isn't that big, and while the frame looks quite thick and ornate, I don't imagine it will be too heavy for me to lift down off the wall.

I'm wrong.

When I try to slide it up the wall off its hook, it won't budge. Not even slightly. It's like it's been permanently stuck on.

'What the? Why won't you come down?' I ask the ruddy thing in annoyance, as though it can answer.

I hook my fingers under the base and try to pull it outward. It moves slightly, but not much. There must be a latch or something holding it at the base as well. I press my cheek against the wall and try to slide my hand in behind the painting, feeling around for a latch, but it's very tight in there.

Suddenly, there's a noise behind me. A creaking floorboard?

I turn around, expecting to see one of the kids.

'Ryan? Alfie?'

But there's no one there.

I put my hands on my hips. 'Boys, are you hiding from me?' I step back out into the entrance hall.

The front door is wide open and I can clearly see all three of them playing cricket next to the car.

Odd.

I walk out onto the porch and squint at the sky. It's seven o'clock, there's probably only about half an hour of daylight left. If that. Time to call it a day.

There are lights in the front three rooms of the house, and in the bathroom. They work, and Antoine did say the grape growers paid the electrical bills, but I'm reluctant to overuse them. I'm not sure proper maintenance has been done on the electrical wiring. Best to get an electrician in to check they're safe before I use too much power.

By eight o'clock the boys and I have showered and changed into our pyjamas. We've arranged our sleeping bags and pillows in a circle on the floor in our new bedroom and are sitting on them. I've put a packet of Arnott's Delta Creams in the middle and handed out cups of milk from the esky as our supper.

Ryan and Alfie are holding torches under their faces, illuminating their milk moustaches.

'This is so cool,' says Ryan. 'I've never stayed in a haunted house before.'

I feel my brows knit as I turn to him. 'Who said it was haunted?'

'That guy who was here,' Ryan responds.

'The funny man wif a ponytail,' Alfie agrees with a mouth full of biscuit.

'He was a funny man, wasn't he?' I groan. 'I wouldn't take anything he says too seriously.'

As if to mock my words, we hear a strange sound from the heart of the house. Almost like footsteps going up the stairs. The soft scuff of a sole, the gentle creak of the wood underfoot.

We all freeze. The boys' eyes go as round as the biscuits they're eating. And then, as one, we all scramble out of our sleeping bags and race into the foyer.

The boys train their flashlights on the stairs but I go one step further and turn on the light. Electrical safety be damned.

I need reassurance.

Sure enough, the staircase is bare.

'What's up there?' Ryan demands.

'Just more rooms.' I try to sound casual.

There's a wooden landing at the top of the stairs and I can just make out a few doors beyond. There are cobwebs everywhere, smudge marks on the walls, and bits of the staircase are missing.

Antoine is right. It doesn't look very safe. All the same, I resolve to take a good look around up there in the morning, just to satisfy myself.

'I heard footsteps,' Ryan whispers, as though we might be overheard.

'It was probably just the wind,' I offer.

He shakes his head. 'Didn't sound like the wind.'

'Maybe it was another mouse.'

'A mouse goes squeak-squeak, Mummy.' Charlie tries to educate me. 'Squeak-squeak, like that.'

'It didn't sound like a mouse.' Alfie shoves his hands on his hips and eyes me sternly.

'Well, maybe it was just all in your imaginations.' I try again, this time injecting more confidence into my tone. They don't buy it. In fact, Charlie shakes his head and walks back into the bedroom.

'But you heard it too, Mum, the footsteps,' Ryan protests. 'Didn't you?'

I sigh. 'Yes, I guess I heard it too.'

'So what do we do now then?' Ryan nervously pushes his glasses onto the bridge of his nose, glancing around like something's about to jump out of the shadows.

Suddenly Alfie's face lights up. 'Call Ghostbusters,' he suggests in all seriousness.

I clear my throat. 'I, er . . . don't think I have their number.'

'Why not?'

I put my hand at the base of their spines and give them a gentle push towards our bedroom.

'It's classified information. Known only to the Australian government and the Queen.'

'That's bogus,' Alfie tosses his head. 'Just google it.'

Kids these days! Too much bloody access. I give up the fight and change the subject.

'Come on back to bed.' I turn off the foyer light and we make our way to the bedroom guided by their torches. Charlie is already back on his sleeping bag, three biscuits in hand.

'I don't think I'll be able to sleep now,' says Ryan as he gets into his makeshift bed. 'Not if there's a ghost wandering about.'

'Look,' I sigh, 'I know we all heard something but I'm sure it wasn't actually a ghost. I'm certain we'll find a logical explanation for the noise in the morning.'

'Like what?' Alfie demands. 'What else can sound like that?'

'It was Mitch,' says Charlie.

Our gazes swing as one to my three-year-old. 'Mitch?' I repeat.

'Mmmm,' Charlie responds absent-mindedly. He has pulled apart his biscuits and laid the six halves in front of him. He picks up the first one and carefully licks the vanilla cream from the inside. He's so absorbed in what he is doing, I don't think he realises what a stir he's caused.

'Charlie,' I say slowly, 'who is Mitch?'

'The man,' says Charlie, completely unconcerned. 'Outside.'

Alarm shoots off in my head like sparks from flint striking steel. 'There's a man outside?' I jump up and gingerly pull my makeshift tent curtain back a few inches. It's pitch black out there. I can't see a thing. We're in the country, for goodness sake. There's not a street lamp or car light to penetrate the darkness. My heart is almost stabbing at my ribcage. I have my phone on me, but there's no signal out here. It's not like I can call the police or anything. Damn it! I knew I should have taken those karate classes back when I was at uni.

I take a deep breath. Okay, Grace, get your shit together. If you can't see anything out there, how did Charlie see someone?

'Charlie, where did you see this man? Can you come to the window and point to him?'

Charlie shakes his head. 'He's gone home. It's dark now. He wants to sleep.'

'I see.' I release the tent curtain and come back to the sleeping bags. 'Charlie, when did you see this man?'

Charlie looks at me blankly.

'Did you see him just now?'

'Nup.'

'Did you see him when you were cleaning the window?'

He shakes his head.

'Did you see him when you were playing outside?'

He nods vigorously. Bingo!

I turn crossly to the other boys. 'Did you two see a man outside this afternoon?'

'No,' they both say in unison.

'We were playing cricket the whole time,' adds Ryan.

'Did Charlie go off and play by himself for a while?' I demand. 'I told you not to let him do that – to call me if he wanders off.'

Ryan shakes his head. 'He was with us the whole time, just outside the front of the house.'

'I said he could play.' Charlie nibbles on the tip of his biscuit. 'But Mitch don't want to.'

I look back at my older boys. 'Are you sure you guys didn't see anyone out there this afternoon?'

'Sure,' says Alfie.

'Positive,' says Ryan.

We turn back to Charlie. He shoves the last half of a biscuit into his mouth in one go, wipes two sticky hands down the front of his pyjama T-shirt and then gives me a smile full of crumbs. I try not to wince as I consider the possibilities.

Was this the beginning of an imaginary friend?

Charlie has a teddy called Tip, whom he sleeps with every night. He often tells me what Tip is saying. Could this just be taking it to the next stage? I grab Tip, who is seated, even now, on top of Charlie's pillow.

'Does Mitch know Tip?'

Charlie frowns.

I try a different tack. 'Have they met each other? Would Mitch and Tip play together, do you think?'

Charlie thinks for a minute. 'No. Mitch is a man. He don't play with toys.'

'Right.'

The other possibility is that my son is talking about that weird guy who was here when we first arrived. I hope Antoine didn't hang around after I thought he had left.

'Charlie –' I pause. 'What does he look like?'

Charlie gives me a blank stare and picks up his cup of milk. Slurping noises ensue.

'Does he have a ponytail?'

Charlie abruptly lowers the cup and gives me a look, as if to say, 'Come on, Mum, you're better than this.'

'He not a pony,' Charlie reprimands me. 'He's a man. I said that.'

'Yes you did,' I respond with a sigh.

I'm so frustrated. I think all mothers should be given a key to the back of their children's heads when they're born, so that every now and then, when the occasion demands it, they can open them up and take a good look at what's really going on in there.

Somehow, I don't think I'm going to get to the bottom of this tonight. And to be perfectly frank, if we do have a stalker, I'd rather find out in the fresh light of day than when I'm about to go to sleep in an old house that's allegedly haunted.

I glance over at Ryan and Alfie, who have slid down into their sleeping bags. Alfie has already fallen asleep, and Ryan looks on the verge. For all their talk of ghosts, they certainly faded fast.

Unfortunately, Charlie doesn't look as sleepy as he should. I suspect it's something to do with all the sugar he's consumed, and my ongoing interrogation.

'Come here.' I open up my arms and we lie down together. He snuggles in, head under my chin, smelling like shampoo and Arnott's Delta Creams. Some things never get old. He plays with my hair, which I have forgotten to tie up after my shower.

'I like your hair, Mummy,' whispers Charlie. 'Don't tie it back no more.'

'I have to tie it back,' I smile. 'So it doesn't get dirty when I'm working.'

'You wear it out sometimes,' pipes up Ryan with a yawn. 'Like at Daddy's funeral.'

That's because Carrie was there and I wanted to make sure I looked good. For some reason, leaving my hair down always makes me feel younger, prettier and a little more carefree. 'That's because it was a special occasion,' I tell Ryan. 'I leave my hair down on special occasions.'

'Oh,' says Ryan, taking off his glasses and rubbing his eyes. 'Do you think maybe the ghost might be Daddy come to see us? He never said goodbye before he died.'

Uh-oh, how do I deal with this one?

'Maybe it was,' I bite my lip. 'But even if it wasn't, I know that your father loved you very much, Ryan. He will always be watching over you.'

'I know,' says Ryan with a quiet reserve I recognise as his 'brave' voice. I want to reach over and pull him into my arms too, but I know from his tone he will only resist. Jake's death has hit Ryan the hardest because he understands it the most. Silence finally descends on our little group and I whisper, 'Goodnight, boys.'

'Goodnight, Mummy.' Ryan yawns and rolls over.

'Goodnight, Mummy,' says Charlie, and then after a pause he adds, 'Goodnight, Mitch. See you in the morning.'

Chapter 10

Ghost
Music and lyrics by Michel Beauchene
Copyright 2017

My life is one late night party
Lots of booze and a cloudy head
Baby there's no structure in my day
I sing songs for pay
And create juicy scandals for bread

I'm living fast out in LA
Sydney and New York when I choose
I never stay too long in one place
Don't think I can face
That I've really got nothing to lose

When I was young I wanted to sing
I didn't realise what it would bring
I know that I'm searching for something in all the chaos
I just don't know what

I didn't think it would be like this
Not quite knowing who to trust like this
Singing in the spotlight yet so invisible
Loud but invisible

I'm like a ghost, a sad ghost
Darling, all I am is a ghost, a sad ghost
A lonely ghost
A singing host
I am a ghost
I am a ghost

The line between gossip and real life is all a blur
And if I do meet a nice girl
She tends to prefer my world
Rather than learning who I am
Not that I can blame her
The truth is I only like to flirt
I keep my cards close
Because I suppose
Deep down I'm scared about getting hurt

When I was young I wanted to sing
I didn't realise what it would bring
I know that I'm searching for something in all the chaos
I just don't know what
I didn't think it would be like this
Never knowing who to trust like this
Singing in the spotlight yet so invisible
Loud but invisible

I'm like a ghost, a sad ghost
Darling, all I am is a ghost, a sad ghost
A lonely ghost
A singing host
I am a ghost
I am a ghost

Chapter 11

I wake up determined to make the new day better. Scott is coming to do his valuation on Tuesday, so I have two days to make Gum Leaf Grove as presentable as possible. Now, I know I can't work miracles, but I can certainly show this place's potential by cleaning it up and tossing out as much junk as I can. If I'm going to sell, I really want to get the best possible price.

But first things first.

Breakfast.

Our sleeping bags, which seem to function as both beds and a dining table, are the perfect spots to scoff milk and Weet-Bix, the boys' staple. I would kill for a coffee but am still not keen on testing any power points. I decide I'll drive into Dunsborough again this afternoon and call an electrician.

'Can we go outside now?' Ryan demands, shoving his empty bowl into my hands.

'For a little while,' I concede. 'We've got a lot of work to do today. Remember I said we're making a big pile of junk?'

'Yes,' he groans.

'Okay. Go.'

All three boys jump up and race outside.

I know I'm going to end up doing most of the work myself, but if I can get them interested, even for ten minutes, that's ten minutes I don't have to do. What's the point of having three boys if you can't get them to do *something*?

While they're off having their fifteen minutes of freedom, I clean the breakfast dishes in our bathroom, roll up the sleeping bags and take down my tent curtain. Once again, I marvel at the transformation I have affected in this room. All it needs is a lick of paint and it'll be just about good to go. If only the rest of the house was like this.

Well, the room across the hall shouldn't be too bad. I wonder if I'll be able to take down the curtains myself. I walk out of the master bedroom, across the hall and into the room in question. Let's call it the sitting room. I think it has to be the room from the photograph of Jake's mother and her female friend. The one with the green couches. I'm sure they were right –

My thought breaks off and my feet stop dead.

The painting – it's moved.

As in, it's opened, like a cupboard.

I can now see that the badly scratched and dented gold frame is hinged on one side, with a latch on the other. I can see that unless you knew the latch was there and undid it, the painting would feel like it was permanently stuck on.

Framed into the wall in the space behind the painting is a pigeonhole divided by two shelves. The top shelf is empty. The second shelf has a small leather-encased ring box. The bottom one has a box on it too, a bigger wooden box with a latch but no lock.

I feel like I'm in an episode of *Scooby-Doo* or something.

I mean, *really*, a hidden space, camouflaged by an old painting that mysteriously opens in the middle of the night? Maybe I should call Hollywood. I wonder if I'll get to star in the movie. I'll insist upon Ryan Gosling being my leading man, of course, and some sort of romantic thread being woven into the plot. Perhaps he could be the detective I hire when the clues become too complicated.

Okay, I've got to stop. This is not a laughing matter. There's a secret compartment in our sitting room that opened by itself.

But that's ridiculous.

Who's been in here?

The boys?

It's too high on the wall for any of them to reach the latch. They'd need to stand on something, and there's no furniture in the room.

Besides, I was with them all night, and I don't recall any of them getting up even to go to the toilet. I'm a pretty light sleeper, particularly when it comes to people stepping over me.

So that leaves . . . the ghost.

I cough in derision.

I mean, for starters, even if ghosts were real, they are reputably ethereal in nature. As in, they've got no substance. They can't actually open anything, or pick anything up. Can they? A shiver passes through me, and I wonder in horror whether that was me or the ghost.

Just as I conclude that I'm definitely losing my mind, another possibility reveals itself.

Antoine.

This time I'm angry.

The fact that he was inside the house when we arrived indicates that he has a key and can come and go as he pleases. He was also suspiciously against the idea of us staying here, inventing stories about ghosts and such. Perhaps he returned in the middle of the night to get whatever it was he was protecting. You know, snuck in and robbed us.

My gaze flicks back to the pigeonhole in the wall and I notice again that the top shelf is empty. Was there something there before? Has it been taken?

It seems like the most logical explanation. The question is, what to do about it? Do I contact Antoine and accuse him?

Seems pretty extreme. I've got no proof of anything. At the very least, though, I could demand he give me his key. But what if it wasn't him who came in during the night? What if it was one of the other growers who had heard on the grapevine, pardon the pun, that there were some new owners in town snooping around their secret cubby hole? All the locals around here know each other, maybe Antoine told someone about us after he left yesterday. Maybe Scott, Sean or Bob had told someone. If the Fletchers knew the Bowmans, other families might remember them too. Maybe . . .

Abruptly, I snatch up the ring box on the middle shelf and open it.

Empty.

I mean, apart from the bed of white felt with the slit in the middle of it. Out of curiosity, I pull it out and am immediately rewarded by a message written in blue ink on the white cardboard base of the box.

Yours, Now and Always.

Well, that's romantic. Did Mr Bowman give this ring to Mrs Bowman? And if so, where is the ring now? I snap the box closed and put it back on the shelf, my belief that we've been robbed only intensifying.

Perhaps a trip round to Oak Hills this afternoon was a good idea. Didn't Antoine say he worked in the cellar door? I could sound him out subtly, see if he looks guilty.

I groan.

This is not how I had envisaged my holiday unfolding.

The boys and I are only here for a week. I have so much cleaning to do, but I want to squeeze in some fun things too, like the beach and the chocolate factory. I really don't need to be chasing French men around the south-west, trying to discover what nefarious activities they or their friends are up to. I have quite enough on my plate, and decisions to make as well. Like, to sell or not to sell. I mean, if we want to keep this place as a holiday home, I can just clean up the front end of the house and do some electrical maintenance. On the other hand, selling could mean I can work part-time. Be there when my kids come home from school. Afford more therapy for Alfie, and have more time for it.

Do you know how many books I've bought on ADHD?

How many of them do you think I've had time to read?

None.

Right now, I'm just winging it. Blundering my way through my son's concentration issues and hyperactivity – trying every bloody thing that's recommended to me by teachers and therapists alike. There's no order to any of it, it's as random as his disorder. Do I really want to continue like this? No plan, no program, no control. Is that really how a good mother behaves? I think of my own mother, who gave up the ability to control her life – surrendered it to alcohol. I know this is not the same thing, but I can't help but draw parallels. I never want to be like that. I never want to let the tide of life run away with me. And yet, is parenting perfection really attainable? How can you be the best mother in the whole world without a guidebook?

To distract myself from this depressing question, I step forward and take the wooden box from the pigeonhole. May as well see what's in there, if anything. I open the box.

Fake passports?

A gun?

A magic lamp?

No.

It's just a bunch of old letters, still in their torn envelopes. Most of them are postmarked . . . yep, twenty-odd years ago, and all addressed to the same person.

Alice Bowman.

Jake's mother?

The letters were sent to a post-office box in Dunsborough. I can't help but wonder if it was one Alice had separately from her husband or business.

I open the oldest letter. It is only one sheet. Handwritten, in blue cursive script.

Dear Alice,

This feels so old-fashioned, but I guess, as you say, your husband may pick up the phone if I call. I know writing to me at night helps you feel better. So please keep doing it. Don't stop. I'm your sister, after all. I want to be there for you. Treat me as a diary, if you will. Or a safety deposit box. Every secret you send to me is safe.

I wish I wasn't so far away. I don't like thinking of you all alone out there with that idiot. Are you sure you are okay? You're not holding anything back from me, are you?

I'm sorry, but I have to ask this question again. Are you certain you want to stay with him? You don't have to, you know. Divorce seems like a huge step, but I'll help you. You can even live with me for a while. Jake too. I love that boy as much as my own. He's a smart kid. Resilient, too. He'll make new friends in Melbourne, I'm sure of it. There's plenty of room in our house for both of you. I've even spoken to Frank about it. He's as worried as I am, Alice. And he's willing to help. Tell David you want a trial separation. If nothing else that might knock some sense into him. I'm telling you, Alice, with alcoholics, pleading does nothing. You've got to shock them into realisation!

That's where I stop reading. I know where this is going. In a flash, I know all of Alice's concerns, all of her worries. I know why she wanted to leave her husband and also why she felt like she couldn't. All of a sudden, Jake's childhood feels like a page from my own history. We could be cut from the same cloth. Why didn't he confide in me about any of this? He knew my mother was an alcoholic. He knew I would understand. I wouldn't have judged or condemned. If anything, I would have loved him more because I would have known how much he needed it.

And now, here I am feeling betrayed . . . *again*!

How can one man manage to hurt someone in so many ways, and then continue doing so even in death?

'Geez, Jake,' I say out loud. 'Have you ever heard of giving it a rest!'

I jump at the sudden stampede of incoming feet.

'Mum, Mum! There's a dead roo in the vineyard,' yells Ryan.

I quickly fold the letter up and stuff it back into its envelope. 'I hope you didn't touch it,' I say as they all appear in the doorway, flushed with excitement. I put the envelope back in the box with the others and shut the lid.

'We poke it with stick,' says Charlie. 'All the magnets crawled out.'

'You mean maggots.'

'Yeah, magnets.' Alfie wiggles his fingers next to his face in a distinctly hair-raising manner. 'And then –'

'*Gross.*' I put up my palm to stop further explanation, wondering for the ten million, nine hundred and eighty-eighth time how I ended up with three boys. 'Please, just leave it alone. Allow that poor animal to decompose in peace.'

'We're not going to bury him?' Alfie demands, clearly disappointed. 'I can dig. I can dig a big hole.'

'A big, big hole,' Charlie adds, stretching his arms wide. 'So he fits.'

'With what shovel?' I ask Alfie pointedly.

'Er . . .' As he tries to answer, Ryan walks further into the room and is staring up at the painting in amazement. He grabs both sides of his glasses as though the lenses might be faulty. 'Mum! What have you done?'

'Well, funny you should ask.' I preen a little. 'I've been having a bit of an adventure myself. As you can see, I've found a secret compartment in the wall.'

Alfie immediately forgets what he is saying and his eyes, along with Charlie's, grow round like jar lids. 'You have?'

'Yep.'

'You got treasure?' asks Charlie, pointing at the box in my hands.

'Sort of,' I wince. I point at the jewellery box in the wall. 'That one is empty, and this one –'

Alfie snatches it off me and opens it. 'It's nothing,' he tells the others dismissively. 'Just envelopes.' He shoves it back into my hands. 'Can we go outside again?' He starts to hop, on one foot and then the other.

'No.' I rub my hands together. 'Now we start cleaning.'

'Awwwww!'

'But if you're all good and do your jobs, we might go to the beach this afternoon.'

'The beach!' they exclaim and start jumping. The idea is clearly a winner. Hopefully, I'll be able to pop in at Oak Hills while we're out. Having sealed the deal, I manage to get them to help me roll up the carpet in the sitting room, the same way as yesterday. We drag this into the foyer, then haul both carpets out onto the front porch. I still don't know how I'm going to dispose of them, but that's a problem for another day.

Next, I pull an old chair in from the dining room. I stand on it and unhook the curtains. The boys have fun watching them fall and then dragging them out to join the carpet.

After that, the boys clean the windows while I sweep and mop the floorboards. Of course, as is so often the case with children, what worked well one day doesn't always have the same success the next. Alfie, in particular, is not interested in the task and more keen on annoying his brothers. It's not long before he and Ryan are fighting.

'Mummy! Alfie wet my shoes!'

'Did not!'

'Mummy, Alfie keeps wiping in my space.'

'Do not!'

'Mummy, I hate Alfie! Why can't he just stand in one spot?'

As I can hardly refer Ryan to Alfie's paediatrician for clarification, I put my broom down and wipe the sweat from my brow. 'Okay, Alfie, I think it's time you got your own window.'

I march him out of the sitting room and into the dining and kitchen area. There's another room adjoining this one. I assume it's a private dining room, as was common in coach inns back in the day. It's empty, unless you count the half-inch-thick layer of dust on the floor and the spider webs on the cornices. The window is large, undamaged and curtain free. Perfect.

'Alfie, this window is all yours. In fact, this whole room is yours. What would you like to do first?'

'Play pirates.'

'I meant which part of the room would you like to clean?'

Alfie huffed. 'Nothing.'

My eyes dart about the room, searching for some element that might appeal to him. 'How about the spider webs? You could use the broom to sweep them all away. Be careful of redbacks, though.'

I say this even though I've already checked all the spiders present in the room. No dangerous predators as far as I can see, but my warning is enough to trigger Alfie's interest.

'Will it be dangerous?' he asks.

'Very!'

We fetch a broom from the stash in the kitchen and he immediately hops astride it and starts galloping around like a cowboy on horseback. I have no hope that he will do any work at all. Or even that he'll stay here and not come back and pester us within minutes. But I leave him to it and get back to my own task. Better to take the chance while I have it, even if it's only for five minutes.

I get stuck back into sweeping the sitting room while Ryan continues with the window and Charlie plays with his Thomas train on the sill. Before long, I've swept and mopped the floor twice. As I stand back to admire my work I realise I haven't heard a peep out of Alfie in ages. I check my watch.

Shoot! It's been close on half an hour.

I lean my mop against the wall and hurry out of there, only just registering Ryan's voice behind me.

'Mummy, what's the matter?'

'I'm just worried that –' I skid to a halt in the doorway of the private dining room.

Alfie is still galloping around on his horse, yelling, 'Coooeeee!' on every turn.

The room, however, is immaculate. The floor is swept. The webs are gone. The skirting boards are dust free; in fact, they almost look like they've been wiped. Even the smudges on the walls have vanished.

'Alfie,' I say in awe, 'what have you done?'

Alfie jumps off his horse and, flushing slightly, stands to attention. 'Nothing.'

'Alfie,' I try to lighten the tone of my voice, 'you're not in trouble. I just want to know how you did this.'

'Did what?' Alfie blinks.

'The room.' I wave my hands impatiently. 'The webs are gone –'

'I used the broom,' Alfie smiles. 'And I had to kill some.' His voice becomes smugly satisfied. 'They tried to run, but I got 'em all.'

'I can see that,' I swallow. 'But where's all the dirt and the dust?'

'We swept it all up and tipped it outside.'

'We?' I raise my eyebrows.

'Mitch and I.'

I'm completely lost for words.

Completely.

I can only gape at him.

'*Okay*,' he amends, folding his arms and sticking out his hip. 'He did *most* of it, but I helped.'

It's lucky I am standing in a doorway so I can grab the frame for support. Meanwhile, Ryan gasps, though more in excitement than fright. 'You saw the ghost!'

'Yeah!' Alfie tells him proudly. 'And I didn't scream or nothin', even though he was pretty scary.'

'He was scary?' I repeat weakly.

'He's really big and his skin looks like it's melting.' Alfie pulls his cheeks down so I can see the red skin beneath his eyeballs. 'He says he can't go outside because the sun burns him.'

'So he's a vampire as well,' Ryan whistles.

'Maybe,' agrees Alfie. 'He didn't ask to suck my neck. But he did look hungry.'

'Okay, that's enough.' I straighten my shoulders. 'I'm going to sort this ghost thing out once and for all.'

Both boys look at me, startled. 'How?'

'I'm going upstairs.'

'Huh?'

'Why?'

As I turn back to the kitchen, Charlie emerges from the sitting room and joins us. He points excitedly towards the stairs. 'You go up there, Mummy? You go up there?'

'I certainly am!' I say with gusto. 'And if I had a pitchfork I'd take it with me.'

'But it's not safe,' says Ryan, as Charlie bends down to rummage around in a wood crate beside the kitchen counter.

'Which is why all of you are staying down here.' I point at each of them in turn. 'I'm going up on my own. If you hear me scream . . .'

I break off. What should they do if they hear me scream? What if there is an axe murderer up there, masquerading as a ghost/vampire, hiding evidence of his dirty deeds in secret compartments? I blink at the sheer absurdity of my thoughts. More likely to be some teenage prankster trying to mess with our heads. All the same, I square my shoulders. I'll take a weapon.

As if to echo my thoughts, Charlie stands up. 'Here, Mummy.' He's holding up an item of silver cutlery. 'Pitchfork.'

'If only it were bigger,' I nod. 'I'll take the broom instead.' I walk back into the private dining room and retrieve it from where Alfie has left it on the floor.

'But you didn't tell us what to do if you scream,' Ryan whines, pushing his glasses up the bridge of his nose. He's starting to sweat. I can tell he's getting scared.

'Look, don't worry. I'm going to be very cautious. I'm just going to peek up there and if I see anything at all –'

'Like a zombie,' Alfie giggles gleefully.

More like the unmade bed of a squatter.

'– you are all to run to the car.'

'Then what?' Alfie demands.

'I'll run downstairs and join you and we'll go get the police.'

'Do police arrest ghosts?' Ryan's voice is a little shaky.

'If they break the law,' I say firmly.

'Awesome!' Alfie pulls a fist down in front of his face.

'Alrighty.' I put a foot on the first rickety step. 'Time to give Mitch his marching orders.'

Chapter 12

The stairs aren't that bad. I mean, there are a few steps missing, and a couple wobble under my feet, but the central landing is intact and in my opinion perfectly serviceable. The boards creak under my feet, but I make it to the second floor fairly easily and completely unscathed. I'm beginning to think that Antoine has exaggerated the safety issue just to keep me from investigating further.

Ha! Foiled after one night.

The floors are timber up here, too. An old and very dirty oriental rug graces the centre of the landing. I walk around it in case the boards beneath are damaged, and enter the first of the four upstairs rooms.

'Mummy, what do you see? What do you see?' yells Ryan from below.

'Nothing yet!' I call back, scanning what appears to be an empty bedroom.

There's a wardrobe against one wall. No bed, but a shadow on the plaster indicates where a headboard used to be. There's a set of modern venetian blinds on the window – much the worse for wear, I might add. Several slats are missing, and those that remain look nasty – rusty and cobweb-ridden.

I move on to the second room. This one has no furniture at all. It's completely bare of anything except dirt and mice droppings. Some of the floorboards are also damaged. Not critically – I don't imagine I'll fall through if I step on them, but I'm not quite game to try it. The damage does have me wondering about termites, though.

The third room is small and nasty. It is, I imagine, what used to be a bathroom. I'm not surprised the vineyard workers chose to maintain the one downstairs instead. The inside of the toilet bowl is completely black. The bath enamel is cracked all the way through – filling it with water would be a mistake. Not that you could, given that the taps are gone, and so is the faucet. The tiles are mouldy, cracked and the most disgusting shade of orange I have ever seen. I shut the door to the room behind me. The handle almost pops out as I do so; it's hanging there by one screw.

Oh dear!

The final room is rather small for a bedroom, so I figure it must be a study or another office. There's an empty bookcase against the back wall, but apart from that . . . nothing.

And no one.

There's no sign that anyone has been up here in ages.

Seriously?

I rub my temple. I was so sure I was going to surprise our intruder up here. After hearing those footsteps on the stairs last night, and then finding the painting opened up this morning . . .

I bite my lip.

So if there's no one up here, and there's no one down there, who the hell cleaned up my private dining room? Alfie?

It's not that I don't think my child is one in a million. Because he is. He's a very special kid. But even in proud parent mode, I can't bring myself to believe he cleaned that room, all in one go, completely unsupervised. He has ADHD, for goodness sake. He literally can't focus. I check the rooms one last time and then slowly descend the stairs.

'What's wrong?' asks Ryan. Alfie's off banging cutlery with Charlie.

I rest my case.

'Nothing,' I say slowly. 'There's absolutely nothing up there. Just four empty rooms.'

'Can we see?'

'No. I'd still prefer that you guys didn't play upstairs. Some of the floorboards are damaged.'

Despite getting his compliance, the butterflies hatching in my stomach continue to increase in numbers. What the hell is going on here?

Am I really dealing with the possibility of a ghost? I say 'possibility' because I want to keep these ricocheting thoughts within the realm of 'this might not be happening.' Even though it is.

It totally is.

The hairs on the back of my neck stand up in slow succession, as though my sixth sense has just woken up.

I honestly do not know how to deal with this.

'Mummy,' Ryan tugs on my sleeve, 'are you okay?'

Hell no.

'Of course,' I reassure him. After all, I'm a mother first, a freaked-out woman second. 'In fact, let's go to the beach early.'

'Woohoo!' He runs off to tell the others while I make a mental note to drop in at Oak Hills on the way. There have got to be more answers than the ones currently scaring me shitless. It's about time I had another chat with Mr Antoine Can't-Remember-His-Last-Name.

'Change into your bathers then put your clothes back on top,' I instruct the kids. 'Come on, Charlie,' I hold out my hand, 'I'll help you.'

I end up helping Alfie too, because he gets distracted halfway through changing.

However, eventually we're all in the car, beach bag in the boot. I've packed sandwiches for lunch, biscuits and water bottles. We'll have a picnic after our swim. Hopefully I'll be sufficiently relaxed by then, after my conversation with Antoine.

Oak Hills is a two-minute drive north down Rickety Twig Road. I use this time to think about the questions I'm going to ask.

'You know that ghost you mentioned, is he called Mitch?'

'Does he like cleaning?'

'And what's with the vampire tendencies?'

They sound completely unhinged, even to my unsettled mind. The important question is, 'Do you know of any secret compartments in the Bussells' old coach inn?'

That's what this is really all about. Not some creepy ghost. Antoine must have told another grape grower about us. Another grape grower called Mitch, who came back to retrieve his belongings from the secret hole in the wall and decided to stay for a spot of cleaning.

Argh!

I refrain from slapping my palm to my head as my reasoning unravels into absurdity again.

As I turn into the Oak Hills property I see a fork in the dirt track. One is unmarked, probably leading to the residence, and the other has a sign directing visitors to the cellar door. I take this route and not two minutes later am parking in a red gravel car park framed by logs. The cellar door is a good-looking building, made mostly of stone with a wooden roof. It's flanked by native floral varieties, and a creeper climbs lazily across one side and up to the gutter, the leaves are a dark velvety green, pretty and delicate. My mood lifts a little.

I turn around in the driver's seat to look at my boys. 'Now, we're not staying here long, but I do expect you to behave. No fighting, yelling or running inside, okay?'

They nod unanimously and I unlock the car. The back doors practically burst open as my sons jump out, shoving and pushing each other in an attempt to be the first on the gravel.

'Beat you losers to the door!' cries Alfie and they're off.

Seriously?

Do my kids speak Japanese or something?

Didn't I just say . . .

What's the point?

I get out of the car and hurry to catch up. Luckily, once they're through the double doors they halt, looking around in considerable awe.

To be honest, it is rather intimidating.

The left wall is completely glass, looking straight out onto a gorgeous section of vineyard. The bar on the back wall is long and shaped in a stretched 'S', with stainless-steel spittoons in the curls at each end. There's a young woman behind the bar, wearing the same black Oak Hills polo shirt I saw Antoine in yesterday. She is serving a middle-aged couple who are reverently tasting a red in large wine glasses. After swirling and sniffing, they tentatively touch the drop to their lips before permitting a whole mouthful to wet their palate. I can see I'm going to have to wait a while to speak to the attendant.

I scan the rest of the room. There are only two others present – two women in their mid- to late-thirties, seated on one of the many burgundy couches arranged around the room. To my surprise, they also have children with them. One of the ladies, an attractive brunette with a great smile, has twin boys who look to be around three years old, seated on the polished wooden floorboards at her feet. They are playing with a couple of plastic trucks and a handful of Matchbox cars. My sons immediately walk over.

'Hey,' says Ryan. 'I like your trucks.'

'Do they make engine noises?' asks Alfie.

'Yeah,' says one of the boys, pushing the button on the side to demonstrate. The toy makes a revving sound and he imitates it as he drives the truck across the floorboards. Charlie sits down next to him, watching closely. I know that look. He's waiting for an opportunity to take the truck for himself.

I quickly walk up to the group.

'Sorry,' I say to the ladies, who have stopped talking to smile at my intruders. 'Didn't mean to interrupt.'

'Not at all.' The blonde woman stands up. 'I shouldn't be taking such a long break.'

I notice for the first time that she's also wearing a black Oak Hills shirt.

'Have you come for a tasting?' she enquires politely.

'Er . . . no,' I quickly reply. 'I'm actually here to see Antoine. I met him yesterday. Is he around?'

'It's his day off.' She wrinkles her nose. 'Is it something I can help you with? I'm Bronwyn. My husband and I run Oak Hills, so if you have a question about our wine I'm sure I could answer it.'

'Thanks.' I smile back. 'I'm Grace, by the way. It's nice to meet you. I wanted to talk to Antoine about Gum Leaf Grove, actually. Do you know when he will be working there again?'

The two women exchange a look and laugh.

'Ant is a lot of things,' Bronwyn explains, 'but a vineyard worker is not one of them. He's strictly in the wine industry for the prestige and the pomp, not the dirt and the bugs.'

'Oh,' I frown. 'So what was he doing at Gum Leaf Grove yesterday then?'

'I have no idea,' Bronwyn shrugs. 'My husband, Jack, does have a couple of blocks over there, but he wouldn't send Ant over to inspect them. And even if he did, Ant would most likely refuse. He's a winemaker, you know.' Her lips twitch. 'Son of Gaston the Great.'

'He did say that,' I agree. 'Among other things.'

She must have caught the derision in my voice because she laughs again. 'Did he ask you out?'

'No,' I hesitate. 'But he did talk about the ghost.'

'The ghost of Gum Leaf Grove,' the brunette muses with a sentimental sigh. 'Wow, I haven't heard mention of that since I was a teenager.'

My heart plummets and I look from one woman to the other. 'So you guys know about this ghost?'

Please don't tell me it's real. Please don't tell me it's actually a legitimate rural legend. That would be just my luck – woman is stripped of all her material possessions by her evil ex-husband, then inherits his haunted house, which proceeds to take her soul as well.

Just super.

'Not me,' Bronwyn holds up her hands in denial. 'I know nothing about it. But then, I haven't lived here practically my whole life.' She glances at her friend with raised eyebrows. 'Eve?'

Eve blushes as though she's been caught doing something embarrassing. An awkward smile curls her mouth as she looks up at me. 'Gosh, I don't know if I can remember the whole story.'

'There's a story?'

'Yeah.'

'Well, don't leave us in suspense.' Bronwyn puts her hands on her hips. 'You've got me all curious now too. Does Claudia know about this? My sister in-law,' she tells me. 'And Jack?'

Eve winces. 'Probably. We all used to hang out at the,' she lifts her hands to make air quotes, '*haunted mansion* in our early teens. You know, scaring ourselves silly and doing all the things teenagers do when their parents aren't around.'

Bronwyn grins. 'I can't believe Claudia didn't tell me. I thought I knew all the Rickety Twigg myths and legends.'

'Well, we were all much older by the time you came on the scene, and I guess by then the story had lost its power.' Eve shrugs. 'Besides, after the accident Chris had there . . .'

'Gum Leaf Grove became famous for something else,' Bronwyn finishes for her.

I am a little curious about the accident they are referring to but I know my boys may not stay happily occupied forever.

Alfie, in particular, is highly unpredictable. So I don't ask questions, hoping they will move back to my original query soon. At last, Eve turns to me and says, 'But I suppose you want to know about the ghost.'

'If you don't mind telling me.' My voice sounds a little breathless. After all, I'm the one who's living in the 'haunted mansion' now.

Eve glances quickly at the children to make sure they aren't listening. Ryan is giving orders for a big car chase. None of them are even vaguely interested in what the grown-ups are talking about. Thank goodness. Eve turns back to us.

'Someone was murdered there,' she whispers. 'Strangled to death in the front sitting room late one evening just after dinner.'

Goosebumps prickle down my arms and across my chest. I've never known anyone who was murdered. I've never even known anyone who's known someone else who was murdered. I'd kind of lulled myself into this subconscious belief that things like that don't really happen in my life, or even on its outskirts. That I'm immune.

Guess I was wrong.

'Who?' I barely get the word out. 'Who was murdered? Do you know their name?'

Eve frowns. 'Now that's stretching my memory. It happened when I was a little kid, and I've never been much good at remembering names.'

'Was it Mitch?' I blurt before I can stop myself. 'And was he a neat freak?'

Bronwyn laughs. 'Strange trait for a ghost.'

'You're telling me.' I throw her a quick derisive look before refocusing my attention on Eve, whose brow has furrowed.

'I couldn't say for sure on either score. Again, I'm not very good with remembering names, and by the time the story became urban legend the mundane details had been edited out. However,' she pauses, 'I do think it was a woman who was murdered. Something to do with jealousy or unrequited love.

You know, the classic crime of passion that makes excellent ghost story fodder.'

Was Mitch short for something? Mitchell? Michelle?

But my boys said they definitely saw a man. I don't think they would get that part wrong.

Eve was still talking. 'The story goes that the ghost of the person who was murdered has haunted Gum Leaf Grove ever since, seeking an opportunity for revenge.'

Of course they have.

Couldn't possibly go up to heaven and have a cup of tea with the saints after that terrible ordeal. No, they had to stay on earth and wallow in self-destructive misery.

I release a heavy sigh.

'And the people who lived there before?' I enquire. 'The ones who died in the car accident. What about them? Are they part of the story?'

Eve's brow wrinkles. 'I don't know anything about a car accident. But apparently the last family who lived there were driven out of the place by the horror of it all, and that's why it's been vacant for over twenty years.'

She's so sketchy on the details, I can't help the frustration bubbling behind my ribcage. How were they driven out exactly? What horror? Did the ghost appear and demand they leave? Did it give them nightmares till they couldn't take it anymore? I'm about to ask when Eve fills in the gap for me.

'That part probably isn't true, but I guess people had to come up with some reason why the place has been vacant for so long.'

Bronwyn looks at me thoughtfully. 'So if you don't mind me asking, why are you so interested in the ghost?'

'My boys have inherited Gum Leaf Grove from their late father, Jake Bowman,' I tell her. 'He was the son of Alice and David Bowman.'

Eve tucks a strand of dark, curly hair behind her ear. 'Those names do sound familiar. But again, you're testing my memory. My older sister Tash or my mum might know more.'

'When did Jake pass away?' Bronwyn's tone is concerned.

'A few weeks ago.'

'I'm sorry,' they both say at the same time.

'Thank you,' I answer politely. It's my standard response when anyone offers condolences. It would be too disrespectful to add, 'Don't be,' but it's hard not to think it.

As nice as these women seem, I feel like coming here has only made things worse. Instead of getting answers, I've ended up with more questions, and a second helping of doubt. I had been hoping that Antoine had made up the ghost to keep me from discovering his secret compartment. The last thing I wanted to hear were more rumours.

Should I tell them about the secret compartment? The hole in the wall that revealed itself? It sounds surreal even to me. I decide the fewer people who know about it, the better. So I shift the conversation into small talk.

'So, now that you own Gum Leaf Grove,' Eve says, smiling, 'any plans on living there?'

I grin. 'I'd love to move. But I don't have the money to make the house liveable. And I couldn't quit my job in Perth.'

'What do you do?'

'I'm an accountant.'

'You could try and get work in Dunsborough or Busselton,' suggests Bronwyn.

'I could,' I nod. 'But I don't think the market's very good right now. It would be a risk giving up my position.'

'And with three boys . . .' Eve nods. 'I understand your need to play it safe.'

I glance at my watch. 'I should get going,' I say. 'Come on, boys.' The three of them ignore me, intent on their high-stakes car race, until I utter two magic words. 'Beach time!'

It's a gorgeous afternoon and the section of coast I choose is nearly deserted. There's only one other person there – a well-cooked lady sitting under an umbrella. She's reading a magazine with a gorgeous blonde pouting on the cover – a garden variety Elle Macpherson coming into her first bloom. My lips curl in amusement at the words sprawled across the model's ample chest. '*Why I dumped Michel Beauchene: Keysha finally reveals the truth*'.

Who has a name like Keysha anyway? Does she come with salad? Seems appropriate, given her figure. Two carrot sticks and one lettuce leaf with maybe a light vinegar dressing for lunch, just before her spin class. Even as I laugh at my private joke, I can't help questioning why anyone would tell the intimate details of their love-life to a gossip magazine.

What is she looking for? A few more likes on Facebook? A discussion on Twitter about how he never understood her needs?

I'm sure someone will say it.

Someone always does.

When I think back on the dissolution of my own marriage, not that many people knew the ins and outs of all of it. But I still found what little knowledge they had an ordeal to get through in itself. Our mutual friends had to choose a side. I had the lion's share of support, given that Jake had cheated on me with my best friend. However, it was still excruciating – the pitying looks, the guarded questions, the sympathetic smiles and, more often than not, the well-meant advice that showed they didn't really get what I was going through at all.

I pass the woman on the beach, expecting her to look up and smile, but she's so absorbed in her reading material she doesn't notice us. I shake my head. Keysha's tragic love-life far too titillating? I'm briefly assailed by pity for Mr Beauchene, but it's only fleeting. I've never heard of him, but I suppose he'll be on *Ellen* next week, telling everyone why Keysha was the problem.

I lead my boys closer to the shoreline, where we dump our things and run into the water. It's just what I need. Nothing like the ocean to wash the day's filth off both mind and body. Later, I sit in the sand, the water lapping at my feet, watching my kids jumping in the shallow waves. A sense of calm suddenly envelops me.

All this time, I've been thinking that I'm alone.

But I'm not.

I have them.

My three gorgeous little guys – a cause to sink my life into. Other mums at my work, mums with only two kids, and a husband to help, say, 'Grace, I don't know how you cope. With *three*! And all on your own. How do you do it?'

On bad days, I think there's no method to my madness. I'm just trapped on this rollercoaster that doesn't stop. I couldn't get off even if I wanted to. I have no choice. I have to make do, keep going, hope for the best.

Put it in God's hands.

And then I realise that's my secret. Love and faith. Turns out, you can do anything with love and faith.

Which is why, I decide firmly, the ghost of Gum Leaf Grove doesn't scare me at all. Suddenly, I hear a faint ringing noise. I glance back at our bags. Shit! Is that my phone ringing? Do we have a signal here?

I jump up, spraying sand everywhere as I race to catch the call.

It's Rachel. 'Sis!'

'Why haven't you called me?'

'I –'

'Are you all right?'

'Yes, I –'

'I've been trying your phone for the last two days but there's been no answer.'

'There's –'

'I was about to get in the car and drive –'

'Rachel,' I interrupt her firmly, 'there's no signal at Gum Leaf Grove. That's why I haven't called. Everybody's fine.'

'Oh.' She calms down a little before snapping, 'Well, you still could have called when you drove into town. I assume you had to get supplies.'

'Yes,' I sigh, dropping back down in the sand, 'sorry. I've just been a little under the pump here. There's a lot going on. The property is amazing, but . . .'

'But . . .' she prompts.

'I think I'm going to sell it.'

'You think or you know?' she asks shrewdly.

'I think I know,' I cheerfully compromise.

'Okay,' Rachel puts on her most objective voice, 'tell me about the place.'

'Well, it's old. Lots of history. Big rooms. There's the most gorgeous-looking stone fireplace in the front sitting room, and the view from the master bedroom window – Wow!'

'Darl,' she interrupts my gushing ten minutes later, 'I think you've fallen in love with it.'

'Fallen in love with it?' I guffaw. 'Hardly.'

'Well, you're talking about it like you'd like to live there.'

I would like to live there. With the proper renovations, a brand-new kitchen, some experience with running a B&B and a live-in gardener, it would be perfect. But we all know none of that's going to happen.

'It's a pipe dream,' I tell her. 'Besides, there are plenty of other things to fall in love with around here instead of an old building that's falling to pieces.' Too late, I realise my mistake.

'Like who?'

'Huh?' I dig my toes into the sand and wince. Idiot. Idiot. Idiot.

'Like who *around there* might you fall in love with?'

'Nobody. I don't believe in love, remember?'

'Cut the bullshit, I'm onto you. Who is it?'

I can see there's no point in avoiding the question. My sister has been known to nag to the brink of insanity. Or perhaps further than that.

'There's a . . .' I pause. 'A good-looking real estate agent who will handle the sale.'

She whoops. 'Well, that's an interesting dilemma.'

'How so?'

'You love the house but can't see the real estate agent without selling it.'

'Oh please,' I protest. 'It's not like that at all. I've considered the pros and cons of keeping the property and I feel that selling the place is the best option. I can't afford to do it justice myself. The proceeds of the sale will make a huge difference to our life in Perth.'

'I see.'

Her smug tone annoys me and I find myself getting defensive. 'I want to start being more of a mother, Rach. I'd like to work part-time for a few years if I can. Just so I can be more present in my children's lives. God knows they need it, especially now. I'm all they've got left.'

Rachel clears her throat, a signal that she's finally decided to get serious. 'They've got me too, you know. And Ron. And their cousins. And . . .'

'If you say their grandmother I'll have to cut you off right there,' I protest.

'Well, they *do* have her,' Rachel says softly. 'She's dying to meet them, you know.'

A stab of guilt slices through my ribcage as I do a quick head count of my kids. It's a habit I repeat every five minutes when we're out and about. The three of them are building sandcastles. Charlie is lying flat on his belly, digging the moat. They don't have a care in the world.

I suppose, at some stage, I should let the children meet their grandmother. Going through Jake's family photographs has made me see the fragility of life, the importance of knowing your roots before they disappear. Gum Leaf Grove was once a hub of life and family. Now it's just a dead carcass, waiting to be cleared away. It's so easy to lose your past, but impossible to get it back.

'I know you don't trust her,' Rachel is saying. 'But you haven't seen her. You haven't spoken to her.'

'I *have* spoken to her,' I argue back. Four years ago.

'Try again.'

I sigh. 'Look, Rach, I'm not heartless. I will let her meet the kids, one day, I promise. But they've just lost their father. I'm just not in the right frame of mind to be bringing her back into my life. I've got enough people to take care of already.'

'She's not expecting you to take care of her.'

I snort. 'It might not be what she's expecting, but it's what will end up happening.'

'She's changed.'

'So you keep saying.'

'Grace, ever since you were a teenager you've been taking care of other people. First me, then your selfish prick of a husband and now your kids. Maybe it's time to let someone take care of you.'

'Are you honestly suggesting that she's going to do that?'

'If you give her a chance.'

I pause, squinting at the sun and feeling the sting of tears. 'I just don't believe that, Rach,' I say. 'She abandoned me when I was eighteen. We begged her, you and I. Do you remember that? I can't go back to the way things were. Can we please just drop this?'

'Okay,' she agrees at last, and then after a pause adds, 'I much prefer talking about you falling in love anyway.'

I choke. 'It's more of a crush. An unrequited crush, with a touch of insanity. I set no store by it.'

'All the same, it's a shame you'll have to come back to Perth,' Rachel muses. 'Long-distance relationships never work.'

'Will you stop?!'

We don't speak for much longer. I ask after her hubby and children and then we hang up. While the boys are still occupied, I take advantage of the fact that I have a signal and ring an electrician as well. He agrees to come out tomorrow morning, leaving me pleased with the productivity of the afternoon, even though I've spent most of it on the beach.

As I call in the kids and start packing up our things, I can't help but dwell on my conversation with Rachel.

Am I interested in Scott?

I've sworn off love. Hung up my saddle. At least, I thought I had. Surely this is no more than a bit of holiday fever?

The question is still on my mind when Scott knocks on my door on Tuesday to do the valuation. He looks slick and purposeful. Collared shirt rolled up at the elbows, grey slacks, and a black leather document folder under one arm. He moves his sunnies from his eyes to the top of his head, freezing me with a bone-liquefying smile and a deep masculine voice that makes my heart patter just a little bit faster.

'Hey there, Grace. How are you?'

Shit.

I am interested.

Chapter 13

I've made sure I look better than the last two times we met. I've put on fresh jeans and the best of my tops, which actually isn't too bad. It's a pale pink number made out of a light soft cotton material, with split sleeves that end at my elbows. I usually dress it up with accessories, but unfortunately I didn't think to bring any with me. Instead, I've left my hair down and put on all the make-up I had in my handbag, which isn't much – some eye shadow, blush, lip gloss. Not that I would have been heavy-handed if I had packed more. I want to give him the impression that this is how I normally present. This is how Grace Middleton, accountant, mother of three, usually looks when she's expecting to meet someone of moderate importance.

As I greet Scott, I feel a couple of little hands at my waist. Ryan's head pops round my body to see who I'm talking to.

'Oh,' he says when he sees Scott, 'so that's why you left your hair down.'

No. No. No.

The smile on my face crystallises as Scott lifts an enquiring eyebrow.

'Er . . . Ryan –'

'She only wears her hair down on special occasions,' he tells Scott.

Shut up. Shut up. Shut up.

'Otherwise, it tends to get dirty.'

I grab Ryan by the shoulders and spin him full circle. 'Thank you, Ryan. I think that's quite enough about my hair habits. Where are your brothers?'

'They're playing cars down the back.'

'Perfect! Why don't you go join them?'

'But –'

'I've got to talk to Scott about the house.'

'But –'

'It's very important grown-up conversation.'

'Okay, okay.' His shoulders slump and he walks off.

'See ya, mate!' Scott calls after him.

Man! I thought Ryan was half asleep when I told him that stupid stuff about my hair. Sometimes that boy's brain is like a magnet. Except all the wrong things stick to it.

Turning back to Scott, I give an unsteady laugh. 'Kids, right?' I fish a hair tie out of my pocket and in two yanks my hair is back up in its no-nonsense ponytail.

That's right, Grace! *No nonsense.*

Scott's lips twitch suspiciously. 'Shall I come in?'

Heat steams my cheeks as I realise he's still standing on the porch. 'Sorry – er – yes, of course. Come in.'

I stand back as he passes over the threshold, the faint scent of his woody aftershave wafting gently under my nose.

'So, this is it.' His knowing gaze scans the area as he peeks first into the master bedroom and then into the sitting room. 'Wow. I see you've been tidying up. It's looking great.'

He walks into the sitting room and looks in blatant curiosity at the hinged painting. 'What have we here?'

'I discovered it a couple of days ago,' I say proudly. 'A hidden safe.'

'So it would seem.' He rotates the painting on its hinges. 'How clever.'

'Would you like a drink before we start?' I ask. 'I've got water or juice boxes.'

He laughs. 'I'd love some water.'

I return with two bottles from the esky to witness him closing the jewellery box and placing it back on the shelf inside the safe.

'It's empty except for the romantic message,' he says. I'm a little taken aback that he felt comfortable enough to have a look while I was out of the room.

'Er . . . yeah.'

He takes the water from me, opens it and sips. 'Thanks. Have you looked in the other box?'

I'm surprised you haven't, I want to snap back, but don't. After all, I did lead him in here and show him the safe. Maybe he thought permission to look was implied. Besides, what's wrong with him looking? I have nothing to hide, even if Jake did.

'There's just letters in there,' I say at last.

'Read any of them?'

'One, partially,' I reveal. 'Most of them are to Alice, from a relative of hers, I think. They're quite personal, so I didn't think I should read the rest.'

'I can understand that.' He nods and I find myself warming to him again. 'This situation must be hard for you, the house having belonged to your husband's family rather than your own.'

'It is a little strange.'

'I'm sure you'll figure your way through it. You seem like a very capable woman.'

I feel a jolt of pleasure at the compliment.

'So,' he turns his attention back to the rest of the room. 'Do you plan on giving it a paint as well?'

I hadn't really considered doing this. We're going home in five days. I have to go back to work. I might be able to get the front two rooms patched and painted, but what's the point if I'm not doing the rest of the house as well?

'I'm not sure I'll have time,' I say slowly. 'I wanted to give my boys a bit of a holiday before we return to Perth.'

'That's a real shame,' he says. 'It'd really bring up the value of the house.'

'You think?'

'Definitely. Along with a few other easy repairs I can think of, just off the top of my head.'

'I'll show you the rest of the house,' I suggest.

'Sure.'

I gesture for him to follow me as I walk out of the room towards the kitchen. 'This building has a lot of historical significance in the area,' he says from behind me. 'This could be quite a sought-after property, especially if you make some cosmetic improvements.'

As he takes in the state of the kitchen, he adds, 'I can see, though, that some jobs might be harder than others.'

'What if I don't do any renovations?' I ask.

He throws a grin over his shoulder. 'You'll just get less money for it. Perhaps a lot less.'

Right.

I'm about to ask him for a ballpark figure when he interrupts my thoughts with his own question. 'So, do you know much about the previous owners, Alice and David Bowman?' It seems like a strange question to ask – it doesn't have much bearing on the market value of the house. But I take it as a sign he's just being friendly, which causes my heart to flutter ever so slightly.

'No, actually,' I say with a smile. 'They had already passed away by the time I married Jake, so I never got to meet them.'

'Oh, right.' His expression becomes cautious and he avoids my gaze as he walks on into the hall. It doesn't take a rocket scientist to connect the dots. He clearly knows something, but figures it's too awkward a subject to raise on a first date – I mean, first *meeting*!

I hurry after him and say with a sigh, 'You've heard about the ghost, haven't you?'

He stops in the storeroom, turns and blinks. 'The ghost?'

'The spirit of the person who was murdered here.'

He veils his eyes. 'So you know about the murder.'

'Yes, and the whole thirst for revenge business,' I add.

'Revenge?' He looks startled. 'Who is after revenge?'

'The ghost!' Has he been listening? I tell him about the strange noises we've heard in the night, and the room that Alfie couldn't possibly have cleaned by himself, and how the safe had opened when I was asleep.

'Now that safe,' he shakes his finger, 'is a very elaborate contraption. I wonder if Alice and her husband put it there or the previous owners did.'

I can't help but notice that he's written off the first part of what I've said, which is frankly quite annoying. The fact that I've been trying to persuade myself for the past day and a half that it's all nonsense is beside the point.

'That's not all, you know.' I tap my foot, my hands moving instinctively to my hips. 'There are a few other things that I can't quite get my head around.'

'Like what?'

'Like yesterday morning, I had an electrician come over to check the wiring.'

'That's a good idea.' He nods his approval. 'So what are the issues?'

'That's the thing,' I spread my hands. 'There are none. In fact, the electrician said some of the wiring looks brand new.'

'That's good, isn't it?' Scott shrugs. 'It means Jake was doing some maintenance while he was alive. Have you checked with his lawyer?'

'Not yet.' I fold my arms, rubbing the backs of my elbows. I'm feeling a little bit stupid right now. 'I would have called his lawyer if I had a signal out here. Unfortunately, I have to drive into town to use my mobile. It's very inconvenient.'

'And a little unsafe,' he says gravely.

'The circumstances could be better,' I agree.

The smile he gives me seems to be one of understanding. 'Yes. Sounds like you've been under a bit of pressure lately.'

A bit?

I want to laugh hysterically.

I settle for a choke. 'You could say that.'

'Well, then you should do something fun in Yallingup while you're here.' His voice is soft and soothing, and does strange things to my insides.

'We already have,' I say, regaling him with stories of our trip to the beach on Sunday.

He nods. 'I'm glad you're getting some time out. Raising three kids on your own –' he pauses to look at me steadily, and the mood in the room seems to shift from small talk into something else, '– that takes a certain kind of strength.'

'They're worth it,' I smile.

'I can tell you're a good mum.' He nods, putting his file down on the shelves behind him. 'But do you get any time for yourself?'

'You mean to read a book or get a pedicure?' I ask sheepishly. I don't like to say 'no' outright. It feels too much like I'm asking for sympathy or something. Besides, I don't resent my kids for the time they need from me now. When they're older I'll probably have more time to myself than I want.

'I mean, to date,' he corrects me.

'To date, I've not had a pedicure,' I squint at the dirty ceiling, 'probably in about eight years.'

'No,' he puts a hand on my arm, sending a jolt through it like it's just been jacked, 'I mean, time to date *someone*.'

'*Oh.*'

Okay. I know I've been mildly crushing on this guy, but even I'm surprised when he makes this move. Somehow, it feels too soon. Maybe I'm just being paranoid. After all, I haven't been in the dating game since before Jake and I got married. What do I know about the niceties of courtship anymore? And this is what I wanted, right? I wanted him to notice me as a woman.

'So,' he prompts gently, looking deeply into my eyes, 'do you?'

Just then a phone rings, snapping the connection between us like scissors cutting through tape. I hastily step back out of his reach, confusion overtaking my senses as the 1990s bell trills loudly from down the hall.

Briiingg-briinggg! Brinnggg-brinngg!

'I thought you said you had no signal out here,' Scott says.

'I – I don't,' I say quickly. 'That's not my phone.'

'Well, then where's it coming from?' He picks up his file and leaves the room. I follow, the heat from the previous moment still fading from my frazzled body.

We find the phone on the floor of the office plugged into a telephone point in the wall – a dodgy-looking one just above the skirting board. The telephone is one of those old white office-style consoles. Rectangular in shape, with large grey number buttons on the side and little speed-dial ones along the bottom. A few handwritten names are on the small white labels beneath them.

'I swear that wasn't there before,' I say as it continues to ring.

'Well, aren't you going to answer it?' he says.

'I guess so.'

I reach down and pick up the whole unit, then lift the receiver to my ear.

'Hello?'

'Congratulations,' growls an unimpressed male voice. 'Now you're bloody connected to the whole world. You can ring out any time you like. Happy?'

'Who is this?'

There's a short pause before he snaps gruffly, 'Telstra.'

The dial tone sounds and I pull the receiver away from my ear and look at it in disgust. I mean, I've heard people complain about Telstra's customer service, but this is ridiculous.

'Everything okay?' Scott murmurs.

'Fine, I think.' I replace the receiver on the console and put the phone back on the floor. It looks like it was just fished out of the open box on the ground next to it. I can see that there's a whole heap of other old office stuff in there too. My boys must have been messing around in here. Damn it! I told them not to open anything.

I look up at Scott. 'Another thing to ask Jake's lawyer about, I guess. It seems I've got a landline.'

'Positive news,' Scott agrees. 'Shall we check out the second storey?'

'Sure.'

And just like that, we're back to business and I'm left wondering if I imagined our conversation about my love-life.

I show him upstairs, the three rooms and the cringeworthy bathroom, and then lead him outside as well. The boys, who are playing cricket out the front, drop their bats and balls and decide to follow us.

'What do you think of our house?' Ryan asks, falling into step with him.

'Interesting,' responds Scott with great diplomacy. 'Very interesting.'

'Have you told him about the ghost yet?' Ryan addresses me.

'Actually I have.'

I peek at Scott, waiting for his response, but he says nothing, ruffling Charlie's hair and quickening his step.

Behind the house is a weed-ridden area of gravel that seems to have settled unevenly in some places. Beyond this is another long single-storey building in much worse shape than the main house. A couple of the windows are broken, offering no protection from the elements. As I walk behind Scott and peer into the rooms I spy a couple of birds in there, and piles of dead leaves on the floor. Who knows what's living under those. From the shape and style of the building, it looks like it was probably the stables back in the day. However, it's been converted into three bedrooms and another very, *very* dilapidated bathroom. Scott opens the door to the bathroom and looks in. One glance is enough. He shuts the door again.

'Nice.'

Overstatement of the year!

The boys giggle.

'So what do you reckon?' I stand back, arms folded. 'Overall.'

'I reckon . . .' Scott's voice trails off. He's looking behind me, back at the main house. I turn around and follow his gaze up to the second storey. 'You were saying?'

'I reckon . . . there's a secret room up there.'

'What?'

That was definitely the last thing I expected him to say. Even the boys, who can ignore commands screamed at them from less than a metre away, stop skipping around and stand still at his barely audible announcement. They turn and stare at the back of the house.

'Look.' He points at the second storey, moving his finger across the building. 'One, two, three rooms. But check out the last room.'

'Yeah?'

'Does it seem bigger than it should be to you?'

I tilt my head. 'It's hard to tell from this angle. Maybe if we walked round the other side.'

But Scott keeps talking. 'And it's also got two windows facing us.'

I look at the darkened windows with drawn blinds. There's no seeing inside from here. But wait a minute. The final room, the one with the bookcase, only has one window in it. And it's north-facing, not on this side.

Tea cups and banana bread!

'There's a secret room!'

'There's a secret room!' The kids jump up and down like I've just announced we're having chocolate for dinner. 'Let's go see! Let's go see!'

'I think the grown-ups will be checking it out on their own first,' I say firmly. 'The stairs are too dangerous for everyone to come up.'

'Awwww!'

Scott barely gives the kids a second glance. He's already moving towards the house. I have to hurry to keep up with him. I'm grateful that he's noticed this, but he seems a little too eager about the find. Maybe it's just that the only man who has influenced my life in recent times is Jake. No wonder I have trust issues.

But is Scott trying to influence my life? Maybe. Maybe not. He didn't actually ask me out back in the house before. It was more of a preamble to that.

Or was it?

I don't know why I'm worrying about my love-life when there's a secret room to be discovered. I firmly push the wayward thoughts out of my head and increase my pace to keep up.

He goes first, negotiating the steps much more quickly than I can. I enter the room a few seconds after him. Yep, one window, north-facing. And on the back wall is the bookcase. The bookcase!

'Look.' He points at the floor and I can see scratch marks in the wood where the bookcase has been dragged across it. He's already on one side of it, pushing, before I finish the thought.

The shelving moves easily. I can see now, that it being empty and all, I probably could have easily shoved it across myself. Why didn't I notice the scratch marks on the floor before?

Too busy looking for ghosts in the walls, no doubt.

Suddenly, the bookcase is out of the way and there it is, in all its glory.

The door to the next room.

Chapter 14

It's locked.

I mean, of course it's locked. The powers that be wouldn't allow us to just walk in there, would they? No, that would be just too bloody reasonable.

'So,' Scott sighs, his hands on his hips as he rocks back on his heels. 'I guess we need to get a locksmith out then.'

'I guess.' I look at the rusty old keyhole in frustration. The door doesn't even have a knob. It's just a flat insurmountable pane stubbornly standing in our way. 'Or you could just bash it down.'

Scott runs his fingertips down the hard wood panel. 'It feels pretty solid to me. I think a locksmith would be quicker and cleaner.' He takes his hand away and faces me again. 'I have a mate who does this sort of stuff. I could probably get him out here tomorrow as a favour, if you like.'

I know this is a good deal, but my reply still comes out frustrated. 'I guess.'

He pauses, watching me. 'I can also come and assist him if you like.'

I blink in surprise, realising I'm acting like a baby. I lift my chin. 'You don't have to do that.'

'It's important to you.'

'Yes, but it's a bit beyond the call of duty, isn't it?'

I want to bite back the words as soon as I've said them. Seriously, Grace! If the man wants to be your knight in shining armour, why stop him? It'd be like Cinderella saying to her fairy godmother, 'Hey, don't worry about the dress. I'll just wear what I have on.'

He grins, almost seeming to read my mind.

'Well, I can't complete my valuation till I've seen all the rooms, so it makes sense for me to return.'

'Right.' I nod, folding my arms defensively across my chest. I feel colour rising up my neck.

'That,' he leans in a little closer, 'and I wouldn't mind seeing you again.'

Our eyes meet and I feel my mouth turning up in that silly, gag-worthy smile often employed by teenage girls looking at pictures of Justin Bieber.

'Muu-uuumm!' yells Alfie from downstairs. 'Have you found it yet?'

'Is there a vampire coffin inside?' Ryan adds.

'Pitchfork!' shouts Charlie in battle-cry mode. 'Pitchfork, pitchfork, pitchfooorrrk!'

I tear my gaze from Scott's as reality slams into me at full throttle. I call through the doorway, 'No vampires. Just a door. Pitchforks at ease. I'll be down in a minute.'

I turn back to Scott, straightening my shoulders to boost my confidence. 'So I guess I'll see you tomorrow morning then.'

'Yes you will.'

He leaves soon after, and I feel a complete sense of anticlimax in his wake. I still don't know the market value of the house, but I now have a secret room to contend with. It just seems to add more lunacy to an already comical series of events.

Why do people have secret rooms anyway?

My inner bitch chimes in – *to hide something that won't fit in a secret compartment, of course.*

What won't fit in a secret compartment?

Well, frankly, lots of things.

A chest full of gold bars.

A priceless artefact from ancient Egypt.

A dead body – the corpse of the ghost who haunts this place now.

I shudder involuntarily. It's like that old saying about someone stepping over your grave. The metaphor seems just a little too close to home right now. Besides, surely I would smell a dead body if it was there. Even twenty years later, there'd still be the residual stench of rotting flesh, right? And the room might not even have been concealed back in the day. Without the bookcase in front of the door, it's perfectly obvious there's a room there. Someone moved that bookcase into position in recent times, I'm sure of it.

I make my boys a picnic lunch and we share it on the weed-ridden lawn out the front. I stare into the vineyard while I eat, letting the kids' playful chatter slip into background noise. Rows and rows of bare trunks blur in my vision. I know it'll only be a few more months before the vines are leafy and green, but their baldness now seems cold and ominous to me.

What's in that room?

While the boys eat their lunch, I go back inside to further examine the contents of the secret compartment, looking for clues. I take the ring box off the shelf and turn it over in my hand, looking for markings on the leather covering.

Nothing.

I open the box. On the back of the satin-lined lid is the name of the jeweller: John Ritz and Co. I look at the handwritten message under the cushion again, but it gives no more hints.

I shove the ring box back on the shelf and retrieve the box of letters instead. I don't bother to read the rest of the first letter, opening another instead.

Dear Alice,

I've made inquiries at the local high school. They have a place there for Jake when you're ready to move. You can send the completed enrolment forms to me. Shall I mail them with my next letter, or is it still too soon?

The rest of the letter goes on about the quality of the high school, how nice the teachers are, blah, blah, blah. I open a third letter, dated a couple of months later. Apparently Alice still hadn't decided to move.

Dear Alice,

I've also cleared out the study. My friend Margaret is downsizing. She's giving away the beds her kids used to sleep in to the Salvos. Shall I snap them up? They seem in reasonably good condition. We'll buy new mattresses, of course. You just need to hurry up and set a date.

Again, the letter goes on with more preparation suggestions. I glance at the signature at the bottom. It's from a woman named Carmen. I flick back to the other letters I've opened. These are from Carmen too. Are they all from Carmen? I riffle through the envelopes and they're all addressed in that same neat cursive script. Yes, they are all from Carmen, Alice's sister from Melbourne, who appeared to think Alice was going to leave her husband and move in with her. Had Jake moved to Melbourne in his late teens? He never mentioned it. Then again, he never mentioned a lot of things.

I open a fourth letter. This one is dated three months on from the last message.

Dear Alice,

I'm sorry but I'm starting to get a little frustrated with you. Are you ever going to move to Melbourne? You keep saying that you need more time to appease David, but I think something else is going on. What aren't you telling me, Alice? Why won't you leave him?

Now that's interesting!

I'm about to read on when I hear a car outside. *Damn it.* I quickly fold up the letters, stuff them into the box and put it back on the shelf. Has Scott returned? Did he manage to get the locksmith to come earlier? I walk through the foyer and out onto the porch. The kids have long since come inside, and are playing in the sitting room.

But it's not Scott's car that I see. A ute with 'Oak Hills' written on the side is parked beside my beat-up Holden. A tall, lanky man, whom I recognise immediately as Antoine, steps out.

'Bonjour, madame. How are you today?'

'Er . . . good thanks.'

'I believe you wish to speak to me.' He strolls up the driveway, glancing around as though he owns the place. 'Bronwyn informed me you had a few questions.'

It's not the first time I feel cross just looking at him. He's dressed as before, in his Oak Hills cellar door uniform, his hair tied sedately at his nape and that jaunty hauteur in his gait that never ceases to aggravate me.

'Well, yes, actually I do.' I put my hands on my hips.

'Then ask away.' He spreads his hands. 'I am at your service.'

I find this statement even more annoying. He's already made it clear that my interests rank far below his own.

'What were you doing here on Saturday?' I demand. 'Bronwyn told me that you don't work in the vineyard.'

'Well, no,' he looks aggrieved. 'That would be preposterous. Can you imagine me in the vines? I leave such tasks to those more rustically inclined.'

My jaw slackens. 'I beg your pardon?'

'No need to apologise. Tell me, have you had a chance to become better acquainted with the ghost?'

'No.' I fold my arms. 'Though it has certainly tried to become better acquainted with me. Why are you here, Antoine? It seems to me like you know something. Why don't you just come right out and tell me already, instead of beating around the bush?'

He actually looks rather pleased with my demand. 'Aah, madame, I do have something to tell you. Or show you, actually.'

'What?'

He holds up his hand and a piece of metal winks in the sunlight. My hand goes to my chest as I gasp.

It's a key.

'I believe there is a room you're trying to get into.'

'How did you – Where did you – *You know about the room!*'

He shrugs smugly. 'Please, madame, you said only seconds ago that you think I know something. Turns out, I know *everything*!' On this extravagant boast, he marches past me into the house. It takes a couple of seconds for me to recover from this announcement before I turn on my heel and hurry after him.

He knows everything! That'd be right, wouldn't it? The French man with an ego the size of China knows what's going on in my life, but I don't. He's already mounted the unsafe stairs. I glance in at the kids, who haven't left their game in the sitting room. They are all seated on the wooden floor, setting up a battlefield for an impending war. Instead of the little plastic soldiers they use at home, they've commandeered the old cutlery from the kitchen and created factions. It's dessert spoons against soup spoons, with the teaspoons as spectators. I step in briefly and pick up the box of yet-to-be-drafted butter knives and slip them under my arm.

'Awww!!!'

'We don't want any real weapons in this battle, thanks,' I say. 'Carry on.'

I shove the knives back on a high shelf in the kitchen then

return to the stairs. Antoine's already at the top, looking down at me impatiently.

'Are you coming or not?'

'Coming,' I nod and climb up, performing what is now becoming a familiar dance routine to dodge the unsafe bits. Side to side, two steps up, two steps left, skip the next one and so on, all the way to the top. I'm panting by the time I enter the room.

'You've really got to do more exercise,' Antoine muses, and then without further ado slips the key into the lock. He hesitates before turning it, looking back at me, a slight smile on his face. 'Are you ready for this, madame?'

Trepidation flutters in the pit of my belly. Should I be worried? What's he got in there?

'Ready for what?'

'Gum Leaf Grove's biggest secret.'

I have no time to process this before he turns the key and the door swings open.

'Tah dah!'

There's the jerking sound of a chair scraping against the floor as someone inside stands up. I stride into the room and shock hits me like a slap.

There he is.

Standing right there in the centre of the room, cool as you please.

I'm too stunned to do anything.

Clearly, this is Mitch.

I mean, who else could it be? It's the only thing that makes sense.

I realise with perfect clarity that there is a man in my house. And that there has been this whole time.

Not a ghost.

Not an imaginary friend.

But a man, hiding right here in this room.

I clench my fists as fear and anger jostle for supremacy.

He's huge. At least six foot four, tall, broad, and his face . . .

It's the kind of face you wouldn't forget easily. The scar is the first thing I notice. Alfie was right. It does look like the skin on the right side of his face is melting. It melts all the way down his neck, until it disappears behind the collar of the checked flannelette shirt he's wearing. And yes, it does look redder and rawer than the smooth, untarnished skin of his left cheek, but I can't for a second say that he's not handsome.

The most startling, piercing blue eyes stare at me over a chiselled nose and a sculpted mouth that neither smiles nor sneers. His hair is a golden brown and sits in long, wavy layers around his face. I can't decide if he is in need of a cut or if this is the style he is currently affecting. I decide to opt for the former, given the stubble on his chin, which suggests that grooming isn't a priority for him right now.

He's looking at me like he's waiting for something.

'Well?' Antoine's long, tentative drawl interrupts my thoughts, and I turn and snap at him harshly.

'Well what? Who is this guy? And why are you hiding him in my house?' My shock has finally subsided enough to loosen my tongue.

Antoine laughs out loud. 'You don't recognise him, madame?' He walks over to Mitch, flicking his chest triumphantly with the back of his hand. '*Tu pensais qu'elle te reconnaîtrait et ce n'est pas le cas!*'

Mitch tears his gaze from me and looks down at Antoine in annoyance. '*Attention, Antoine. Ce n'est pas le moment de se moquer de moi.*' His voice is dark and smooth, like a long black, no sugar. I could easily listen to him all day. It's probably because he's speaking French, though – such a romantic language. It makes me think of classical music and patisseries.

Grace, focus!

Abruptly, I round up my thoughts, which seem to have scattered like seagulls caught stealing fish and chips.

'I don't recognise him,' I inform Antoine curtly. 'However, my sons tell me his name is Mitch.'

Again, they both look at me. They seem to be waiting for something. For what? Is there a penny around here that's supposed to be dropping? I frown at them, smelling a conspiracy.

'Should I recognise him?' I glance sharply from one to the other. 'Who is he?'

Antoine's expression is gleeful, like a gambler who just won a bet. 'Absolutely no one of importance, madame. A veritable vagabond, if ever there was one. We just thought you might see the family resemblance.'

'What family resemblance?'

Antoine straightens to his full height, trying to align his face closer to Mitch's, even though the larger man dwarfs him by at least a foot. He flits a finger between himself and the man behind him. 'You don't see our DNA connection?'

I squint at them. 'No.'

'Mitch is my cousin, madame. Surely you must be able to tell?'

It could have been Winnie the Pooh claiming kinship with a pirate of the Caribbean.

'No,' I repeat bluntly.

'There, you see,' Antoine addresses Mitch with another smug smile. 'I told you that you couldn't hold a candle to me. *Tout le monde n'est pas obsédé par le monde de la musique.*'

'*Parfait. Alors, qu'elle est mon histoire? Pourquoi suis-je ici?*' Mitch sounds exasperated. At least, I think he does. It's hard to tell, given his romantic French dialogue. But he is definitely standing over Antoine intimidatingly, like he'd dearly love to snap him in half. Then again, who wouldn't?

'*Patience. J'y viens,*' Antoine answers him, then turns to me. 'I am so sorry about this, madame. Mitch had nowhere else to go and I didn't know that you and your family were going to appear. After all, Gum Leaf Grove has been vacant for twenty years. I didn't see a problem with allowing my cousin to squat here while he gets back on his feet.'

I fold my arms. 'Can you see a problem now?'

'Of course.' He spreads his hands. 'When do you and your boys intend to leave?'

'When do *I* intend to leave?' My blood is starting to boil.

'Yes,' Antoine blinks. 'That is what I asked.'

'I'm not the one who's going,' I snap. I wave a hand in Mitch's direction. 'He is.'

Mitch opens his mouth to say something, but Antoine flicks him in the chest again with the back of his hand. '*Joue le jeu.* Let's think about this for a moment, madame. Is it really necessary that he go?'

'Absolutely.' I glare at him. 'I can't have a strange man I don't know living in the same house as me and my children.'

'But he won't trouble you,' Antoine explains. 'He doesn't even speak English.'

'What?' I blink.

'*Est-ce vraiment une bonne chose de lui dire?*' says Mitch crossly.

'He doesn't speak English. He's just arrived from France,' Antoine rushes on, his eyes darting between Mitch and me. 'He, er . . . came here to get a job in a winery. But unfortunately the language barrier is a bit of an issue.'

'You don't say.' I can't stem the derisiveness in my tone.

'I know, I know,' Antoine nods. 'I did tell him the odds would be against him. But unfortunately, madame, he's not that bright.'

'*Bon, tu as fini?*' says Mitch, but Antoine continues without even glancing back at him.

'My point, madame, is that he'll be quiet as a mouse, all holed up here in his room. You won't even notice him. We can even re-lock the door, if you like.' He holds up the key in front of my face, but Mitch takes it and puts it into his own pocket.

I shake my head vigorously, rubbing a frustrated hand across my brow. 'No, no, no. He has to go.'

'But he has nowhere else to stay,' protests Antoine.

'What about your place?' I demand.

'My place?' Antoine seems horrified. 'I already have a friend in the spare room, there is no space for Mitch. Besides, he and my friend will not get on well. The two of us have a very active social life and this Neanderthal is not very socially adept, you know, especially with the ladies.'

I look at Mitch and he stares back at me impassively. *'Je me demande ce qu'elle pense de moi.'* At first glance you wouldn't suppose he had much subtlety about him. He's so large and raggedly dressed, but that voice of his, combined with those eyes . . . those French vowels just tingle all the way down my spine.

'All right, all right.' Antoine snaps a finger in front of my face and I realise I've spaced out.

Mitch smirks at him.

'Might I at least appeal to your sympathy?' His cousin tries a different tack.

I switch my gaze to Antoine. 'What are you talking about?'

'He's down on his luck.' Antoine lifts his hands dramatically. 'Cast adrift by life and facing utter ruin.'

'I'm sorry to hear that, but –'

'He's got no money.' Antoine seems unnaturally pleased by this fact. 'Not a cent.'

'I see –' I try to move him along, but he seems to be warming to his theme.

'Poor as a beggar. It's not like he could buy a Porsche and never offer his cousin a ride in it. No siree!' Mitch folds his arms in resignation as Antoine throws up his own dramatically. 'Couldn't afford a phone either, to maybe call up his cousin and check on him – his faithful cousin, who never did anything but be there for him when he needed a friend more than family. His exiled cousin, who –'

Antoine yelps in pain as Mitch accidentally steps on his foot while reaching across to point firmly at the wall.

I glance in the direction he is indicating. There, hanging on a hook, is a tool belt.

'*Dis-lui que je travaillerai pour elle,*' Mitch says to Antoine.

Antoine hops on the spot, whining, as Mitch points to the belt again.

'He says he'll work for you,' Antoine says. 'He'll fix a few things and do any other odd jobs you want done, if he can stay in this room a little while longer.'

'Free labour?'

'Yes.'

It's my turn to look Mitch up and down – assessing those large, strong shoulders, generous biceps and strong pectorals. I've got to say, I love the way the colour in his neck rises up during my inspection till a faint flush fills the portion of his face not already red from scar tissue.

'All right,' I say at last. 'He seems capable enough.'

The truth is, I could do with an extra pair of hands around here. Hands that are larger and stronger than mine. For some reason, the thought puts a blush in my cheeks and I bite my lower lip in embarrassment.

'Well,' Antoine seems pleased. 'It's all settled then.'

'Not quite.' I raise my chin. 'I think we ought to establish some ground rules.'

'Such as?'

'You need to be actively looking for another place for him to stay.'

'Of course.'

'And as soon as the jobs run out, he's got to go.'

'Absolutely.'

'And he needs to work hard. I'm not going to give him the easy tasks.' I pause, and then decide to test my power. I look at Mitch, holding his gaze. 'Tell him I want him to fix the stairs.'

'*Elle veut que tu répares les escaliers,*' Antoine says.

Mitch nods.

'And clean out the office and the kitchen, too.'

I wait for Antoine to translate, but there's silence, so I break eye contact with Mitch and turn to look at him. 'Go on, tell him.'

'Huh?'

'Tell him in French.' I roll my eyes impatiently.

'Oh, sorry, madame,' Antoine quickly apologises and then looks ruefully at Mitch. '*Tu comprends tout ça?*' Antoine looks up at the giant behind him.

'*Bien sûr,*' Mitch responds. '*Dis-lui que je l'aiderai autant que possible.*'

'He will help you in any way he can.'

'Good. In return, he can stay here and I'll let him eat whatever we're eating, which,' I grimace, 'will mostly be sandwiches because hot food is kind of impossible right now. At night, I would prefer he continue to sleep up here, and that he keeps to himself as much as possible. And tell him that I intend to sell the house. That's why we're cleaning it up.'

While Antoine translates all of this, I look around the secret room. There is a mattress on the floor in one corner with a pillow and doona. Opposite this is a bar fridge, which, much to my disapproval, appears to be turned on. There's a telephone sitting on top of it – another 90s throwback, a twin to the one in the office. No wonder Antoine turned up in such a timely fashion. Mitch must have heard Scott and me move the bookcase and called him, knowing his days were numbered.

There's also a worse-for-wear-looking duffel bag on the ground filled with clothes that look like they might need washing, and some sort of speaker with a mobile phone sitting on it. I assume he's using it to listen to music rather than make calls. The most surprising item in the room, however, is the guitar case leaning against one wall.

I walk over and touch it gently. 'Does he play?'

The rapid to and fro of French dialogue ceases instantaneously at my words.

Antoine coughs. 'Very rudimentarily, madame. He needs a lot of practice. I always tell him, greatness comes to those who embody perfection.' He tilts up his chin and pushes out his chest. It takes all my strength not to giggle at his implication.

'There is one thing my cousin does request, madame, if you are agreeable.'

I frown suspiciously. 'Agreeable to what?'

'He has no desire to . . . er . . . socialise with anyone other than yourself.'

'Well, I'm not planning on throwing any parties anytime soon,' I scoff.

'Of course not, madame. However, should you have any visitors, I'm assuming that Mitch will make himself scarce. He's, er . . . a little embarrassed.'

'Embarrassed? Embarrassed about –' And then I immediately bite my tongue, stunned at my own insensitivity.

Of course, this is all about his scar. By its rawness, I can tell that it's a recent injury. He's probably still getting used to it. In fact, maybe it's the reason he's down and out, 'cast adrift by life and facing utter ruin'. I inwardly roll my eyes again at Antoine's melodramatic explanations. But it must be all connected. I can understand that he might be feeling the loss of his perfect skin. But honestly, the man needs a flaw. His charisma is so visceral that I had all but forgotten about any markings on his face. He'd be *too* good-looking if he didn't have a scar.

Hollywood perfect.

Rock-star divine.

Can't have poor Ryan Gosling feeling inadequate; I need him to put out another movie.

'I'm sorry.' I look away, feeling my cheeks heat up at my wayward thoughts. 'He must have been through hell to get a scar like that.'

'Yes, it was very traumatic, madame. He is still working his way through it.'

'I see,' I say, then pause, hoping for further hints on what this means, but none are forthcoming. Instead, Antoine dusts off his hands.

'Anyway, I must go, madame. I cannot, after all, be baby-sitting my cousin all day. I do have a job.' He says this as though I invited him over and proceeded to take up all his time with unnecessary chatter. It puts me in mind of something. As he steps forward I move in front of him to bar his path. 'I just have one more question.'

'Go ahead,' Antoine gestures graciously.

'The ghost.'

Antoine's eyebrows rise. 'What do you wish to know?'

'You made it all up, didn't you? So I wouldn't go upstairs and discover your little . . .' I glance cynically in Mitch's direction, 'big secret. It was all a trick, wasn't it?'

Antoine's lips curl in amusement. 'No trick, madame. The ghost is very real. I can even tell you her name.'

I start. 'What?'

'Alice Bowman,' Antoine reveals promptly. 'Her name is Alice Bowman.'

Chapter 15

So typical of Antoine to drop a bombshell just as he's walking out the door. I'm too shell-shocked by the revelation to ask any questions. After all, I've been under the impression that Jake's mum died in a car accident. Perhaps that was just another lie. It's only after Antoine drives off in a cloud of red dust that I think to ask who murdered her.

A very unwelcome thought occurs to me.

Jake?

Is that why he was so secretive about his past? What if the whole time he was married to me he was hiding from the law?

Come on, Grace. You don't really believe that, do you?

I mean, Jake was selfish, self-absorbed and inconsiderate, but I don't think he was a murderer. It's much more likely that he just didn't want to discuss the fact that his mum was murdered. Perhaps because it messed him up badly. I can definitely attest to that.

Jake was messed up.

Nobody becomes a selfish bastard for no reason. Evil people aren't born evil, they're created when they eat what life dishes out to them.

I rub my suddenly aching head. I can't imagine what Jake went through. He was so young and vulnerable. One minute his mum was there and the next she was ripped abruptly from his life.

I sigh.

Maybe I can imagine it.

I wish that he'd told me, and I'm angry that he didn't. I knew so little about the man I was married to. A man who seemed so different from the one being revealed now. This new Jake seems so much more human, now that I can actually see the demons that were standing around him.

I hear footsteps on the porch behind me and jump involuntarily. With demons, ghosts and Antoine's parting revelation in my head, it's no wonder I think there's a villain behind every corner.

Ironically enough, it's Mitch.

The porch seemed bigger before he stepped onto it, filling it with his presence, which, frankly, he seems to have a lot of.

'Oh, er . . . hi.' I stuff my hands in the pockets of my jeans, feeling awkward. It's hard to make small talk with someone who doesn't speak the same language. And I've never been very good at charades.

He gives me a crooked smile and I'm sure I see a twinkle in his eye, as though he's laughing at me. I scuff my sneaker.

Without a word, he walks right past me, picks up the roll of carpet it took me and three boys to carry out and slings it over one shoulder like it's a surfboard or something.

I fold my arms in jealous exasperation and watch him carry it down the porch steps with a light, easy jaunt, as though he's flaunting his masculinity.

So you're strong. Big deal. Try giving birth!

He sets the carpet down on the ground at the side of the house.

'Er . . . why are you putting that there?' I ask uselessly.

He ignores me and comes back for the other roll, then the broken outdoor chair and the cracked pots littering the front of the house.

'Er . . . excuse me!'

That's when I realise he's making a junk pile, at probably double the rate I could do it. The front porch is starting to clear into a nice open space.

'Oh.' My exasperation morphs into pleasure, until I see the state of some of the timber boards that have been exposed by his efforts.

Damn! Almost half of them need to be replaced.

While I'm frowning at the boards, my kids come running out onto the porch.

'Hey, watch yourself!' I call. 'Those boards over there are broken.'

Ryan stops, puts his hands on his hips and examines the work Mitch has just completed, like a foreman doing the rounds.

'That looks better,' he decides, pushing his glasses up his nose. 'You done well, Mummy. Better than yesterday.'

'What do you mean, better than yesterday?' I say indignantly.

'When you got tired and had to take us to the beach.'

'That's not why we went to the beach.'

Ryan shrugs and says matter-of-factly, 'If you say so.'

Over his head I see Mitch strolling back towards the porch and realise that I'd better formally introduce them and set some boundaries. I don't want them getting under his feet all the time.

'Guys,' I begin tentatively, 'this is –'

'Mitch!' They almost bowl me over as they streak towards him like he's some long-lost uncle, fresh home after years of exile.

Puh-lease!

News starts flowing fresh and fast.

'Yesterday we went swimming!'

'Mummy found a secret room!'

'There's a dead kangaroo out back that needs to be buried. Can we dig a hole?'

'A big, big hole.' This last one is from Charlie, who spreads his chubby little arms out as wide as they can go and looks up at Mitch with eyes as large as the image in his imagination.

Mitch merely grins, scooping Charlie up and putting him on his shoulders. He hands Ryan a cracked bucket, Alfie a gnome that's lost its head and, with the hand that's not holding one of Charlie's ankles, picks up the bundled-up curtain I recently took down.

Show-off!

Then, just like that, they all troop off to the junk pile to add this booty to it. It's like watching Gandalf and three hobbits.

'Er . . . boys?' I call out tentatively. They completely ignore me. I'm just their mother, after all. No one of importance. 'Ryan, Alfie, Charlie?'

Their attention is completely focused on Mitch as they fight over his attention, speaking a word a millisecond. Mitch merely nods or grunts. They don't seem too concerned about his lack of verbal response, though. He manoeuvres them about with a tap on the shoulder or a point of the finger. They are like bees circling a hive, and they continue to buzz for the next two trips, from the junk pile to the porch and back again.

There's not an ounce of restraint in their faces, and I can't help but wonder how many times the boys have run into Mitch without my knowledge. I chew pensively on my lower lip. This guy is related to Antoine, so I wouldn't put any stealthy behaviour past him. What about the painting, for example? Did he open that up for me?

Why?

What was on the top shelf?

Guess I'll have to wait for his cousin to return to get to the bottom of those questions. All the same, I can't help but watch in admiration as he somehow manages to carry on a whole conversation with my boys without even saying a word.

They return to the porch and I realise in shock that it's clear of everything except an old park bench that would actually look really nice with a fresh coat of paint and a couple of outdoor cushions. It's amazing what a bit of space can do to open up a place and a person's mind.

Mitch clears his throat and I look up. He touches each of the boys' heads. 'Ryan, Alfie, Charlie.' He puts his hand on his own chest, 'Mitch.' Then he points at me.

Oh! I haven't even told him my name.

'Grace,' I say quickly. 'It's Grace.'

His lips turn up in a smile that seems more intimate because it hasn't been diluted by chatter. Then he slowly repeats my name. 'Grace.' I feel the intonation tingle all the way to my toes.

Wow.

I can see why the kids are drawn to him. He's magnetism personified. I close my hand over my left wrist where my pulse is jumping like a terrified grasshopper.

I don't know what's the matter with me this week. Maybe it's the country air or something, but my emotions seem to be all over the place. First Scott, now this guy. It's ridiculous. I haven't needed a man in my life for years. Scratch that. I haven't *wanted* a man in my life for years. It's too complicated and restricting, and just not worth the pain.

Right?

I grit my teeth. What I really need is to go out and buy myself a slab of chocolate or a tub of ice-cream. Maybe even a bottle of wine . . . or two. I'm sure that'll fix the problem!

In the meantime, I force myself to give Mitch a casual thumbs up. 'Er . . . good job. Now, shall we go inside?' I point at the door. 'Inside?'

He nods and we all walk into the house.

'So.' I rub my palms together, searching for a way to explain what I want done next. I know I told Mitch to fix the stairs, but I have to source some wood for that before he can get started. In the meantime, I have to dream up something else for him to do.

Mitch, however, doesn't seem to be waiting for orders. He doesn't stop walking until he gets to the kitchen, and my traitorous sons follow him. I find myself coming into the room last, only to witness him doing exactly what he's been doing outside – handing out junk to the boys to be removed.

There's an old lamp, a pile of rags, and weevil-eaten telephone books from 1992, 1993 and 1994.

'Mummy,' says Ryan impatiently, 'you're in the way.'

I realise then that I'm standing in the doorway. 'Sorry.' I step aside, right into Alfie.

'Why aren't you working?' he demands as he files past.

'I'm –'

'No sleeping on the job!' Charlie shakes a finger at me and I hastily back up, right into Mitch, who's coming the other way.

'Oh.' Butterflies fill my ribcage as our bodies collide. I spin around. 'Sorry.'

Instead of stepping away, he grabs me by the shoulders and moves me behind the counter, where there is a tonne of junk in the cupboards. And yes, I get what he means, but he's kind of in my personal space and I have to regain some ground on the leadership front. 'You do realise I'm supposed to be the one giving the orders around here,' I throw peevishly in his direction.

There's no response, of course, but at least he's not standing so close to me anymore. That kind of messes with my internal wiring.

Soon we've got a bit of an assembly line going. Mitch and I are sorting and the kids are slowly carting rubbish outside, happy as three Larrys.

Typical.

'You're just showing me up now,' I say out loud.

Mitch looks up and meets my eyes. I know he can't understand me, but the silence is doing my head in. It feels good to get the words out. I point in the direction the kids have gone. 'You're too good with the boys. I've lost all their respect.'

He looks puzzled and taps his lips.

'I know, I know,' I sigh. 'You can't speak English.' My mouth kinks. 'Funnily enough, that actually makes you very easy to confide in.'

He shrugs as though he's realised I'm talking to myself, and returns to the task of pulling things out of cupboards and setting them on the damaged countertop.

'I don't actually get much adult conversation,' I admit casually as I join him at the counter and start sorting the junk into two piles, one for removal and one to keep. 'I have one sister who usually calls me on a weekly basis just to make sure I haven't killed myself . . . or one of the kids,' I add with a wicked chuckle. 'And then there are the people at work. One is my boss, so I don't like to get too personal with him, and the rest . . .' I swat my hand. 'It's usually chit-chat about the weather, to be honest.'

I realise he's completely emptied two of the cupboards. The counter is starting to get overcrowded. So I grab a cloth and the Spray N Wipe I bought in Dunsborough and start wiping them down. Might as well clean them up before putting the good stuff back in.

'I'm actually excellent at talking about the weather,' I tell him emphatically. 'Most people will just say "It's cold today, isn't it?" Or "Thank goodness it's stopped raining." But I can usually add a little extra, like, "Time to revamp the wardrobe," or "Excellent weather for soup, right?" The problem is, you need to be able to talk about more than just the weather if you're considering dating again.'

I sneak a peek at him to see if there's any reaction to what I've said. But he's just going about his business, emptying a third cupboard, completely ignoring me, and yet keeping me company all the same. Chatting to him like this feels insanely natural for some reason, so I keep going.

'You need to be able to carry a conversation for at least the length of a meal,' I explain. 'And I don't want to be one of those boring mothers who only talks about their children.'

I shake a finger at him. 'It's very easy to do, you know. I once went to this so-called "girls' night" with some of my sister's friends and we spent the first hour at the bar discussing which vegetables our kids will and won't eat and why. Can you imagine?'

I know he's not imagining it, but it's nice to pretend he is.

'The thing is, the best conversation to bond over is interests and hobbies. My problem is, I don't have any hobbies. Unless you count making Halloween costumes for under five dollars, or dinner with only four ingredients.'

Mitch continues unpacking.

'I know you have a hobby. Music, right? I saw your guitar.'

As he's transferring an armful of junk to the counter, an old kettle with a chewed-up cord drops from his arms and hits the floor with a loud *thwang*!

'I'll get it,' I reassure him as he looks down nervously. I bend and retrieve the item and put it on the counter.

'So I'm sure you would talk about that, right? Women are always interested in music.'

No response. In fact, he seems to be working faster.

I sigh. 'I think about the things I used to talk about when I was in my early twenties. Movies, books, where to go for the next holiday. I thought I was so sophisticated.' I laugh. 'But isn't sophistication about knowledge?'

This time, I don't even look up for his reply, which I know is not coming. I keep talking. It's nice to unload my thoughts without stressing about sounding like an idiot.

'I was pretty dumb back then.' I bite my lip. 'Married the first guy who swept me off my feet, which is another reason why I'm worried about re-entering the dating game. I'm not a good judge of character.' I pause. 'How do you tell when someone is real?'

Mitch's hand stills over a pot with no handles as though he's considering it, and then abruptly he moves it to the pile I've made for rubbish.

'Jake was so nice in the beginning, you know. Caring, considerate, loving. I never could have imagined how he would change. How he would hurt me the way he did.' I shrug. 'Actually, I never could have imagined any of this. This house, the vineyard. The ghost of Gum Leaf Grove.'

I start picking out the best of the white dinner plates. There are about ten that aren't chipped or cracked. I place these in the cupboard I've just cleaned.

'And then on the other hand,' I point out, 'maybe it's best not to know everything that went down in Jake's life. I don't want to ruin the shiny image the boys have of their father. I just want to protect them. They are my everything, you know.'

'Grace.'

I jump, as he suddenly turns to me, reaching out with his hand. For a moment, a crazy infinitesimal moment, I think he's going to caress my cheek. My heart leaps into my throat and I gasp, then suddenly his hand moves up and flicks something off my head. I look down and see a large black spider on the old linoleum floors.

'Gross!' I squeal and he promptly steps on it. 'Thanks,' I say.

'*De rien, mon cher.*' He smiles and the tilt of his mouth is utterly infectious, like when one of the boys smiles after they've just presented me with their latest art project. I can't help but grin back.

For a moment, we just look at each other and I feel a wave of understanding pass between us that is about more than a squashed insect on the floorboards.

Foreigners.

Why is there an immediate misperception that they're deep because they don't speak English?

Probably all he's thinking about right now is what's for dinner.

Dinner!

I slap my palm to my head and glance at my watch. It's nearly 5.30. The boys will be nagging in a few minutes. I had been intending to duck out earlier and get a roast chicken and some salad items. All I have in the house is bread, spreads and biscuits.

'Damn!'

Mitch watches me as I start pacing, one hand on my hip, one palm still to my forehead.

'We've got nothing to eat. Do you think the shops in Dunsborough will still be open?' I groan. 'Probably not, right? The kids will kill me if we have sandwiches again. Maybe I should go out anyway and get takeout. It's not like pizza ever gets old, even though I'm sick to death of it.'

Mitch frowns at me in concern.

I'm not used to men looking at me this way. I mean, occasionally it happens in the check-out when I take too long to pay for my shopping, but that's usually because I'm trying to stop Charlie raiding the lolly display. I swear, it's like a Venus flytrap for parents. Actually, scratch that, those looks at the check-out are probably one hundred per cent exasperation. Concern doesn't come into it.

Maybe Mitch is worried because he can't understand a word I'm saying. Am I stressing the poor man out?

I quickly clear my throat and mime someone eating. 'Food,' I say quickly. 'Food for tonight.'

'*Oui*.' He nods.

Abruptly, he turns and leaves the room. 'Hey!' I demand. 'Where are you going?'

I have a bad feeling that he's taking control again, like the last two times he walked away from me.

I stumble after him, nearly tripping over the junk that's overflowed onto the floor.

'*Mitch*.'

'Grace,' he responds, but doesn't turn around. Damn his flannelette shirt!

He takes the stairs two at a time, skilfully avoiding the dangerous bits without even looking down. I do my hippitty-hoppity staircase routine behind him, taking twice as long. By the time I reach the top, he's got his little bar fridge open.

Are you kidding me?

He pulls out a tray of sausages, a bag of onions and a tub of margarine.

'Wait a minute, how are you going to cook those?'

He grins at me, which doesn't steady my fluttering heart. I follow him back downstairs, feeling like Jack scampering after the giant. Just as I fear, he's headed straight for the stoves in the kitchen and is putting an old frying pan on the coils.

'No, no, no!' I protest. 'You can't. Those things are dinosaurs. They might be dangerous. You'll set the house on fire.'

I put a hand on his arm and am momentarily distracted by the firmness of his bicep beneath his shirt as he turns on the ancient stove.

'Mitch, stop.'

I cringe, waiting for the spark – the explosion, the *kerklunk*! I want to step back but he puts his hand over mine, holding it pressed into his arm, so all I can do is hide behind his body and peek around it. Nothing happens.

Unless you count the sizzling of butter in the pan and the intimate invasion of my personal space. I suddenly realise how close we're standing. He looks down at me, jiggling his eyebrows. I roll my eyes and manage to yank my hand free. 'How is that stove even working?'

The kids, of course, choose this moment to come running in.

'Sausages!'

'Mummy, Mitch is cooking sausages.'

'Really? I didn't know.'

'I love sausages,' says Charlie, as if this is a fact that's been up for debate for centuries. 'Big, juicy sausages.'

'Yum, yum, yum,' Alfie sings.

'Mummy,' Ryan looks at me reprovingly, 'the stove is working.'

'Yes, well, it is now,' I say defensively. 'But it could break down any minute. We can never be too careful. It must be thirty years old at least.'

The bloody butter keeps sizzling and my mouth starts watering at the smell.

'Don't worry,' Ryan assures me. 'If it breaks, Mitch will fix it.'

'Oh, he will, will he?' I snap. 'I wonder if there's anything he can't do.'

Is it my imagination or do his shoulders shake ever so slightly? He's got his back to me, so it might just be a trick of the light.

The kids don't deem my comment worthy of a response, and I have to say, after Mitch puts the sausages on and the smell of fatty, succulent pork wafts under my nose, I don't give it any further thought. Instead, I snatch up the bag of onions and start slicing them. You know what they say.

If you can't beat 'em, join them.

Chapter 16

I call Scott the next morning to tell him I no longer need the locksmith, and am chuffed that he sounds disappointed.

'But don't you want to see what's in the room?' he asks.

'I, er . . . found a key among the junk in the kitchen.' I feel a momentary pang at lying, but Antoine did say that Mitch wanted to stay under the radar. And after all the work he did yesterday, and the excellent dinner he cooked for us last night, I feel like I owe him.

There's a pause on the other end of the phone. 'So you got into the room then.' The restrained curiosity in his tone is almost tangible, so I put him out of his misery.

'The room was empty aside from some more junk. It was nothing special, trust me.' Again, I'm lying. How can you call a fridge full of sausages 'nothing special'?

'Well, I still need to finish my valuation,' Scott says brightly, 'so perhaps I'll come over anyway to do that.'

I love that he's so eager, and am almost persuaded to change my plans but decide against it. I've already mentioned the chocolate factory to the kids – taking it back would be akin to murder.

'Actually,' I apologise, 'I was going to take the kids out this morning. We, er . . . got a lot of cleaning done yesterday, so I've decided to give them a reward. This is supposed to be their school holidays, after all.'

'Oh, of course,' Scott agrees. 'You'll be wanting a break too. How much longer are you in town?'

'Just a few more days.'

'That's a real shame. Your kids seem to really love it here.' He pauses. 'Are you sure you want to sell?'

I'm a little taken aback, and I'm sure he can hear it in my pause because he laughs. 'Yes, that's the real estate agent talking. You'd think I didn't want your business.'

'Do you?' I ask tentatively. 'Want my business, that is?'

There's a soft sigh on the other end of the line and then he says with quiet conviction, 'My problem is that I would love to take you out some time, and how am I supposed to do that if you go home to Perth?'

'Oh.' My voice is shaky, and a streak of heat rushes through my body. I have no idea what to say. Do I try to sound coy, or admit that I'd like to go out with him too, if only I didn't have commitments in Perth?

'There's something about you, Grace,' he adds while I'm still making up my mind. 'Something I haven't seen in a very long time.' He hesitates. 'If there's any chance you're staying, any chance at all . . .'

'You'll be the first to know.' I aim for honesty in a rush, unable to believe this is actually happening.

'Great,' he responds warmly. 'In the meantime, does 9 am tomorrow suit you?'

It takes me a second to realise he's talking about the valuation, not a date. *He's only dating you if you're staying in town, Grace.* He's made that pretty clear.

So we're officially *not* dating.

Though it's been established that we would if we could.

'Nine is perfect,' I say quickly, because my head is starting to hurt. We say our goodbyes and I hang up, rubbing my temple. Come on, Grace. It's a little much to get stressed out over *not dating* someone.

I'm starting to find being in Yallingup a little unsettling. Not only was my mother-in-law murdered at Gum Leaf Grove, I'm also sharing the place with a complete stranger who doesn't speak my language, and now I have a potential boyfriend waiting in the wings.

Key word: *potential.*

Not actual, or even eventual.

It's a good thing I'm leaving. I shouldn't be disappointed. I need to get back to Perth – to less-confusing normalcy.

My job. School runs. Therapists' waiting rooms.

Life as a single mother, without any aspiration to change that status. That's real. That's life.

Thoughts of routine make me think of Rachel and I instantly want to call her to give her an update. Not about Scott, I tell myself quickly. She doesn't need to know about that – she'll just tease me. But the rest – definitely. A lot has happened since we last spoke. I sit down on the corner of the desk and pick up the receiver again. I dial my sister's number.

'Hey, you!' Rachel sounds really pleased to hear from me. 'You at the beach again?'

'No, I'm at the house. We have a landline now.' I give her the number that's stuck on the top of the phone. 'I'm pretty sure that's it. You'll have to test it later.'

'Sure will,' Rachel agrees. 'How did you get a landline?'

I fill her in on the *Alice in Wonderland* sequel that has become my life, leaving out the part about officially *not* dating Scott.

'This is unbelievable,' is Rachel's first response, which makes me feel utterly vindicated.

'Thank you!'

'So this French guy was hiding in a secret room in your house?'

'Yep.'

'And now he's living with you in return for free labour?'

'That's right.'

'Where is he right now?'

'He's –' I break off as Mitch walks into the room with a bucket of sugar soap solution and a sponge. He's been making his way round the house since breakfast, scrubbing marks off the walls. For someone who's not getting paid for his labour, he is extremely conscientious.

I glance nervously at him but he doesn't even look at me, merely puts his bucket down on the desk next to me and starts scrubbing. Today he's wearing just a white tank top without the flannelette shirt over the top, so I can see the muscles in his arm bunch and flex as he scrubs.

Damn it!

I look away.

'He's in the room with you,' accuses Rachel.

'Er . . . yeah.'

'Well, tell me more. What does he look like?'

'Rachel, I can't.'

'Why not? You said he doesn't speak English. He won't understand a thing you're saying.'

'I guess.' I try to work some moisture into my mouth. 'He's, um . . . just cleaning some spots in the office. Never seems at a loss for something to do . . .'

Mitch draws the sponge up the wall and his bicep forms a beautiful, sculptured bulge. My jaw drops open again.

'Grace?' prompts Rachel.

'Sorry, what was I saying?'

'You were saying that you think he's very good-looking,' Rachel tells me slyly.

'Well, you know, if you like them tall and muscular,' I admit.

'*I knew it!*'

'You tricked me,' I accuse her. 'You tricked me into telling you he's hot. That is grossly unfair and not very sisterly of you.'

I whirl around as Mitch suddenly turns to re-dip his sponge in the bucket. Knowing my face must be beet-red, I go to the window and pretend to look out.

Rachel doesn't spare me. 'So what does the real estate agent think of him?'

'The who?'

'Scott. Don't play dumb. He can't be happy you're now living with another man. A *hot* man.'

'It's only been one night! And actually I don't plan on telling Scott that someone else is living here.'

'Why not?' Rachel jokes. 'You want to date them both? Grace! I never thought you were that kind of woman.'

I groan. 'Why did I call you again?'

'Because you needed a sounding board. So I'm happy to put the question out there for you.'

'What question?'

'If they were competing for your heart, who would win?'

I gasp. 'No one is in contest. Believe me! My, er . . . tenant needs a roof over his head and he just wants some privacy. As for Scott, well, I can't date him because I live in Perth, remember?'

I don't mention that Scott has told me he wants to take me out, or that Mitch cooked me dinner last night. Those two points will just confuse the issue, and my sister doesn't need any further encouragement.

'Actually,' Rachel sighs, 'that reminds me, there's something I should warn you about.'

Her tone has changed, and the hairs on the back of my neck instinctively stand up. 'What is it?'

'Mum is in town. As in Perth, not Yallingup.'

My heart struggles over the next beat before returning to normal. I try to keep my voice light. 'So is she there for a visit or something? Are you catching up with her?'

'I've already caught up with her,' Rachel says. 'She was over here yesterday. And we had a long chat. It's not a visit, Grace. She's back for good.'

I clutch the phone a little tighter. 'What do you mean she's back for good?'

'She's given up her rental in Melbourne, and now she's looking around here for a place to stay.'

'Well, let her look,' I say firmly. 'There's no need for us to get involved.'

I can't help but think back to the last time we all lived together. Mum's constant cycle of sobriety, depression and then drinking. Apologies, followed by more moments of weakness. The lies. The excuses. The dishonesty.

Rachel's voice interrupts my thoughts.

'I haven't gotten involved . . . well, not exactly.' There's a strange lilt to her voice that arouses my suspicions.

'What's happened?'

'When she was here she noticed the mail I've been collecting for you and asked me why your stuff was here.'

'What did you tell her?'

'The truth.'

'*Rachel.*'

'Well, I felt sorry for her,' Rachel rushes on. 'She's dying for news of you, Grace. And you won't talk to her at all.'

'There's a reason for that,' I say, wishing my sister had held her tongue. I know she's a psychologist and she thinks Mum is her special project, but does she have to try to make her *my* special project too?

'Well, it's not a big secret, is it?' Rachel rushes on. 'That the boys have inherited Jake's old childhood home, and that you love it?'

'I don't love it –'

'Of course you love it. You couldn't stop talking about it the last time you were on the phone, and the only reason you're not keeping it is because you can't afford to.'

'Yeah, but that's life,' I shrug. 'You win some, you lose some. Running a bed and breakfast in the south-west is just a fantasy, Rachel. It's not real.'

'But that's just it,' Rachel says quickly. 'Maybe it could be real.'

Uh-oh.

'What are you trying to tell me?' I ask, slowly and suspiciously.

'Mum sold the family home. She made a lot of money,' Rachel says slowly. 'She gave me a cheque the other day. I reckon,' she pauses, 'if you saw her, she'd give you a cheque too.'

'Why?'

'Why do you think?' Rachel says earnestly. 'To reconnect with you. To make it up to you.'

'She can't just buy her way back into my life.'

'Grace, you know she doesn't mean it like that.'

'Well, how else am I supposed to take it?' I demand. 'Look, tell her I said thanks, but I don't want her money.'

'Now you're just being stupid,' Rachel scolds me.

'Rachel, she's an alcoholic. And sure, she may be recovering and in a good place right now, but you can't trust her. We've been down this road before.'

'But how is taking money from her going to harm you?'

'It's the obligation that comes with it,' I explain. 'She'll want something in return. Something that I don't want to give. Or she'll try to have a say in how I spend it or something. I know her.'

My mother always thought she knew what was best for us, from how to dress to what to eat. For my first disco at school, she bought me a dress to wear even though I'd told her I wanted to wear my denim skirt with a nice top. I ended up wearing the dress to please her, and feeling awkward all night. The dress was pretty, but it wasn't my style, and wearing it took the shine off the whole evening.

That was what my mother did.

She took the shine off things.

It was Dad who held the family together, smoothed out the disagreements and tended to wounded pride. It was no wonder we were so lost without him.

'This is a trick, Rachel,' I tell her implacably. 'An unadulterated trick. I haven't heard one apology from her. Not one word about how she shouldn't have abandoned us. Until she takes responsibility for what she did, I don't want anything to do with her.'

'Okay, okay,' Rachel says. 'I just thought I'd put it out there, for both your sakes.'

'Fine, it's out there, but it's never going to happen.'

And that, I think, was my key mistake.

I should never have said never.

Chapter 17

After I hang up, I feel like kicking something. If only Mitch hadn't carried all those old plastic crates out to the junk heap.

I just can't believe it.

I can't believe Mum is trying to bribe her way back into my life. That's exactly what this hypothetical cheque is. A bribe.

She's trying to reinstate herself without even admitting she ever did anything wrong. How can you believe someone won't hurt you again when they've never even said sorry, never shown any remorse for what they did?

It doesn't work that way.

If you get shot, you take the bullet out. You get the bullet out and clean up the wound and let it heal. You don't just put your shirt back on and hope no one notices you're bleeding. The wound would just get infected. That's exactly what's happened with Mum and me. We're infected.

I want the bullet out, she wants it to stay in. Hidden, so she doesn't have to admit she shot me in the first place.

Nobody wins.

I've been staring at the phone a long time. Suddenly I feel a hand on my shoulder. I turn to see Mitch holding a steaming hot mug emitting the sweet aroma of something I don't dare believe is real.

'Coffee!' I gasp. 'You made coffee?'

I wrap my hands lovingly around the mug. I'd been so absorbed in my conversation with Rachel, I hadn't even noticed him leave the room.

'You're a legend.'

Mitch doesn't respond but he smiles at me, that achingly endearing smile of his that gets right into my bones and warms me up from the inside.

When you can't actually speak to someone, you rely a lot on body language to get to know them. I've noticed that Mitch has three different smiles. They don't appear often, but when they do it's pure magic.

There's the grin he reserves for the boys when he's goofing around with them; the cheeky, mischievous twist of the lips he does when he knows he's got the better of you (as seen with the sausages and onions yesterday); and lastly, there's this smile.

It's personal.

It's the smile that makes me believe that after just two days, we might actually be friends.

I smile back at him over the rim of my cup and take a deep sip. I shut my eyes as the coffee slides down my throat like liquid love. I can't help but groan in ecstasy.

'This is exactly what I needed. Thanks.'

'*De rien, mon cher,*' he responds, a hand going into the hair at the back of his head as though he's embarrassed.

He walks out of the office and leaves me to enjoy my coffee. I glance around the room and notice what a good job he's done – and not just with the walls. The room is clean and bare except for the desk and the filing cabinet. He's even taken down that horrible half-broken set of venetian blinds. Now the sunshine streams into the room, filling it with light. Outside, I can see the kids playing cricket beside the vineyard. Apart from their cheering, all I can hear are birds. To my horror, I find myself tearing up.

It's not because of my mum, though I'm certain the news about her has contributed to my heightened emotional state. It's because I'm standing here in a room I didn't clean myself, holding a hot cup of coffee I didn't make, and drinking it without interruption.

That sort of thing doesn't happen to Grace Middleton.

That sort of thing is a miracle.

A pure, bona fide gift from God.

Who knew such a simple pleasure could bring all my walls crashing down. I brush away the tears with the back of my hand and tell myself to stop being stupid.

There's nothing to cry about.

Everything is going well for me right now. Better than well! I'm about to make a killing on this house – much-needed funds for my kids. Best to focus all my thoughts on that, and not get bogged down in old fantasies and lost causes.

I take some time to polish off my coffee and wipe my eyes before slipping outside and back into real life.

'Time to go to the chocolate factory,' I announce. 'Mummy needs some chocolate.'

The statement brings instant results. The boys drop their balls and bats with a shriek of 'Woohoo!' and tear off to the car like it's a race to get there. I wish the words 'Time to shower' had the same effect.

Through a series of hand gestures, I manage to tell Mitch that we're going out. I think he understands what I'm saying. He certainly doesn't seem too concerned as I get in my car and drive off with the kids. It's kind of weird leaving him in our house like that – a little too intimate, really. But he was there before us and has been there all along. It's kind of silly to feel awkward now.

Isn't it?

Once we're out on the main road, thoughts of Mitch recede. The country air refreshes me and gives me some perspective.

Gum Leaf Grove is a means to an end. Its sale will make the

next few years much easier. I have a job and a semi-stable life back in Perth. I can't let my mother confuse the issue.

Even if I had the money, starting a B&B in the south-west would mean pulling the boys out of school and starting over in a new town without friends or family support. And what do I know about running a B&B, anyway? I mean, it's a very romantic notion. It makes me think of homemade cookies, horseriding and playing hide-and-seek in the vines. However, I'm pretty sure that's what the guests experience, not the owners.

Also, running a B&B wouldn't be a one-woman show. I'd at least need to hire a cook. Then there's the cleaning of the rooms, doing the laundry, marketing, website design and administration. I'd need help for sure. And who's to say we'd even get any customers.

Don't be such a pessimist, Grace. You know you'd get customers. You've seen the photos.

I brush aside the images that flash through my mind of Gum Leaf Grove in its heyday. After all, I'm no Alice Bowman.

Then again, that might be a good thing.

Considering she's dead.

I flash back to that photo of her in the sitting room with her arms around her friend, smiling happily at the camera. How did she get from that to murdered?

Like a black-and-white movie pulled straight from the Hollywood archives, I see someone's fingers closing around her throat, her eyes bulging, her hands scratching like claws against their relentless grasp.

Ugh!

I shake my head and blink rapidly, trying to toss away these morbid thoughts.

'I see the sign. I see the sign!' pipes up Ryan. If it wasn't for him I'd have completely missed the turn-off.

As we pull into the car park and I find a bay, Alfie says crossly from the back seat, 'Mummy, are you sure this is the right place?'

I kill the engine and examine my surroundings. 'Sure is.'

'It doesn't look like a chocolate factory.' Ryan lowers his glasses and peers over the rims like an old man.

I have to admit, the building itself is not very Willy Wonka-like. It's modern and square, like a giant Lego block that's been dropped in the middle of a forest.

'Don't worry,' I swivel in my seat to address Ryan, 'this is definitely the right place.'

We get out of the car and walk in. The smell of chocolate hits us first, then we see the tables of product that dot the long hall. There's chocolate of all kinds, shapes and sizes. Simple blocks are stacked like gold bars on the first display, which is enough to get my mouth watering. On my left is a long counter showcasing bite-sized delectable delights in a myriad of designs and flavours. Behind this is floor-to-ceiling box shelving, like the honeycomb of a hive, filled with bags and bags of different kinds of chocolate.

My boys look like they're about to start licking the floor so I quickly lead them over to the large tasting bowls full of buttons – milk, dark and white chocolate. Each silver basin is equipped with a large plastic spoon so patrons can hygienically sample a handful.

My youngest holds out both hands, and looks like he's died and gone to heaven as I place milk buttons in one palm and then dark buttons in the other.

He brings both hands to his mouth at once. His next words, 'Can I have some more?', are muffled by chocolate.

I laugh. 'Today you are Charlie *in* the Chocolate Factory.'

We do a bit more tasting and I buy a couple of blocks. There are some delicious condiments on the other side of the store, and a cafe with an ice-cream section. The cafe tables spill out into an alfresco area edged by a lovely stretch of lawn and bushland beyond. Not a bad spot to relax if you've got time on your hands. I get ice-creams in cones for the kids and a coffee for myself, and we go outside to enjoy the beautiful spring sunshine.

The boys finish their ice-creams in record time and start 'hunting kangaroos', using long sticks for rifles, while I take my time over my coffee. My mind wanders back to Alice Bowman's murder. I still can't believe Jake didn't tell me about it.

His mother was murdered.

That's a big deal.

That's something that changes you. It's not something you just get over. My own mother wasn't murdered, but her alcoholism changed the way I viewed the world, my perception of family and level of trust. I can't see how Jake losing his mother couldn't have affected him too.

I wonder what Jake would have been like if his mum hadn't been murdered. Would he have married me? The girl who was happy not to talk about 'the parents'. Who liked to keep the past in the past, childhood secrets buried and forgotten.

Out of sight, out of mind.

I look at my phone and am pleased to see that I have reception. I google 'Alice Bowman's murder', not expecting to find much. After all, it was twenty years ago; not many papers were online back then. Surprisingly, I get a few hits – in fact, there's a whole page of related stories and reprinted articles. Some are ten years old, some are more recent.

As I scroll down and scan the headlines, the truth hits me with a sick swoop. Jake's father was the murderer.

Chapter 18

Archived article from 13 February 1996

Town in mourning after alleged murder-suicide in Yallingup

Today the town of Yallingup paid its respects to local business-woman Alice Bowman. Ms Bowman, a prominent member of the community and a distant descendant of the pioneering Bussell family, was laid to rest in a small cemetery behind the historically significant Anglican church, Saint Andrews. Disbelief and anger more than sadness were rife among the attendees, who felt this terrible tragedy could have been prevented.

Ms Bowman was allegedly murdered just one week ago by her husband, David Bowman, who later took his own life. The couple owned well-known bed and breakfast Gum Leaf Grove in Yallingup.

'We all knew he was an alcoholic and that they were having problems,' family friend and local Elise Gregory told *Southern News*. 'You just never know how involved you're supposed to get in other people's problems.'

By all accounts, David Bowman was a quiet man who mostly kept to himself. He was a frequent patron of the Dunsborough Tavern and was spotted there more or less on a daily basis. By contrast, Alice had a large network of friends and was well respected by other business owners in the area. There was no known history of domestic violence, though the Bowmans' marriage was considered to be in crisis.

'He hadn't contributed much to the running of Gum Leaf Grove in recent times,' Alice Bowman's best friend, Deborah Hanen, reported. 'Alice was always complaining that she had to do everything herself.'

Staff who worked at the bed and breakfast told journalists that the couple's relationship was tumultuous at best.

'We often heard them fighting in the morning because he was out drinking late the night before. Never any violence, though. Just raised voices and slamming doors,' Gum Leaf Grove's cleaner Celeste Brown told *Southern News*. 'I felt so sorry for their son Jake, who spent most of his time trying to stay out of their way.'

In fact, it was their son (age 17) who discovered his mother's body at 9 am on 27 January 1996, in the sitting room of the family home. Jake had been out at an Australia Day party the day before. He returned home late and went straight to his room so as not to disturb anyone.

Forensic investigators ruled that Alice Bowman died of traumatic asphyxiation by strangulation. Police later found David Bowman's body in his car, which was parked outside the house. He had committed suicide by consuming an overdose of sleeping pills and a bottle of vodka. A note to his son was also discovered on the front seat of the car, apologising for his own weakness and for accidentally killing Jake's mother.

While Jake Bowman was present at his mother's funeral, he did not attend the wake presided over by his aunt, Carmen Hastings, who advised *Southern News* that Jake was completely overwrought after everything that had happened.

It is uncertain what will become of the family business, Gum Leaf Grove, which still has bookings well into the new year.

'Jake will inherit everything,' his aunt said. 'However, given what's happened here, I'm not sure he'll want to stay.'

Chapter 19

Wow.

An unnerving feeling of sorrow and pity for Jake washes over me. It must have been horrific.

Finding his mum like that, then realising it was his dad who'd killed her, and that he was dead as well.

And the note from his dad.

Oh, the note.

Events and scenes from our marriage slide in and out of my mind as I fill in the blanks. Unexplained reactions. Extreme behaviour. A complete and utter lack of sensitivity.

I can just imagine the cycle of neglect that was his child-hood. Two parents absorbed in their own problems. His father an alcoholic in denial. His mother an overworked wife and a victim of abuse. It was no wonder Jake's emotional wellbeing had fallen through the cracks. After the death of his parents, he must have packed it all away and just run . . . right into my unsuspecting arms.

'Hi, Grace.'

It's the woman I met at Oak Hills the other day. My head snaps up like I've been caught looking at nude pictures of Chris Hemsworth.

'Er, hi . . .' I say, feeling my face heat up like water on a gas stove. I hope she can't read minds. 'Eve, isn't it?'

There's a woman standing next to her holding a tray with two coffees. She is older than Eve, with darker eyes and much less height.

Eve nods. 'And this is my mum, Anita,' she adds, following my gaze.

'Nice to meet you,' I say, even though I am dearly wishing they hadn't walked over at this precise moment.

'Sorry to interrupt you,' Eve is saying, 'but it looks like my kids have conscripted yours.'

I look across the lawn and see Charlie handing Eve's two sons a long stick each. Ryan yells, 'Move out!' with a slicing motion of his right hand. The boys immediately fall into line and start frogmarching across the lawn.

'Actually,' I chuckle, 'I think it's the other way round.'

Eve smiles back. 'Maybe you're right.'

'Kangaroo hunting,' I explain. 'It's a very serious matter.'

'It sure is,' she grins. 'Do you, er . . . mind if we join you?'

That's when I realise I've rudely left them standing next to my table without inviting them to sit down. Being school holidays, all the other outdoor tables are taken. I'm hogging a four-seater all to myself.

'Oh, sorry! Where's my head? Please, sit down.' I hurriedly gesture at the chairs in front of me.

'So,' Eve asks cheerfully as they take a seat, 'what have you been up to since we last spoke?'

Airing secret rooms. Letting a stranger move in with me. Officially not dating a real estate agent. Ghost busting.

'Er . . . cleaning,' I say at last. 'Lots and lots of cleaning. We're preparing Gum Leaf Grove for sale.'

'You own Gum Leaf Grove?' Anita's eyes widen with interest. 'I knew the previous owners.'

'You did?' Eve raises her eyebrows. 'You never told me that.'

Anita gives a rough sigh. 'It was tragic what happened to them. The murder. The suicide. You and your sisters were too young at the time. I shielded you from it.'

'Did you go to Alice Bowman's funeral?' The words rush out before I can stop them.

Anita winced. 'Yes, it was a terribly sad occasion.'

'Wait!' Eve says and turns to me, stricken. 'Alice Bowman. That's the name of your ghost. The name I couldn't recall?'

'Yeah,' I give her a small smile. 'She was my ex-husband's mother. Antoine told me a few days ago.'

'Ghost?' Anita's brow wrinkles. 'What are you talking about, Eve?'

'The ghost that haunts Gum Leaf Grove is Alice Bowman,' her daughter says, as if it's obvious. 'Her story was turned into an urban legend, Mum. It was all around school, and every slumber party I ever went to.'

Anita sniffed. 'So much for shielding you! I can't believe the insensitivity of the kids who made up those stories. Especially about a victim their parents would have known.'

'Where is the cemetery?' I ask, suddenly seized by a mad desire to go and visit her grave. 'The one where Alice is buried.'

'It's behind an old church,' Anita informs me. 'Heritage listed and no longer in use by a parish. Actually, it's functioning as a museum now.'

'I know the one,' Eve says. 'It's just off Caves Road, after you pass the turn-off to Canal Rocks. I forget the name of the road, but I think it's signposted because it's a tourist attraction. The museum is called "Memory Lane". It's got first-settler memorabilia and a winemaking history sort of theme.'

'Sounds interesting,' I say, wondering how I'm going to sell this to the boys, because we are definitely going there next.

Anita groans and leans in confidentially. 'It's actually a terrible museum. I don't know why they didn't shut it down years ago. I expect it's because Doris Caffery will likely die if she doesn't have a cause.'

'Who is Doris Caffery?'

'Yallingup gossip, lobbyist and freeloader,' Eve smirks. 'Bronwyn says she comes to Oak Hills every Wednesday for the free cheese and crackers.'

'Free cheese?' I grin mischievously. 'My boys love cheese. It's always good to know where the freebies are.'

As if my words have just triggered a siren, all the boys come running back to our table.

'Mummy,' Ryan's face is flushed red with exertion, 'can we have another ice-cream?'

'No time,' I say brightly. 'We're going now.'

'Aawww! We can't go now.'

'Oh yes we can.'

I was one hundred per cent right about my boys' reaction to the idea of a museum visit.

'What's a mooseem?' asks Charlie from his booster seat.

'It's boring! That's what it is,' says Ryan. 'It's a building full of old stuff that nobody can use anymore.'

'Like my cot?' asks Charlie, who only moved into a bed three months ago.

'Sort of,' I throw over my shoulder.

I glance in the rear-view mirror and see Charlie's face screw up in disgust. 'I no want to look at cots! That's stoopid.'

'I didn't say there'd be cots,' I said. 'Just old things.'

'That's more stoopid,' responds Charlie categorically.

Surprisingly, Alfie is not completely against the idea. 'Will there be dinosaur bones there?' he demands, rubbing his little hands together as though he's itching to get chiselling on a fossil.

I clear my throat. 'Unlikely. But . . .' I rack my brain for something potentially exciting. 'There might be . . . an Aboriginal spear, or a stuffed . . . echidna.' I have no idea if echidnas are even native to the area, but they have spikes, which I know is infinitely appealing to Alfie, who seems to find the pursuit of sharp, dangerous objects a form of thrill seeking. I bite my lip and keep my gaze firmly on the road ahead, hoping I'm not raising a serial killer. An appalling thought occurs to me in an instant. Is being a murderer genetic? If so, these kids have some awful DNA.

Ryan, who is in the seat next to me today, lowers his chin into his chest and looks at me reprovingly. For an aching moment, I can almost see my father in that gaze, and a lump forms in my throat. It's the same look he'd use to make me squirm.

'You're just making that up,' Ryan throws at me. 'Like the time you told us the dentist's room has rides in it.'

'What?' I say defensively. 'The chair goes up and down. It's totally a ride.'

'It's not a ride.' Ryan is outraged. 'The dentist wouldn't let us play on it anyway.'

'Yes, well, he was a bit of a stick in the mud,' I concede, remembering the cranky old codger glaring at me when Alfie told him to 'make it go faster'. 'But we mustn't let one bad experience spoil all the rest.'

Ryan is all seven-year-old outrage. 'There were no other rides at the dentist.'

'Weren't there?'

'No!'

'Oh well,' I grin flippantly as I turn onto Caves Road, 'it doesn't matter because we're going to the museum anyway.'

'Memory Lane' is exactly where Eve told me it would be. After getting onto Caves Road, I just follow the brown tourist signs to my destination. As I pull into the gravel car park I notice that there's only one other car there. Obviously, this tourist attraction isn't that popular.

The church is smaller than the average house, but tall, and constructed of giant limestone blocks with a tiled pitched roof. It's a quaint, pretty-looking building with beautiful stained-glass windows. There's a plaque out the front denoting its Anglican heritage and giving the name of the priest who held the final mass there, which seemed to occur right around the time Alice was murdered. I wonder if he was the one who presided over her funeral.

Behind the church is the graveyard, unprotected by a fence of any kind. It's not huge, but big enough that it would take at least a couple of hours to read every headstone.

Somehow, I don't think my boys will be keen on that plan. I wonder if the museum will have a map of the headstones that I can refer to.

The arched back door of the church is open and a blackboard next to it reads: 'Welcome to Memory Lane. Adults $20 Children $10. Tours available.'

Are they kidding? What have they got in there? Gold-plated kangaroo paws? And what do they mean by 'tours available'? The church looks like I could walk around it in five minutes.

I look back at my boys. Ryan and Charlie are pulling faces and dawdling. Alfie is shooting finger pistols into the trees.

'Good news, boys. I don't think we'll be staying. It's a bit pricey.'

I grab Charlie's hand to help him keep up, and lead the boys into the museum. It smells like damp that's never been aired. I look up at the stained-glass windows and realise they can't be opened. My nose wrinkles. What I'm smelling here probably dates back to the first vineyard.

The boys have already moved forward. They are standing in front of a woman who has her head down on the reception desk and is gently snoring. Her hair is grey with streaks of white, pinned in a messy bun. The displays behind her appear to be as boring as the boys expected – glass cabinets filled with coins, china and silverware. There are some mannequins dressed up in old, yellowing linen, and a didgeridoo leans in one corner, propped against an ancient wheelbarrow that was clearly purchased from the 'early settler' hardware store.

Charlie pokes the woman. 'No sleeping on the job.'

The woman whimpers and turns her head over, resting her other cheek on the crooked arm she is using as a pillow. Her blue knit cardigan looks as ancient as she is. 'Go away, Harry,' she says in a croaky voice. 'I'm not in the mood.'

'My name's not Harry,' Charlie says, and pokes her again.

Meanwhile, Alfie has taken two pencils out of her stationery holder and is tapping them on the side of the desk like drumsticks.

'Alfie, stop that,' I hiss.

The woman's head jerks up at the noise and she finds herself eye to eye with Charlie, who is looking disgruntled. 'In the mood for what?' he asks.

With a flustered gasp, she straightens, patting her chest in search of her glasses, which are dangling from a plastic chain around her neck.

'Do you have any dinosaur bones?' Alfie chucks the pencils aside and grabs her stapler.

I take it off him before he can do any damage.

'Or echidnas?' he presses her further.

She draws her glasses onto the bridge of her nose with an unsteady fumble and peers through them.

'Welcome to Memory Lane.' She tries for a smile. 'I'm Doris Caffery.' She scans my brood. 'That'll be fifty dollars, please.'

Daylight robbery!

'Er . . . actually, we aren't here to see the museum –'

'Yes!' Ryan draws his hand down in a fist pump.

I glare at him and continue. 'We're here to see the graveyard.'

'*What?* Awwwww!' Ryan wails.

'Ssssh.' I shove him behind me. 'A member of our family is buried there. We're just not sure which one is her grave, and I was wondering if you could help us.'

'Your best bet is to take the graveyard tour, which, lucky for you, leaves . . .' Doris checks her watch briskly, 'in five minutes. The guide will be able to handle all your questions.'

'You can't just point out our relative's grave if we give you her name . . .?' I begin futilely.

'Definitely not.' Doris seems horrified. 'That would completely ruin your experience.'

I sigh. 'So how much is the graveyard tour?'

'Well, as it so happens,' Doris says brightly, 'this week when you purchase entry to the graveyard, you receive a complimentary ticket to the museum and a free graveyard tour as well.'

'And how much is that?'

'For all of you,' her finger does a tight circle, 'fifty dollars.'

I roll my eyes. *Come on!* 'I'm sorry, but that's very expensive.'

'Fine.' She purses her mouth. 'Forty dollars.'

I fold my arms.

'Thirty?'

'I'll give you ten,' I say.

'Sold.' She stands up and rips off four tickets from the reel pinned to the side of her desk as I pull a ten-dollar note from my purse. 'Thank you for supporting local history.'

'So wait,' Ryan's eyes widen in horror, 'now we're going to the museum *and* the graveyard?'

'Yep.'

'This is the worst day ever!'

I have to agree with him, especially when Doris announces that she will be our tour guide for the afternoon. I'm beginning to wonder whether there really is a tour or if she just made it up to get into my purse. I guess she has to keep her job somehow.

'This way, please.'

The boys drag their feet as she leads us into a large display room, which is basically the rest of the church, and starts rattling on about the origin of this and the discovery of that.

'Yallingup was first put on the map when its caves were discovered in 1899 by European settlers. We have some rocks that come from some of the first explorations.' She stops at a glass display case that is indeed full of rocks.

'You've got to be kidding me,' says Ryan.

Charlie attaches his mouth to the side of the glass like a suction cup on an octopus tentacle. Why do all kids love doing this? I find it disgusting.

'Charlie, no!' I pull him off the glass under Doris's disproving stare.

Doris walks on, clearly expecting that we will follow. 'Over here we have some very exciting jars of soil. Rich in minerals unique to the Mediterranean climate and maritime influence – taken, I believe, from our most successful vineyards.'

Behind her retreating back I see Alfie shaking the hand of Dr Tom Cullity (region pioneer). It detaches from the mannequin at the wrist.

Oh shit.

Luckily, Doris hasn't turned around yet. I hastily snatch the plastic hand from Alfie and try to reattach it. It refuses to click back into place, so I slip it into the large pockets of Dr Cullity's coat just as Doris spins around to see what's taking me so long.

'Is there any chance we could skip the museum and go straight to the graveyard?' I ask. 'I don't think my boys are going to go the distance in here.'

Doris seems somewhat put out by this request. 'But I haven't shown you the wine glass that held the very first wine that was ever drunk in Yallingup . . . or was it Cowaramup? It doesn't matter. It's basically the Holy Grail of the Margaret River wine region. Tourists come for miles to see it.'

Uh-huh.

I glance around at the empty room.

'Maybe we'll catch it another day.'

When it's not so crowded.

With a 'humpfth', she leads us outside and into the graveyard, which, I have to say, has not been very well maintained. The pathways are weed-ridden and unswept. The grass around the graves is patchy, and interspersed with sections of red-brown dirt and gravel.

I am immediately taken with the ornate headstones, however. Some are large and arched, others are shaped like crosses, raised on blocks and flanked by statues of angels. Several are above-ground stone graves with little wrought-iron fences around them.

But all the graves seem to be empty of tributes. Their stone vases are overgrown with weeds, or full of muddy water. After glancing at a few of the dates, I figure these people's relatives must have moved on by now, or perhaps no longer know that these graves are here.

'The oldest grave is from 1902,' Doris is saying. 'It belongs to a man by the name of Richard Appleby, who died in an exploration venture into Ngilgi Cave, which was first discovered by Edward Dawson in 1899 and at the time was known as Yallingup Cave.'

'Can we go now?' asks Ryan.

'So, er . . . would you know where Alice Bowman's grave is?'

Doris spins around in surprise. 'You're related to Alice Bowman?'

Ryan surprises me by revealing that he's been paying attention to the random discoveries I've made over the past few days. 'She's our grandma, isn't she, Mummy? The one in the photos we found.'

'Yes.' I nod and turn back to Doris. 'Do you know of her?'

Doris is affronted. 'This job requires extensive knowledge of local history. It would be remiss of me not to know her story.'

'Was my grandma special?' asks Ryan.

Doris meets my gaze sharply and I quickly shake my head. She looks down at Ryan again. 'Very special. In fact, her grave is the only one here that still gets visitors.'

I assume she's referring to occasional visits from Jake, until we find ourselves in front of Alice's headstone. There's a giant bunch of fresh white roses in the immaculately clean stone vase. The grass around her grave is free of weeds, and the headstone itself is unmarked by black spots and perfectly clean. Someone has clearly been looking after this little plot, and the flowers are too fresh for them to have been from Jake.

'Who visits this grave?' I ask Doris.

'No idea.' She shrugs, but looks evasive.

'You must have some idea,' I insist. 'Don't they pay entry?'

Doris looks a little guilty, then lifts her chin again. 'Fees were only recently instated due to, er . . . the economic downtown and flagging business profits. But in any case, the person or persons who visit Alice's grave come after hours.'

I fold my arms. 'When is the museum open?'

'Every day except Wednesday, 9 am to 4 pm. But they come on Monday or Tuesday. Every week.'

'If you never see them,' I frown, 'how do you know they come Monday or Tuesday?'

'Because on Monday morning the flowers at her grave are dead or wilting, and when I come in on Tuesday morning they have always been replaced with fresh ones. I can only assume it's done on Monday or Tuesday when no one is around.'

I have to confess, I am completely nonplussed. Whoever is doing this is extremely dedicated. Alice must have really meant something to them.

'How long has this been going on?' I ask Doris.

'Ages,' Doris spreads her hands. 'Ever since her funeral, I think.'

'And it's every week?' I clarify. 'There's never been a break in the pattern?'

'Never.'

'And you really don't know who is bringing these flowers?' I prompt again.

'Well,' Doris lowers her voice confidentially, 'you didn't hear it from me, but apparently Bob Fletcher purchases a bouquet from Sally Merlin's florist in Dunsborough every Monday evening just before his bridge game with friends in Yallingup.'

Bob Fletcher.

I remember the day we met, and Bob saying Ryan had his 'grandmother's eyes'.

Wow. It made sense.

Ryan is touching the headstone. 'It must be awful to die,' he sighs.

'I'm not going to,' announces Alfie. 'I'm going to live forever and ever.'

'Me too,' agrees Charlie.

'You don't get a choice, dummy,' says Ryan, and I can tell from his eyes that he's thinking about his dad.

'Come now, Ryan. Don't be rude to your brother.'

Ryan's face screws up. 'But he's just being dumb. He's always being dumb.'

'He's not.' I squeeze his shoulder. 'He's just younger than you are. It takes a bit longer for him to understand.'

'Don't you think that if he had a choice, Dad would still be alive?' Ryan demands of Alfie, who looks stricken.

'Alfie,' I bend down to his level, 'everybody has to die at some point, whether they like it or not. It's just the way things are.'

We are all silent for a moment. I offer up a small prayer for Alice's soul and, belatedly, Jake's as well.

'Well, if I have to die,' Alfie perks up again, 'I'm gonna die fighting a crocodile or something really cool like that.'

'Well, I hope you're not going to start picking fights with crocodiles any time soon.'

'Oh no, I'll wait till I'm really old,' he assures me. 'Like when I'm ten!'

'What a relief.' I exchange a look with Doris and she leads us back to the museum.

It's hard not to feel a little unsettled by the day's revelations. As I drive back to Gum Leaf Grove, I can't help but wonder about Bob's devotion to Alice.

He's been visiting her grave weekly for the last twenty years, leaving flowers every time. Out of love? Or guilt? Maybe both.

Then there's David Bowman, who was an alcoholic and a lout, but not the violent sort, according to the *Southern News* . . . until one day something made him snap. Suddenly, I think I know what that thing was.

Alice was having an affair.

Chapter 20

As I pull up outside our house at Gum Leaf Grove, the first thing I notice is that the junk pile is gone.

There's only a flattened patch of dirt in its place. I climb out of the car slowly, shading my eyes from the evening light as I stare at the empty space. By contrast, my boys burst out of the car like firework rockets on a floating barge and run towards it, exclaiming, 'Where'd it go? Where'd it go?'

Is it my imagination or does the garden in front of the house also look a little neater? I narrow my eyes, trying to work out what's changed. The path has been weeded. The bushes have been pruned. And all the dead trees, of which there were many, have been removed.

Did Mitch do all this while we were out? Who is he? Superman?

Let's not answer that.

I climb the porch steps and enter the house. I hear hammering, and look up. He's sitting on the stairs, replacing the wobbly step with a new board. He's wearing a white tank top, a pair of butt-hugging blue Levi's, and looks exactly like an advertisement for a soft drink until he turns his head to greet me and I see the scar. Not that I'm in any way repulsed by it. It just brings me back to reality, reminding me that he's a person, not a fantasy. He pulls out the three nails he's been holding between his lips and says, '*Bonjour, Grace.*'

'*Bonjour*, Mitch,' I say cheerfully. 'You've been busy, haven't you?'

He gives a nod with a dart of the eyes that indicates he's merely nodding because that's all he knows to do.

'Yeah, me too.' I swing my arms jovially. 'Solving crimes and finding out that my mother-in-law had an affair with my real estate agent's boss. Go figure.'

He stares at me blankly and I swat my hand. 'Never mind.'

I tilt my head to one side, wondering how to broach the issue of the junk pile when he can't understand a word I'm saying.

'Er . . .' I point towards the front of the house. He stares back at me dubiously. I gesture for him to descend the stairs. 'Can you come here, please?'

He points to where I'm standing.

'Yes, down the stairs.'

He nods and complies. 'Great job, by the way.' I fill in the awkward silence as he carefully avoids the holes where he's pulled up boards. 'And I love what you've done with the garden. This free labour thing is really working out for me. I'd forgotten how good it is to have a man about the house.'

He finally reaches the bottom of the stairs, and I instantly feel dwarfed as he towers over me, broad shouldered and smelling like sweat and man. I suddenly find myself making stuttered excuses.

'Not that I'm implying you're my man. J-just that you are *a* man who is in *this* house.' I chew on my lower lip. 'Why am I still talking? You don't understand me anyway.' I give my head a little shake and reach over to take his hand, intending to lead him to the nonexistent junk pile and point to it in a 'What the hell?' kind of manner.

But as I turn to lead him outside, I'm jerked back – his feet seem to be nailed to the floor. I look over my shoulder. He's just standing there, looking at our joined hands in shock. I feel a momentary zing of pleasure as I realise *this time* I'm the one who has unsettled him.

Wait.

I've unsettled him.

Oh crap. He thinks I'm coming on to him.

'No, no, no, no, no.' I shake my head as he looks up and meets my eyes, his own intensely questioning. I try to pull my hand away but he tightens his fingers around my palm so I can't let go. Really, Grace, you have got to learn your social dos and don'ts. Like, don't grab the hand of the guy who can't speak English. He might think you want him.

I swallow hard.

Brain, please do not go there.

I hastily gesture towards the front door, and do a two-finger walking motion with my free hand. 'Now, don't freak out. I just want to show you something.' I point towards the front door. 'Can I show you something?'

I try walking again and this time he follows. His fingers loosen slightly, allowing my palm to gently graze the inside of his as we move, almost the way our lips would if we –

Grace!

I flick the thought away in absolute horror.

You have seriously got to get a grip!

I lead Mitch out onto the porch and then down the steps. We walk across the garden. The walk seems miles too long for my peace of mind. I can't remember the last time I held hands with a guy. I'd forgotten how intimate it was. Maybe this 'lead the way' thing wasn't such a good idea after all.

At last, we get to the now-vacant patch of dirt where my kids are still playing.

'Hey, Mitch!' they call. 'The junk pile is gone.'

'Somebody stole it.'

'Do you think it was aliens?'

I am finally able to drop his hand as he ruffles their heads and fires pretend handguns at Alfie, who is firing back at him. I'm always amazed at the way he is able to hold the boys' interest without saying a word. You'd think they'd be bored with him by now.

'The junk,' I say, trying to regain his attention as I point at the ground and then spread my arms wide. 'The huge junk pile that was here. Where is it?'

'Oh.' He nods his understanding, then says, 'Antoine.' Then he mimics someone driving a car.

'Are you telling me that *Antoine*,' I do a 'lift and carry' mime, 'put all that stuff in a trailer and drove off?' I do the driving mime. 'As in, to the tip?'

He nods and points to himself as well, indicating, I assume, that he helped.

I look at him incredulously. 'Even so, I find this very hard to believe.'

His shoulders shake with mirth and then he takes his phone out of his pocket. Flicking it on, he presses a few buttons and shows me a photo. There's a picture of a very disgruntled-looking Antoine sitting in an Oak Hills ute, with an open trailer hooked to the back.

'Wait, is that a coffee in his hand?'

My eyes narrow in on the disposable cup Antoine is holding, before examining the tray of the ute and the trailer. They are both full.

'He didn't help you load up at all, did he?'

I glance up, but Mitch is swinging Charlie between his legs. I wonder if Bronwyn knows that Antoine has been using the Oak Hills ute to help me out. Damn it! I only just made friends with her.

I shake my head. 'That guy is going to get me into trouble. I suppose I'd better call and thank him.'

Mitch follows me back to the house and returns to the

stairs. I go into the office and pick up the phone, dialling the number that Antoine gave me the last time he was here.

'Good afternoon, Oak Hills Cellar Door.' The French accent is very clear.

'Antoine,' I exclaim with relief, 'it's Grace. Thank you for taking away all my junk today. There was really no need for you to go to so much trouble.'

'Yes, you are absolutely right, of course,' Antoine agrees bluntly. 'It was completely above and beyond, and I never would have done it had Mitch not insisted.'

'Mitch insisted?' I repeat, a little nonplussed.

'Got it into his head that it was a hazard and not safe for the kids to play near.'

'Oh.'

'Too many sharp edges. Said *I* had to remove it.' Antoine flicks this bit of information at me as though he's asking, *Can you believe it?*

'I'm, er . . . sorry –'

'Yes, well, it is all very well and good for him, sitting pretty in his little hideaway, sending me off to bring food and wood and trailers like I'm at his beck and call, which,' he adds severely, 'I am not! I have a life, you know. I'm not one of his staff. And you would be very kind to tell him that.'

'Er . . . Antoine, I can't tell him that. He can't understand me.'

'Of course he can't,' he grumbles between clenched teeth, 'because I must play translator as well. *Inconsidere!* I am beginning to think I should never have volunteered my help when he came to me.'

I'm finding my 'thank you' a little hard to deliver when the giver is so obviously loath to receive it. 'Well, I appreciate your time anyway,' I say tentatively. 'I hope you didn't use the Oak Hills equipment on the sly.'

'Not at all,' Antoine assures me. 'They were available and Bronwyn was completely okay with it.'

'Then I should call her and thank her as well.'

He gives me her number and I'm grateful to get off the phone to him and call someone a little saner. Bronwyn is very gracious.

'Absolutely no trouble at all. The trailer was just sitting there today, and I know how hard it must be for you with three kids all on your own. To be honest, I've never seen Antoine so disconcerted. He's never gone this far for a woman, and he's chased a lot of skirts.' She pauses and then asks tentatively, 'Are you two dating?'

'*No!*'

'Oh.' She seems confused, and I realise that Antoine hasn't told her about Mitch. I think this is a little over the top. I mean, I know Mitch wants privacy, but surely he wouldn't object to people knowing of his existence per se. I decide to keep his secret, however, given it seems to be so bloody important.

'He's just being kind,' I tell Bronwyn.

'Okay,' she chokes. 'I'll let Jack know. He's been trying to get Antoine to help clean out our sheds for weeks!'

We chat a little further, then I put down the phone, marvelling at the fact that, despite having been in Yallingup only five days, I seem to have two girlfriends and three potential suitors. Living here would be fun. It's a shame our holiday is almost over.

I get up and go outside to check on the boys – not a moment too soon.

They've been digging in the red dirt exposed by the absent junk pile like it's beach sand. They've made a series of tracks and channels, and even filled some of them with water gleaned from a tap on the side of the house.

'Oh, man!' I cover my gaping mouth as Charlie stands up and grins at me. His once-white shirt is now red and wet, and moulds beautifully to his little pot belly. 'Look!' He holds up two fists, opens his fingers and lets the mud fall out.

'You are disgusting,' I tell him solemnly.

'I making a mountain, Mummy.'

'It's not a mountain, Charlie,' Ryan says patronisingly, 'it's a volcano.'

'I'm doing the lava,' says Alfie, scooping mud from a bucket.

'We are never going to be able to use those clothes again,' I say, though clearly no one cares. I allow them ten more minutes of play before announcing that it's clean-up time.

'Awww!'

'We need to get you washed before dinner.'

I help them remove as much dirt as they can by rinsing their feet under the outdoor tap and brushing loose mud off their clothes. Then we traipse gingerly around the front of the house, up the porch steps and into the master bedroom.

'Okay, who's up first?' I enquire as I swing open the door to the ensuite.

Mitch, who is standing in front of the mirror, spins around with a start, steam rising off his bare skin like he's just stepped out of a volcano himself.

I shriek, yank the door shut and jump away from it like it's going to bite me.

'What's a matter, Mummy?' asks Charlie.

'She just saw Mitch's penis,' Ryan tells him.

'I saw it too,' says Alfie. 'It's big and hairy like a –'

'Can we please not talk about Mitch's penis?' I snap. 'Especially while he's just in the other room. It's very rude.'

Alfie shrugs. 'Sorry.'

'All right, everybody out.' I give them gentle shoves back towards the hall.

'I thought we were going to have a shower,' protests Ryan.

'The shower is not free at the moment,' I tell him testily. 'You've got ten more minutes outside. But not in the mud. Go play cricket or something.'

'Yay!' They all make a run for it, and I head straight for the phone in the office.

I dial Rachel's number and she picks up after five rings.

'Hello?'

'Thank goodness,' I cry. 'I need your help.'

'Shit! Grace. What's happened?'

'It's an emergency! I need internet. Can you google something for me?'

'Of course,' Rachel's voice comes back to me, breathless as she moves quickly through her home. 'I'm sitting in front of my laptop right now. What is it? Fire away.'

'Okay.' I take a deep, calming breath. 'Can you google the French translation for *I'm sorry I saw you naked*?'

Chapter 21

I wake up the next morning with a splitting headache. Turns out calling your sister for help isn't always a good idea, especially if she won't give you the goods until she gets a full debrief of what you saw, to whom it belonged and whether it meant anything.

Of course it didn't mean anything, other than that we really, *really* need a working lock on that bathroom door. Or at least a 'Do not disturb' sign.

I should have realised that at some point, Mitch has to wash. I mean, when I first met him he didn't smell. So he must have been cleaning himself on the sly. Like maybe when we went out to the beach, or into town. But now that we know he exists, there's no need for any more sneaking around.

Though I wish he would.

I am never going to get that image out of my head.

I mean, *never*.

All that sculpted muscle, gleaming in the steam. How am I supposed to function? How am I supposed to look at him and not see hot, wet abs, tight taut butt and hard, defined calves. Maybe I'll just stay in bed all day. Maybe I won't get up. Maybe I don't need to.

I rub the sleep out of my eyes and look around.

There are banana peels scattered on the floorboards around me. It looks like the kids have already had breakfast and started playing. I sigh. There's absolutely no need for me to rush. No need for me to –

'Mummy, Scott is here!'

Oh shit. I completely forgot he was coming today. What time is it?

I sit up, wrench the sleeping bag off my legs and bolt into the thankfully empty bathroom. I know it's empty because the door is wide open. I'll be looking for that clue from now on!

My phone is on the shelf above the sink. I check the time. Nine o'clock. How did I sleep that long?

'Mummy!'

'I just need five minutes,' I call. No time for a shower. Or make-up. Double damn! I swallow two Panadol, then throw on some jeans and a T-shirt, drag a brush through my hair and another over my teeth. It'll have to do.

I open the master bedroom door, which I never normally keep closed – did Mitch do that? – then launch myself out of the bedroom and into the foyer.

Scott is standing there with his black document zip file, looking as handsome as ever, surrounded by my three boys. They all have their necks bent at ninety degrees as they gaze up at him in consternation.

'Did you bring a shovel?' Alfie asks pointedly. 'Because we still have a dead body to bury.'

Scott hears me come into the room and looks up with some relief.

'Oh hi, Grace.' His face breaks into an attractive smile and I feel that familiar jolt of pleasant awareness whenever he's around.

'So sorry.' I walk forward and we shake hands. 'I overslept.'

'It's all right,' he winks. 'You're on holiday.'

'Boys, do you want to go play outside?'

'Nope.'

'Well,' I look at them sternly, 'you *need* to go and play outside.'

'Awww!'

'I need to talk to Scott for a moment – important, boring stuff about the house.'

'O-kay.' They run off.

I glance surreptitiously towards the stairs and see that Mitch is not there. He must have made himself scarce when Scott showed up, as Antoine said he would do. Not that I have a problem with that. I'm just a little sad that his scar is such an issue. I mean, I really don't think it detracts from his looks. It makes him rather unique. Even the burn marks I glimpsed on his arms and shoulders yesterday didn't give me any sense of repugnance. Maybe it's the pity he doesn't like.

'Grace?'

'Sorry.' I wince and look at Scott, realising he's been trying to ask me something. 'Got a bit of a headache this morning.'

'Oh, that's no good.' He's all concern. 'Do you need any painkillers? I've got some in my car.'

'Thanks,' I say, touched, 'but I've already taken some. What was it that you asked me while I was off with the fairies?'

'It wasn't so much a question as a compliment.' His eyes are laughing again. 'The house is looking great. I love what you've done with the porch, and I see you're working on the stairs now. I didn't realise you were such a DIY Wonder Woman.'

'Oh, I . . .' I rub my temple as I realise I've been roped into Mitch and Antoine's subterfuge. 'A friend has been helping me. Off and on.'

Damn. I feel bad concealing this from Scott. I count him as a friend. More than that, if I'm honest. I feel a blush creeping up my cheeks as I remember our last conversation when he said he'd love to 'take me out sometime' if I wasn't going back to Perth.

'Well, shall we take a look around?' he asks. 'I'm dying to see what's in the secret room.'

I take him through to the kitchen first and show him how much junk we've removed. The problem is, now that it's tidy you can really see how much repair work is needed, including the fact that there's no kitchen tap.

'We could market this place as a renovator's dream,' Scott suggests. 'The kitchen is like a blank slate just waiting to be redone. Buyers will come with their own tastes and plans.'

This should be good news, but I don't especially like the thought of someone changing Gum Leaf Grove too much. Particularly by bringing their 'own ideas'. I have a few myself, and it's hard to give up the fantasy of putting them into action.

'You seem to be using the stove.' He points to a greasy pan and a small stack of pancakes on a plate.

Mitch made pancakes for the kids! Exactly how long have they been up? I look at the utensils crossly. 'Er . . . yeah,' I mumble.

'I'm surprised it's still working.'

'So was I!' I return grumpily as I rip off a bit of pancake and stick it in my mouth. I am starving and these are . . . *heaven*! Wait, is that maple syrup further down the bench? I'm about to reach for it when Scott says, 'And where did this fridge come from?'

I spin around and see that Mitch has brought his bar fridge downstairs.

'Er . . . it's secondhand. I picked it up at a garage sale in town. Do you want a pancake?'

Scott shakes his head. 'No thanks.'

I'm actually dying for the rest of the one I've started munching on – maybe with some maple syrup this time – but I don't want to hold Scott up, or for him to see me eat when I'm this hungry. That's a truth better reserved for a third or fourth date. I catch myself on the thought.

Does that mean I'm still thinking about dating him – after we've officially decided not to? Or am I just thinking about dating full stop? If I didn't know any better I'd think I was starting menopause or something. My hormones are all over the place. I need to stick with the program.

Charlie. Alfie. Ryan.

They're enough boy trouble for now.

'Can we go upstairs?' Scott interrupts my thoughts.

'Sure.' I smile.

I take him up the half-repaired stairs and he explores the second level in silence. The other rooms haven't changed at all since he was last here, but he walks through the third bedroom into the secret room with a low whistle.

'Wow. It's quite a big space back here.'

I notice that Mitch has removed his guitar and his clothes – to where, I have no idea. But the mattress and bedding are still there. I wait for Scott to comment on them, but he doesn't. Instead, he asks, 'When were you planning on returning to Perth?'

'In a couple of days,' I tell him. 'I might do a little more cleaning and gardening before then, but that'll be about it before you put it on the market.'

We leave the room and go back downstairs, where he unzips his little folder and pulls out some paperwork. We discuss market value, commission and strategy, and I am pleased to note that my sale prospects aren't looking too bad.

'I'll be honest,' he says solemnly. 'Across the board, the housing market is not great for sellers right now, but you have a very sought-after location so it may even out. If you leave me a key, I can handle it all from this end after you head back to Perth.'

Just as I'm about to sign the paperwork, there's a crash and a scream from outside. Ryan tears into the house, his little face white as a sheet.

'Mummy, come quick!'

I drop the pen. *Oh shit.* 'What's happened?'

Without a word, he runs back through the house and out the front door. I vault after him, vaguely aware that Scott is right behind me; panic slams my heart against my ribcage and blood pounds in my head. I follow Ryan down the steps of the porch and around the back of the house.

What is it with kids and accidents? It ages me at least two years every time something like this happens.

Ryan leads me to the old stables. Charlie is sitting on the ground outside the building, crying. I double my pace to get to him, kneeling down and examining his little body, lifting his face to mine with a hand under his chin. He doesn't appear to be hurt.

'Not him!' Ryan yells. '*Alfie.*'

Of course. When is Alfie not the centre of a disaster?

'Where?' I look up.

'In there!' Ryan points rapidly at the window of the room at the end of the building, almost like he's having a fit. 'He can't move.'

'What?'

Adrenaline shoots through my body. I lunge towards the windowsill. It takes me a second to locate him because the room is dark and full of junk, but when I see him my knees nearly give way. He's on the ground, moaning and covered in blood. As a scene snapshot, it could easily fit into a horror film.

'Alfie! Alfie!' I cry, gripping the sill in frustration. He doesn't respond, but continues to moan. 'I'm coming in,' I say, even though I have no idea how. I'm pretty positive I'm not going to fit through the window the way Alfie did. I dash to the door and shake the rusty handle.

Locked, of course.

'Is the key in the house?' Scott asks urgently. 'Shall I run and get it? Where is it?'

I'm about to turn around and tell him when I suddenly feel two hands grab my upper arms and move me to one side, then a large solid shoulder hits the door with a loud thwack.

The rusty lock gives way and the door flings open.

'Mitch!' says Alfie weakly from the floor as the French

squatter strides in and says, clear as an Aussie on a summer's day, 'You're going to be fine, little man.'

If I wasn't so overwrought I might have said something, but instead I just watch in gratitude as he lifts Alfie into his arms and carries him outside.

In the light of day, my son looks even worse. There's a huge gash in his forehead that is weeping blood in streams down his face. In fact, the entire front of his dirty shirt is soaked with it. He looks like he's fallen face-first on an axe.

Shit.

Is that what he did?

'What happened?' Mitch demands of Ryan.

'We saw a shovel in there.' My eldest wrings his hands. 'So we got the window open and Alfie climbed onto the sill and jumped in –'

'– without looking for a safe place to land first,' I finish with a sigh of futility. ADHD kids never look before they leap.

'Mummy,' Alfie moans, 'my ankle hurts. I can't walk.'

'You're not going to,' I assure him, glad he's at least still conscious. 'Does anything else hurt, apart from your head?'

'No.'

'Who are you?' Scott joins our circle.

Mitch glances at him impatiently. 'A friend.'

'I don't recall seeing your car.' Scott tries to continue the conversation, but Mitch is already carrying Alfie towards the house.

'We need something to stop the bleeding,' he says as I stumble after him.

'I'll get a towel,' I say.

'I'll meet you at his car,' Mitch replies.

'My car?' queries Scott as he brings up the rear.

'You were going to drive them to the hospital, weren't you?' Mitch flicks back.

Scott blusters. 'Of course.'

I race into the house, grab a towel and dash back outside. I wind it carefully around Alfie's head as Mitch continues to hold him. He is crying now, the shock having subsided and the pain setting in.

'Am I going to die?' he asks in a small voice.

A gentle smile touches Mitch's mouth. 'Not likely, mate.'

Alfie wipes his tears, red with blood, on the backs of his hands. 'Good, 'cause it was supposed to be a crocodile that kills me.'

'Oh, Alfie.' I don't know whether to laugh or cry.

Scott clears his throat. 'Grace, we better get going. He needs to get that seen to.'

Mitch puts Alfie in the car and steps back. My little boy immediately tries to lie down, but I stay him with a hand on his shoulder. 'I think it's better if you sit up.' I put his belt on for him. I'm about to get into the car when I remember the other children.

'Ryan, Charlie.' I look around for them. They are both peeking from behind Mitch's legs. Charlie has two hands wrapped around one of Mitch's kneecaps, his eyes wide, his dirty, plump cheeks streaked by tears. Ryan is trying to be braver, but I can already see the guilt in his little face. He blames himself. Just like his mother.

I look up at Mitch, a question in my eyes.

He lays a large hand on each of their heads. 'It's okay, I've got 'em. You go. We'll be fine.'

I nod and lower my gaze to the kids. 'Don't worry, Alfie is going to be okay. I'll call you after we've seen the doctor.'

The drive to Busselton emergency passes in a blur. I'm so glad I'm not driving. My mind is wholly absorbed with Alfie. I'm so tuned in to every whimper or movement he makes, I can't focus on anything else. I intermittently squeeze his hand and murmur, 'You're going to be fine. What's a little knock on the head anyway?'

Amnesia

Brain damage.

Concussion.

I turn off my inner physician and ask Scott, 'How much further?'

'Another five minutes.'

We don't speak again until he's pulling into the car park, right in front of the emergency section. I think Alfie's twisted or broken his ankle, so Scott picks him up and carries him in.

It's a good day. There's hardly anyone in there, just a screaming infant and his distraught parents. I think he might have croup. They are seen to first, but we don't have to wait long before a triage nurse calls us up. She's a cheerful-looking sort with a round face and a friendly smile.

'So, what's happened to this little fella?' she asks.

As I explain, the words rushing out, she comes around her desk to examine Alfie. She looks at his ankle first, then asks if she can unwrap the towel from his head. She does it just enough to have a quick peek.

'Yep, you've done a good job there, young man.' She looks up at me. 'If you'll just excuse me for a moment, I'll go and check when the doctor will be available.' She disappears through two large swinging doors with metal plating on the bottom. It's such a strange thing to focus on, but for a couple of seconds it keeps me sane.

'Am I gonna have an operation?' Alfie starts crying. 'I don't want an operation. I'm only five.'

'I know, sweetie,' I assure him. 'I don't think you'll be having an operation. But you might need some stitches.'

'Stitches!' he cries. 'What's that? Does it hurt?'

I curse my big mouth.

'Not a bit,' says Scott, who is sitting next to me. 'When I was your age I had some in my arm after I fell off my bike. It was nothing. I can show you my scar if you like.'

Alfie eyes him with extreme distrust, but mutters, 'Okay.'

Scott rolls up his sleeve to reveal a thin red line on his forearm.

Alfie's eyes momentarily light up. 'I'm gonna have a scar too!'

Just then the nurse returns. 'The doctor will see you in about ten minutes. Would you like to come through to our emergency ward? We have a bed he can rest on.'

'Thanks.'

Scott picks Alfie up and we follow the nurse into the next section of the hospital. The smell of antiseptic cleaning fluid assails me. Everything is white, stainless steel or that pale colour that is neither blue nor green. The hall is lined with railing and curtains to divide up the beds. She takes us to the last bed, where the curtains are open.

'You're lucky,' she says to Alfie. 'This is the only bed with a TV.'

She raises it into the half-reclining/half-sitting position and turns on the TV. Scott settles Alfie onto the bed and I sit down in one of the visitor's chairs.

'While we're waiting,' Scott murmurs, 'I'll just phone work and ask them to cancel the rest of my appointments this morning.'

I throw him a look of gratitude. 'You're a lifesaver. I'm so sorry about all this.'

'Don't be.' He shakes his head. 'It's not your fault. Things happen.'

'Still, I hate ruining your day. Will you get in trouble?'

'Hardly,' he grunts, then adds, 'Well, Sean won't be happy, but I'm used to him giving me a hard time.' He lowers his voice confidentially. 'We don't get along very well.'

'That's a shame,' I say with equal discretion.

'Probably,' he says with a smile. 'But there's nowhere else I'd rather be than here.'

My heart does a little somersault as he turns on his phone and walks out of the room. Alfie, who hasn't had access to a television in five days, is already engrossed. His injuries can't be that serious.

I take the opportunity to pull out my own phone and catch up on my messages.

There are a couple of missed calls from Rachel and at least fifty junk emails from every loyalty program I've ever signed up to. My eyes skim down the list, looking for a name instead of a company. And then I stop.

There's a message that's two days old. It's from my boss. With trembling hands, I open it.

Private and confidential
AQS and Sons
21 St Georges Tce,
Perth 6000

Dear Grace Middleton,

Termination of your employment by reason of redundancy

The purpose of this letter is to confirm the outcome of a recent review by AQS and Sons of its operational requirements and what this means for you.

As a result of the economic downturn, the position of Financial Accountant is no longer needed. Regrettably, this means your employment will terminate. This decision is not a reflection of your performance.

Your employment will end immediately. Based on your length of service,

There's more, but I stop reading. I don't need to see my redundancy package to know that it's not going to be much. I've been with the company less than a year, so it's not surprising they've chosen to get rid of me first. I really should have seen this coming. I knew morale was down, that there was a sense of unease in the office, but I chose to focus my worrying on my children. I mean, come on, their dad just died! I was trying to keep everything as normal as possible for them. School projects, sports carnivals, after-school therapy, excursions, housework, cleaning, homework and the million other things that come with being a single mother who goes to work for money, not ambition. Inheriting this house was a big distraction, too. I realise with self-recrimination that I really should have paid more attention. I could have prepared for this. I could have started looking around for another position, just in case. I could have –

'Everything okay?' Scott walks back in and sits down beside me. 'You look like you've just seen a ghost.'

Wouldn't be the first time!

I click my phone off, wondering if I should tell him. He's just helped me bring my injured child to Emergency. I know he cares, but surely it's too soon to dump my financial problems on him as well.

Suddenly, he reaches over, takes my hand and squeezes it. 'I know you're worried about your son. But trust me, he's going to be okay. The doctors will take care of everything.'

He smiles down at me, that lovely mixture of concern and admiration in his eyes. I feel a gentle welling of excitement behind my ribcage that I haven't felt since my early twenties. The bloom of first love, that anticipation that comes before a new romance, the tingling taste of maybes. I blurt the truth. 'I just lost my job.'

His brows knit. 'Huh?'

'Sorry,' I cringe in embarrassment. 'I shouldn't have dumped that on you. Forget I said anything.'

'No, it's okay.' He squeezes my hand again and I realise in delight that he's still holding it. 'I'm just surprised, that's all,' he says ruefully. 'That was the last thing I expected you to say.'

'While you were on the phone I checked my email,' I explain. 'And there was one from my boss. My position has been terminated.'

'What a lovely way to tell you,' he responds sarcastically. 'They could have done it in person.'

I bite my lip. 'I have a feeling a lot of us got the chop. We were warned there was going to be a review. I was just hoping stupidly that –'

'Well, of course you were,' he responds without needing me to finish. 'I mean, not stupidly, but . . .'

'Naively?'

'Optimistically,' he supplies with a chuckle.

'It's the worst time for this,' I admit glumly. 'If only it happened a couple months from now, after we'd sold Gum Leaf Grove. We'd have some money to fall back on. As it stands, I won't be able to make rent in a month, unless you get *really* lucky with selling our house.'

'I'm not saying it won't happen. You can sell a property in under a week. But I won't lie to you,' his mouth twists, 'the market is pretty slow at the moment. Average sale time is eight to twelve weeks, if not more.'

'Mummy,' Alfie grumbles, 'is the doctor coming yet?'

I take my hand from Scott's and put it over his. 'Soon, darling. Another five minutes, tops.'

'My head is hurting really bad.'

'I know. Do you want me to get into the bed with you?'

He's never looked more pitiful or more gorgeous. His big blue eyes wet with tears, his lower lip trembling. He nods and I kiss his freckled nose. I get up from my chair and recline in the bed beside him, still holding his hand.

I glance back at Scott, who is looking thoughtful. He catches me watching him and meets my gaze seriously.

'Why not just stay at Gum Leaf Grove . . . now that you don't have to go back?'

Chapter 22

I stare at Scott, immediately overwhelmed by an onslaught of internal protests.

That was never the plan.

The house is a dump.

What about school for the kids?

What will I do for money?

Before I can put a voice to my thoughts, the doctor arrives.

After studying Alfie's forehead, Dr Helen Mason announces that she will be gluing Alfie's wound closed, rather than stitching it.

Alfie is scandalised. 'That's not going to work!'

I can tell he's picturing a Glu Stik, like the blue one in his Lightning McQueen pencil case. 'It's a special glue,' I tell him.

'Designed specifically to hold skin together,' Dr Mason assures him. 'And it won't hurt much when I'm putting it on.'

'Are you sure?'

'Absolutely.'

She turns to me. 'The important thing is not to get the wound wet for at least twenty-four hours. I'm going to dress and bandage it, but he'll need to wear a waterproof cap in the shower.'

'Will do.'

'The glue should fall off after five to ten days, which is enough time for the skin to heal.'

Alfie folds his arms mulishly. 'Will I still have a scar? Because I need to have a scar.'

The doctor's lips twitch. 'You will most definitely have a scar. It will be quite red at first, but that will fade over the next few months.'

Alfie considers this for a moment. 'I suppose that's okay.'

With a wry smile, the doctor turns back to me. 'Just keep a close eye on him over the next forty-eight hours. I don't think he has concussion, but if he starts displaying any unusual symptoms –'

'Such as?' I prompt.

'Vomiting, bleeding from the ears, blurred vision, mood swings, headaches.'

'Sure.'

'Anything not quite right – and it will be obvious – please bring him straight back.'

'Okay.'

'As for his ankle, I believe it's just a sprain. I'll wrap it today, and he should keep his weight off it for at least forty-eight hours. Ice and elevation will also help with the pain and swelling. If he's really complaining, a mild oral painkiller is fine.'

'I have a question,' says Alfie. 'Are you going to wrap a bandage around my head?'

'That's right,' the doctor confirms.

'Can you wrap my whole head?' asks Alfie. 'I want to pretend to be a mummy and scare my brothers when I get home.'

'*Alfie.*' I give him a stern look. 'I don't think you should ask the doctor to do that.'

'Awwww, but it would be awesome.'

'You'll have to wait till Halloween.'

Dr Helen winks at me, then says to the nurse in attendance, 'Let's start prepping for the wound closure.'

Half an hour later it's all done, and Alfie and I are safely ensconced in the back seat of Scott's car.

'Well, that was relatively easy,' he comments as he starts the engine. 'I was expecting much more drama.'

'I still think she should have wrapped my whole head,' pouts Alfie. 'She had enough bandages. I saw two whole rolls.'

'Yes,' Scott agrees. 'It was very ungenerous of her.'

'Don't encourage him,' I smile.

'I could not encourage him all the time if you move down south,' Scott suggests coyly as he drives out of the car park.

'It's a lovely thought,' I admit nervously. 'But a massive step.'

'Didn't say it was going to be easy,' Scott agrees.

I allow the subject to drop. As much as I like Scott, this is not something I want to discuss in front of Alfie, or to be pressured into. It's not like we're in a relationship. We haven't even been on a date yet. I know how my son would feel about living in the country and I don't want to get his hopes up. Luckily, Scott seems to take my cue, and breaks the silence by saying, 'You hungry?'

Before I can open my mouth, Alfie answers for me. 'Yes!'

Scott immediately pulls up at a bakery on the side of the road. He leaves us in the car and ducks in to buy a box of sausage rolls and pies for lunch.

While I'm sitting silently with my own thoughts, memory strikes me like a bolt of lightning. I've been so caught up in Alfie's injuries and losing my job, I'd completely forgotten about Mitch.

English-speaking Mitch.

Double-crossing Mitch.

Two-faced pretender Mitch.

And I've left my kids with him!

Suddenly, I'm frantic to get home. Winding down the window, I poke my head out to see if Scott is coming back. Not yet. I sit back against the seat, clenching my fists, wondering if I should go and grab him, tell him not to worry about the food.

'Mummy, what's the matter?' asks Alfie.

'We need to get home,' I say shortly, my mind racing as revelations flit across my consciousness.

He's not even French, for goodness sake. His accent is more dinky-di than mine.

The things I told him because I thought he couldn't understand.

Thick, gooey embarrassment oozes out of my pores like treacle. In the kitchen, in the office! I told him about Jake. He knows about Mum. I told Rachel he was hot. *In front of him!*

I want to dissolve into the upholstery of the seat. Humiliation Central just got a new resident.

'Grace, are you okay?' Scott has returned. He's opened the passenger door and is holding the box out to me. 'You're looking a little green.'

'I just haven't eaten in a while,' I admit.

'Well, feel free to sample one in the car,' he smiles.

'Oh no,' I say hastily, 'I'll make a mess. Let's just get home *quickly.*'

'Sure.' Scott nods. A few seconds later we're back on the main road and I'm watching his speedometer, thinking, 'Geez, he could go *a little* faster.'

'So, just out of curiosity,' Scott starts up conversation again, 'who's that guy looking after Charlie and Ryan? I thought I heard Alfie call him Mitch. Is that his real name?'

'I assume so. Why do you ask?'

'No reason,' Scott shrugs. 'I'm more interested in why he was at your house?'

'He's been working for me,' I reply tightly.

I really don't want to get into the rest of it, and be forced to explain what a bad mother I am for the umpteenth time. I just want to get home. But Scott wasn't joking when he said he was curious.

'Working for you,' he repeats. 'Doing what exactly?'

'Fixing the stairs and . . . a few other bits and pieces.'

'So he's a handyman for hire?'

'Something like that,' I reply, realising I have no idea what or who Mitch is, and I've opened up my home to him.

I'm suddenly relieved to be returning to the property with Scott. At least I'll have some back-up if I need to physically remove Mitch. Though, honestly, if they got into a fight, I'm not sure Scott would win. I rub my temple. Let's not get ahead of ourselves. I'm sure Mitch is not the violent sort. This is probably just some elaborate practical joke that got out of hand. I mean, what other explanation could there be?

'Can we go any faster?' I ask.

'I'm doing the speed limit,' Scott jokes. 'You must be hungry.'

As soon as we pull into Gum Leaf Grove, I see that the Oak Hills ute is there.

Of course! He's called in his lackey to protect him.

As I step out of the car, the front door opens and Antoine emerges, bright as the sun. 'Madame! We have been worried sick. You should have called and given us an update.'

Yes, I should have. In all the excitement, I completely forgot.

'How is Alfie?' Antoine continues, all concern.

'He's fine,' I say tightly. 'Just a sprain and a cut on the head. Nothing to have a song and dance about.'

Scott steps out of the car and hands me the box of hot pastries so he can carry Alfie in. He gives me a look that clearly says, 'How many guys do you have roaming around your property anyway?'

Embarrassed, I clear my throat. 'Scott, this is Antoine. He's –'

'A close friend of the family.' Antoine whisks down the steps and takes the box from me. 'And such a lovely family they are.' He touches Alfie's knee. 'My dear boy, you really must be more careful. You've had everyone in such a spin.'

'You're weird,' Alfie tells him frankly.

Antoine tuts before turning to saunter back up the steps, holding the box aloft like it's a tray of hors d'oeuvres.

'How do you know this guy?' Scott asks as he follows me into the house, Alfie in his arms. 'Doesn't he work for Oak Hills?'

I'm saved from having to reply by Antoine's enthusiastic call. 'Wait till you see what we've done with the kitchen. A stroke of genius, madame! You'll be so thrilled.'

I walk into the kitchen/dining hall to see they've moved the desk from the office into the space, and brought the park bench in from the porch to use as seating on one side. The other side is flanked by the two folding chairs I had in the boot of my car.

'Of course,' Antoine clasps his hands, 'it is not ideal, but we must have somewhere to eat our meals.'

Mitch is standing on the other side of the desk, playing some sort of game with Ryan and Charlie. He straightens abruptly when he sees me, and our eyes lock together like two magnets.

It takes all my willpower not to scream at him.

The screaming is instead done by Ryan and Charlie, who race up to Alfie as Scott is setting him down on the park bench and aligning his legs along the length of it.

'Can we see your stitches?'

'Did you have an operation?'

'Did you get a needle?'

'Was it a big needle?'

Alfie lifts his chin and looks patronisingly at one and then the other before simply saying, 'I'll have a scar.'

Ryan and Charlie gasp. 'You're so lucky.'

'Is he okay?' Mitch asks, his voice the gentle rumble of a train passing through a valley. I feel my shoulders stiffening at the clear Australian twang.

'He'll be fine,' I snap. 'Thanks for asking so plainly, so eloquently, so –'

'Madame,' Antoine interrupts, 'were you going to eat these before they get cold?'

I turn to him impatiently. 'Yes, I –'

'Excellent. I'll just put some plates out.'

He puts the box on the table and walks around the kitchen counter to the doorless cupboards. 'Were you staying, Mr, er –' He looks pointedly at Scott over his shoulder.

Scott frowns. 'Hunter. Scott Hunter. Call me Scott.'

'Don't feel the need to put yourself out,' Antoine adds as he pulls the white plates I rescued the other day off the shelves. 'As you can see, Mitch and I have the situation well under control.'

'What situation would that be?' I fold my arms.

'Madame,' Antoine puts his hand over his heart, 'I am fully aware of your independent spirit, but in emergencies you must learn to lean on your friends. It is imperative that you don't overburden yourself. Tell her, Scott.' He puts the plates on the table.

I think Scott's exasperated expression must mirror my own. 'Grace –' he begins.

'Yummy!' Ryan and Charlie squeal as Antoine flips open the box.

'You must have appointments with other clients this afternoon,' Mitch speaks up as the boys dig in. I turn instinctively towards him, still trying to process the sound of his voice. 'You're the real estate agent, right? Here on business? We're sorry your meeting was interrupted.'

Scott straightens his shoulders, seeming to sense that he's being challenged. 'And you're the handyman,' he throws back at him. 'Your work must have been interrupted too.'

'I wasn't working today.' A militant glint momentarily lights Mitch's eyes, the implication of his blunt statement dropping like a stone into a deep cavern. I blink, trying to figure out what to say. Am I supposed to be making excuses for why Mitch is here? Do I tell Scott he actually lives upstairs?

But maybe he won't be soon. Not after I'm through with him.

'Well,' Antoine saves the day, 'I must say, these pies are divine. Madame?' He holds out the box to me. 'Care to try one?'

'No thank you.' I push it aside impatiently.

'Do I know you from somewhere?' Scott's eyes narrow on Mitch. 'Because you look familiar. I can't quite pinpoint it, but –'

'He's my cousin,' Antoine declares with a wave. 'Everyone notices the resemblance.'

'I beg your pardon?' Scott blinks.

'Family,' Antoine titters. 'You can't choose who you get assigned. It is horrendously inconvenient.' He holds out the box to Scott. 'One for the road?'

'No thanks.' Scott glares at him. 'Grace,' he turns to me, 'can I see you outside for a minute?'

'Sure,' I agree, only too happy to march out with him.

Once we're out by the car he turns and says, 'I'm sorry, I really needed to talk to you and I didn't want to do it in front of them.'

'Don't apologise,' I assure him. 'This is completely fine.'

More than fine!

'I've still got your papers for selling the house in my brief-case,' he begins.

'Oh yeah,' I nod. 'I never signed them, did I?'

'No, you didn't.' He hesitates. 'Given our discussion at the hospital I'm wondering if you still want to.'

'I –'

I stop, realising I don't know what I want now. Everything has changed. The plan was always to sell Gum Leaf Grove. I was going to make a mint and take the money home to improve life for the boys.

But what would improve life for the boys? Going back to our two-bedroom unit with no backyard and living on unemployment benefits? They love Gum Leaf Grove. So do I. I haven't been able to stop fantasising about living here since we first arrived. Sure, it's a bit of a dump at the moment, and I've got no money for big improvements, but it's not unlive-able, as the last five days have proven.

'What are you thinking?' Scott's eyes are darting across my face. 'Have I been too forward?'

'No, no,' I shake my head. 'I'm just thinking about the house. Whether we can live in it long-term the way it is.'

He sighs. 'It does need work, and you're lucky we're heading into summer – I'm sure you'd get water coming in when it rains. *But* if you're not spending money on rent . . .'

'I might be able to renovate slowly and cheaply.' I smile. 'You're not wrong.'

'Listen.' He takes my hand. 'There's no need to make a decision right this second. You can think about it. Make up your list of pros and cons and get back to me.'

I breathe a sigh of relief. 'Okay.'

'I'll give you a call in a couple of days, if you like.'

'That would be perfect.'

His eyes seem to darken as he stares down into mine. 'There is, of course, that other reason I want you stay in town,' he adds softly. 'And I'm hoping it might make it onto the pros list.' Spontaneously, he leans in and kisses me.

It's a lovely kiss. Soft, gentle, promising. It's been a while since any man has been this close and, I have to say, it feels very nice.

'So am I on the pros list?' he asks as he slowly pulls away. 'Definitely.'

My cheeks burn as he gets into his car and drives off. I turn around to see Mitch standing on the porch. I don't know how long he's been there, both his large hands resting loosely on his hips as he squints peevishly at Scott's plume of dust.

'Well, he's a tosser if ever I saw one.' He eyeballs me. 'What the hell are you doing kissing him?'

It lights the match on my temper.

'Are you kidding me? You lying, manipulative piece of work!'

He shoves his hands into the pockets of his jeans with a grimace and casually walks down the steps towards me as though I've just pointed out a crumb on his collar. 'I suppose this is about the fact that I can speak English.'

'What about the fact that you're not even French?' I march up to meet him.

'Well, if Antoine's anything to go by, would you want to be?' he asks ruefully.

'Don't joke about this!' I shove a finger in his face, which he catches and draws away. I snatch my hand out of his like I've been burned.

'Sorry.' He takes a step back, hands up in surrender. Though how a six-foot-four musclebound giant can surrender to anyone is beyond me.

'You're right.' He nods as I tilt my head back so I can see his face. 'I'm a bastard. It was a cowardly thing to do. I shouldn't have pretended.'

'Damn right you're a bastard! You made a fool out of me. I never would have said the things I said to you if I'd known –' I break off, making a low, guttural growl of frustration at the futility of hindsight. 'You tricked me. I thought you were deep, for goodness sake!'

'Grace –'

I square my shoulders and cut him off. 'Pack your things and get off my property.'

His eyes widen. 'But –'

'Why'd you do it anyway?' I throw at him. 'Why did you pretend like that? Was it some big prank hatched between you and your cousin?'

'No,' Mitch shakes his head firmly. 'Definitely not. It wasn't about playing a joke.'

I rub my temple. 'Shit! Is he even your cousin? Or is that a lie as well?'

'Unfortunately, that's not a lie.' Mitch winces. 'He is my cousin – my uncle's son and, you know, he told you the truth when he said I'm in a really tight spot at the moment.'

'Poor you.' My voice sounds so sarcastic I almost flinch at the venom in it.

'The language thing was spontaneous,' he rushes on. 'Antoine's idea. I guess he thought it would be easier for me if I didn't have to speak.'

'Easier than what?' I pounce. 'Telling me the truth?'

'Yes.' He looks incredibly sad, and for a moment, just a moment, I feel sorry for him. 'I . . . I don't like talking about what happened to me.' He looks away, off into the distance, as if wishing he were anywhere but here.

My gaze roves across his profile, taking in the scar and the horror it represents.

How easily I had forgotten the trauma he must have been through, even though I see it every day. Red, shiny and maybe even still painful. I guess not talking about it would help him put it aside, escape it for a while. Pretend it's not there. I imagine whatever happened to him was a nightmare he would not like to relive. Maybe that's why he was at Gum Leaf Grove in the first place – squatting in the upper bedroom, hiding from his memories.

'Don't look at me like that.' His voice is hoarse. 'I don't want your pity.'

'Okay,' I say slowly. 'No pity. But at least I understand why you did it now.'

'I'm sorry,' he says again.

I sigh. 'Well, it was a bit extreme. If you didn't want to talk, you didn't have to lie. You could have just told me certain subjects were off limits.'

'I know.' He holds up his hands. 'It was dumb.'

'It was cruel,' I correct him, turning my gaze to the vines. 'I am so embarrassed.'

'Why?'

'You have to ask?'

'Grace, look at me.'

I refuse to turn around.

'I enjoyed every one of our conversations. I don't regret them.'

'I bet you don't.' I look skyward in self-mockery. 'Nothing like a little in-house entertainment to keep you laughing all week.'

My face is burning.

'No.' He walks towards me, grabbing me by the shoulders and forcing me to look at him. 'Remember that day when we were in the kitchen and you were telling me about . . . your life.'

I shut my eyes and groan in agony.

'You asked me a question.'

I don't actually recall asking him anything, but I guess I must have because he's waiting for me to remember. I squint at him and shake my head.

He laughs. 'You asked me, "How do you tell if someone is real? Who is real?"' He looks around as though he's asking the universe, and his hands drop from my shoulders. 'And you know what, I thought in that moment, thought and just couldn't say . . .' He takes a deep breath. '*You're* real. You're one hundred and fifty per cent refreshingly real.'

He steps back as though putting a fence between us, and I think at this point we kind of need one. The air has thickened up like smoke and I can't seem to tear my gaze from his eyes.

I know he's wearing me down, trying to make me like him so I'll change my mind. I have to be firm. I'm a mother. I've got priorities.

'You still can't stay here.'

'Grace –'

'I don't trust you anymore. I don't want you around my children.'

'Grace, you know I didn't mean you or the boys any harm. I would never do anything to . . .' He breaks off. 'I just want to help you. I'll do as much free labour as you want. Anything, just name it.'

'All I want,' I throw at him, 'is your honesty.'

'I know you do.' He runs a shaky hand through his hair, not daring to meet my eyes. It's clear. I've got him.

'Then tell me.' I fold my arms. He looks up sharply and as our eyes connect I put the challenge out there. 'What did happen to your face?'

I know it's a cruel test, but it's the only way I'll know his true measure, by making him do the one thing he said he wouldn't.

For a moment, I don't think he's going to respond. He becomes utterly still, and his eyes glisten in a way I don't like. I'm just about to retract my challenge when he starts to speak.

'It was a car accident.' The first words come out stilted. 'In Sydney. I was driving and . . . arguing . . . with my brother. He was telling me what a dick I was becoming because . . .' he swallows, 'I was. I was becoming a self-absorbed, shallow prick with sights set only on ambition. I know because after this happened –' he points at his face, '– it became pretty clear how many real friends I had.' He shoves his hands in the pockets of his jeans and looks at the ground. 'I was driving too fast because I wanted to be anywhere but stuck in a car with my conscience. I didn't make the turn. I crashed into a wall and the car exploded.' He stops, and then with difficulty opens his mouth to keep going, but I put a hand on his arm.

'It's okay. You don't have to say more.'

He looks down at me and whispers, 'I thought I was going to die.'

I swallow. 'A reasonable assumption.'

'But somehow,' his crooked smile appears for a split second, 'I managed to get myself and my brother out. We were taken to hospital. I was there for three months. He . . .' His voice cracks. 'He's still there. His injuries were much worse than mine.'

He drags his gaze from the dirt and fixes it upon me again. 'This wake-up call has come at such a price. I don't know how to forgive myself for being the one who suffered the least when I was the one who deserved it the most.'

There's such agony in his face that I want to take him into my arms, hold him close and comfort him, try to ease some of the suffering in those dark, lonely eyes. But it's not my place, so I say instead, with some restraint, 'From the deepest pain comes the greatest strength.'

He snorts. 'Does it?'

'Oh yes.' I smile through tears. 'Trust me. I know.'

He stops talking and we just gaze at each other, understanding passing between us like water lapping on the shore.

Finally he asks, 'Do you still want me to go?'

The rat! He knows I won't kick him out now. Why do I have to be such a soft touch?

You can't forget that he lied to you, Grace.

He also cooked me dinner.

Made me coffee.

Cleaned my house.

Fixed my stairs and looked after Ryan and Charlie when I had to take Alfie to emergency. From the moment we met, he's been saving my bacon. And now he's told me about one of the most difficult experiences of his life. At least I understand him.

'All right, all right,' I groan. 'You can stay a little longer.'

'Yes!' Like a little boy he rushes forward, wraps his arms around me and vaults me into the air, spinning around in glee. Clearly he has none of the scruples I had earlier.

I scream, clutching his shoulders. 'Hey, put me down!'

'Sure.' He lets my body slide down his and I get the unmistakable impression that he did it on purpose, going by the grin spread across his face.

'You're crazy.' I catch my breath and step back.

'Thanks,' he counters, just as Ryan and Charlie come running out of the house, dusting pastry crumbs off their T-shirts.

'Are you done arguing yet?' asks Ryan. 'Cause Ant says we're not allowed to come out until you're done fighting.'

'Yes,' I roll my eyes, 'we're done fighting.'

'Now you get the shovel out the room, Mitch?' Charlie points at him earnestly. 'So we dig hole. Big, big hole for the kangaroo.'

With a laugh and a nod, Mitch holds out his hand to Charlie, who manages to wrap his little one around just two of Mitch's fingers. The pair of them trot off. I expect Ryan to follow but he looks up at me, confused. 'Mummy?'

'Yes?'

'What were you and Mitch fighting about?'

I choose my words carefully, knowing that Mitch is staying on. I don't want to make it a big deal, and yet I have to be honest. I don't want the kids to think it's okay that he was pretending.

'Mitch,' I pause. 'Mitch can speak English. He's always been able to speak English.'

Ryan looks at me funny. 'Well, duh,' he says.

Suspicions click into place. Mitch is very hands-on with the kids. Although he doesn't appear to speak, he seems able to get what he means across to them. Maybe when I leave the room or can't hear, he's been speaking English to them. My eyes narrow on Ryan.

'So Mitch has been speaking normally to you when I'm not listening.'

'Yep.' Ryan looks off in the distance, like he's itching to quit this conversation and catch up with the others.

I gasp and put my hands on my hips. 'But didn't you think it was a bit weird that he doesn't talk in front of me?'

Ryan's expression becomes wary and he lowers his voice to a whisper. 'Mitch says he's a bit shy around girls. I get that.'

'Oh, you do, do you?'

'Yeah, and I told him that it was okay. He doesn't need to say anything.' My sensitive son pauses thoughtfully and scratches his chin. 'Maybe if you aren't so bossy to him and just be quiet for a while, he'll talk to you more.'

I can do nothing but gape as he turns and strolls off to join the others. When I recover from my stupor, my gaze zooms in on Mitch's retreating back.

I swear if that man isn't careful, he's going to be digging more than one grave with that bloody shovel.

Chapter 23

Even though Mitch has sworn he'll wait till Alfie can be present before he digs the 'big, big hole', my middle child is still wholly dissatisfied at having to stay indoors while his brothers are out scouting the area for a possible gravesite. It's actually quite problematic having a sick child and no television. He does nothing but complain. On a positive note, however, I am absolutely certain that his head injury has had no lasting effects.

To distract him, I help him into the office, where I set him up in the folding chairs – one for his bum and one for his foot. Then I call my sister.

'Hey, Rach, got a minute?' I put Alfie on the phone. 'Tell Aunty Rachel what happened today.'

I smile as I walk out of the room. Sometimes, being my sister is a pretty raw deal. While Alfie is distracted, I am able to clean up the dining room. There's flaky pastry all over the floor, and some dirty plates that I wash in the bathroom, given the kitchen sink is still unserviceable.

Half an hour later, Alfie is ready to get off the phone. This time I'm able to palm him off to Mitch, who is back to fixing the stairs. Turns out, Alfie is excellent at passing the nails.

Ryan and Charlie continue to scout for a gravesite in front of the office window. Apparently, this is very dangerous work.

'Next time give me a little more notice before you require me to babysit,' my sister says when I pick up the receiver to thank her.

'But if I'd given you the full explanation myself, it wouldn't have been nearly as suspenseful,' I reply jovially.

I can hear the smile in her voice as she responds. 'You guys certainly sound like you've been in the wars. Did he really cut his head open and sprain his ankle?'

'Absolutely, but Scott got us both to the hospital easily enough.'

'So Scott was there,' Rachel muses, as though this is an interesting titbit that I'd conveniently left out.

'Didn't Alfie mention him? He's been sweet today. Bought us all lunch as well.'

'No, Alfie didn't say anything about him, but he did mention Mitch. Said you guys had a big fight on the front porch. How is that possible when the man can't talk to you?'

Damn!

I suppose I was going to have to tell her sometime what a gullible fool I've been. I take a deep breath. 'Mitch can speak English.'

'Huh?'

'Mitch can speak English! He's not even French. He was pretending, just to get out of talking.'

'That's ridiculous. Why would he want to get out of talking?' Rachel sounds even more confused.

'I didn't mention this because I didn't think it was relevant to his personality – and I still don't – but he kind of has this burn scar on part of his face, and a little on his shoulder and arm. He was in a car accident earlier this year and he didn't want to have to relive the experience by talking about his injuries.'

'That's no good.' Rachel is putting on her 'I'm a professional psychologist' voice. 'It's always better to talk about these sorts of things rather than bottle them up. Grace, he probably has post-traumatic stress disorder. I mean, look at how you found him, squatting secretly in a room upstairs. One of the classic symptoms of PTSD is avoiding people and places that remind you of the trauma.'

'That's what I was afraid of.' I tilt my head. 'But it's pretty extreme, isn't it, for him to hide from the entire world. I mean, the entire world can't remind him of his trauma, surely?'

Rachel ignores the question. 'Does he have difficulty sleeping? Concentrating? Perhaps he's been having flashbacks or nightmares.'

'I wouldn't know. We sleep in separate rooms. Separate floors, actually,' I hastily remind her.

'Of course.' Rachel still seems distracted by her professional diagnosis. 'Does he seem depressed? Easily irritated? Withdrawn?'

I sigh. 'Do you want me to get him? Maybe you can interrogate him yourself.'

'No,' Rachel seems thoughtful. 'You don't want to push him. He'll just clam up like a . . .' She seems to be searching for the right word.

'Clam?' I suggest cheekily. Rachel immediately recognises my teasing.

'Funny,' she says sternly. 'You need to be more understanding, Grace.'

'Me?' I protest. 'What about him? I can't believe you're not even slightly mad that he played such an awful trick on me.'

'No, you're right,' Rachel agrees. 'That wasn't very nice of him at all. PTSD is no excuse for being a liar. So what are you doing? Kicking him out?'

'I tried. It didn't work.'

'What do you mean it didn't work?'

I sigh. 'Compassion kicked in.'

'You're not serious.'

I pause. I know why she's worried about me. I'm worried about me too. I've been lied to before, more than once, and the fallout has not been pretty. The truth is, I don't want to trust Mitch, but there's something distinctly vulnerable about him that makes me drop my guard. Like if I didn't, I'd be turning my back on a wounded animal.

'I don't know what to tell you, Rachel. I mean, I know he's just played the worst trick on me, but he seemed genuinely distressed by it and kind of out of it. Like –'

'He's going through a personal crisis,' Rachel filled in for me. 'That's exactly why you need to be careful.' She exhales slowly. 'Then again, I guess it's only for a few more days.'

'Er . . .' I bite my lower lip. 'It may be a tad longer than that.'

'How much longer?'

'Not sure. Maybe indefinitely.'

'*Grace*, have I missed something here? Something between the hospital run and the practical joke?'

'Yeah,' I smile, enjoying the shock value. 'I lost my job and Scott kissed me and suggested I stay at Gum Leaf Grove. Not that I would ever base that decision on whether I'm seeing him.'

'What!' Rachel gasps. 'Hold on a minute. Back up a little.'

'I lost my job –'

'No, to the kiss, dummy,' Rachel interrupts me again. 'I can't believe you didn't open with that. How long have we been on the phone for?'

I shrug. 'You were kind of preoccupied with Mitch.'

'Yeah, and I thought you were too.'

'Mitch and I are different.' I roll my eyes. 'He's more of a friend. A *reluctant* friend and semi-employee. There have never been any romantic overtures.'

'We'll discuss *that* again later.' Rachel doesn't seem convinced, but she moves on. 'Right now I'm more interested in what's happening with Scott.'

'He was with me when I found out my position at AQS was terminated.'

'So it was a sympathy kiss.'

'No, the kiss was much later, when we were discussing whether or not I should still sell Gum Leaf Grove.'

'Can you please just start at the beginning?'

'I'm trying to.' I sigh in exasperation. I tell her about the job review I didn't take seriously enough. The email at the hospital. The choice between my expensive home in Perth or the free dump in Yallingup.

'I know you don't think it's a dump,' Rachel protests. 'It's a project. Your project. And now you don't have an excuse not to take up the challenge.'

'Don't I?' I scoff, going through my mental bullet-point list of worries.

Rachel counters easily enough. 'Applying for jobs in the south-west is not harder than applying for jobs in Perth. You will get one. They also have great schools in Busselton, and in Dunsborough too. Smaller ones, in which kids like Alfie might get more attention. There are also therapists, dentists and doctors in those towns. You're not moving to the desert or a third-world country, Grace. As for the house, have you spoken to Mitch about it?'

I flip my hair back indignantly. 'His opinion has no bearing on my decision.'

'You're misinterpreting my question,' Rachel responds smugly.

'Oh.'

'He's your free labour. I think you've got a good thing going there. If he stays on too, helping with the renovations, there's really no reason you can't make this happen.'

'I guess,' I say reluctantly.

'You *know*,' Rachel reprimands me. 'Imagine it. With his help, you could get a fresh coat of paint on all the walls in the main house before I send your furniture down.'

'Hang on a minute. *What?*'

'Well, I can't come to you,' Rachel tells me. 'But I could certainly help out at this end – supervise the removalists doing the packing and getting everything on the truck.'

'I can't ask you to do that.'

'Why not? It's just a few phone calls and then letting some professionals into your house,' Rachel assures me. 'Think of it this way, whether you're there or here, someone has to look after the kids. You can't do both, Grace.'

I chew on my lower lip. 'This is all moving too fast for my liking. Pardon the pun.'

'Pardon granted.' Rachel responds promptly. 'But you do need to make a decision. So what's it going to be? Should I ring the removalists?'

I squeeze my eyes shut like I'm making a wish.

What's the worst that could happen?

The kids hate their new school.

I can't get a job.

We have to survive on toast and baked beans because it's all we can afford.

It's not like we haven't been there before. In fact, right after Charlie was born, it was almost that exact scenario. We got through it then. We could get through it now.

'Okay.' I open my eyes.

'Okay what?' Rachel enquires.

'Call them.' I suck in a breath. 'Call the removalists. We're moving to Gum Leaf Grove.'

Chapter 24

Subject: Re: New Song

From: Nicholas Cooper <N.Cooper@CooperAgency.net.au>

To: Michel Beauchene <MBprivate@Beauchene.com.au>

Monday 2 October 2017

Mitch,

Thanks for your email! I was so relieved to receive it. I've been practically at my wits' end with worry. It is marvellous to hear that you're on the mend, and even writing songs again.

Firstly, however, there are a few scheduling issues that we must address *immediately*.

A. Your movie deal

B. Your record deal

C. Your upcoming 'No Holding Back' world tour.

Now, while of course a severe car accident and burns to 20 per cent of your body are certainly just cause to cancel these items, or delay them, I advise strongly against it. We need to keep the 'Michel Beauchene' brand alive and fresh in the eyes of your fans. Even with the enormous amount of talent we have here at the Cooper Agency, we can't do that without your physical presence.

While you haven't yet raised the issue, I know you must have some concerns about your change in appearance. No one can relate more than myself when it comes to body imperfections, trust me. However, I wanted to bring to your attention a few pertinent facts. Make-up these days is highly advanced, and if that doesn't work, there's always CGI to fall back on. I hear the work graphic artists can do is absolutely amazing. And that's only while we wait for you to decide on a cosmetic surgeon, which I have already taken the liberty of scoping out for you. Please find some reputable names and references attached to this email. I would be more than happy to arrange a discreet appointment for you. No trouble at all.

Now, in response to your new song. I received the music and lyrics you attached, and I've got to say, Mitch, I'm impressed. Very impressed, and super excited.

The song 'Ghost' is of itself just fantastic. No doubt about it. I just have a few concerns that I think would be good to address before we present the song to the record label to be considered for your next album.

A. The lyrics feel a little – just a touch – depressing. You might want to tone down the self-pity and perhaps refer more to how happy you are to be a singer.

B. Please don't take this the wrong way, but it's not very sexy. I really feel there should be more appeal, again in line with the 'Michel Beauchene' brand, which involves you being one of the sexiest men alive. Fans will be expecting a little more rawness in the beat, perhaps some overtures in the lyric and more moaning, where appropriate. Not as the ghost, of course, but in a sexual fashion, if you know what

I mean. What am I saying? You're the writer. I'm sure you get it absolutely!

C. The title, 'Ghost', also comes off a tad too modest. I think something like 'Superstar' or 'Cosmic Angel' might be a little more appropriate. Of course, you'd have to adjust the chorus to reflect the new title, and maybe also some of the lines in both verses. Nothing major.

Otherwise, overall, I think the song is an absolute winner and I'll be holding on to it in the bottom drawer of my desk until we can talk about it again.

I'm wondering also, if it's not too much trouble, if you could possibly send me a comment I can give the media regarding your break-up with Keysha. I realise she's not a priority right now, but she's been doing a string of interviews concerning the fact that you can't have children. This, along with everything else, is highly disruptive to your brand and reputation. I just thought it might be appropriate to send a response that includes the fact that she cheated on you. None of my business, of course. Just a thought.

Now, please, take your time getting better. Put your feet up. Let absolutely no one tell you what to do or disturb your peace. It's all about you, my friend, and I have your back 150%.

Thinking of you,

Nicholas Cooper
Cooper Agency

PS. If you could respond by Friday with that comment, that would be perfect. No pressure.

Chapter 25

After deciding we're going to stay at Gum Leaf Grove, the next move is to tell the kids. The following morning at breakfast I bite the bullet.

'What do you guys think about living here?'

Three cherubic faces look up from their bowls of Weet-Bix in shock.

'You mean, we don't sleep in a bed ever again?' Alfie is clearly thrilled. 'It's camping . . . forever?'

'No,' I say slowly, 'we're going to move your beds and all your toys here. Aunty Rachel is going to pack everything up for us and send it. We're going to start a new life.'

'Yeah. Awesome!'

'Epic!'

Ryan and Alfie both have their fists in the air above their heads. Charlie looks over at his brothers, realises he's slightly behind schedule and puts his hands in the air too. 'Yeah!' he adds for good measure, and gives me a grin.

Breakfast progresses in a torrent of excitement. So much so that I wish I'd broken the news to them after they'd eaten. It's hard enough keeping Alfie on task under normal circumstances, let alone when he's just received news that his childhood dreams are coming true.

'We can build a fort out the back and Mitch can dig us a trench,' says Ryan.

'It's gotta be deep,' Alfie says firmly. 'To keep our enemies out.'

'A big, big trrrench,' agrees Charlie firmly.

'Thanks, boys,' Mitch smiles. 'My back is hurting already.'

'And in the winter when it fills with water,' Ryan's eyes brighten like stars, 'we can use it as a moat.'

'Mitch will build us a boat,' Alfie announces.

'A big, big boat,' says Charlie.

'When does Mitch have his day off?' enquires Mitch. They pointedly ignore him and start discussing fort defence tactics and battle plans.

'Okay, okay,' I hold up my hands, 'eat your cereal.'

I spend the rest of the meal reminding them to put food in their mouths.

Finally, breakfast is done. The boys, including Alfie, who hops along on one foot, go into the sitting room to plan the layout of their fort using Alice's cutlery.

I help Mitch gather up the dishes.

'So, moving in, huh?' He looks at me quizzically. 'That's new.'

'Yeah,' I nod. 'I lost my job in Perth. I found out yesterday. So there's no real need to go back. Might as well stay here.'

He raises his eyebrows. 'Might as well?'

I sigh and abruptly voice my worst fears. 'You think I'm crazy, don't you? This is too fast.'

'I didn't say that.'

'Normal people make these sorts of decisions after months and months of mulling. I've done it in a week, if you even count the past few days, when I didn't think I was going to stay.'

'The length of time taken to make this decision has no bearing on whether or not it's a good one. It's all about whether you've considered all the variables.' He pauses. 'Have you considered all the variables?'

Mitch seems to be taking this far better than I am. Then again, why shouldn't he? He's not the one turning his life upside down. He's just a bystander, enjoying the show.

'Variables, variables,' I mutter under my breath. 'There are so many of them. Finding a new job. Finding a new school. Finding new friends.'

'I think you've already got the last one covered and the first two are just administrative issues.'

'I'll be living on a vineyard with absolutely zero knowledge about wine.'

Mitch smirks. 'You'll learn. You know how to drink, don't you?'

'Do I know how to drink?' I scoff with all the false bravado of a one-glass wonder. I get drunk on vapours, and a headache before I've even finished a glass. 'Well, I'm certainly going to start,' I grimace. 'I'll need something to take the edge off living in this house.'

'You love this house.' He closes up the box of cereal and puts it in one of the doorless cupboards.

'It's a dump,' I remind him frankly. 'There's not even a kitchen sink, for goodness sake. There's water damage in the ceiling, so we know this place leaks like a tap when it rains. The only functional bathroom is my ensuite. *And,*' I shake my finger, 'I use the word "functional" very loosely.'

'You'll fix it all, slowly,' he shrugs. 'With my help.'

'And then there's –' I stop, put my hands on my hips and really look at him. He's wearing his flannelette shirt and ripped jeans that I believe are from the result of actual wear and tear rather than trying to be on trend. The 'hard times' Antoine spoke of briefly are certainly evident in his attire. However, I'm sure – no, I'm *positive* that Mitch could get a *paying* job somewhere and his own place of residence fairly quickly if he wanted to. So why is he digging his heels in about moving on?

PTSD, Rachel's voice whispers in my head. *He's got PTSD.*

'What?' Mitch asks self-consciously when I continue silently staring at him.

'Are you okay?' I ask.

'Er . . . yeah,' he responds, like I'm asking a question so obvious it must be a trick. 'I'm fine.'

'But what are you doing here, Mitch? What are you *really* doing here?'

'I'm being your handyman.'

'Yes,' I say slowly, 'but that's just a temporary thing, right?'

'Right.'

'So then . . .' I press him again, 'how long were you planning on being a handyman . . . for free . . . just to stay in a leaky room?'

'I don't know.'

'I'm not saying I'm not grateful,' I add hastily, 'but you must have some plans, or a life to get back to. You can't intend to hide in my dump of a house indefinitely.'

'Why not?'

I give him a knowing look. 'Because it's not normal.'

He folds his arms. 'What's not normal about it?'

'Are you kidding me? Avoiding the public, hiding like you're ashamed of something, cutting yourself off from the world.'

He scratches the back of his head. 'I'm just taking a break . . .'

'I know you've been through a lot with the accident and everything,' I concede. 'But what does your family think about all this?'

'My family?'

'Yes, your family,' I confirm impatiently. 'I mean, apart from Antoine, who is a *special case*.'

Mitch grins. 'Very special.' I can tell he's trying to sidetrack me with humour, so I press home my point.

'I'm talking about the people who really care about you. Do they even know where you are?'

'Yes.'

'And they're happy about it?'

'Yes.'

'Sorry, what?'

'Yes, they are.'

I have to do a double take. 'They are? They're happy that you're . . . you're . . .'

'Getting away from it all.' He looks at me in amusement. 'Yes, Grace. They are. This is what's best for me right now. Staying here. In this house. With you and your family.'

Is he honestly giving me the whole truth?

'Are you sure?'

'Yes.' He seems exasperated. 'And I want to be here too. So stop worrying that I'm going crazy and put me to work, unless you intend to change your mind about moving here.'

'I wasn't going to,' I say uncertainly. 'Despite the variables.'

'There are plenty of them, and the stakes are high,' he agrees. 'Face it, you need me. So why fight it?'

Because I care about you.

The thought comes unbidden and it takes me a moment to shake it off. Of course I care about him. In living here, in helping me out, he's become a sort of friend. He knows more about my day-to-day life than Rachel. It's not inappropriate to care about the wellbeing of a friend. I mute the warning bell that's ringing in the back of my head, the one that reckons I'm oversimplifying this.

'So what do you say?' He smiles boyishly at me. 'Am I going to help you with this insanely crazy decision you've made or not?'

I throw up my hands. 'Yes you are.'

The first thing we sort out is what we need to do in the seven days before my furniture arrives. It seems pretty obvious. All the broken floorboards need to be fixed. The walls and ceiling need to be patched and repainted. We decide to make downstairs a priority, as that's where I plan to live for now. I don't really want the kids falling down the stairs in the middle of the night.

The next morning I head out to the hardware store and pick up wall-repair supplies and a wad of paint colour cards to mull over.

I decide the office and the storeroom will be the boys' bedrooms. Ryan can have the office to himself and Alfie and Charlie can share the storeroom. We've already taken most of the junk out of the office. However, the box of photos is still in there, along with a few other keepsakes from Jake's childhood. I decide to move them into the spare room upstairs, out of the way of our patching and painting operation.

I pick up a discoloured eight-by-ten-inch photograph in an old frame and pause to examine it. The picture is of Alice and the woman from the other photograph I discovered on our first day at Gum Leaf Grove. This time both women are standing outside Flinders Street Station in Melbourne with massive grins on their faces. They look younger, maybe late twenties, early thirties, and like they've just come back from a big adventure, or are about to embark on one. I can see the family resemblance much more clearly in this picture, and the location pushes a puzzle piece into place for me.

Melbourne.

Is this Carmen? Is this Alice's sister?

I chew on my lower lip as I think back to Jake's funeral. It was a small affair done Carrie's way. The ceremony short, the food fancy and her eulogy more about her than about him. All of her family were there, but the only blood relatives of Jake's were his sons. I don't recall seeing anyone fitting Carmen's description. Were he and his aunt estranged? Does she still live in Melbourne? Has she even been notified of his death?

Oh crap. Was it my responsibility to tell her?

I try to put the thought out of my mind but all morning my brain keeps returning to it. Eventually I find myself in the sitting room, retrieving the box of Carmen's letters from the safe. I'll use the return address on these letters to find her phone number online. Hopefully it's still current. And if not . . . at least I tried.

As I pull the box from the safe, a face suddenly appears in the window beside it. I shriek and drop the box on the floor.

'Hey Mum!' Alfie's muffled voice comes through the glass as he eyes me gleefully. 'Did I scare you?'

'Yes you did!' I put a hand to my chest to calm my heart. *'Don't do that.'*

'Sor-ry.' He grins.

I know he's not sorry at all as he disappears back into the garden yelling to Ryan and Charlie. 'I scared Mummy so much she nearly fainted.'

I look down and see that all Carmen's letters have spilled out of the box and over the floor.

Damn it.

I bend down to pick them up. As I do, I notice one envelope that's different from the rest. It is addressed to Jake, not Alice. I suck in a breath, wondering how I could have missed this. Snatching it up, I pull out the single folded sheet and begin to read.

Dear Jake,

Because you aren't taking my phone calls, I'm resorting to sending this message the old-fashioned way. I know that you think I am protecting someone who doesn't deserve to be protected. However, I don't think knowing who your mother was having an affair with would be of any benefit to you right now. This is not what your mother would have wanted for you. You have entry to an amazing university and that is where you should be – living your life. Sell the house. Sell the business. Staying there, among the memories, is not going to help you. Nor is looking for someone to blame. The police have told us repeatedly, this is a cut and dried case. Even if your mother was having an affair, that person is not directly linked to her murder. They were not present at the scene. You must let this go and move on with your life.

Please call me. If there is any way I can assist you, I would like to.

Aunty Carmen

I finish reading the letter just as Mitch walks into the room, a bucket of plaster in one hand and a spatula in the other.

'You all right?' he enquires when I meet his eyes. 'You look like you've seen a ghost.'

His phrasing couldn't be more appropriate.

'What do you know about the ghost of Gum Leaf Grove?' I ask, wondering why I've never bothered to grill him before.

'Alice Bowman?' His lips rise in the corners. 'Antoine's pretty fond of passing on local rumours, but I also had those letters to read when I first moved in here.'

I raise my eyebrows. 'You've read them?'

'Well,' he winces apologetically, 'when I arrived at this house they had already been abandoned for twenty years. I wasn't overly concerned about invading anyone's privacy.'

His logic is sound enough, but I'm not going to tell him so. Something else has just occurred to me. 'You're the one who opened the painting that first night we arrived,' I accuse him.

He grins. 'Yeah.'

I punch him in the arm. 'That wasn't funny. I was so creeped out by that.'

He rubs his arm but doesn't look the least bit repentant. 'I wasn't trying to be funny or creepy.'

'Really?' I fold my arms, looking doubtful. 'So what about when you appeared to Charlie the first day that we got here and the other boys didn't see you?'

'Firstly,' he protests, 'I didn't *appear* to Charlie.' He lifts his hands to make air quotes for the word 'appear'. 'The cricket ball rolled into the vineyard. Charlie ran after it and we had a very brief chat under cover of the vines before he went back to his brothers.'

I give him a pointed look. 'So you weren't trying to make me believe this place was haunted and scare me off.'

'No.' He shakes his head. 'Most of the time I was just trying to be helpful. To be honest, I opened the safe because I thought you might find the contents interesting.' He looks away, as though he's embarrassed. 'Especially after I heard you and the boys going through those old family photographs in the office.'

My brow furrows. 'I don't know how someone as large as you is able to move around so silently.'

'Well, I can't reveal all my secrets.' His eyes twinkle. 'But in this case, the office window was open. Sound carries well in still country air.'

I roll my eyes. 'But how did you even know the safe was there?'

'It was open when I got here,' Mitch responds, and then adds after a pause. 'To be honest, Grace, I don't think I was the only one to read those letters over the years.'

I think about Eve and how she said she used to hang out here as a teenager. Who knows how many giggling girls have read them, in addition to the vineyard workers and anyone else who has explored the abandoned house?

'What about the top shelf?' I ask, remembering my earlier suspicions. 'Was there something there too?'

'If there was, someone took it long before I arrived.' Mitch shrugs.

'There's just one thing left to explain.' I pause.

'What's that?'

'The secret room.'

'It's not a secret room,' Mitch laughs. 'Never was. When you and the boys arrived, Antoine went downstairs to distract you and I pulled the bookcase over the front of the door and then locked it from the inside.'

I choke. 'It never occurred to you to maybe come downstairs like a normal human being and just ask me if you could stay a few more nights?'

He has the decency to look ashamed. 'No.'

'No?' I repeat.

'Well, would you have said yes?'

I sigh. 'Probably not.'

'I had nowhere else to go.' He gives me an apologetic look. 'I thought it was better to stall and plan my next move.'

'Like pretending you couldn't speak English?' I demand, hurt by his deception all over again.

He shuts his eyes and winces. 'You haven't still forgiven me for that, have you?'

I avoid the question. 'How do you know how to speak French anyway?' My eyes narrow. 'Your accent is completely Aussie.'

He meets my eyes squarely. 'I was born here, but my parents are French. My family migrated to Australia when my older sister was two. I've spoken two languages since I was a little kid.'

'You have a sister?' He's never mentioned her before.

He hesitates. 'Her name is Adele. You'd like her.'

I turn and look at him suspiciously out of the corner of my eye. '*Why?*'

He laughs. 'You both like to speak your mind.'

A smile breaks across my face. 'In that case, I'd love to meet her.'

'Maybe one day you will.' The way he says it is kind of wistful, like he doesn't actually believe it will happen. The mild prick of rejection causes my warmth to retract a notch. Mitch and I don't have a permanent commitment to one another. It's not surprising he doesn't believe I'll meet his family one day. Still, I thought our friendship was more than just an accommodation deal.

Perhaps not.

I pull my gaze from his and glance back at the letter and envelope I'm holding. 'I'm sorry but I'm going to leave you to it for a minute. I've got a phone call to make.'

Mitch catches my arm as I attempt to walk by and heat shoots through me. 'Grace,' he asks, 'are you still mad with me . . . about the French thing? Because I thought I explained –'

'No, Mitch,' I say slowly. 'I'm not.'

'Really?' It's clear from his tone that he doesn't believe me.

'Really,' I repeat, and reluctantly he lets go of my arm. I walk out, glad to see a worried expression on his face. I don't get to confound Mitch often, so I have to take my moments when I get them.

I head straight to the office because I actually do need to make a call. Two, actually. The first one is to my sister. After a quick catch-up, I ask if she can look up Carmen's return address for me, considering I haven't got access to the internet myself. Five minutes later, I have a Melbourne phone number scribbled on the back of Jake's letter. There's no guarantee it's current but it's definitely worth a shot. I pick up the phone again and dial carefully.

After five rings, a woman answers. 'Hello?'

'Hi, is this Carmen?' My eyes flick to the envelope with her full name on the back. 'Carmen Hastings?'

'Er . . . no. This is her daughter, Margaret. She's just in the other room, though. Do you want to speak to her?'

'If you don't mind.'

'Can I ask who is calling?'

I'm sure Carmen won't recognise my name, but she does, from the wedding announcement Jake put in the paper when we got married.

'I never thought I'd get to meet you,' Carmen admits when she gets on the phone a minute later. I can hear her age in her voice, which is gravelly and slightly breathless. 'How is he?'

My skills at sharing bad tidings must be improving, because I manage to convey the news about Jake without stumbling over my words or having to go back and re-order my sentences.

There is a long pause when I finish speaking, then she says, 'Thank you for telling me. How did you get my number?'

'I found your letters at Gum Leaf Grove,' I reveal. 'All of them. The ones to Alice and a final one to Jake.'

She sighs. 'It was such a sad business, you know. All so unnecessary.'

I wait for her to continue.

'There are so many times when I wish Alice had just come to Melbourne with Jake instead of getting mixed up in the problems of another man.'

'Bob Fletcher?' I suggest.

'You know of him?' Carmen is shocked.

242

'Sort of.'

'You're not saying he confided in you?' she demands. 'I made him promise to tell no one that he had an affair with my sister.'

'Oh no. Not at all,' I assure her. 'I just did a little digging and connected the dots. He leaves flowers at her grave every week.'

'Silly man,' Carmen snorts. 'He felt so guilty after it all happened, but I thought it would be better if Jake never found out who his mother was sleeping with. It wasn't like Bob fought me on that either. He was still married at the time. His poor wife had just lost her son. She didn't need to find out her husband had been planning to leave her for another woman. All a confession would have achieved was more pain for everyone.'

'So he and Alice were in a relationship?' I prompt.

'It started a few months after Bob lost his son, Edmund. Instead of drawing them together, grief pushed Bob and his wife apart. It happens sometimes – they grew distant from one another.'

After my experience with my own mother, it isn't such a leap for me to understand this.

'It was Alice who provided him with comfort and support,' Carmen continues. 'She shared his loss because Jake and Edmund had been best friends. She and Bob became closer, and, I guess he started to comfort her too. Being married to an alcoholic wasn't easy. They were like two lost souls who each understood what the other was going through.'

I can see exactly how this lonely pair would find a lifeline in each other. I also realise why Alice took so long to come clean about it. Clearly, from Carmen's anxious letters, Alice didn't tell her sister about the affair immediately. In a small town like Yallingup, it would have been a huge scandal for these two star-crossed lovers to leave their respective partners and hook up – particularly as they were both owners of prominent local businesses.

'In his suicide note, David blamed another man for his loss of control,' Carmen continues. 'This was what put Jake on a mission for revenge. That and the unfamiliar engagement ring they found on her finger after her death.'

Was that the ring that was supposed to be in the empty jewellery box?

I want to ask Carmen about it, but she's still finishing off the story. 'Jake realised that I knew who had given Alice that ring. I was the logical person for her to confide in. And she did tell me about Bob, the night after he proposed. When I wouldn't tell Jake what I knew, he froze me out.'

'So I gathered from your letter.'

'You must understand,' Carmen tries to explain, 'the last thing Jake needed was this tragedy dragging on. I didn't want him to dwell on what he couldn't change. What he needed was a fresh start, not a vendetta.'

'He did start again, in Perth,' I inform her dryly. 'When he married me, he never mentioned his past at all. It was like it didn't exist.'

'I'm sorry you're finding out about all this now,' Carmen apologises. 'It must be very disconcerting. To be honest, I thought Jake had sold his parents' business a long time ago, but it sounds like he never did let go of what happened there.'

I fill in the blanks about Jake's life after leaving Yallingup. She sighs when I'm done. 'I know there's no love lost between you, but Jake did have a rough time of it when he was young. He basically raised himself, you know. As much as I love my sister, I think at times she was neglectful of him because of what she was going through.'

I had figured out as much myself, and while I didn't personally need nice memories of my ex-husband, I knew that my boys would. One day, they would ask questions about his childhood, and want to know more about him as a man. I wanted to be able to give them the full picture. So I say impulsively, 'If you're ever in Yallingup, please come by. I know my boys would love to hear more about their father and grandmother.'

'Thank you.' Carmen sounds pleased. 'I would love to meet them too.'

I put the phone down a few minutes later, feeling like I made the right decision to contact her. I leave the office and walk down the hall to the storeroom, where Mitch and the kids have just finished removing the shelving from the walls. Well, Mitch has removed the shelving. Charlie, Ryan and Alfie have used the loose planks to make a track on the floor for their toy race cars.

Now that the walls are bare, the room is looking much more spacious. The window seems bigger too, even though it hasn't changed at all. Of course, all the nicks and dents are more visible now. Patching is the obvious next step.

I make the mistake of asking the boys what colours they want their rooms to be. They don't even look at the wad of paint sample cards I picked up at the hardware store that morning.

'I want a blue room,' Charlie responds. 'All blue. The floor as well.'

'Red for me,' Ryan says, shaking his head.

'My room is gonna be black,' Alfie announces. 'Like the Batcave.' He pauses. 'Can I also have a trapdoor?'

I look at Mitch, who has his arms folded across his chest, one hand covering his mouth. I glare at him but he still looks suspiciously like he's about to laugh.

'Maybe you boys should ask your mother if she's got any ideas about what colours *she'd* like to paint the house,' he offers.

Ryan looks at me with narrowed eyes. 'You're not going to choose pink, are you?'

We settle it in the end. I'm not entirely sure how. I think Mitch bribes them with sausages. We decide to do the boys' rooms a light shade of blue and the rest of the house an extremely light beige called 'latte'.

Once the decision is made, I feel a quiet sense of joy wash over me. The act of painting the house in colours we have chosen is like marking Gum Leaf Grove as our own. Not scrubbing the past out, but building upon it – making the future brighter and better. I know this is the beginning of a new chapter in my life and I can't wait to see how it pans out.

Chapter 26

True to his word, Scott calls a couple of days after Alfie's accident. I feel giddy as a teenager when I pick up the phone and hear his voice.

'Hi, Grace.'

'Hi, Scott.'

There is an awkward pause before we both start talking at once, then have to stop to decide who is going to speak first. It's like the kiss has thrown our natural rhythm out of kilter, though neither of us dares mention it. Instead, I tell him that Alfie's head and ankle are much better, and that I've decided not to sell the house.

'So unfortunately I won't be signing any contracts with Fletchers,' I finish.

'At the risk of sounding like a disloyal employee, I have to say that's great news,' he responds cheerfully.

'My furniture arrives in five days,' I tell him. 'In the meantime, I want to give the ground floor a quick facelift.'

'Need any help?' he asks. 'I'm pretty handy with a paintbrush.'

'Only if you've got time,' I say, touched by his offer. 'We've mostly got it under control.'

'We?'

'Oh, you know.' I fumble over the words. 'I've got Mitch helping out, and possibly Antoine on his day off.'

'The handyman and his French cousin.'

I catch his disapproving tone and reply uncertainly, 'Well, yeah.'

'Just be careful,' he warns. 'There's something not right about those two, especially Mitch. I can't quite put my finger on it.'

'What do you mean?' My eyes narrow and I hold the phone closer to my ear, glancing around to make sure Mitch isn't within earshot.

'Doesn't he come across a little arrogant to you?' Scott asks.

'Not really . . .'

'How long have you known him?'

'Er . . . not long. About a week.' I realise I should probably tell him that Mitch is living upstairs. I open my mouth to do so when he sidetracks me with another question.

'And has he always been a handyman?'

'I'm not sure.'

I think about Antoine's brief bio. He said he was fresh from France and looking for a job in a winery. I know he's not fresh from France. So the winery business is probably all a lie, too. I realise with some difficulty that I don't actually know much about Mitch.

The real Mitch.

'Well, just be careful. I'm sure I've seen him somewhere before.'

'Sure. I'll be careful. I –'

'I better get going. I'll talk to you soon, okay?'

'Er . . . okay.'

'Bye.'

'Bye.'

And then he's gone. I look at the receiver in dissatisfaction. Despite offering, he didn't actually make a time to come and help me paint, he didn't give me a chance to explain about Mitch and, most importantly, he didn't ask me out. To be honest, I'm a little confused. I mean, we did kiss. I didn't imagine that. He did say he wanted to date me if I stayed in town. I told him I'm staying. So why didn't he get the ball rolling? Not that I know how I would swing it if he did. I mean, I can't go out with him without getting a babysitter – a *proper* babysitter who I trust.

Not Mitch, but a girlfriend, like Eve or Bronwyn. Although I'm not sure that hitting them up for babysitting so early in our friendship would be a good move.

Oh well, perhaps dating Scott would be too stressful for me right now anyway.

I never suspected for a second that Scott hadn't wanted to talk long because he was planning a surprise pop-in the next day.

Mitch and I are in the office. I am on a stepladder trying to pull the curtain railing off the wall so I can put a roller blind up instead. I've already managed to unscrew most of the fixings, but some of them are a little stuck, so now I'm in the 'yanking' phase.

'Here, let me do it,' says Mitch just as I give it one almighty tug. The rail pops off the wall, taking me with it.

'Oh no.' My body tips back and I fall directly into Mitch's arms. It could have been a scene straight from a 1950s movie, if only, right at that moment, a little voice didn't announce, 'Mummy, Scott is here.'

To my horror, Mitch turns around, still holding me, bride-over-the-threshold style, to greet the newcomer. Scott is standing in the doorway with Ryan, a huge bunch of flowers in his hands. He looks as uncomfortable as I feel. I struggle to get back on the ground, but for some reason Mitch's hold on me seems to tighten.

'Is everything okay?' Scott enquires. I can feel my face flaming redder by the second.

'Oh, I nearly fell off the stepladder, that's all.' I quit struggling and look up at Mitch in exasperation. 'Will you put me down?'

'Nearly fell?' Mitch grunts. 'I suppose I only *nearly* caught you then.'

'Something like that.' I avoid his gaze as I dust my hands on my tracksuit pants and pat the frizzy bits of hair coming loose from my ponytail. I must look an absolute fright. I have my worst clothes on and no make-up. In fact, I probably look worse than the first time Scott and I met. I've just reset my reputation back to zero.

'How are you, Scott?' I lift my chin uncertainly. 'I wasn't expecting you.'

'Yes, sorry to drop in unannounced.' He smiles and holds out the flowers. 'After our talk yesterday I just wanted to give you a little housewarming gift.' He holds up a large white cake box. 'And I brought celebratory donuts for the boys!'

'Yay!' Ryan jumps up and down. 'Can we have them now, Mummy? Can we? Please!'

'I guess it is almost time for a coffee break,' I grin.

'Good idea,' says Mitch.

Scott's face turns from good natured to annoyed. I don't actually blame him. 'Oh, don't let us interrupt you if you're on a roll,' he frowns. 'You can keep going, if you like.'

'Not on a roll.' Mitch shrugs and leads the way into the kitchen.

I watch in helpless frustration. Mitch knows that Scott is here to see me. Why can't he give us some privacy?

Scott puts a hand on my arm to slow me down.

'I hope this guy is pulling his weight for what you're paying him,' he murmurs quietly. 'Let me know if you need me to give him a motivational talk.'

Mitch – a slacker? The concept is laughable, even apart from the fact that our arrangement isn't financial. I quickly reassure Scott.

'Oh no, that won't be necessary. I think he's just a big fan of donuts.'

They certainly cause a ruckus once Alfie and Charlie get wind of them.

'I'm having the one with the rainbow sprinkles.'

'Aww, I want that one.'

'You have the jam donut.'

'No, I'm going to have the chocolate one!'

'Coffee, Scott?' Mitch offers, rummaging around in my kitchen like he lives here. Which he does, but there's no need to be so bloody obvious about it. I can feel my nerve-endings starting to tingle.

First he gets out the mugs and the coffee powder. Then he picks up the water jug and fills the little pot we use for boiling water.

'I'll do it.' I try to take the pot from him as he turns to the stove, but he dodges my hand.

'No, it's fine,' he says. 'You go sit down. Take a break. That jam donut isn't going to last long, and you didn't have much for breakfast.'

I cringe.

'You had breakfast together.' Scott's voice is flat. 'You must have gotten here early.'

I neutralise my facial expression and turn to explain, but Mitch gets in first. 'I live here.'

'You live here?' Scott says, but he's looking at me.

'Upstairs,' I say quickly. 'In one of the spare bedrooms.'

'You didn't tell him?' Mitch sounds amused. 'Why didn't you tell him?'

I wince. 'I meant to. But it hasn't been that long. It's a very recent thing.'

'A week tomorrow.' Mitch noisily taps the teaspoon on the side of the mugs as he distributes the coffee powder. 'Do you take sugar, Scott?' he asks.

'Yes,' Scott responds impatiently. 'Grace –'

'What about milk?' Mitch asks.

'No thank you,' says Scott, turning back to me. 'Since when –'

'Not even a little?' Mitch interrupts again.

'I said no.' Scott sounds angry now.

'Sorry,' Mitch responds cheerfully.

'How did this come about?' Scott has his eyes trained on me. 'I didn't realise you were renting rooms.'

'Well, it is a bed and breakfast,' murmurs Mitch.

'It *was* a bed and breakfast,' Scott corrects him. 'Now it's just a derelict home with more falling apart than sticking together.'

'*Scott*,' I gasp.

'Sorry,' he quickly apologises. 'That came out wrong. What I meant was, you're hardly running a business here. Are you?'

'No,' I say, trying to stay calm. 'But he is just my tenant. He pays rent with labour. It's strictly a business arrangement. We don't really get much into each other's space . . . at all.'

'Except that one time,' says Ryan, just when I think the kids are too absorbed in their donuts to be listening. 'When you saw him naked.'

'*Ryan.*'

'What?' His shoulders slump. 'Was that another one of those things I was supposed to keep a secret?'

'Another?' Mitch repeats curiously. 'How many secrets do you keep for your mother, Ryan?'

'Well –'

'It's not a secret.' I hastily interrupt my son. 'Nor did I ever say it was.' I try to laugh it off, because Scott's face is turning red. 'It's just something embarrassing that happened to me. That's all.'

'She screamed 'cause she saw his penis,' Alfie tells Scott, as if he didn't have enough information already.

'It's a big, big one,' Charlie reveals, stretching his arms wide to demonstrate the size, which would probably be more accurate for a whale.

'He might be exaggerating . . . slightly,' Mitch murmurs, a mischievous smile twisting the corners of his mouth, though he doesn't look up from preparation of the coffee.

A tidal wave of mortification rolls through me. What must Scott be thinking right now? This is a disaster!

'Guys,' I hiss. 'That's *enough*!'

I turn to Scott. 'The incident occurred because I didn't realise the bathroom was occupied. It was an accident.'

But he doesn't seem to be listening to me. His cheeks are flushed and his hands have curled into fists.

He clears his throat. 'You know what, you guys enjoy these donuts. I should probably get going. I've got a stack of paperwork to get through at the office before a home open this afternoon.'

Mitch brings our steaming mugs over and sets them on the table. 'So soon?' He feigns innocence. 'I only just finished making your coffee.'

'I misjudged how much time I had.' Scott glances quickly at his watch. 'I'll have to skip it this time.'

'What a shame,' Mitch replies with a complete lack of regret.

'I'll walk you out.' I glare at Mitch over my shoulder before I follow Scott out to his car. He seems very stiff around the shoulders, like he's trying to contain his anger.

I really should have told him that Mitch was living with me. Now it looks completely dodgy.

Oh, Grace! How on earth do you get yourself into these situations?

Scott turns to open his car door, hesitates, then spins back around.

'I have to know. Did I read you all wrong? Did I not make it clear that I was interested in you?'

'Yes, yes,' I vigorously nod my head. 'You did. You did make it clear. And you didn't read me wrong. I am interested in you. Totally interested.'

'Then what's with . . .' He makes an irritated gesture towards the house.

'Mitch?' I roll my eyes. 'He's just my tenant. *Really.*'

'Does he know that?' Scott asks acidly.

'Of course.' I blink. 'The bathroom incident was a one-off. And it was very embarrassing for us both. Trust me. No romance in it at all.'

I make a cutting motion with my hands, displaying the extent of my mortification.

'I never expected to find him in there. He scared me half to death. That's why I screamed.'

A slow grin spreads across his face. 'That would have been pretty funny.'

'The kids thought it was hilarious.'

'Still, I don't trust him,' Scott says. 'I told you that yesterday and I feel it even more strongly today.'

'Well, our arrangement is only temporary,' I explain. 'He'll be gone soon.'

'So you're still up for a date with me then?'

I smile. 'Why wouldn't I be?'

'Great,' he nods. 'I'll call you when I get back to town.'

I blink in surprise. 'You're going away?'

He groans. 'Just for a few days. I know I said I was going to try and help you with some painting, but unfortunately Bob wants me at his Margaret River branch till Friday.'

'That's okay,' I shrug. 'These things happen.'

He tucks a strand of hair behind my ear. 'I'm glad we had this talk.' His fingertips pause just before they reach my chin and he leans in for a quick kiss.

'See you soon.'

As Scott drives off in a swirl of dust, I turn and march straight back into the kitchen. The boys have finished their donuts and have gone back to whatever game they were playing before

Scott arrived. Mitch is innocently clearing rubbish from the table.

I stop in front of him with my hands on my hips. 'What was that all about?'

He looks up cautiously. 'What was what all about?'

'The way you were acting just now.' I throw out a hand. 'You were deliberately provoking him.'

'He deserves to be provoked. He's an idiot.'

I gasp. 'You don't even know him.'

'Neither do you. You shouldn't go out with him.'

'Right, because you get to decide who I date?' I snap.

'No, that's not what I'm saying.'

'Then what are you saying?'

He takes a deep breath. 'I just think a woman like you deserves a whole lot better than a guy like him.'

My eyes narrow. 'A woman like me?'

'I know you're feeling the pressure. You think it's time for you to re-enter the dating scene and you're even a little nervous about it.' I cringe at his insight, remembering our 'conversations' when I thought he couldn't understand me. This guy knows too much. I'm an open book and he's read every page.

'But maybe,' he continues with a tentative tilt of his head, 'you should wait just a little longer.'

'Wait,' I scoff. 'For what? My children to grow up and wrinkles to set in?'

'Not necessarily, but I do think it's a bigger decision than you think it is.'

'Wow.' I can't believe he's being so patronising. Is he questioning my responsibility to the kids? 'I don't need you to tell me to put my children first, thank you very much. I would never risk their needs for anyone.'

'I know.'

'If I did start dating someone, I wouldn't introduce them as a regular presence in their lives until I was sure that person was genuine. As in, they're not just going to break my heart and leave the second there's trouble.'

'Wise move,' he nods. 'So what about me?'

My brow wrinkles. 'What about you? You're a friend, there's no danger of you breaking my heart.'

'Of course.' He stiffens.

'All I mean is, Scott is a lovely guy. I have seen nothing in him to make me suspect he's looking for a cheap fling. So if I want to date him, I certainly will. The rest is none of your business.'

He says nothing for a moment, a muscle working in his jaw.

'Okay then,' he says at last. 'I'm sorry, I shouldn't have said anything.'

'Apology accepted.' I lift my chin.

'All right then.' He nods abruptly and turns to go. His back is so stiff he might as well have a broomstick up his T-shirt. At the sight, my anger dissolves, leaving me dissatisfied and grumpy.

'Mitch, wait.'

He stops and turns around. 'What?'

'Are we okay?'

He bites his lip. 'Sure.'

'Because the last thing I want to do is ruin this friendship.' I walk over and lay a hand on his arm. 'I didn't mean to snap at you. I know you're just being caring. I'm just so sensitive about this issue. You know that.'

'I do.'

'Friends?' I hold out my hand. He looks at it for a moment and then, with a rueful smile, takes it.

'Friends,' he agrees.

Chapter 27

With just three days till the furniture arrives, we've still got a lot of work to do. So Mitch calls Antoine to enlist more help. I'm not sure it's the best idea, but I suppose beggars can't be choosers.

Antoine arrives around mid-morning, apologising for being late. 'Obviously, I meant to get here early as agreed,' he explains. 'But when my alarm went off at 6 am, I discovered to my horror that it was still dark. Getting up before light is simply unnatural, madame, so I went back to sleep for another couple of hours.'

He looks around at the room we've painted and nods his approval. 'You seem to have done a good job so far. At this rate, there may be nothing left for me to do but give you a few pointers. I'm extremely good at noticing areas of poor quality. It's the perfectionist in me, you see.'

'Ant,' Mitch growls warningly, 'pick up a paintbrush.'

'All right, all right.' Antoine holds up his hands. 'There's no need to get tetchy.'

After an hour of 'assisting', however, all he's done is lay down a few drop sheets, choose his brushes and select some music to work to, using Mitch's little sound system. Having some pop songs playing in the background does put a bit more bounce in my step, but it only makes Antoine procrastinate even further as he flicks through Mitch's extensive library, wondering what to play next.

The kids make me laugh when they all start grooving. Especially Charlie, who wiggles his little bum out of sync with the beat, his mischievous smile making me just want to eat him up.

'I can dance,' he tells me.

'Yes you can.' I grab him and press two kisses to each of his gorgeous little dimples.

Antoine sighs. 'Well, I'm glad someone is having fun. This is back-breaking work. Should we rest, madame, and Mitch can make us all a coffee?'

Although Antoine has only been there a short time, Mitch and I have been painting since 7 am, so I concede to his suggestion.

Just as we walk into the kitchen, I hear the phone ringing in the office.

'Hey, Grace, it's just me, Bronwyn.'

'Oh, hi, Bronwyn,' I say with genuine pleasure. 'How are you?'

'Fine thanks. Antoine told me yesterday that you're moving in.'

'Yep.'

'I just wanted to offer you our trailer again, if you need it,' she says. 'Now that we're going to be neighbours, I thought I'd just be . . . well, neighbourly.'

I smile at her generosity. 'Thank you so much, that's really sweet. I don't need it right now, but I'll let you know if that changes.'

'Yes, please do, and just give me a shout if there's anything else I can help with. Even if it's just to watch the kids for a couple of hours.'

'Wow, thanks.' I'm touched. 'I'll keep that in mind. There is so much to do in the next few days. I still have to work out where I'm sending them to school.'

It's a worry that has been close to the forefront of my mind. My main concern is Alfie, who consistently performs at the bottom of his class due to his concentration problems. His teacher in Perth is pretty sensitive to his needs. I'm really hoping we will find a school in Dunsborough that will be just as supportive of ADHD students.

'Well, my kids go to South West Primary, which is a lovely community,' Bronwyn is saying. 'Eve's kids go to kindy there too, and her sister, Phoebe, is one of the teachers. It would be great to see you at pick-up and drop-off. Someone else to hide behind when the PTA volunteer scouts come a-hunting.'

I laugh. 'I didn't know you had kids.'

'They were up at the house when you dropped in at Oak Hills that time. I have Brendan, who is seven, and Sabrina, who is five.'

'Good to know. I'll have to check South West Primary out.'

'Please do. Us country girls have to stick together.'

'For sure,' I reply, feeling a little zing as I put down the phone.

I can't believe this is real.

I'm actually doing this.

I'm uprooting my safe, normal life in Perth to live in the sticks.

I'm a country girl.

Hear me roar.

The next couple of days pass in a flurry of stress, adrenaline and hard work.

Alfie's ankle has more or less healed now. He's walking easily – no running, though – and his head wound is all but forgotten. The cut is still visible, but it no longer troubles him.

I haven't found a job yet, but I've started asking around and staying on top of local advertisements. Once I have my computer here, I'll be able to spruce up my résumé and start sending out applications. School is sorted, too. On Bronwyn's advice, I checked out South West Primary in Dunsborough. Ryan and Alfie start there on Monday. I spoke with their new teachers yesterday – a little longer to Alfie's, so I could explain his ADHD issues.

I called Alfie's therapist in Perth to cancel his ongoing treatment, and asked her to recommend reputable counterparts in Busselton. I'll investigate those next, once I sort out our home.

Our furniture arrives tomorrow, and I'm feeling trepidation and excitement. Having our stuff here is going to make everything oh so permanently real. I wander through the house, taking in the dramatic changes we've affected since I first got here. A sense of hope lifts my energy levels.

I head for the porch to call everyone in for dinner. The kids are playing outside while Mitch finishes painting the handrail. I was helping him until I stopped to make spag bol. From a jar, not from scratch, of course.

As I approach the screen door I stop to take in the scene outside. Sitting on the steps of the porch, their backs to me, are Mitch and Ryan. Side by side, like two old men having a beer and chewing the fat. Well, Mitch has a beer, Ryan has his blue water bottle. They both toss back at exactly the same moment.

'So I'll tell you a joke,' says Ryan.

'Okay, sure,' says Mitch.

'Knock knock.'

'Who's there?'

'Knock knock.'

'. . . Er . . . Who's there?'

'You got it wrong.'

'Did I?'

'Yes,' Ryan sighs. 'You're supposed to say, "Knock knock who?"'

'Are you sure? I don't think that's how it normally works.'

'Yes it is.'

'Really?'

'Yes, you say "Knock knock who?"'

'Okay, if you say so.' There's a grunt as Mitch takes another swig of beer. 'I'm ready this time. Start again.'

'Knock knock.'

'Knock knock who?'

'*Not yet!*' Ryan slaps his palm to his head and I cover my mouth to contain the laugh that wants to escape.

'What are you talking about?' Mitch's voice is comically defensive. 'I did it exactly as you said.'

'You only do it the second time.' Ryan groans like he's speaking to an imbecile. 'Don't you know how knock knock jokes work?'

'I thought I did,' says Mitch.

'It's always knock knock, who's there? Then the answer. Then the answer with "who?" *O-kay?*'

'Okay.' Mitch takes a deep breath. 'Hit me with it again. I'm ready.'

'Knock knock.'

'Who's there?'

'Knock knock.'

With exaggerated aplomb, Mitch answers, 'Knock knock who?'

'Knock knock.'

Mitch groans. 'Okay, now I know you're just having a lend of me.'

Ryan giggles and I'm about to join them when he adds in that quiet voice I recognise as anxiousness, 'Mitch.'

'Yeah.'

'I'm a little bit scared.'

My hand stills on the doorknob.

'I mean, not heaps scared,' says Ryan. 'But just a little.'

'About what?'

'Going to a new school,' he whispers. 'Don't tell Mum.'

My heart squeezes. I want to run out there and hug him, but I don't.

'Why would I do that?' Mitch quizzes him. 'Women need to be kept guessing, let me tell you.'

Ryan grins at him and I flip from sympathy to extreme indignation. Kept guessing my arse!

'Alfie isn't nervous.' Ryan's expression drops and he self-consciously adjusts his glasses. 'Why can't I be more like him?'

'Mate, Alfie nearly topped himself last week. He's not afraid of *anything*. That's not necessarily a good thing. Sometimes a little bit of caution pays off.'

'I guess. But what if I don't make any friends?'

'You'll make heaps of friends, trust me. There's no one who couldn't like you.'

'You're just saying that because *you* like me,' Ryan says dismissively.

'Well, why do you think I like you?' Mitch asks.

Ryan shrugs, trying to look like he doesn't care, but I know he secretly does. Even I'm waiting with bated breath.

Mitch bumps his shoulder. 'Because you're really good at cricket, hunting kangaroos and painting. You're a good older brother, especially in emergencies. You remember every single thing that anybody ever says or does *and* . . .' he pauses dramatically as he builds up to his finale, 'you tell the most amazing jokes.'

Ryan laughs. 'You don't believe that.'

Mitch grunts. 'Yeah, that last bit was a fib. Your jokes could definitely use some work.'

I open the door then, and as it creaks on its hinges they both turn around guiltily, as if they're wondering how long I've been standing there.

'Er . . . I'm going to go back to playing cricket.' Ryan leaps up and dashes off, presumably to avoid any difficult questions.

'Hi,' I say shrewdly after he's gone.

'Hi,' Mitch says in an equally loaded tone.

'So, er . . . thanks for what you said to him just then.'

'You overheard?'

'Most of it.'

Mitch shrugs. 'He's a good kid. Just needs a little more self-confidence.'

It's amazing hearing this insight into my child from another adult – it feels like validation. I walk over and sit down beside him, suddenly in a chatty mood.

'So the house looks great,' I say. 'The latte colour came up really well.'

'And the floors?' he prompts me.

'You did a great job.'

'Thanks, mate.'

He's been calling me that ever since we had that conversation in the kitchen about me 're-entering the dating scene'. I regret having been so blunt with him, because it seems to have changed the dynamic of our relationship. He's withdrawn from me slightly, and I'm not sure I like it. I got so used to him being open and honest and speaking his mind, shoving me out of the way and being up in my personal space. And now he just . . .

I don't know.

Maybe it's just me.

But I feel like he's building walls around himself and I'm worried it's not just the PTSD talking.

It's sad, because I really like Mitch. I don't know how I could have achieved any of this without him.

'So what's next on the list?' he interrupts my thoughts.

'What list?'

He taps his head. 'Your mental renovations list.'

I purse my lips. 'The kitchen.'

'Good idea. And then?'

'The bathrooms. They all need to be completely gutted and redone, including my ensuite. I'm thinking cream and peach, something soothing.'

He winces. 'Yeah, the current colours are a bit of a slap in the face.'

'Aren't they? I also want to do something with this garden.'

'Like . . .?'

I sweep a hand to the right. 'I'd plant kangaroo paws there – at least three different varieties. And on this side –' my hand moves across the scene, 'lilac hibiscus and cushion bush.'

'Been doing some research.' He looks at me with raised eyebrows.

'A little,' I admit, wrinkling my nose. 'I am starting to get a bit excited about living in the country.'

'It's not a crime, you know,' he laughs. 'There's no need to be ashamed.'

'I know,' I lift my chin. 'Though sometimes I can't help but feel like it's all a bit too good to be true. Like a fairytale.'

'More like a ghost story,' he grins.

Something occurs to me for the first time. 'You know what I'd love to do? Return the sitting room to the way it used to look. I've got the photos and it looked amazing. It'd be nice for the boys, too. A way they can get to know their grandmother.'

Without getting into the unfortunate side of her life.

He nods. 'That sounds like a really nice idea.'

'It'd be a big project, though.' I tilt my head. 'Sourcing all the unique bits and pieces, I mean.'

'Well, you know what they say,' he tells me after finishing the last of his beer. 'Everything is available on the internet.'

I groan. 'That reminds me, I really need to get onto hooking up the house. Every time I want to get online I have to go into town.'

He winces guiltily. 'My mobile has reception if I stand on the other side of the vineyard, right on the fence line.'

I gasp, outraged. 'That would have been useful to know *five days ago*, Mitch!'

'I thought you knew,' he protests. 'How else do you think I managed to call you after I plugged in your landline?'

'That was you!' My eyes widen in sudden remembrance of the gruff Telstra voice.

Mitch doesn't meet my eyes. 'I didn't like Scott implying the house was unsafe.'

'*Unbelievable.*' I punch him in the arm.

'Ow!' He catches my hand and says slowly, with a dark, teasing timbre in his tone, 'I'm sorry, but you've seriously got to stop hitting people who are twice your size.'

For a moment, just a second, I get this paralysing sense that he's going to pull me into his arms and kiss me. The premonition is so tangible that I can't move. I can only stare back at him while he holds my wrist in his hand, gently rubbing his thumb over my thrumming pulse.

Oh no. This can't be happening.

I don't have feelings for Mitch, do I?

But that's insane. He's my tenant. My friend.

I've always been interested in Scott. Always.

I can't possibly be interested in two guys. There's got to be something dishonest about that.

Shit.

Am I a slut?

Mitch must recognise the confusion on my face because he drops my hand and looks away. The teasing light in his eyes has been replaced by bleak shutters.

'So I was speaking to Antoine this morning,' he says tightly. 'His roommate is moving out.'

'Oh.' I rub my wrist, trying to keep the trepidation out of my voice.

'So,' he nods his head slowly, 'it might be time for me to move on.'

I freeze.

Too soon.

Way too soon.

I need him.

He must see the utter dismay in my eyes because he holds

up a hand. 'Don't panic. I'll stay on for at least another couple of weeks. Help you get a few more things done. I just wanted to give you some notice, that's all.'

'Sure,' I smile, trying to pretend I'm not feeling utterly bereft – and not just because he won't be here to help me renovate. 'It's great that you're getting on with your own life again.'

He nods. 'I think it's time. I mean, you were right. I can't squat here forever.'

'I guess not,' I agree, wishing I felt better about this.

Why don't I? A couple of days ago I would have been happy for him. Now I can't help but wonder. Is there a woman in Mitch's life? Someone waiting in the wings for when he gets back on his feet? Come to think of it, where is Mitch's life? It's definitely not in France. I know so little about this guy. As much as I have confided in him, there's so much he's held back from me. Maybe it's better that he's going.

Before I can say anything more, Charlie comes out of nowhere and launches himself at Mitch.

'Charlie! What the?' Mitch peels him off his body and looks down into his flushed little face, cheeks like ripe cherry tomatoes. 'What are you doing?'

'Alfie lost a tooth!'

'What?'

I turn and see Alfie running towards us with a gappy grin, his little tooth held proudly aloft between thumb and forefinger.

'I pulled it out myself,' he announces. 'Because it was really wobbly.'

Ryan is just behind him. 'I can't believe you just did that!'

Neither can I.

'So does this mean I get money from the tooth fairy now?' asks Alfie, who has never lost a tooth before, but has witnessed two years of his older brother finding coins under his pillow. He once left a toenail under there in an attempt to garner some interest from the fairy kingdom. It was a gross find when I was making his bed.

'Yep.' I smile. 'You'll finally get some tooth-fairy money.'

'Awesome!' Alfie leaps gleefully. 'I'm putting it under my pillow right now.'

The boys all run into the house and I realise, with poignant dismay, how much they're going to miss Mitch when he goes.

I look at Mitch. He looks at me.

'Should we go in for dinner?' he asks, with a sadness that belies the normalcy of the question.

I sigh. 'Seems as good a time as any.'

Chapter 28

Rachel calls at 10 am to let me know the removalists have just left Perth. I can't say I'm sad I didn't spend one more night in that house. I'm not going to miss it, or my grumpy landlord.

'It all went really smoothly, Grace. Not a single hiccup,' she says. 'Now I'm just waiting on the cleaners to make everything spick and span before I hand the keys back.'

'Perfect,' I smile. 'What do I owe you?'

'A holiday in Yallingup, of course!'

We hang up and I go back to the kitchen, where the plumber has just finished fitting my new sink. It looks kind of comical, actually – a shiny stainless steel basin and brand-new tap sitting in an old, stained, ugly-looking counter. I turn my attention to the doorless cupboards. I have to throw out a few more of Alice's things, otherwise there won't be enough room for my stuff when it arrives. As I go through the cupboards, I'm half hoping her engagement ring might turn up in the bottom of a jar or something. I never did get around to asking Carmen where it was now. Though I imagine if it was in the jewellery box in the safe, some local teenager would have pinched it years ago. Not that it really matters, of course. If I were to find the ring, I'd never add it to my own jewellery collection. Didn't she get murdered with it on her finger? Not exactly a lucky charm.

Mitch is at the back of the house, preparing the laundry to eventually house my washing machine. The tiles in there aren't the best, but I've decided to keep them for the time being, so he's been re-grouting all morning.

The kids have pitched the tent I brought down with me in the space behind the house. At the moment, it's a Stormtrooper base that's under Jedi attack. I can hear the sound effects of blasters, and Ryan yelling, 'Fall back, fall back! There's too many of them!'

Just after midday, I start making sandwiches for lunch when I hear a rap at the front door. The removalists can't be here already, surely? It takes at least three hours to get to Yallingup from Perth.

I dust off my hands and make my way quickly through the house, freezing halfway across the foyer when I see her standing on the porch.

An avalanche of emotions hits me as I take in her face. The uncertain smile. That familiar tilt of her head beside her droopy, less-than-confident shoulders. Even her smell is familiar. The breeze carries it in as it blows through the door.

'Grace.'

'Mother.' My voice is terse, hostile. Not at all inviting.

And yet she asks, 'Can I come in?' The drawl of her American accent brings back a rush of memories. Not all bad. But I can't trust them.

She is dressed in the slightly off-kilter hippy style she always used to affect when we were growing up. Jeans, a multi-coloured knitted poncho and a velvet hat on her greying dark curls. My mother is tall and willowy, so she's able to carry off her own brand of fashion effortlessly. I'd forgotten that about her.

'How did you get this address?'

'Rachel told me . . . sort of.' She plays with a ring on her right hand. 'She told me you moved to a property called Gum Leaf Grove in Yallingup. Once I drove into town, I just asked around. I was pointed here by some locals.'

'Why have you come?'

She pauses. 'Are we going to have this whole conversation through the door?'

'If we have to.'

'I'm not here to cause problems for you, Grace,' she sighs. 'Quite the opposite, in fact. Please let me come in. This won't take long. I'll leave as soon as I've said what I've come here to say.'

I hesitate, grit my teeth and march forward. I mean, seriously, did she have to come today of all days, just when I need everything to run like clockwork? I unlock the flyscreen and step back so she can come in.

'We'll talk in the kitchen,' I say. 'It's the only area with seating.'

'That's fine.' She nods quickly.

We get to the kitchen and I gesture to the park bench. I sit opposite on a folding chair, feeling about as natural as plastic. I haven't seen my mother in half a decade, and close up I'm starting to notice the difference in her appearance. The extra wrinkles, the strands of white in her hair, and something else. The tarnish of life. A weathered look about her countenance.

All that drinking, perhaps?

Her smile is slight as she catches me studying her. 'Are you checking to see if I'm sober?' she asks. 'I am.'

'Well, I suppose that's a plus. Given you drove here.' I know the cynicism in my voice is cruel, but I can't seem to help it.

'I've been sober for four years now.'

'Congratulations,' I say stiffly. Rachel has told me a few times that she has remained sober for a while. But to be honest I hadn't really believed it. I've lived through so many false starts and broken promises.

As though reading my mind, she adds, 'It's different this time.'

'Okay,' I respond slowly.

'This time I actually want to get better.'

'And all the other times you didn't?' I raise an eyebrow.

'Not really.' Her clasped hands twist together. 'I couldn't face life without your father.'

That's when I lose my cool.

'You didn't just lose him, Mum. You lost us as well. And not because we died.'

'I was being a bad mother,' she says firmly. 'At the time, I thought leaving you girls was the better option.'

'Not drinking was the better option!'

'I know.' She takes a deep breath and focuses her gaze on her hands like she's reciting a practised speech. 'I've joined Alcoholics Anonymous. They run a twelve-step program to keep you on the straight and narrow.'

I stay silent and wait for the rest.

'My sponsor says she thinks I'm ready to tackle step nine.'

'Which is?'

'Making amends to the people I've hurt.' Her eyes meet mine, filling but not quite overflowing. I suck in a stilted breath as she says the words I thought I'd never hear from her.

'Grace, I am so sorry. I'm so sorry for letting you down. For not being your mother for all those years.'

I'm not prepared for this. I'm not prepared for her apology because I thought it would never come. In all the years of our separation, she's never once owned her actions. Never.

Maybe Rachel was right. Maybe this time it's different.

'I also want to give you this.' She holds out a cheque. The sum is substantial. On instinct, I thrust it back.

'I can't.'

'Yes, you can. It's mostly from your father anyway. Half the money from the sale of our home. I gave the other half to Rachel. Think of it as the money I owe you for all the missed years of love.'

I choke. 'You can't exchange money for love, Mum. It's practically a paradox.'

'Then take it because you need it.' She smiles. 'I know you do.'

I hesitate. She's just apologised and offered me thousands of dollars. What is it with this year of unnatural benefactors?

'Please.' Her face has taken on the expression of a wounded animal, and it feels churlish not to take the cheque. I mean, it has come with the apology I always wanted. It seems to be in good faith. And she said she'd go as soon as she'd said her piece, so . . .

'Okay. Thank you.'

'Good.'

'There's just one other thing I wanted to ask you.' The money has been in my hand less than five seconds. I nearly curse out loud.

'Am I allowed to meet the children?'

It takes all my willpower not to shove the cheque back at her and ask her to leave.

I know she's just apologised. But when you've been upset with someone for as long as I've been upset with my mother, it's hard to take that first sorry and go, 'Okay, I trust you now.'

'Please?' She raises her clasped hands to her chin. 'It'll only take a minute. I know they're here and I just . . .'

I know what she 'just' wants. It's written all over her face. And I can see that, in fact, it is the real purpose of this visit. Not the money, not the apology. The kids. Her legacy. The balm to her soul. The chance to start again with people who don't know her or what she was. A clean slate.

I don't blame her. Of course that's what she wants. Who wouldn't? The question is, do I allow it? Do I risk it? Do I dare risk her disappointing them?

I'm still trying to get my head around the dilemma when Mitch walks into the room, flannelette shirt rolled up to his elbows as he wipes his hands on a rag.

'Well, that's all done,' he says before he looks up. He freezes when he sees my mother in the room. 'I'm sorry, I didn't . . . I didn't realise you had visitors. I'll come back later.'

'No, don't go,' my mother says. 'I was the one who –' She stops and squints. 'Do I know you?'

'I don't think so.' He shakes his head and takes a couple of steps back, half turning back the way he came.

Her eyes narrow in concentration. 'I'm sure I –' She breaks off. 'Wait!'

He quickly turns back towards her.

'You're –'

'Call me Mitch.' He suddenly strides forward, more confidently this time, hand outstretched.

'Er . . . of course.' Her voice is trembling and girlish, and she puts her hand in his in a kind of dazed manner, like she's been knocked out and has just come to.

'It's *amazing* to meet you.'

I watch them dubiously, wanting to snap my fingers in front of my mother's face. I mean, I know I haven't seen her in a while, but she was never shy when it came to men. Quite the opposite, in fact.

'Grace.' She tears her gaze from Mitch with some effort. 'What is *he* doing here?'

'Mitch is my tenant and handyman.'

'Tenant?' she blinks. 'Handyman? But –'

'Mummy!' There's an ear-splitting shriek from outside. After Alfie split his head open the other week, I'm not about to stop and ask questions.

'Er . . . wait here!' I order and dash outside to find that the tent has caved in with all three boys in it. I'm sure Alfie pulled out the central pole on purpose. 'It's okay,' I say. 'I'll just find the zipper.'

I fluff around with the plastic, little bodies laughing as I accidentally grab one of them.

'Again, Mummy. Again?' cries Charlie.

'No, no,' I say. 'We've got to get you out. It's a very busy day today, you know. The movers are coming and I haven't got time for games.'

There's also the fact that I have an unwanted visitor in my kitchen who I want to dispose of as quickly as possible. The boys tumble out of the tent.

'Mummy, we're hungry.'

'Is lunch ready yet?'

'Can we have apples?'

'No, you –' But I'm too slow. They're already running towards the house. Damn it! I sprint to catch up.

I don't reach them, however, till we're all in the kitchen again. It takes my mother and Mitch a second to turn around. They seem deep in conversation for two people who just met. But I'm more concerned that my boys are now in my mother's personal space, heads tipped back as they examine her.

'Who are you?' asks Ryan.

She gasps in delight. 'Hello, little ones!' She gets down to Charlie's level. 'I'm your grandma.'

Great.

Just great.

'Grandma!' Ryan's eyes widen like saucers. 'Are you back from the dead?'

'No,' Francine scoffs. 'Just from the lolly shop.' She reaches into her handbag and pulls out three packets of Skittles.

'Yay!'

Now I'm never getting rid of her.

Mitch pulls me to one side. 'She told me she's your mother?' he prompts.

'Yes.'

'But she's American.'

'Didn't I mention that?'

'No,' he says shortly.

I know he knows the rest. He overheard me talking to Rachel in the office that time. There's no need to tell him she's an alcoholic. I can see it in his face. A muscle moves in his jaw and his gaze flicks back to me with something like worry in his eyes.

Suddenly there's a loud honking coming from around the other side of the house. The kind of horn that could only belong to a very large truck.

Oh shit.

My eyes widen. 'The removalists are here.'

After that there's no time to think. Everything is happening so fast. Beds are coming in. Chairs are being carried past me. A dining table. A couch. My fridge. Followed by yet more boxes – all carefully and systematically labelled. Man! These guys are amazing. They've somehow managed to categorise my life. For the first time in ten years I feel organised. I'm actually disappointed that I have to unpack it all.

I spend the next couple of hours showing two burly Italian men where to put what. They can barely speak English.

They wave Mitch's help away, so he gets busy in the bedrooms, reassembling furniture. As for my mother . . . she keeps the kids out from underfoot. I would say that I'm grateful to her, but that would mean admitting that introducing her to my babies had some positive benefit. I'm not ready for that yet.

Let's face it, anyone can hand out Skittles and tell classic nursery tales as if they actually wrote them. And if I'd known my boys would find the naughty things I did as a child so fascinating, I would have told them myself.

'She didn't really eat your lipstick, did she, Grandma?' I hear Alfie gasp in glee as I walk past. She has them munching on a late lunch as she regales them with tales from the 'olden days'.

This last story is true – it wasn't my finest moment. In my defence, I was only two, and my mother used to wear bright red lipstick. Nothing says strawberry lollipop like a bright red stick.

'Oh yes she did.' Grandma's voice is wise and lyrical, like she's spinning yarns from old folklore. 'She was terribly sick afterwards.'

Puh-lease.

I have to admit, it's a stroke of genius when she takes the boys outside to teach them how to play hopscotch. I never would have thought of it myself – hopscotch being such a lost art and all. I don't know many kids who play it these days. I should have known, however, that anything to do with jumping and throwing stones would appeal to my boys.

By the time the removalists leave it's four o'clock. Mitch and I take another hour making up beds, hooking up the TV and unpacking the essentials. By the time that's all done, I'm exhausted – that deep, satisfied tiredness that makes your bones tingle when you stop moving. I flop down on the couch, amazed that I have a couch to flop down on after going without one for two weeks.

Two weeks!

How on earth did I manage?

The movers have positioned this miraculous piece of comfy softness in the sitting room opposite my old scratched coffee table, next to Alice's amazing fireplace. Beyond the coffee table they have set up my TV unit, which Mitch is hunched over, trying to get the DVD player to work.

'I don't think this is the right cable,' he mutters, but I'm too busy melting into the couch to respond. It's funny seeing my stuff here in this auspicious room – almost like they're ten per cent better quality just from being moved. I've rescued my things from suburban banality and brought them to this place of fantasy – furniture heaven.

My mother appears in the doorway and with a sigh I sit up. Time for phase two of our argument?

'No, no,' she smiles, 'don't get up. I just thought I'd let you know that I brought some soup with me, and some bread rolls.'

'Soup?' My mouth waters instantaneously.

'Pea and ham. It's in the fridge,' she explains. 'We can warm it up and have it for dinner.'

Pea and ham soup!

I used to have it all the time as a kid. Wordlessly, I get up and follow her into the kitchen, where she already has a pot on the stove and bread rolls on a chopping board. Oh my goodness, it smells divine!

'I told you not to move,' she scolds.

I say nothing – I had to see this to believe it. We've got a proper dining table again and my boys are sitting around it, bashing plastic cups impatiently on the table. Even Alfie is seated, which is a first. He never sits at the table waiting for his food, even when he's starving. He's always under it, draped across the chair on his stomach or doing laps around it.

They mustn't realise we're having soup.

Mitch comes into the room looking pleased with himself. 'Done! It's working. We have in-house entertainment.'

'And you're just in time for soup,' Francine announces as she places a steaming bowl on the table. 'Grace, this is yours.'

'Thanks,' I say, and sit down without hesitation. 'I'm starving.'

'Sometimes,' Charlie whispers huskily behind his hand to Mitch, 'Mummy eats lipstick.'

'Is that right?' Mitch's lips twitch as he sits down.

The soup is exactly how I remember it. Chunky, tasty and full of a homespun warmth. I'm halfway through my bowl before I notice that the boys, who are horrendously fussy with their food, are carefully pushing spoonfuls into their mouths and licking their lips. They're not even spilling any.

This can't be right. They do know this food is healthy, right?

I put my spoon down and ask cautiously, 'So, what do you guys think?'

'How come you don't cook this, Mummy?' asks Alfie. 'Grandma says it's bushranger soup.'

'Good for kangaroo hunting,' says Ryan.

'And rock climbing,' adds Charlie, oblivious to the soup wetting the tip of his nose.

'And building forts.'

I look quizzically at my mother, whose attention is focused on Mitch. 'Do you like it, Mitch?' she asks him.

'It's delicious. Thank you.'

'It was Grace's favourite soup growing up. She actually wasn't a very fussy child. Very easygoing, which is a trait you may have noticed in her as an adult.'

Huh?

It's almost like she's trying to recommend me as a friend, or . . .

Oh no.

This situation is confusing enough without her getting involved.

My spoon clatters into my bowl. 'Er . . . Mother –'

'Grace, why must you call me Mother in that highly formal way?' She smiles at Mitch. 'We're not English.'

'Mum –' I begin again, without success.

'I noticed a foldaway bed in the foyer,' Francine cuts me off as she slides into a chair with a bowl of her own. 'Who does that belong to?'

'That's the bed for our cousins,' Ryan tells her. 'For when they sleep over.'

'How handy,' my mother smiles. 'I've got to start thinking about where I'm going to sleep tonight. You don't happen to know any good hotels around here, do you, Grace?'

My eyes widen. 'You didn't organise any accommodation for tonight?'

'No.' Francine doesn't meet my eyes. 'I just thought I'd . . . wing it.'

'Wing it?' says Ryan. 'What does that mean?'

It means, she thought she'd try her luck staying here.

'It means,' Francine pats his hand, 'that I thought I'd be spontaneous.'

Ryan's brow wrinkles. 'I don't know what that means either.'

'It means,' Francine laughs, 'that I thought I'd have an adventure.' She looks up, but instead of eyeballing me she glances at Mitch. 'And what a fabulous adventure it's turning out to be.'

Mitch breaks off a piece of bread and shoves it into his mouth as though he's trying to keep himself from speaking.

'*I know!*' Alfie sits bolt upright in his chair. 'Why doesn't Grandma have a sleepover here?'

Why not indeed? Seems so logical, doesn't it?

She's got me cornered and she knows it. I can hardly kick her out at this hour, after she's looked after the kids all afternoon and fed us dinner. I grit my teeth.

'You can take one of the rooms upstairs, if you like,' I say. '*Just for tonight*. There are some spare bedrooms right next to Mitch's.'

'Next to Mitch.' She smiles sweetly at him. 'How lovely. I think I will.'

I feel the trap snap shut behind me. Mitch chokes on the bread he has stuffed into his mouth and reaches for his water.

'Slowly, slowly, dear.' Francine refills his glass and turns to the kids. 'Let this be a lesson to you, boys – don't eat too fast.'

My boys giggle. Kids always love it when a grown-up gets into trouble.

'Grandma, why you talk funny?' asks Charlie.

'You mean my accent?' Francine presses a hand to her chest. 'That's because long, long ago, when I was a little girl, I used to live in New York, in America.'

'In the olden days?' prompts Ryan.

'In the olden days.'

'Why did you come to live here?' asks Alfie.

'It's a long story.'

'Will you tell us the story?'

'Maybe in the morning.'

I try to shake off the unease delicately curling itself around my shoulders. It's only one night. She'll be leaving in the morning. It's a temporary arrangement. She's not moving in or anything.

There's nothing to worry about.

Chapter 29

After dinner, it's shower time. I spend the next hour washing the kids and getting them ready for bed. Ryan is excited about having his own room. Yesterday, I told him that he got it because he's the oldest, which it turns out was the wrong thing to say. He's been patronising Alfie and Charlie all evening, adding, 'You don't understand because you're too young,' to almost every conversation. Alfie looks like he's about to kill him.

'Okay, boys,' I clap my hands. 'Now that all your books are here, we can have a story before bed.'

'Yay!'

After rummaging through the box of books, Alfie announces, 'We want Mitch to read it.'

Mitch is sitting on the couch, reading the back of one of my romance novels. He quickly puts it down when he hears his name.

'Guys,' I say warningly, 'I don't think you should bother Mitch. He's tired. It's been a long day.'

I've never expected Mitch to participate in the bedtime ritual, and now that I know he's leaving in a couple of weeks

I'd really prefer he didn't. I've started trying to wean the boys off him by continually redirecting their attention. Not that it's had much of an effect. Alfie's attention shifts as often as the second hand on a clock anyway.

'I don't mind,' says Mitch tentatively.

'Yeah!' cry the boys. Before I can open my mouth, they dash over and crowd onto his lap and beside him. What's the point in saying no now?

I leave the room to help my mother clean up in the kitchen.

'He's so good with them,' she comments as we carry the dishes to the sink.

'I guess.'

'Such a lovely man.'

I decide to make my position clear before she gets any ideas. 'He's my tenant, Mum. I've already told you. He's staying here in exchange for free labour. Nothing more. In fact, he's leaving in a couple weeks.'

'I know,' Francine scoffs. 'I wasn't trying to imply anything.'

Yes you were.

'I was just thinking that you're single and he's single.'

I screw up my face. 'How do you know he's single?' I haven't dared ask him that question myself.

'I . . . er . . .' Francine prevaricates and then adds hastily, 'Well, isn't it obvious? No wedding ring.'

'He could have a girlfriend,' I suggest.

Francine snorts. 'Believe me, if a man like that had a girlfriend, she'd be in your face twenty-four-seven about him living here.'

'O-kay.'

Francine tosses her head. 'Just saying.'

We are quiet for a moment as I fill my lovely new sink with hot water. It seems so luxurious.

'Thanks for letting me stay,' Francine says quietly, grabbing a tea towel. 'I know you don't want me to.'

'It's just one night,' I say tightly.

'Yes,' Francine agrees. 'Just one night.'

When the dishes are done, Mitch and the boys emerge from the sitting room.

'All done,' announces Charlie.

'And time for bed.' I smile at him. Tucking them all in turns out to be uneventful. Instead of the usual onslaught of 'We're not tired' and 'We don't want to go to sleep', they go willingly, eager to try out their new bedrooms.

I tuck them into bed, kiss them and turn out the lights. They might be out of bed again in five minutes, but at least it's a good start.

This is the point in the evening when Mitch and I would usually say goodnight. He'd go up to his room and shut the door and I'd take a folding chair into the sitting room and read, or have an early night. Given our arrangement, I didn't wanted to muddy the waters with further interaction. Hanging out with him every night in a big house, even in the presence of three sleeping boys, might have been a little . . . not so professionally distant. Though I wonder whether we've actually been as 'professional' as we should have been during the day.

However, now there's a TV in the house, and also my mother. So what am I going to do? Dismiss them both like school children?

I'm just about to suggest we watch a DVD when Francine says, 'So, Mitch, the boys say you have a guitar in your room.'

His eyes flick up, showing some surprise and just a little bit of caution. 'I do.'

'I love music,' Francine gushes. 'I'll listen to anything, from classical to pop, rap to rhapsody.'

He nods noncommittally and says, 'It's getting pretty late.'

It's actually only 7.42 pm, but I immediately agree. 'It's been such a long day.'

'You wouldn't mind playing me something, would you?' says Francine. 'I would love that.'

You can't be serious.

I'm astounded. You can't just ask a stranger to play for you. Who does that?

'Mum,' I protest, 'I don't think Mitch really wants to. I mean, Antoine says his guitar skills are rudimentary at best. He can't take requests or anything.'

Mitch, who is about to address my mother, closes his mouth and turns back to me. 'I beg your pardon?'

I look at him uncertainly. Can't he see I'm trying to get him out of a tight spot? 'I was just trying to explain to Mum that you're not an expert.'

'Yeah, but I'm not incompetent.' He folds his arms.

My jaw drops. 'I didn't say you were. I just –' I break off, not wanting to put my foot in it even further.

'Well, if he's not incompetent, Grace, let him sing us a song.'

'First you want him to play his guitar and now you want him to sing as well?' I look at my mother like she's sprouted another head. Perhaps she might suggest he add a little dance routine with it next. 'He's not a performing monkey, Mum.'

She stares back at me innocently, then turns to Mitch. 'I didn't mean to offend.'

'Not at all.'

I turn in surprise to see Mitch is going upstairs. He returns with a guitar and an iPad I've never seen before. I wonder what other gadgets he's got in that black duffel bag of his.

He turns on the iPad and goes into what appears to be an extensive library of sheet music. Song after song after song – all different types, varieties and genres. He hands the device to me with a challenge in his eyes. 'Pick anything you like.'

'Er . . . okay.'

I flick through the music. Half the songs I don't recognise, the rest are a variety of hit pop songs from a myriad of different artists I don't keep track of. Music charts aren't my thing, but I will sing along to the radio in the car sometimes. I mean, who doesn't?

'Give me that,' says Francine, snatching the device from me. Mitch sits down on the couch with his guitar and thrums a hand tentatively over the strings. I tilt my head and really look at him. He looks awfully comfortable with the instrument . . .

'This one!' announces Francine in a sudden burst of inspiration. I look over her shoulder and see that the song she has chosen is 'Amazing Grace'.

This is not a surprising choice. It was one of my father's favourite hymns, and it's the song I was named after. It has a lot of meaning for her, and memories for me. Maybe she's trying to build another bridge between us. But is it really right to use Mitch to do that?

'Mum –' I protest.

'He said any song.' Mum lifts her chin haughtily at me and passes the iPad to Mitch, who takes it from her and stands it on the coffee table in front of him. 'Is that song all right?' she asks him sweetly.

Mitch looks at the song for a minute and then up at me. 'It's perfect.'

I stifle a groan. This is going to be unbearable.

And then Mitch starts to play.

He tentatively plucks the all-too-familiar notes with a gentleness I hadn't expected. 'Amazing Grace' is such a firm, solemn song. I'm used to church choirs and soaring notes, pomp and ceremony. But he distils the notes to barely a whisper, and when he finally starts to sing, I'm floored by the humble timbre of his voice.

'*Amazing Grace, how sweet the sound. That saved a wretch like me.*' There's a slight catch in his voice at the word 'wretch', and I can feel the very fibres of his humanity tingling over my skin.

'*I once was lost, but now am found. Was blind, but now I see.*'

His voice is enfolding me, pulling me in and holding me close. There's an unmistakable welling in my heart, like he's filling it up, note by note. To my horror, a wetness starts to sting the backs of my eyes.

'*'Twas Grace that taught my heart to fear, And grace, my fears relieved; How precious did that grace appear, The hour I first believed.*'

The song goes on but I don't hear the lyrics anymore, I just look at him, absolutely mesmerised by the rawness and beauty of his talent.

When he finishes, I sit and stare at him, unable to speak. My mother has tears openly streaming down her face. She walks over and kisses him on the cheek.

'Thank you,' she says.

His gaze travels from my mother to me, seeking my opinion.

I lift my hands helplessly. 'Pardon the pun, but that was *amazing*.'

His smile is wide and boyish, his eyes sparkling like I've just given him the best present ever.

'Have you thought about taking it more seriously, making a career of it?' I add. His smile wavers slightly, so I rush on. 'I really think you could do this professionally if you put the work in. You've got so much raw talent.'

'*Raw* talent?'

The look in his eyes suggests that I've offended him, which was not my intention at all. I try again with maximum positivity in my voice.

'You've got great tone, Mitch. You should really nurture it.'

'Great tone,' he smiles slightly. 'What does that mean exactly?'

'Actually,' I admit, feeling my cheeks heat a little under his steady gaze, 'I'm not too sure. But I did watch *The Voice*, back when I was breastfeeding and had time to sit on the couch.'

'You watched *The Voice*.'

'Yeah, you know,' I say enthusiastically, 'that singing competition where the contestants get coached by industry professionals? I reckon they would definitely say you have great tone. Or huge potential. Or something like that.'

'Something like that?' Mitch's voice is faint.

'Yes. I forget all the buzzwords.' I glance at my mother, who looks like she's trying not to burst out laughing. Desperately, I pass the ball to her. 'What do you think, Mum?'

'I think you know a lot more buzzwords than I do,' Francine chuckles.

Thanks for nothing!

While I'm still glaring at her, Mitch slides his guitar off his lap and then back into its case. 'You know what,' he stands up, 'I think I might go upstairs and work on my tone, or . . . something.'

Now *I know* I've offended him. 'I didn't mean for you to work on it immediately,' I blurt.

'I know,' he chuckles. 'But I'm feeling inspired.'

'Er . . . okay. Good.' I nod.

He picks up his guitar and leaves the room. I round on my mother as soon he disappears up the stairs. 'You could have helped me out, you know. I was just trying to encourage him.'

'I'm sorry, darling.' She finally gives in to her laughter. 'I was having way too much fun just watching.'

After that train wreck, I decide to play it cool on Saturday morning by not mentioning the incident at all. The boys make it easy by rising early and casting enough chaos in their wake that there's no time for awkward small talk anyway.

'The tooth fairy came!' Alfie comes running into my bedroom at first light. Given the tooth fairy forgot the night before, this is news indeed.

'What?' I jerk upright in bed. I didn't put any money under his pillow last night, either. I completely forgot. Again!

'She did? When?'

'Last night.' He frowns at my stupidity. 'See?' He waves the note gleefully in my face. 'Ten bucks!'

He runs out of the room, holding it aloft.

Ten bucks!

I never leave more than a dollar or two.

I toss the covers back and swing my feet to the floor. Man,

it's nice having a bed again! Ten bucks, however, is going to cause problems.

As if on cue, Ryan's voice rings out from the kitchen.

'Mum! How come Alfie got ten bucks from the tooth fairy?'

I stagger into the kitchen to sort it out. Five minutes later my mum and Mitch both make an appearance, because the noise still has not settled.

'The *tooth fairy* gave Alfie *ten dollars*,' I inform them both sternly.

'Ten dollars!' my mother squeaks. 'But doesn't the tooth fairy normally –'

'Give only a dollar or two,' I fill in for her. 'Yes, she does.'

'Wow.' Mitch scratches the back of his head, his eyes darting this way and that. 'Maybe the tooth fairy won lotto and only had large notes and no loose change –'

'Regardless of whether the tooth fairy is flush with money or not,' I interrupt stiffly, 'the tooth fairy should have asked her banker whether spending all her winnings on one child was a wise investment.'

'Yes,' he looks sheepish. 'Perhaps the tooth fairy should have done that. Of course, if the banker hadn't already gone to bed and forgotten *again* that the tooth fairy was visiting, perhaps he/she would have done so.'

'The banker,' I say crossly, 'was tired and can't be expected to be on the ball all the time. If the tooth fairy really wanted to –'

'I don't care,' Alfie cuts me off crossly. 'I've got ten dollars!'

'You'll have to share that money with your brothers,' I say sternly. 'It's only fair. The tooth fairy doesn't win lotto all the time.'

'Awwwww!'

Debate finally settled, I offer everyone breakfast. We all sit down to Weet-Bix and milk and discuss our plans for the day. Ryan and Alfie start school on Monday, and I have their uniforms but I need to get them some new shoes and hats for the summer term. Also, Alfie's lunch box cracked in the move, or maybe he stepped on it – I'm not sure. Whatever the case, I need to get him a new one of those as well. I announce that I'm taking the boys into town to get some things.

'Shall I start taking the tiles off the walls in the boys' bathroom while you're out?' Mitch asks.

'Don't you want a day off?' I ask, surprised. 'I'm not a slavedriver. You can take the weekend, you know.'

'I know.' He smiles. 'But I'll feel silly sitting around doing nothing.'

I swallow. 'No worries. Knock yourself out.'

I turn to my mother. 'I suppose you'll be heading off then?'

'Very shortly,' she nods. 'But I was thinking –'

Here we go.

'– that if you want, I could come with you to the shops.'

My eyes narrow. 'Why?'

'To give you a hand. Trying on shoes with three boys is no easy feat.'

I have to admit, I wasn't looking forward to it. Trying to get one boy to comply while keeping the other two from playing hide and seek between the shoe racks isn't exactly a fun time. It would be amazing to have another set of hands, and after witnessing her Mary Poppins routine yesterday I'm sure she would be competent.

I can't ignore that niggling feeling of doubt still tapping on the side of my head, though. Mum has been sober before. She's fallen off the wagon before. I can handle it because I'm expecting it. But if she makes my boys fall in love with her and then lets them down, I'll be furious – not just at her, but at myself, for letting it happen.

She can read the indecision in my face. 'I'm still leaving, Grace. It's just one morning at the shops. We're not popping in at the pub afterwards or anything.'

I blanch.

'Sorry.' She looks away. 'You didn't deserve that.'

No, I didn't.

I'm angry, but for some reason her pleading softens my resolve. Clearly, this holds some meaning for her. It seems churlish to turn her down when all she'll be doing is helping me out. Big time.

Ten minutes later the five of us head out to Busselton. It's a surprisingly smooth morning, if you don't count Alfie completely emptying a shelf in Kmart while I try to find sneakers in Ryan's size and Mum chases Charlie through the boots and thongs.

When we move on to lunch boxes, Mum ends up buying them all one – 'her treat' – despite the fact that it was only Alfie who needed one.

'When am I going to get this opportunity again?' she asks.

I roll my eyes, seeing the question as both a trap and a bid for sympathy, but let her help them pick the most expensive lunch boxes in stock. They're all licensed, of course – Spider-Man, Pokémon and Thomas the Tank Engine. If it had been me buying they would have picked a colour, not a superhero.

The nagging for food begins at the check-out.

'Mummy, we're soooo hungry.'

'We're starving to death.'

'You're not starving to death,' I protest. 'You only had breakfast an hour ago.'

'We need to have hot chips.'

'You *need* to have hot chips?' I repeat contemptuously.

'If we don't eat something soon we'll die.'

They clasp their hands under their chins like the orphans in *Oliver Twist*. Oh please.

'Let's have morning tea,' says Grandma, who can do no wrong. 'My treat.'

I swear, if this woman says 'My treat' one more time . . .

'Come on, Grace.' Her eyes twinkle at me. 'You can have a cappuccino.'

Ha! The magic word. She should have opened with that.

We walk into a cafe in the shopping centre and grab a table. As we pick up our menus, I hear someone calling my name, and look up to see Bob Fletcher.

'Oh, hi, Bob.' I lift my hand in an awkward half-wave. It's hard not to feel a little uncomfortable now that I know about his secret affair with Alice. 'How are you?'

'Fabulous,' he grins. 'I had a meeting with a client in Busselton this morning. Just grabbing a coffee and then it's back to the office.'

'Right.'

I expect him to walk on then – it's not like we know each other that well – but he lingers by our table, so I feel compelled to introduce him to my mother.

'Bob, this is my mother, Francine. She's in town for a visit.' I turn to Mum, who is examining us both with some interest. 'Mum, this is Bob. He owns Fletchers, the er . . . real estate agency that was going to sell Gum Leaf Grove before I decided to stay.'

He holds out his hand to Francine, who shakes it politely. 'Lovely to meet you, Bob.'

'Likewise.'

'Sorry the sale agreement came to nothing,' I add. 'I didn't mean to waste your agency's time.'

'Not at all.' He spreads his hands and his smile seems to widen. 'I think it's very romantic that you decided to stay in town for Scott.'

'Huh?'

'He told me you two are seriously dating.' He leans in conspiratorially. 'I'm very happy for him.'

'Uh, thanks.' My automatic response barely covers my surprise.

He straightens. 'He deserves to meet someone special, and it's good for Alice's grandkids to have a strong male influence in their lives. Their grandmother would have wanted that.'

The way he says it momentarily distracts me. Bob's feelings for my late mother-in-law are written all over his face. The love and regret in his eyes are palpable. Their timing may have been bad, but I believe they truly loved each other. Perhaps if Bob and Alice had managed to get together, Jake might have turned out a different person. And David Bowman might have had a chance to start again. Bob ruffles Ryan's and Alfie's hair awkwardly. 'Well, enjoy your lunch! I'll see you when you're next in Dunsborough visiting you-know-who.'

He gives me a wink, as though he's aware this will be sooner rather than later, and totters off, swinging his briefcase like he's just sold the largest property in town.

I stare after him in shock. Scott told him we were dating. No, *seriously* dating.

We've kissed. Had a few flirty phone calls and talked about seeing each other.

But we haven't actually been on a single date. He knows that, right?

Not that I'm averse to dating him. I'd really like to. I just thought that maybe I'd be more aware of whether I was or not.

'Mummy?' Ryan's brow is wrinkled. 'What is dating?'

'It means being really, really good friends.'

'Oh,' says Ryan, slowly digesting this.

'So Scott, huh?' Francine looks up from her menu to eyeball me. 'You never mentioned you were *really good friends* with anyone in the area.'

I pick up my own menu firmly, giving her a pointed look. 'I'd rather not talk about it.' I lower my voice. 'Especially here.' My eyes flicker towards the children.

'Very well,' Francine shrugs. We order coffee, cake and a mandatory basket of hot chips and the subject is allowed to drop. I should have known that her compliance would be short-lived, however.

•

Not five minutes after we return to Gum Leaf Grove, she corners me in the kitchen. I'm unpacking a box of dinnerware. Mitch is taking tiles off in the bathroom and the kids are playing hopscotch outside.

'So who is this Scott character anyway?'

I nearly jump out of my skin at her sudden appearance at my elbow.

'Huh?' I prevaricate. 'Shouldn't you be packing? I thought you were leaving this afternoon.'

'Soon. I want to know what's going on with you.'

I give a choked sort of laugh. 'Nothing is going on with me.'

'Why didn't you tell me you were seeing someone?'

'It never came up.' I walk away and sit down at the table, where there are some tea towels to be folded. She follows me.

'Don't you think I would want to know if you were in a relationship?'

'You've never cared about that information before.' I glare at her, thinking about her no-show at my wedding, her absence at the birth of each of my children and during my volatile divorce.

'I realise I haven't been a very involved mother in the past –'

'Try *not at all*!' I snap back.

Her face seems to shrink slightly. 'I have a lot to make up for, Grace. *Obviously*. But can't you see I'm trying?'

'I never asked you to try.'

'Just please tell me. Is it really too much to ask?'

I heave a sigh. 'Scott is the real estate agent who was going to sell this house before I decided to stay.'

'And . . .'

'He asked me out.'

'So you're in a serious relationship?'

'I wouldn't call it serious.'

'So you're just dating.'

'Well, we haven't exactly been on a proper date yet.'

My mother groans in frustration. 'Grace, are you seeing him or not?'

I put down the tea towel I'm folding. 'It's complicated.'

I look up to find my mother staring at me. Her lips are pulled in a taut line. 'You are terrible.'

'Terrible?'

She pulls out a chair and sits down opposite me, clearly getting ready to tell me off.

Okay, she does not get to scold me! Particularly as I've done absolutely nothing wrong. Since when is my love-life everybody else's business? First Mitch, now her.

'You don't seem to realise it, but you are stringing along two men.'

'What?' I scoff. 'No I'm not.'

'Yes, you are,' my mother insists. 'I can see not one but two men vying for your attention here.'

I frown. Sure, Scott may be after me, but with Mitch, it's more like the other way around. He's leaving in two weeks. And he specifically told me that a 'woman like me' should 'wait'.

Ha!

'*Grace.*' My mother is trying to reclaim my attention. 'This is serious.'

I roll my eyes. 'Surely you're not suggesting Mitch again.'

'Who else would I be suggesting?'

Thank goodness she hasn't met Antoine!

'Well, I don't know.' I refuse to meet her eyes. 'But this is just silly.'

'Why is it silly?'

'Because he doesn't think of me that way. He's my friend.'

'Honey, darling, sweetheart, that's the only way he thinks of you.'

There's a sudden kick in my chest. 'No, he doesn't,' I scoff, but my voice wavers tellingly.

'I've seen the way he looks at you,' says my mother. 'More importantly, I've seen the way you look at him.'

I ignore that last bit and attack the first. 'He doesn't *look* at me.'

'Why shouldn't he?' my mother argues back. 'You're gorgeous. Those eyes, that hair. You don't look like you've ever been pregnant in your life, or that you actually eat . . . We'll talk about you putting on weight later. Right now I think you need to wake up, Grace. You're not that old. You're thirty-five. So stop acting like you're in your twilight years.'

'That's not how I act.'

'No, you're right,' my mother finally agrees. 'How you act is naive. He's more than just your handyman, Grace. Blind Freddy could see that in a fit. You rely on him for everything. Is that really fair?'

'I . . .'

'And then what about this poor Scott guy, who thinks you're his girlfriend? Does Mitch know about him?'

'Yes, and he's fine with it.'

Francine snorts. 'You can't lead them on, darling. It's not right. You need to decide if you're dating Scott or not. If you are, then ring him up and go on a date. I'll even look after the kids for you.'

I quickly shake my head. 'I couldn't.'

'Yes, you could. I'm right here, offering my services.'

'But –'

'You know the kids are perfectly comfortable with me.'

'I guess,' I admit reluctantly.

'So,' my mother prompts me, 'go and find out whether you actually want this man. And if not, then let him go. Don't lead him on. He deserves better than that, and so does Mitch.'

I throw up my hands. 'I have never been ambiguous with either of them.'

'Are you sure? It seems to me that you're neither here nor there. Or that this Scott character is playing some kind of game with you.'

This gives me pause. 'What kind of game?'

'I don't know.' My mother spreads her hands. 'You're the one who knows him. Doesn't it seem weird to you that he's telling people that not only are you seriously dating, but that you moved towns for him?'

Not just weird. Downright presumptuous!

'Call him. Find out what's going on.' My mother's voice suddenly sounds alarmingly like Rachel's. High-pitched, bossy and . . . annoyingly correct.

'Okay, okay,' I agree. 'I'll call him.'

'Now.'

'*Okay.*'

I get up and go into Ryan's bedroom, where our only connection to the outside world is still located. I'm really going to have to get a line set up in the kitchen, and maybe get my modem hooked up.

I sit down on Ryan's bed and fish my mobile out of my pocket, where I have Scott's number saved. Then I dial out on the ancient landline.

He picks up almost immediately, making me freeze with stage fright. To be honest, I had been expecting it to go to voicemail.

'Hello?' he repeats in his low, attractive voice.

'Hi, Scott. It's me, Grace.'

'Grace!' He seems genuinely pleased. 'I was just thinking of you.'

'Oh.' I try to sound aloof rather than nervous. 'Are you back in town yet?'

'Yep, got in last night. How have you been? Has all your furniture arrived okay?'

'Yes, moving day went really smoothly. Actually, I was out shopping earlier and I ran into your boss.'

'Bob?' He laughs and then groans. 'Uh-oh. Did he freak you out?'

I'm relieved he's anticipated this, and feel my bunched shoulders relax slightly.

'I made the mistake of telling him that we've been talking about going out sometime. He's been pestering me to get a girlfriend for ages.' He chuckles. 'We're pretty close. He's been my boss for about ten years. So when I told him, he was so excited, I think he's already planning the wedding. Sorry. I hope he didn't frighten you off.'

'No, no, that's okay,' I assure him. 'Not frightened at all.'

'Good to hear,' he enthuses. 'Because we've got to organise our first date. Hopefully sometime soon?'

'Well, actually,' I take a deep breath, 'my mother is in town at the moment and she's offered to babysit.' Wow. It feels strange saying that – involuntarily natural, and yet not quite right. I'm so struck by my own words that I almost miss his reply.

'How about Monday night for dinner? Unfortunately most of the wineries are closed at night, but we could go to Caves House. It's an old hotel that serves really great food.'

'No problem.'

'I'll book it in then. Pick you up at six?'

'Sounds great.'

I put the phone down and place a hand on my spinning head. I'm not sure if it's excitement or nausea.

I have a date.

Chapter 30

On the first day of school I'm definitely more nervous than Alfie, whose only concern is whether the playground at South West Primary will be as big as the one at his old school.

'And do they have monkey bars?' he demands. 'There's got to be monkey bars.'

Yes, I think, because otherwise where will all the monkeys play?

Ryan, however, is quiet as a mouse on the way there, like he's pulling together his reserves of courage. I'm touched by his brave, pale face. He doesn't breathe a single word to me about his fears, but he's clutching his backpack like it's a shield.

'Everything's going to be fine, you know,' I tell him gently.

Ryan looks at me briefly, then returns his gaze to the scenery out the window. 'I know.'

'I've spoken to your teacher. She's lovely, and she told me she's seated you next to one of the nicest kids in the class. They're going to help you settle in.'

He looks at me a little more hopefully this time. 'Okay.'

Ryan's teacher is actually Eve's sister Phoebe – Ms Maxwell. I met her last week. She's a fountain of energy and optimism, which will be so good for Ryan, who definitely needs a shot of positivity right now. He tends to build things up so much in his head that by the time they actually happen, he's burned all his confidence away in anticipation. Can't think where he gets that from . . .

I have left Charlie, who doesn't start kindy until next year, at home with my mother. It'll be much easier to settle the boys into their new classrooms without him. It's funny how easily Francine seems to be slotting herself into my life. I'm not sure if I should start panicking yet, or give it a little longer.

I walk both boys to their classes, get their bags unpacked and kiss them goodbye. As I return to the car park, I see Eve, Bronwyn and a woman I don't know standing by the kerb under a tree.

'Grace,' Bronwyn calls out, lifting her hand and waving enthusiastically, 'you're here! I was wondering what school you decided to send your boys to.'

'Well, now you know,' I laugh. 'Hi, Eve.'

'Hi, Grace.' She flashes me a sincere smile. 'Great to see you again. Looks like we'll be running into each other a lot more now.'

Bronwyn gestures to the lady beside her, who has been watching me shyly. 'This is Sue. Her daughter, Olivia, is in Ryan's year.'

I hold out my hand. 'Lovely to meet you, Sue.'

'You too.' Sue shakes my hand warmly. 'Welcome to the school.'

'How are the renovations at Gum Leaf Grove going?' Eve asks.

Bronwyn's lips twitch suspiciously. 'Antoine says that, due to his guidance and insight, you've really managed to lift the vitality of the place.'

I snort. 'He said that, did he?'

'Don't worry,' Bronwyn chuckles, 'it's not like I believed a word of it. But it is becoming clear to me that he doesn't have a crush on you.'

'That's . . . er, good.' I chew self-consciously on my lower lip.

'In fact,' Bronwyn looks at me knowingly, 'he's been hinting that you've got someone else in the picture.'

'He has?' I respond casually, but my efforts are ruined by the fact that I won't meet her eyes. Who has he been hinting about? Scott . . . or Mitch? I feel my face going red.

Eve lifts her nose to the wind with overacted intrigue. 'Hmmm, do I smell gossip?'

'Well, if you must know,' I say slowly, 'there is a bit of romance in the air. I have a date tonight with my ex-real estate agent. His name is Scott.'

'Do you know him, Eve?' Bronwyn asks.

'No. Should I?'

'Do you mean Scott Hunter?' Sue's features have sharpened.

'Yes,' I nod. 'Do you know him?'

'I do.' Sue seems to squeeze the words out. 'I'm sorry,' she says before I can ask any further questions, 'I just realised, I'm late for . . . the, er . . . gym. I have a class. I better go. Nice to see you, ladies.' She turns back to Bronwyn and Eve and smiles more warmly at them. 'Here's to a fresh new term.'

Abruptly, she jogs off.

'Was she weird just then?' Bronwyn asks. 'Or is it just me?'

'No, she was weird.' Eve frowns. 'Scott Hunter an old boyfriend, perhaps?'

Damn, I hope not. The last thing I want when forming a new group of friends is to wind up dating somebody's ex.

'I don't think so.' Bronwyn shrugs. 'Besides, Sue adores her husband.'

'Yes,' Eve agrees, then slaps a hand to her head. 'Wait, did you say real estate agent?'

I nod.

'From Fletchers?'

'Yes.'

Eve rolls her eyes. 'Sue's husband is Sean Fletcher, the property manager there.'

'I've met him.' My eyes widen. 'He's Bob Fletcher's nephew. Seemed nice enough, though Scott doesn't overly like him.'

'Well,' Eve says, 'Sue said last week there's been a bit of family drama going on in the office. Bob's looking at the succession plan for when he retires. Sue's husband was supposed to step into the top spot, but now Bob's considering someone else.'

'Scott maybe?' grins Bronwyn.

'I don't know,' I say slowly.

'The plot thickens,' Eve laughs.

'Sorry to cut this short,' Bronwyn looks at her watch, 'but I've got to get back to Oak Hills before Antoine notices I forgot to restock the shiraz in the cellar door.'

'No worries,' Eve smiles. 'It's back to the restaurant for me.' Eve is a chef, I recall. 'What about you, Grace? What are you doing today?'

'Job hunting,' I respond promptly.

'Well, good luck!'

'And have fun on your date.' Bronwyn waves as she starts walking away.

I drive into the Dunsborough town centre and locate a cafe with free wifi. I want to look at job advertisements, and email out a few résumés. While I'm at it, I google internet providers and arrange to have Gum Leaf Grove hooked up. Dancing along the edge of my property, my phone held high over my head, trying to find that sweet spot Mitch keeps talking about, is getting pretty old. It will be nice to be able to get online in peace. Some schools don't go back till tomorrow, and there's a group of what I can only assume are private school girls giggling so loudly at the table next to me I can barely hear myself think.

'Maybe he's, like, gone underground,' one of them is saying. 'Found a cave to hide in or something.'

'Well, if that happened to me, I would *totally* do that,' says her friend, flicking her long hair over her shoulders. 'Can you imagine! He must look like a Batman villain now.'

I close my laptop in frustration. I'm not going to get much more done with them talking so loudly. Besides, I need to find a bank and deposit my mother's cheque.

Or should I hold onto it a little longer?

I pull it out of my pocket and look at it. Was I stupid to have taken this? It's been three days and she's still in my house. Not only that, she's advising me on my life choices.

Then again, maybe I need the advice.

I take out my mobile and call Rachel.

'Did you know she was coming here?' I say as soon as she picks up.

'Well, hello to you too,' Rachel says cheerfully. 'Furniture arrive safely?'

'Mum is here. She's been living with me for the past three days.'

'Wow, really?' Rachel sounds surprised, but not unhappy. 'So what do you think?'

'What you mean, what do I think? I'm totally freaked out. And I'm holding this cheque of hers and I'm seriously considering giving it back. Even though with this much money I could redo the whole kitchen and probably all three bathrooms too.'

'Grace, don't. She'd be so hurt.'

'Yes, but –'

'How's she been?' Rachel interrupts me.

'Fine.'

'Just fine?'

'Okay, she's been quite helpful,' I say grudgingly. 'I've been pretty surprised.'

'Well, why not let her surprise you for a couple more days?' Rachel suggests. 'And just hold on to the cheque for a while if it makes you feel better.'

I decide to take her advice. We chat a little longer, then I hang up and head home.

When I get there, Mum is playing with Charlie in the sitting room and Mitch is in the roof identifying rotten beams that will need to be replaced. Fortunately we don't have termites, just a severe case of age.

To be honest, I haven't seen much of him since Sunday morning, when my mother announced to the kids that she was staying another couple of nights because 'Your mummy is having a night out with her friend Scott.'

The boys were ecstatic. Apparently Grandma, who feeds them hot chips and Skittles, is welcome for as long as she likes. Mitch, however, went up into the roof and has only come down for meals and sleep since then. I know my mother wants me to read something into this, but I'm sticking to my guns and ignoring it completely. Mitch's absence isn't a sign of jealousy. I think it's more indicative of the fact that he just doesn't care.

The day passes quite quickly. I've only unpacked a couple of boxes before it's time to pick up the kids from school again. When I arrive outside Alfie's classroom he comes running out, bag slung over one shoulder, hat completely askew.

'Mummy, guess what?'

'What?'

'I've got a new best friend.'

My heart warms. 'That's wonderful, Alfie. What's his name?'

'I don't know,' Alfie shrugs. 'But his dad drives a tractor.'

'Wow,' I exclaim and ruffle his hair. 'The prerequisite for all good friendships.'

We walk on to Ryan's classroom, where I'm pleased to see my older son engaged in a highly animated conversation with another kid. He doesn't even notice me, but Ms Maxwell does. She comes out of the classroom wreathed in smiles, a piece of paper in her hand. I'm struck for the first time by how good-looking she is, her dark hair pulled back in an elegant knot and the best kind of creamy skin.

'I just wanted to let you know that Ryan had a wonderful first day,' she tells me. 'I know you were a little worried, but he's made so many new friends and he did a great presentation this morning.'

'Presentation?' I'm stunned. *On his first day?*

'Well, we were doing profiles of ourselves today. Filling out a fact sheet and then, if they wanted to, the students shared them with the class.'

'And Ryan presented his?' I'm pleasantly surprised.

'Yes, he did,' she nods enthusiastically. 'And I thought you might like to see what he presented. It's pretty special.'

'Oh?' I take the paper from her outstretched hand.

Ryan has drawn a particularly good impression of himself inside a box that takes up a quarter of the page. The eyes could be better aligned and the hair less green, but otherwise it's his spitting image. I look at the bulleted facts that he's filled in with uneven handwriting. His name, his age, birthday, favourite TV show, favourite colour, favourite food – I laugh when I read 'sausages'. The list goes on. And then I get to the last line, which asks for his personal hero. Next to that he's written:

My mum.

I put my hand over my mouth and gasp, my eyes immediately filling.

'I know, right?' says Phoebe, a hand to her cheek.

As soon as we get home the boys run into the house, screaming out for my mum and Mitch.

'They have three sets of monkey bars. A big one, a little one and a medium one.'

'My desk has a drawer!'

'The canteen sells popcorn at recess!'

'We're going on an excursion to The Maze next week!'

'Oh my goodness, oh my goodness, oh my goodness,' my mother says as she wraps them in her arms. Mitch raises an eyebrow at me. I know I must look a little frazzled, and a bit red around the eyes. 'All settled in?' he asks.

Wordlessly, I pass him Ryan's profile sheet and he scans it. A little smile turns up the corners of his mouth and he glances back at me knowingly.

'So did you cry?'

'Discreetly,' I tell him. 'All the way home.'

Chapter 31

When you haven't been on a real date in just under ten years, you tend to experience a bit of performance anxiety when getting back in the game. I've changed my outfit three times. In the end, I settle on my version of the little black dress, which I usually wear for job interviews or corporate lunches. It's a sleeveless V-necked number with a flowy skirt and a belted waist. I decide to 'date it up' with jewellery and strappy black scandals.

I add make-up, leave my hair out and choose a soft black cardigan to take with me in case it's cold. At five to six, I make my entrance in the kitchen, where the boys, Mitch and my mother are having dinner. All five of them stop what they are doing and stare at me. The sudden attention makes me feel a tad self-conscious.

'What?'

'Mummy, you look beautiful,' says Ryan.

'Do I?'

'Yes.' Charlie licks the back of his spoon. 'Very, very bootaful.'

'He'll be knocked off his feet,' my mother exclaims.

'Thank you.'

Mitch picks up his fork and resumes eating. He doesn't look at me again until Scott arrives.

'Have a good time,' he says quietly.

'I will.'

He doesn't greet Scott at all, and Scott gives absolutely no indication that Mitch even exists. He leans in to place a peck on my cheek.

'You look great,' he says, then takes my arm and leads me out.

I have to say, I'm not at all disappointed by Caves House. It's a lovely double-storey old-style hotel, a combination of timber and brick with a gorgeous stone porch. The tiled roof is framed by dark timber, contrasting with the light-coloured balcony on the second storey. It's surrounded by gardens, and I can hear the gentle hum of happy diners as we mount the stone steps.

'At last,' Scott grabs my hand and tilts his head close to mine, 'I have you all to myself.'

Warmth mixed with uncertainty spreads inside my chest. Tonight is all about making a decision. Do I want to date this man or not? I don't really know him that well. Not like I know Mitch. I mean, I know what Mitch likes for breakfast every morning. What makes him cranky. What makes him smile. Scott is still a bit of a mystery.

'So,' Scott says after we secure a table in the main dining area, 'how was your day?'

The question is so mundane compared to the depth of my thoughts that I almost breathe a sigh of relief.

'Great. Today was the kids' first day of school.'

'And how was it?' he enquires as he fills my water glass.

I smile and launch into the story that made my afternoon. The moment when Ryan's teacher came out of her classroom to show me his profile sheet.

'So then next to personal hero he's written *my mum*,' I say, feeling myself begin to well up again.

'That's really great,' says Scott as he picks up the menu and starts perusing the dishes on offer. 'Just so you know, the steak here is excellent. Some places, it's touch and go, but this chef always gets it perfect if you order it medium-rare.' He wrinkles his nose and looks concerned. 'You don't like your steak well done, do you?'

I pause. 'Er, no.'

'Oh good.' He looks down again and keeps reading.

That's it? Did he miss it? The moment where my son affirmed his love for me? Because I'm sure the 'awww' cue was as clear as day. Maybe it's because he doesn't have kids. It's not that he's insensitive or anything – he just doesn't get it.

Mitch got it.

I bite my lower lip impatiently.

Yeah, but I'm not on a date with Mitch, am I?

I take a breath. 'So, how was your day?'

Crow's feet appear attractively around his eyes. 'Busy but excellent.'

'Well, that's good.'

'I had my usual clients and home opens to deal with, but Bob and I made some time today to go over the business structure. I'll be taking over as principal when he retires, which will actually be at the end of the year.'

I blink, remembering my conversation with Eve and Bronwyn this morning. 'But doesn't he have a nephew who's supposed to take over? Sean, isn't it?'

'That was before Bob and I agreed I would be buying into the business.'

'You're buying into Fletchers?' I raise my eyebrows.

'Fifty per cent,' Scott looks pleased with himself. 'The deal hasn't gone through yet, but we're in the process of writing up the partnership agreement.'

Something doesn't sit right.

'But what about Sean?' I say slowly. 'I thought Bob was really against people selling their family businesses. He seemed almost disappointed when I said I was selling Gum Leaf Grove that day we first met.'

'Bob does like to keep things in the family,' Scott nods, sounding like the attitude has been a thorn in his side for a while now. 'Don't get me wrong, this wasn't an easy deal. I've been lobbying Bob for years to go into partnership with me, but he was so concerned about chopping Sean's inheritance in half he wouldn't sell.' Scott groans. 'Didn't help that Sean kept laying the guilt trip on him.'

'Well, do you blame him?' I ask. 'He probably didn't want his uncle chopping the family business in half.'

'Or me being in charge come December.'

'No wonder his wife gave me the cold shoulder when she found out I was dating you,' I respond dryly. 'It must be rough for her husband. Especially if he's been groomed to run the business his whole life.'

Scott is not very sympathetic. 'Life is all about change. Look at you.' He reaches over and squeezes my hand. 'You're the perfect example.'

I know he's trying to compliment me, but somehow I don't feel flattered. I slip my hand out from under his. 'There's something I don't quite get.'

'What's that?' He smiles like he's talking to a child.

'If Bob wants to keep the business in the family and he's refused to sell for years, how did you manage to persuade him to sell now?'

Scott's eyes flare momentarily before he coughs and looks down at his plate. 'I've worked for Fletchers for ten years. Bob and I have gotten so much closer lately.'

'Right.' I wait.

He fiddles with his fork. 'I simply made him realise that I have his best interests at heart.'

Unease slips across my heart like a fat, unwelcome slug. My face must reflect my feelings because he frowns. 'I thought you'd be happy for me.'

'I am,' I say slowly.

He takes a sip of his water and studies me quizzically. 'You don't sound very positive.'

That's because I'm not. In fact, I'm suddenly getting a very bad vibe. It's nothing to do with whether or not I should be dating Scott. Why the hell is he dating me?

Of all the woman out there, why has he gone for the one with three children? I mean, he's not even interested in my boys. Not truly interested. If his reaction to my profile sheet story is anything to go by, he's not even a kid kind of guy.

More the ambitious business type – making plays and brokering deals. If I'm really honest, I think he's more suited to the city than the country. Where are his small-town spirit and family ties?

A waiter interrupts my train of thought. 'Can I take your order?'

Scott names a main and a side and I just pick something at random because although I've been looking at my menu for the last five minutes, I haven't read a word.

After that, we stay on safe topics – books and movies. Scott does most of the talking. In fact, it's a bit of a one-sided lecture. He seems to be trying to impress upon me exactly how worldly he is and how out of touch I am. Not that I challenge him. Being single and kid-free, he has a lot more time to experience 'culture' than I do. I've never been competitive by nature, so if he wants to win, he can go ahead.

By the time dessert is over, he's started rating countries around the globe. Given I've only been outside Australia twice, I predict another monologue coming my way. In three hours we seem to have exhausted almost all our conversation. I have nothing left to say to him, and if it wasn't for his extensive interest in his own experiences I'm sure we'd be struggling through awkward silences by now. Unbidden, the thought of dining with Mitch flashes through my mind. How different the experience would be – certainly no lack of conversation, no avoidance of 'kid topics', but maybe a few disagreements to spice things up. And looking at the portion sizes, Mitch would have to order at least two main meals in order to fill up. I realise I'm smiling, but not at what Scott is saying.

Damn.

A relationship with the real estate agent is definitely not going to work.

Scott picks up the bill and we leave. When we are inside the car, he starts the engine, places his hands on the steering wheel and glances slowly my way.

'So . . . would you like to prolong the evening? Maybe go back to my place for little while?'

An immediate wave of revulsion streaks through me. There is no doubt in my mind that the answer is no.

I'm ready to end this relationship, not take it to the next level.

I mean, I've just spent a whole evening in his company and I'm bored. Not only bored. I'm suspicious.

We have nothing in common, and his answer about how he persuaded Bob to sell half the business sounded shady to say the least. It's almost like he's hiding something from me.

'Scott,' I bite my lip. 'What is it that you actually see in me?'

'See in you?' he repeats with a nervous laugh. 'Is that a trick question?'

'No,' I say flatly.

He sobers. 'I think you're beautiful, intelligent and funny.'

Did he just pull that from the stock-standard rom-com response file? Not very original.

'And what about my kids?' I ask. 'Do you like my kids?'

'I think they're great,' he enthuses. 'Best-behaved boys in the world.'

I raise my eyebrows at him. '*Really?*'

'For sure.'

Yep. This guy is up to something.

A scene from the last time I was annoyed with him flashes before my eyes. Scott standing in my sitting room, going through my things without asking permission, Alice's ring box in his hand as he says, 'It's empty except for the romantic message.'

I click my fingers.

'You know Alice had an affair with Bob.'

Scott splutters.

'Don't you?' I probe more sternly and he holds up his hands.

'Okay, okay, yes. I recognised Bob's handwriting on the ring box. It didn't take long to put the rest together.'

Anger arcs through me like sparks through bushfire.

'That's how you finally got Bob to sell, isn't it? You're blackmailing him.'

'*No*,' Scott protests.

But my mind is putting the pieces together. 'Bob promised Alice's sister that he would never tell anyone about the affair, and you threatened to go public if he didn't agree to your terms.' I turn away from him and face the dashboard. 'Take me home.'

'*Grace* –'

'Start driving,' I order sharply.

With a frustrated sigh, he puts the car in gear and pulls out of the car park. As soon as he hits the main road, he starts making his case again.

'You've got it all wrong.'

'Which part?' I stare straight ahead. It's pitch black outside except for the beam from his headlights on the country road.

Scott runs a nervous hand through his slicked-back hair, messing it up. 'I'm not *blackmailing* my friend, Grace. I'm helping him get over his pain.'

I snort. Does he honestly believe I'm going to swallow such an obvious spin?

Scott rushes to explain. 'Bob is filled with remorse and guilt over what happened. He wishes there was something he could do to make amends for Alice's death. He blames himself for her murder.'

'O-kay,' I respond. This may be true, but its relevance is dubious.

Scott takes his eyes off the road momentarily to look at me. 'He said he wanted to be there when Alice told David she was leaving him, but she refused. Thought it would be better if she did it alone. She put Bob's ring on her finger and confronted David. Bob is pretty sure that's when her husband killed her. She was buried wearing that ring.'

We pull up outside Gum Leaf Grove and I get out of the car. Scott comes quickly around the vehicle and grabs me by the shoulders.

'Do you believe me, Grace?'

'Yes, but I don't see how Bob's guilt has anything to do with you and me.'

'He's all about keeping it in the family, Grace,' Scott finally blurts in frustration. 'And now he thinks he's going to get a connection to you and Alice's grandkids, the family he should have had. The family he's always wanted to secretly make amends to. It's made my buy-in even sweeter.'

I remember Bob's smile in the cafe when he told me how happy he was that Scott and I were in a relationship.

Good for Alice's grandkids to have a strong male influence in their lives. Their grandmother would have wanted that.

I put a hand to my mouth. 'Okay, so this is blackmail *and* leverage. You told him we were in a serious relationship, maybe even headed for marriage.'

I know I'm right because he's chewing on his lower lip, eyes darting, looking for an out and not finding one.

'Well, I'm sorry,' I say tightly, 'but you're going to have to tell him we broke up.'

'But –'

I start to walk away. 'I don't want to see you anymore, Scott.'

He follows me. 'But you haven't even given us a chance.'

I spin around just before reaching the porch steps, my eyes practically bulging out of their sockets. 'Why would I want to give someone who's just using me a chance?'

I'm seeing red now. Blood bubbling. Fingers tingling.

This is Jake, Take Two.

I've been taken in by a shark again.

I thought I was beyond this but it looks like my horrendously poor judgement is still alive and well. I've been suckered in by another handsome face, a few cheesy lines and some not especially good donuts.

I hate to be a cliché, but all men are liars.

'I'm not just using you,' Scott throws back at me. 'I like you.'

'Rubbish. You're half as interested in me as you are in Bob's business. I'm just a bargaining chip.'

Scott's face hardens. 'It's not like you wouldn't benefit. If we did get married . . .'

I throw back my head in a mocking laugh. 'You can't be serious. Marriage? You had no right to even suggest that to him. We've barely been on one date, and not even a good one at that.'

'Relax,' Scott spits out. 'I wasn't planning on proposing. We could have broken up any time after my deal went through –' He breaks off suddenly, realising he's gone too far.

'Thanks for showing me your true colours,' I toss at him. 'Now get off my property.'

'Grace –' Scott stops speaking as I hear a footfall behind me. He looks beyond me and scowls.

'I think the lady wants you to leave, mate,' says Mitch in a cool voice as he falls in beside me. I want to cry with relief.

'You stay out of this.' Scott stabs a finger at him. 'This is none of your business.'

'If you're upsetting her, it's my business.'

'This is a private conversation,' Scott tries again. When Mitch remains stone-faced, he turns to me. 'Grace, tell him to leave.'

I shake my head. 'I want you to leave.'

Scott's face flushes. He's looking desperate now. 'Can't you see how selfish you're being?'

'Me! Selfish?' I gasp.

'This is my entire career you're holding in your hands.'

'Only because you put it there,' I protest. 'It's not my problem, Scott. It never was.'

'Will you at least not tell Bob we're not together until –'

'Get. Out!' I point at his car. Mitch takes a step towards him and, like the cowardly loser he is, Scott hastily retreats.

'Fine, I'm going,' he says, yanking the door of his vehicle open and glaring at us both. His handsome features are contorted by malice. I can't believe I ever thought him good-looking.

'I won't forget this,' he offers as his final parting shot, then gets into his car and drives off. I watch the tail-lights disappear down my long driveway and rub the goosebumps on my arms. A breath I hadn't realised I'd been holding shudders out of me.

'Are you okay?' asks Mitch gently.

And I'm not.

I'm really not.

But all I have left is my pride, so I lift my chin and nod.

'Yep. Absolutely fine.'

Chapter 32

Subject: Re: Location of Michel Beauchene
From: Scott Hunter <Scott.Hunter@hotmail.com>
To: NineTipoffs <Tipoffs@Ninenews.com.au>

Monday 8 October 2017

Dear Channel Nine News,

My name is Scott Hunter. I'm a well-respected real estate agent in the Margaret River wine region of Western Australia. I happened to see your late news special tonight concerning the disappearance of the singer Michel Beauchene. I confess, I'm not much of a music lover and have not previously followed this man's work. However, I got very excited when I saw the footage of him in past interviews and also the re-enactment of his recent accident and professional opinions regarding what he might look like now.

I am one hundred per cent certain I know his location, and I'm fully prepared to sell my story if we can come to some sort of agreement.

Upfront, I can tell you that Michel Beauchene is not alone. He is living with a woman who has a reputation for leading people on but not following through with promises. I'm sure his fans deserve to know the truth. Please contact me ASAP. If I do not hear from you by 9 am tomorrow, I will be taking this offer to Channel Seven.

Best regards,
Scott Hunter

Chapter 33

I must look terrible when I get up the next morning, because my mum sends me straight back to bed.

'I need to take the kids to school,' I protest.

'You need to take a load off,' she says severely and pushes me back into my room. 'Mitch and I will take care of things around here.'

To be honest, I'm pretty happy to let her do so. I didn't get much sleep last night – I lay awake till 3 am systematically going through a list of self-recriminations.

You shouldn't have trusted him.

You should have seen this coming.

You're a mum with three kids.

What guy is going to come after you, just for the pleasure of taking on all that baggage?

When I decided to move to Yallingup, I foolishly thought more had changed than just my location. I'd started to believe that maybe my life didn't have to be all about the kids. Not that I begrudge them my time or my love. But it would be nice to have someone – an adult – to connect with, to share the joys and sorrows of every single day.

But it's just not possible.

If someone gets into a relationship with me, they're in a relationship with Alfie and Ryan and Charlie too. I can't separate them from my life. But I can't expect some guy who's not their father to embrace them like they're his own.

At that point my mind immediately goes to Mitch.

Wonderful, solid, dependable Mitch, who seems to have done just that.

Truth be told, he's been my rock these past couple of weeks. I couldn't have moved to Gum Leaf Grove without him.

But that's just it.

It was a couple of weeks. A couple of weeks from a guy with PTSD who needed to hide from the world and pretend to be someone else. Playing hero to a desperate mum is just his escape from everyday life.

Permanency was never his intention. He was always going to leave eventually, and now he is. By the end of the month he'll be gone.

It doesn't matter that I might have developed feelings for him. No one is going to carry my baggage long-term. I don't care what my mother says. She's got it wrong.

After all, Mitch was the one who gave me the 'woman like you' talk.

The 'you should wait' speech.

The tactful 'you've got kids so just focus on them' advice.

Wow. I'm such an idiot.

I've totally misjudged one guy and fallen in love with one I can't have.

I didn't want to hear the 'I told you so's last night, so after Scott drove off I thanked Mitch for his help and said I needed to go to bed.

'Are you sure?' he pressed me, as though he could see I was lying about being okay.

But I just nodded my head and said flippantly, 'There's nothing better for disappointment than sleeping it off.'

Well, if sleep is the cure, I didn't get enough. Not even after Mum sent me back to bed. I just lay there listening to the children's rowdy breakfast routine. The clanking of cutlery and noisy conversation – a mixture of fighting and anticipation of the day.

Around 8.15 am the house goes quiet. Mum has taken the kids to school and Mitch, no doubt, is up in the roof again. After another fifteen minutes I give up on sleep and get up to take a long shower.

The hot stream of water against my back does its bit to return the strength to my body. Scott is a manipulative prick, but at the end of the day I haven't lost anything. It's not like I was in love with the guy.

As for Mitch, he's still a good friend. Maybe we'll keep in touch. Hopefully, he'll come visit the boys every now and then after he moves on. And I'll just put this all down to a valuable lesson learned.

I take my time getting dressed and put some make-up on to hide my red-rimmed eyes. I want to show Mitch and Mum that I'm not going to let this get me down.

It's nearly ten o'clock when I go into the kitchen, but my mum and Mitch aren't there. Eventually I find them sitting out on the front porch, where the park bench has been returned to its former place of prominence. Charlie is rolling a car across the boards at their feet.

'Mummy!' he exclaims, jumping up and running over to give me a hug. His beautiful smile immediately gives me a boost.

'What have you been up to?' I ask tenderly.

'I went to school,' he says proudly.

'Did you?'

'Yep. But I didn't stay like Alfie and Ryan.' He pulls a face. 'I just went on da swing.'

'Next year,' I tell him encouragingly.

Francine and Mitch were in deep conversation but they looked up guiltily when I appeared. I know they've been talking about me. I guess I don't blame them.

'So what are you two chatting about?' I raise an eyebrow.

'Grandma says she's gonna kick Scott in the nuts,' Charlie tells me. 'Can I watch, Mummy?'

I make a choking noise before looking sternly at my mother.

'Sorry,' she blushes. 'I didn't realise he was listening.'

'I hope you don't mind.' Mitch glances at me apologetically. 'I told your mother what happened with Scott last night. Between the two of us we've managed to piece together a story that makes sense.'

'Well, if your conclusion was what Charlie said, then you're right on the money.' I give them both a slight smile. 'And you have my blessing.'

'I'm really sorry, Grace,' says my mother.

'It's not your fault.' I wave my hand. 'At the end of the day, I'm glad I had this wake-up call. I really needed it. As you once told me, Mitch,' I glance his way, 'a woman like me has got to be careful.'

He winces and stands up. 'Grace,' he begins, 'there's something I really need to tell you.'

He's still finishing the sentence when a car pulls into the driveway. He turns his head sharply then moves towards the door, but Charlie sits down on his boot and wraps his limbs around Mitch's leg. 'Don't go, Mitch,' he says.

Meanwhile, the car doors fly open and Bronwyn and Eve jump out. Eve is carrying a container of freshly baked goods and Bronwyn has four takeaway cappuccinos in a cardboard cup holder.

'Grace!' She waves and starts walking towards me. 'Sorry to intrude. Your mum told us at school drop-off that your date didn't go well. So we thought we'd come by with comfort food.'

I glare at my mother and she whispers helplessly, 'They asked about it,' as Eve and Bronwyn climb the porch steps.

Bronwyn reaches the landing first, looks up to see Mitch and abruptly stops walking. For a moment she just stares, and then her mouth drops open. Eve, who is putting her keys in her handbag, doesn't raise her eyes until she walks straight into the back of her.

'Ow! Bronwyn?'

She looks at me, my mother and Mitch. The container falls from her hands and lands on the ground with a loud *thwack*.

I jump for it. Luckily, it didn't spill open.

'Muffins!' says Charlie, and lets go of Mitch's leg to run and help me pick them up.

'Ladies, ladies.' My mother bustles to her feet, grabbing both Bronwyn and Eve by the elbows. 'Let me help you get those set up on a tray.' She literally pushes them into the house. 'Bring the muffins, Charlie.'

'Yes, Grandma.'

I hand the muffins to Charlie and he follows them into the house. I turn to Mitch. 'What was that all about?'

He scratches the back of his head. 'We'll just have to wait and see. In the meantime, I really think we should have that chat.'

I study him, loving the way he manages to look so boyishly vulnerable sometimes, despite his size.

'Okay,' I say, waiting.

'You might want to sit down.'

'Okay,' I say again and comply. He sits down next to me.

'So,' he clasps his hands between his knees and focuses on them, rather than me. 'It's hard to know where to start without sounding like a complete egotist.'

I bite my lip to stop myself from smiling. It's funny seeing him looking so bloody nervous. This is going to be good, I can feel it.

'Why don't you just start at the beginning?' I say gently.

'Yeah, good idea,' he agrees, and takes a deep, ragged breath before meeting my eyes. 'I love singing.'

'I can totally believe that,' I say encouragingly.

'It's been my biggest passion since I was a little kid. The guitar too. My instrument of choice, though I've dabbled with others.'

'Right,' I nod. 'So you've decided to make a career of it then?'

'No.' He shakes his head slowly. 'It *is* my career.'

I still.

Of course.

I shut my eyes. No one who sings and plays as well as he does could be a beginner.

Idiot!

'You let me rabbit on about the *The Voice*,' I cry. 'I was giving you music tips and you're a professional.' Now I'm leaning over my knees, covering my face. 'I'm so embarrassed. You must have laughed yourself silly all the way up to your bedroom.'

'No, I didn't laugh at you.' He shook his head. 'I thought you were really sweet.'

'Sweet, my arse,' I scoff. 'You thought I was patronising and presumptuous. My mother did too.'

'Well, kind of,' he chuckles. 'But in a sweet way.'

'Stop talking,' I groan.

'I'm trying to reassure you.'

'Shouldn't I be trying to reassure you?'

He pauses. 'Why?'

'Well, I know the next part of your story.' I sit up straight. 'You had your accident and now you've lost all confidence in yourself. Am I right?'

'You're not wrong,' he says dryly.

'You'll be okay, Mitch.' I pat his knee. 'You're still hugely talented and if you're worried about your face, don't be. To be honest, I barely notice your scar anymore. All I see is you.'

'I know,' he replies quietly. 'All you've ever seen is me.'

'Well, who else would you be?' I chuckle. 'And if you're "down on your luck",' I lift my hands into speech marks to show I'm quoting Antoine, 'well, isn't that what being an artist is all about? Suffering for your craft? I dated an actor once when I was in university.' I make a face. 'It was always feast or famine with him, and nothing in between. He'd get a gig for a couple of weeks and then go for months on end with nothing – always teetering on the edge of poverty. Of course, I don't know how he's doing now. We never kept in touch. Then again, he's no Channing Tatum.'

'Channing Tatum!' Mitch scoffs with what I hope is just a hint of jealousy. 'You like him?'

'Well, I don't know.' I shrug. 'It's not like I would ever get the chance to find out. You just don't meet people like that.'

'People like what?'

'Famous people. People who have too much money and not enough problems.'

'I wouldn't say they don't have problems,' Mitch says solemnly.

'I guess not,' I concede. 'If the tabloids are anything to go by, those people are riddled with psychological issues. I don't think any of them stay in a relationship for more than twelve months.'

'It's the fame,' Mitch tells me. 'It gets in the way, or creates an illusion. They don't know if someone is with them for their career or for them . . . until it's too late. And then when someone who really matters comes along, they're worried that in bringing them closer, the fame may destroy who that person is anyway.'

I blink. 'Wow. I think that's the most insightful thing you've ever said.'

'Thanks.'

I'm about to say something else when Bronwyn and Eve come tumbling back out onto the porch, giggling like a couple of teenage girls. Honestly, they look like they've just tossed back a couple of glasses of wine each. My mother is walking sternly behind them, carrying a plate of choc chip muffins and the coffees on a tray. Charlie must be still inside, playing.

Mum sets the tray down on the upturned wooden crate that we've been using as a makeshift coffee table. Mitch stands up, immediately looking uncomfortable. I know he just wants to get out of there, make himself scarce like he did when the removalists were around. I wish he wasn't still so self-conscious about his scar. There's really no need to be.

'Er, hi.' Bronwyn waves at him as though he's standing far away instead of right there.

'Yeah, hi,' repeats Eve, apparently too flustered to come up with her own material.

Bronwyn thrusts out her hand. 'I'm Bronwyn.'

'Lovely to meet you.' Mitch shakes her hand and she giggles.

What the? I never picked Bronwyn as someone who was shy around men. She seems to be pretty forthright when talking about her husband and Antoine.

'I'm Eve.' Eve also shakes Mitch's hand, holding onto it perhaps a little too long. Mitch looks as frightened as a guinea pig in a cage as he disengages from her grip.

'I think I might get back in that roof.' He points upwards with exaggerated firmness. 'Let you ladies have a yabber.'

'Yeah, yeah,' says Bronwyn. 'We love yabbering.'

'Yeah we do,' Eve agrees soulfully. 'It's our thing, yabbering. Do it all the time.'

'Right,' nods Mitch awkwardly.

'Honey,' my mother ushers him away from the park bench and towards the house, 'I think you'd better go in, like you said.' She smiles at Bronwyn and Eve. 'I'll leave you ladies to it. I need to go check on Charlie.'

'Byeee.' Bronwyn and Eve both wave at Mitch till he's disappeared through the front door.

I eye them both with some concern. 'Are you guys okay? If I didn't know any better, I'd say you were drunk.'

They finally take their eyes off my front door to look at me.

'We're great,' says Eve and then they both walk over and grab one of my arms each. 'How are you?'

'Fine,' I reply, a little startled.

They sit, pulling me down onto the park bench with them in one swift movement. It's a tight fit.

'That's really great,' says Eve.

'Because we think you should forget about Scott,' Bronwyn tells me firmly. 'He's old news. You've put him out with the rubbish, Grace. It's time to move on.'

'I pretty much had,' I assure them.

'There's something you've got to understand,' says Bronwyn slowly, succinctly. 'There's more fish in the sea. *Seriously, Grace*,' her nose is practically touching mine as she stares into my eyes sternly. '*More fish.*'

Chapter 34

Bronwyn and Eve stayed at my place talking crap practically till school pick-up. I just couldn't seem to get rid of them. Every time I thought the conversation was coming to a natural close, they'd strike up some other random topic. I got absolutely no work done, and I think my mum was getting pretty annoyed too, because she kept coming outside and dropping hints. Even when the internet guy showed up around twelve, they didn't make their excuses. I was dying to turn on my laptop and get online, but instead Bronwyn and Eve came inside for lunch.

'You know, something just occurred to me,' Bronwyn said when I finally walked them out to her car. 'I've got a lot of handyman stuff around my house that needs doing, too. I don't suppose Mitch –'

'Bronwyn,' Eve gasped and punched her in the arm.

'Never mind.' Bronwyn smiled sweetly and unlocked her car. 'Maybe I'll get someone else.'

'See you at school,' Eve added as they got in and drove off. I walked back into the house shaking my head. That was by far the weirdest four hours I've spent with friends in a long time.

But perhaps I needed a day with the girls after the train wreck the night before. I'm feeling a lot better now, though not one hundred per cent. I've still got to get through the next two weeks, and keep the feelings I'm developing for the man in my roof under control.

When Alfie and Ryan come home from school I welcome the chaos and noise that drown out the voices in my head. Day two has done much to solidify the school's permanence in their lives and ease any remaining doubts and fears.

As a special treat, Mitch decides to cook sausages for dinner again, lifting Ryan's mood from cloud eight to cloud nine. Alfie is dancing around the table but at one stern look from Mitch, he slips back into his chair. His bum doesn't stick for very long though, so I discipline him next, and then Mum does. After that it's back to Mitch. We seem to have an unspoken agreement to take it in turns.

When I realise what we're doing, a lump forms in my throat. We're behaving like a real family. Like this is who we are. This is what's natural. But Mum is going soon. Tomorrow morning, actually. And Mitch has set his departure date as well. Eventually, it'll be just me again.

All on my own.

This set-up we have now, it's just a temporary fantasy that I've allowed myself to get entirely too used to.

After dinner, I shower the kids, refusing help from Mum, and then put them to bed. I make myself a cup of tea and take it out onto the porch. Being the middle of October, the night air is fresh. I can smell earth and trees – the scent of spring. It's too dark to make out much more than a shadow of the vineyard, but the night sky is lit up with a thousand stars.

I return to the park bench and sit. A gentle breeze raises goosebumps on my skin. I should have grabbed a jumper, but am too lazy to go back in and get one now. Instead I sip my tea to keep me warm. The fluid is soothingly hot as it slips down my throat. After a while, I set the empty mug on the wooden crate and rub my hands across my thighs. Still cold.

The front door creaks gently and a large body cloaked in darkness steps out onto the porch.

'Mind if I join you?' It's Mitch.

I don't think it will be good for my mental health if he does, but I don't know how to refuse without being rude, so I say, 'Sure.'

He sits down beside me, our shoulders brushing as we gaze out at the vineyard we can't see.

'So, I, er . . . just wanted to finish the conversation we started earlier,' he says.

'Oh, you mean about Channing Tatum,' I say cheekily, knowing it will annoy him.

'No,' Mitch groans. 'What is it with that guy? My last girl-friend had a crush on him too.'

'Last girlfriend?' I repeat, trying not to sound too inter-ested. 'Not *current* girlfriend?'

'We broke up six months ago,' he murmurs. 'She cheated on me while I was in hospital.'

I make a face. 'Know how that feels.'

'Jake?' he enquires.

'Plus best friend,' I say bitterly. 'Plus pregnant with Charlie.'

'Bastard.'

'You know what the sad thing is?' I say angrily. 'I actually thought I'd wised up. I thought, hey, I know what to look for now. I'm not going to fall for a liar ever again. Then along comes Scott. Am I an idiot or what?'

'You're not an idiot,' Mitch says with a deep sigh. The wind picks up my hair and flutters it around my shoulders, causing a shiver to streak through me. 'But you are cold.'

He slips his arms around me and draws me onto his lap.

Whoa! I startle in surprise. 'What are you doing?'

'Keeping you warm.'

'Oh.' I hesitate, wondering if I should protest. There are other ways, much easier than this, to keep me warm. Like maybe going inside and fetching me a jumper or a blanket.

It feels too good, being cocooned in his strong arms, shielded from the wind. So I snuggle in, press my cheek on his chest and listen to his heartbeat. I haven't felt this safe since I was a kid.

'You are one of the most intelligent women I know,' Mitch murmurs against my hair. 'Strong but tender. Takes a patient heart to be a mother to three boys.'

I fiddle with the buttons of his flannelette shirt. 'You're not so bad with them yourself.'

'If I could have kids,' Mitch confides, 'I think I'd want ones like yours.'

'You can't have kids?' I'm devastated for him. He would make an amazing father.

'Sporting injury in my early teens,' he says.

'You weren't wearing a –'

'No.'

'Can you still . . .'

'Yes, I'm just shooting blanks.'

I wince. 'I'm sorry. That's terrible.'

'Not as terrible as how I've behaved towards women most of my adult life.' His voice is a deep rumble. 'My girlfriend cheated on me because I deserved it.'

'I can't believe that,' I protest, sitting up and trying to look at him. 'The Mitch I know –'

He pulls me back down. 'The Mitch you know is a changed man. Post-accident Mitch, wake-up call Mitch. I wasn't always like this, Grace.' His voice seems stern, like he's telling me to be careful.

'Does it matter?' I whisper. 'What you were like before?'

'Yes.'

'Not to me it doesn't.'

Neither of us moves and I'm beginning to think that this park bench might be one of the most romantic places on earth. I mean, if I look up . . . and I do, all I can see is stars twinkling down on us in a bright, limitless universe.

I feel Mitch's breath on my cheek before his nose brushes

it gently. I turn my head slightly so that our noses graze in the darkness. Then ever so slowly he tilts his head and our lips meet for the first time.

There's no awkwardness about it.

No false start.

It's like casually walking straight off the edge of a cliff and falling into sweet and utter oblivion.

His mouth angles over mine, his hand cupping my cheek, drawing me closer. My body moulds into his as I wind my arms around his neck, wondering why I've never done this before.

It's Mitch.

Dependable, strong, big-hearted Mitch, who has fit himself so easily into my life that I find it very hard to imagine him not in it anymore. The night covers us like a blanket and I'm not sure how long we sit there, touching and caressing each other without speaking at all. Talking would mean breaking the magic, and I don't think either of us wants it to end.

But it does.

All too abruptly.

Chapter 35

When the cameras first start flashing I don't know what's going on. It's just blinding light after blinding light, straight in my face. There's some sort of commotion happening in the front yard. I can hear voices. Rustling in the bushes. Questions thrown out of the darkness.

'Michel, would you and your girlfriend be prepared to give an on-the-spot interview?'

'What's your name, darlin'? How long have you been seeing Michel Beauchene?'

Mitch stands up. He's got me in his arms so I go up with him. He carries me straight into the house and doesn't put me down till he passes over the threshold. Then he shuts the door with a slam and locks it.

My mother comes running out of the kitchen. 'What's going on?'

'We need to call Antoine now,' Mitch barks. 'They're here.'

'Who's here?' I demand, watching the play of torchlight on the windows in our dark sitting room. 'Who are those people?'

'The media,' says Mitch darkly.

'The media?' I am unable to comprehend, but my mother does.

'I'll call Antoine,' she says, and dashes from the room.

There's a knock at our front door. 'Ignore it,' Mitch says, taking my hand and leading me into the kitchen.

'Mitch, what's going on?'

'We'll call the police as soon as your mother gets off the phone to Antoine. They'll clear them off your property.'

'But why would the media be here?' An icy hand wraps its fingers around my heart. 'You're not a criminal, are you?'

Suddenly, the reason I found him squatting in the secret room makes perfect, sinister sense. He's on the run from the law!

'Not quite.' Mitch winces and steers me to the kitchen table, where my laptop is sitting. I turned it on earlier to check my email and browse the kids' school website, which I haven't had a chance to navigate yet. He gestures for me to sit down, then pulls up the internet browser and googles the name 'Michel Beauchene', which, come to think of it, does sound disturbingly familiar.

'Mitch.' My voice is crackling with panic. 'If you don't start talking soon, I'm going to go outside and demand an explanation from them.'

'Just read,' he says and steps back. I can hear him pacing the ground behind me as I lift a trembling hand to click on the first search result.

My mother comes back in the room. 'He's on his way.'

'Right,' Mitch nods. 'I'll call the police now.'

'No,' Francine shakes her head. 'You stay with her. I'll do it.'

She backs out of the room. There's another knock at our front door, and a tapping on the window.

'Michel, Michel!' someone is shouting. 'Talk to us, please. Your fans are concerned about you.'

The page in front of me is taking a while to load, probably because it features a giant photograph. When the rectangular sections finally come together, I can see it's a photo of Mitch.

Without the scar.

To be honest, I'm not so keen on Mitch without the scar. He looks too plastic, too perfect. Like a genetically modified vegetable. Looks glossy and great on the surface, but the first bite will prove tasteless.

It's not the only photo, though. There are heaps of them.

Mitch on album covers.

Mitch in concert.

Mitch on the red carpet.

Mitch at the Opera House.

Mitch surrounded by fans.

Totally drunk.

Singing at the AFL Grand Final.

I'm starting to feel just a little bit queasy.

My Mitch isn't really my Mitch at all.

He belongs to the world.

'Grace, say something.'

'What do you want me to say?' I ask dully. 'Should I ask you for your autograph?'

'No.'

'Why?' I spin around. 'Wouldn't you give it to me?'

'Please, Grace, I know you're angry.' He looks surprisingly pale. 'I cannot tell you how truly sorry I am for not revealing this earlier. I hate that you're finding out this way.'

I stand up, shaking with rage. 'Anger doesn't even come close to what I'm feeling right now.' The words rip from my lips, raw and bloody. 'You lied to me once and I forgave you, but all along you were *still* lying to me.'

'Grace –'

'I thought you pretended you couldn't speak English because y-you didn't want to talk about y-your scar,' I stammer, the words hard to find and difficult to order in my current state. 'I-I thought it was all about PTSD and avoiding painful subjects. But that wasn't the full truth, was it? You didn't want to speak to me because you didn't want to be lying at every turn about who you really were.'

'You're right.' Mitch's face is naked guilt. 'It wasn't the full truth. But you must know I regretted my actions every day once I started getting to know you.'

The sting across my chest is as sharp as a physical gash. 'I don't care! What am I, a magnet for men who just can't tell the truth?'

'No! You didn't deserve what I did,' Mitch responds hoarsely. 'And after I realised, all I wanted to do was tell you everything. I *was* telling you.'

'Not soon enough,' I throw at him. 'What's going to happen to us now? My kids? Me? We've got the media surrounding our house! They've taken pictures of us.' I cover my mouth, tears smarting in my eyes. 'Pictures of us kissing . . .'

That beautiful moment we shared is now dust in my mouth. It's just the latest scandal in the long list of shocking incidents that make up Michel Beauchene's life – a juicy story for the masses.

He grabs me by the shoulders. 'I'll protect you.'

'Let me go.' I push him away. 'How can you protect me? You can't even protect yourself.'

'Grace, I don't want to lose you. *I love you.*'

I shake my head, backing away. Rejecting the words. 'No you don't. This is all about you.' I stab a finger at him. 'It's always been all about you.'

'Yes, yes, at first,' he agrees. 'I was just a selfish, self-pitying idiot looking for a way out. And then I met you and your kids and you didn't know that other side of me and . . . and . . .'

'You took advantage. We got used. *Again!*' I fill in for him. Tears are falling freely down my face now. My voice is struggling to work, the words coming out in halting jerks. 'Well, guess what, Mitch? Three strikes, I'm out. I'm done. I don't need this crap in my life anymore.'

'Grace, I promise you, I'll fix this.'

'You can't fix it,' I cry. 'It's not fixable.'

There's banging on our door again. Louder this time.

A voice shouts. 'Mitch, it's me! Let me in!'

Mitch goes to open the door a crack. Lights flash behind Antoine as he comes in. He has his jacket pulled over his head so his face can't be seen. Mitch quickly shuts the door behind him.

'I must say,' Antoine scolds, 'this is an outrage. They didn't even ask me my name before they started on you.' He turns a sympathetic smile on me. 'How are you holding up, madame?'

'Don't you dare!' I glare at him. 'You lied to me as well. As far as I'm concerned, you're as bad as he is.'

'My sincerest apologies, madame. We thought it best to keep you in the dark. Mitch didn't have anywhere else to go at such short notice and, if you recall, we didn't know you were coming. And when you did, we thought you were only staying a week. It was supposed to be a temporary and painless situation. You must understand.'

'When I said I was moving in, you could have told me then,' I throw at them both.

'You needed a handyman,' Mitch tries to explain. 'You were so stressed out. I wanted to wait, and it seemed safe to do so.'

'No,' I shake my head, 'I don't want to hear any more of your weak excuses. You played me for a fool. If you're going to leave with Antoine, you had best do it now. And take those bloody journalists with you.'

'If that's what you need,' says Mitch.

'That's what I need,' I reply sharply.

'Okay,' he says finally, and then adds, 'Some of the journalists will probably still stay behind, but the police will clear them off tonight. Keep the doors and windows locked and the kids home from school tomorrow. You may get some phone calls in the morning from reporters. Tell them whatever you want.'

'I intend to,' I snap.

He flinches like I've hit him, but nods solemnly. 'If you need any help, anything at all, please call me. This is my private number.'

He scribbles it on the pad beside my laptop. 'I'm going to do my best to feed the frenzy and calm them down.'

He waits.

I say nothing.

'We better go, Mitch,' Antoine says quietly.

Mitch sucks in a ragged breath. 'Okay, I'll just get my bag.'

He takes the stairs two at a time and my mother emerges from my bedroom, where we've installed a phone. I'm surprised the kids haven't woken up with all the commotion.

'The police are on their way,' she says. 'Is everything okay?'

'No.' My lips tighten.

'Bonjour, madame,' says Antoine cordially, as though he's been invited for morning tea. 'I'm Antoine Beauchene, it's a pleasure to finally meet you. So unfortunate that it's not under better circumstances.'

Flustered, my mother allows her hands to be pressed between his. Mitch comes back down the stairs, his black duffel bag tossed over his shoulder. 'Antoine can bring my guitar and other stuff to me another time,' he says. 'Tell the boys . . .'

My eyes narrow in warning.

'Tell the boys I'm sorry,' he says at last. 'Goodbye, Grace.'

'Goodbye, Mitch – *Michel*.'

Chapter 36

'I'm staying,' my mother says to me at breakfast the next morning. I open my mouth and she raises her finger. 'No buts.'

I wasn't actually going to argue. The photographs of me and Mitch kissing are already on the internet. They're not particularly good – dark, blurry and dodgy as hell. But by afternoon they've hit television screens around the world and are being discussed on peak-hour radio. I'm being painted as the love interest with questionable integrity. 'Questionable', I'm guessing, because I haven't deigned to comment on the whole debacle. Our alleged secret affair is 'oh so romantic', but was clearly kept a secret because I either have something to hide or am not willing to commit.

What a joke.

The phone rings nonstop all morning. Magazines. TV journalists. Bloggers – all wanting my version of events. But despite my threat to Mitch the night before, the last thing I want to do is talk about my gullibility.

My primary concern right now is the kids. I don't want them getting caught up in this, or, God forbid, hurt by it in some way. I keep them home from school, telling them the car won't start. But honestly, I could have said anything. They're just happy to be getting out of schoolwork – until they find out they're not allowed outside.

Ryan is outraged. 'Why not?'

'We've sprayed for snakes,' says my mother as I scramble for an excuse. Thank goodness her brain is functioning better than mine.

'Sprayed for snakes!' Alfie's face screws up in shock. 'I've never heard of that before.'

'They'll be coming out of hibernation soon,' my mother explains quickly. 'So we've sprayed the grass with a potion that will keep them asleep a bit longer.'

Ryan and Alfie's eyes are as wide as donuts. 'Will we fall asleep if we go in the grass?' they ask.

'Yep,' my grandmother nods. 'And you won't wake up till next winter.'

'Crikey!' says Alfie.

The ridiculous story seems to work, for the most part, except when I catch Ryan and Alfie trying to get Charlie to walk outside just to see if he falls asleep or not, the little ratbags! After that I let them 'unpack' the five boxes the removalists have labelled toys, even though I had intended to do it myself while they were at school so I could do some stealthy culling. Now the house is a complete mess, but I'm beyond caring.

I shouldn't turn on the television, but I do. I'm surprised by the amount of information they've managed to find on me. Old high school and university photos flash up on the screen. I wonder where they've got them from until Carrie fronts up for an interview on *Sunrise* to give 'her side'.

Typical.

'Everybody thinks Jake left Grace for me. But the truth is, he always said he felt kicked out of that marriage. She didn't love him. She had her sights set on bigger fish. And this just proves it.'

'*What?*' I swear at the television and flip the channel, but it looks like the story has hit other stations as well.

My ex-boss, Adrian, is on *The Today Show*.

'I warned Grace that it was a bad time to take leave because of the economic downturn, but she just didn't seem to care.' He rubs his chin thoughtfully. 'It was almost like she wanted to lose her job.'

Are you kidding me?

'Grace,' my mother snatches the remote from me, 'please turn that off. It's not doing you any good.' With a click, the screen turns to black. 'You need some time away from that rubbish.'

I know she's right, and I do manage a couple of not very productive hours on housework.

Mitch calls around two o'clock.

'I don't want to speak to him,' I tell my mother, so she takes the call. Despite myself, I pace in the foyer outside my bedroom until she's finished speaking.

'Well?' I demand as soon as she puts the phone down.

'He wanted to know if you were okay.'

'And did you tell him no? Ten times no!'

'Yes,' my mother says solemnly. 'He also wanted to say he was sorry. Again.'

'And did you tell him that I don't forgive him and that I hate what he has done to my family and that I wish he'd never come here and that I –' I choke on my words as the tears begin to fall again.

'He knows, darling. He knows. He's suffering as much as you are, if not more.'

'Good,' I say viciously.

'He also wanted me to tell you that he'll be doing a live interview on *The Latest* tonight. It will air at 8 pm. He's hoping he can take some of the heat off you.'

'Or put more on.' I fold my arms. Of all the prime-time variety shows, *The Latest* is my least favourite. The host, Sally Fielder, is far too simpering for a program that is supposed to be Australia's answer to *The Tonight Show*.

The kids are surprisingly good in the evening. Normally, if they've been cooped up in the house all day, they have cabin fever by five o'clock and morph into mini green hulks over dinner. I think they must sense that something is not quite right. Ryan, in particular, is wearing his 'I'm worried but trying not to be' look.

'Where's Mitch?' Alfie asks after his shower. 'Is he coming home tomorrow?'

'No, Alfie, he's not.'

'But I want him to come home.'

The statement is like a punch in the face for me, highlighting just how stupidly unguarded I've been. They've just lost their dad, and now I've put them in a situation where they stand to lose another man they care about. I have no idea how to respond. No doubt hearing the deathly silence from the bathroom, my mother comes bustling in, grabs the towel from my hands and throws it over Alfie's head.

'Time to get you nice and dry. I'm going to be doing the bedtime story tonight. What shall we have? *Winnie the Pooh* or *Peter Rabbit*?'

Alfie pulls a face. 'I don't like either of those. Can't you just make something up like you did last time?'

'*Monster Trucks in Vegas* it is,' my mother says with aplomb, and I can't help smiling a little as she leads him out of the room.

By seven-thirty, all the kids are asleep and we creep quietly into the sitting room and turn on the television to wait for Mitch's interview. We don't turn on the lights, just sit there in the dark with only the light of the TV illuminating our faces.

I clutch my hands tightly together in my lap as we wait for the earlier segments to roll through, the lighthearted nothingness of it all grating on my nerves. I can't believe how tense I am. I could be giving the interview myself.

And then Mitch walks out across the stage to the waiting armchair next to Sally's desk.

He looks different already. His hair has been cut and it's better groomed. He's wearing a dressy, fitted, dark-blue collared shirt, designer jeans and shiny black shoes that you could see your face in. The scar is the only dent in his Hollywood gloss.

'Michel,' gushes Sally. 'Thanks so much for agreeing to speak to us tonight. Everyone is so relieved at your sudden reappearance.' She stands up to kiss him before they both sit down.

'How have you been?' she coos, and then shoots him a sneaky smile. 'Or should I say *where* have you been?'

'I've been in a little town called Yallingup, located in WA,' Michel responds coolly as he gets comfortable in his chair.

'Sounds lovely, of course,' she laughs. 'But *why*?'

'After I was released from hospital, I got sick of the media hounding me in Sydney, so I left for a bit of privacy.'

Sally sits back a little, clearly registering the dig at her profession. 'Well, as you know, Michel, you and your music are much loved Australia-wide, and indeed throughout most of the world. Are you sure you didn't mistake a little concern for hounding?'

'Nope.' Mitch shakes his head. 'I was being hounded. Plain and simple.'

Sally looks squarely at the camera with mock sternness. 'So there you have it, Channel Nine. Stop pestering Michel Beauchene. He's feeling hounded.'

The studio audience laughs, and when Mitch doesn't follow suit, Sally quickly schools her expression back to sympathy.

'The truth is, Michel,' she says solemnly, 'we all know how much you've been through –' She tactlessly half gestures at his face, breaks off and then starts again. 'The car accident report was just horrifying. How is your brother?'

'He's still on the mend,' Mitch nods. 'But much better. I actually saw him today. He's been released from hospital.'

Sally gasps, either in delight or relief – I'm not sure which she's trying to fake. 'That's excellent news. I'm so glad.'

The audience claps as though a dog just jumped through a hoop.

'Well, we all know you're a very private person, Michel.' Sally clasps her hands on her desk. 'But I have to ask the question just burning on everybody's lips. Who is Grace Middleton?'

Mitch seems to be expecting this question because his expression doesn't change. 'Grace Middleton offered me a secluded place to stay in exchange for manual labour.'

Sally Fielder raises her eyebrows, the expression on her face now less sympathetic and more dubious. 'Excuse me for saying it seems improbable that all Ms Middleton would request from a two-time Grammy Award-winning artist is a spot of manual labour in exchange for board.'

'Grace doesn't follow the careers of music artists, so she didn't recognise me.'

A ripple of snorts echoes through the audience and Sally scoffs. 'Didn't recognise you! Come now, Michel, you must be joking. Are you sure she wasn't just pretending?'

Mitch maintains his calm. 'She didn't recognise me. In fact, when I played a song for her once, she told me that if I had more practice I might be able to make a career out of it.'

Sally titters. 'Very cute.'

'Actually,' Mitch is nodding slowly, 'I think she's right. I've been playing a lot of songs in a genre that I feel I've outgrown now. I'd really like to stretch my wings next year and do things a little differently. I'm hoping my fans will be on board for that. It would be great to take them on the journey with me.'

'Hmmm,' Sally says absent-mindedly, obviously thinking of her next question rather than really listening to his comment. 'That's all well and good, Michel, but it's clear that Grace Middleton has morphed from landlady to lover. We've all seen the steamy photo taken of you and her just yesterday.' To punctuate her words, the blurred atrocity pops up on screen yet again, causing me to shut my eyes before it burns my retinas. When I reopen them, Sally is doing a fanning motion with her hand against her neck. 'Care to explain, Michel? Exactly who is Grace Middleton to you?'

Mitch looks directly at the camera now. 'She is one of the most extraordinary women I've ever met. She changed my life.'

'So are you two an item now?' Sally digs again. 'Dating, wedding plans?'

'No,' says Mitch shortly.

'So the kiss –'

'Is not something I'm willing to discuss on national television,' Mitch returns sharply. 'But I will say this. Grace Middleton was caught in an unfortunate web of my making. I offer her nothing but the deepest of apologies. I want to ask the media, and all my fans, to respect her privacy as I hope they will respect mine in future weeks.'

'I'm sure fans are tweeting about it already, Michel,' Sally smirks, which sounds like a paradox if ever I heard one.

'Well, something else I'd rather they tweet about is my world tour.' Mitch's expression transforms from serious into something I've never seen on him before. His stage face, perhaps. A mix of earnestness, confidence and sparkle. 'It'll be going ahead as planned for November. I'm heading full swing into rehearsals now, and hope to see everyone in Sydney in four weeks.'

'Don't you worry, we're all extremely excited.' Sally enthuses with surprising warmth. 'Great to have you back, Michel.'

'It's good to be here.'

She turns back to the camera to announce the next segment.

After a few moments, my mother picks up the remote and kills the picture. The TV goes dead and I unclasp my hands, which I realise are more or less numb. As I flex my fingers, blood flow recommences.

'So what do you think?' my mother asks tentatively.

'I don't know.'

'You don't know what you think or you don't know whether you'll forgive him?'

'I don't know what *I'm going to do*,' I say crossly, standing up and pacing the floor. 'I feel like a prisoner in my own home. The media are not going to leave me alone until I say something, you know.'

'And whatever you say, they may spin it into the story they want anyway.'

'Exactly.' I put my hands on my hips. 'This is a nightmare.'

My mother sighs. 'Well, now you know why Mitch was so desperate to escape his own fame.'

My gaze snaps quickly to her face. 'You're not honestly trying to excuse what he did, are you?'

'No, sweetheart, I'm just trying to help you understand him. I know he's in a lot of pain right now.'

'So he should be.'

'He knows what he did was wrong. He regrets that he didn't listen to me. I told him to tell you the truth when I got here, but he was just so afraid you'd reject him for it.'

I freeze.

'Wait.' A chill makes me shiver. 'You told him to tell me the truth when you got here?'

My mother's eyes become round, like she knows she's made a mistake.

'You knew!'

'Darling, it's not like we hatched a plot between us,' my mother protests quickly. 'I recognised him. I mean, he's *Michel Beauchene*, for goodness sake.'

I take a step back. 'I can't believe you didn't tell me! You just kept it to yourself.'

'He wanted to tell you himself. I could see he was more than half in love with you and I wanted to give him that chance,' my mother tries to explain. 'And it would have been terrible coming from me.'

'You mean, more terrible than a mass media invasion?' I snap.

'Grace, he said he had it all contained and I believed him.'

'Well, clearly he didn't.' I rub a hand over my eyes. 'I can't believe you would do this to me. On top of everything else.'

My mother flinches. 'Please don't say that. Is it impossible for you to ever trust me again?'

'I don't know.' I bite my lip. 'I don't know anything anymore.'

Chapter 37

It takes a while for things to settle down but they do eventually. I think Mitch's interview did much to calm the hordes. And then I made some threats of my own, causing them to back off completely.

I caught a reporter taking photos of my children in the car park at South West Primary, two days after they went back to school.

I lost it. Bronwyn had to physically hold me back to keep me from assaulting the woman. Eve managed to get her to delete the photo and the school notified the police for me, but I still went home and called her employer.

Once I revealed I was Grace Middleton, I immediately got the attention of their highest-ranking journalist. However, I think he was disappointed with our conversation. 'If you or anyone from your network *ever* takes photos of my children again, I will sue you all the way to kingdom come and back again. And then I'll sell my own story to your competitor about how your network enjoys exploiting innocent children!'

My mother has stayed on at Gum Leaf Grove, but it's more her decision than by invitation. Our relationship is strained at best. Eventually, Rachel shows up to help mend fences, though I can't say she's all that sympathetic to my plight.

'Honestly, Grace, how could you not know you had Michel Beauchene living in your house? His disappearance is the biggest thing since Prince William got married.'

'What do I care about celebrities?' I protest. 'You know me. I don't keep up with anything. I struggle enough with my own life without keeping tabs on others.'

'Yes, I know, but it's not like you live in a bubble. You still have TV, internet and radio.'

'Well, not in those two weeks I didn't,' I try to excuse myself. 'And you know how terrible I am with names and faces.'

'That's a point.'

Rachel stays for a week, and I appreciate the support, but when she leaves Mum and I have still not reconciled.

Mitch keeps phoning, too, but I don't take the calls. My mother talks to him at least once a day, but as far as I'm concerned they've been in cahoots with each other from the start. I'm not in the least bit surprised that she's keeping him informed.

In the first week of November Mitch's world tour begins, and at last I become old news. In fact, with his trekking around the globe, there is a string of new women said to have romantic connections with him, including an American actress who attends the afterparty following his Madison Square Garden concert. I know half the stories are probably made up. However, it still gets to me as I realise what a drop of insignificance I was in Mitch's real life.

I know my friends are getting worried about me. Bronwyn and Eve come over with muffins again after Mitch touches down in England.

'We just wanted to let you know we're here for you,' Bronwyn says. 'Whatever you need.'

'I can't believe he just up and left like that.' Eve shakes her head. 'We really thought better of him, didn't we, Bron?'

'Yes,' Bronwyn sighs. 'He seemed like such a nice guy when we first met him . . . for a superstar, that is. Not in the least bit snobby.'

My eyes narrow. 'You knew who he was from the beginning too?'

'Honey, he's Michel Beauchene. Of course we knew who he was.'

I groan and stick my head between my knees. 'Am I the only idiot in this universe?'

'No, no.' Eve rubs my back. 'He is. For abandoning you the way he did.'

But he didn't abandon me. I told him to go and haven't taken any of his calls since.

The calls stop when Mitch goes on tour, though. And even though I never took any of them, I'm angry that he no longer seems to care how I'm doing.

I try to harden my heart, block my feelings. I don't want to admit the truth.

That I miss him.

I miss seeing him at breakfast in the morning.

Sharing a laugh.

Speaking my mind.

Enjoying the children together.

I don't want to admit that I fell in love with him. That I'm still in love with him. And even though I can't forgive him, I wish I could.

The next day a gardener turns up, unsolicited. He's got a trailer full of plants and starts work without even knocking on my door. I only notice him when I'm about to take the kids to school.

'Who are you?' I demand. 'And what are doing?'

He doesn't look like a reporter in disguise, but I'm not going to take any chances. The gardener raises his head and gets up off his knees as I come striding down the porch steps. 'Don't tell me I've got the wrong property. Are you Grace Middleton?'

'Yes.'

He wipes a sweaty hand across his forehead. 'Then we're fine.'

'I'm not paying you for this mess you're making.' I shake my head.

'The account's already been settled.' He smiles and returns to his work. I watch him in frustration until I see what he's doing.

Kangaroo paws on one side, four different varieties, and on the other, lilac hibiscus and cushion bush.

I cover my mouth with my hands and walk back into the house, where my mum is still trying to find Ryan's other red sock.

Mitch may have stopped calling, but he hasn't forgotten about me. He hasn't moved on. I think I would have burst into tears if Alfie hadn't yelled out, 'Found it!' and all the kids come racing into the foyer.

Somehow I manage to get them to school and drive home again, a weird feeling burgeoning in my chest. A cross between hope and caution. Do I dare forgive this man?

I pass through the rest of my morning like I'm walking through fog. I'm present, but not really there. I'm thinking about the last time I saw Mitch in the flesh, the look of pain and longing in his eyes when he cried out the words *I love you*.

Can I trust that confession?

Is it real?

After lunch, I stare into my tea, wondering if I've made the right decision to guard my heart so completely.

My mother comes quietly into the room. Charlie is playing with blocks on the floor. She pulls the cold cup of tea out of my unresisting hands and takes it to the sink before returning to the table and sitting down.

'Now I realise,' she says calmly, 'I'm not your favourite person right now. But you've either got to get over this or do something about it.'

I'm silent.

'Look.' She takes a deep breath. 'I'm sorry I didn't tell you. I'm sorry I was such a bad mother for so many years. But I'm here now. Please, I'm begging you, Grace, forgive me. Let me help you.'

I look up, my throat constricting, my eyes moistening. 'I do forgive you. I forgave you the second you said sorry. It's the trust I'm having problems with.'

'I know.' She nods sadly, her eyes as wet and glassy as mine. 'I just want you to know that I'm going to stick around as long as it takes to build that up again.' She takes my hand. 'I love you, Grace. Always and forever.'

I burst into tears. 'I love you too, Mum.'

She gets up out of her chair and walks around the table to where I'm sitting. I press my face into her stomach and she wraps her arms around me. We hold each other like we used to when I was a child, and she strokes my hair until I stop crying.

'He loves you too, you know,' she says softly. 'People make mistakes. After the nightmare you've been through these last few weeks, can't you understand how tempting it was for him to escape it for just a month or so? Imagine if being in the spotlight was your whole life. Wouldn't you cling to a lie if it gave you a lifeline? If it gave you the woman you'd fallen in love with?'

I sniff and wipe my tears. 'He's hurt me so much. And yet, the worst thing is, all I regret is never telling him that I loved him back. That I still love him.' My voice cracks. 'So very much.'

'It's not too late.' My mother kneels down beside my chair, catching both my hands between hers. 'You can still tell him. You have his number. Call him.'

'He's on tour,' I say, wiping more tears off my face. 'I'll never reach him. Not now. He's too busy.'

'Just try.'

She gets up, goes to the kitchen drawer and pulls out the notepad where Mitch scribbled his private number. I take the pad into my bedroom. I call the number and, as I suspected, it goes immediately to voicemail.

It feels surreal hearing his voice again. Deep and resonant and yet so far away.

'Hi, it's Mitch. Leave a message.'

'Er . . . hi . . . Mitch . . . It's Grace. Grace from Yallingup,' I feel compelled to add, in case he's forgotten me among the myriad of other women he's been with since then. 'I'm ringing because . . . I just needed . . . I just want to talk to you. It's not urgent. I know you're on tour right now but if you have a chance . . . it would be great if you could, er . . . call me back. Thanks. Bye.'

I come out of my bedroom and my mother is pacing in the foyer. She spins on her heel. 'So?'

'He didn't pick up.'

Her shoulders deflate, but with a smile she adds quickly, 'Don't worry. He'll call back. I know he will.'

I smile weakly. 'Sure.'

After that, I try to busy myself for the rest of the day. I go into the bathroom where Mitch started taking tiles off the wall, and viciously continue where he left off. It's not like I can stuff up demolition, and it's the perfect job for the mood I'm in. I pick the kids up from school at three, help them with their homework and make them one of their favourite dinners. Fried rice.

I try not to focus on the fact that the phone doesn't ring, though I find my feet taking me into my bedroom every hour or so, just to make sure it's not faulty.

It's a Friday night, so I let the kids stay up a little later. We make popcorn and sit down to a family screening of *Finding Dory*. Mitch still doesn't call, but I don't blame him. I do a search online and see that he has a massive concert in Singapore this evening, and the next two nights as well. It doesn't look like I'll be hearing from him anytime soon. I go to bed early but wake around five and can't get back to sleep. After half an hour of tossing and turning, I decide to get up and make myself a cup of tea.

Instead of taking it into the sitting room, I wander out onto the front porch.

I haven't sat out here since the media sprung Mitch over five weeks ago – mostly because I'm scared the paps might take a picture of me in a less-than-glamourous state, which, let's face it, is most of the time. It's been a week since I've seen a journalist, though, so I don't think it'll be an issue stepping outside in my PJs. Instead of sitting on the park bench, however, I walk down the porch steps and take a seat on the timber boards.

The early morning air is balmy. It's finally starting to warm up as we count down towards December. Dim fingers of orange light filter through the vineyard. It's not quite daytime, but the darkness is definitely receding. I can hear the chirping of insects, and a rabbit darts out and then back into the bushes. I sip my tea, trying not to think about what happened on the park bench behind me. That seems like an age ago now.

My thoughts break off as I hear a twig crack on the ground to my left.

I freeze.

'Who's there?'

Seriously, these people never give up!

I wait for another noise. Silence. Just as I'm concluding that I imagined it, there's the sound of leaves crunching underfoot. I put down my tea and get to my feet, nerve-endings splitting, hairs on my arms standing up.

'Answer me now,' I growl. 'Or so help me God I'll –'

A tall, dark figure emerges from the vines and starts walking towards me. I take a step back and am about to scream when his features become clear.

'*Mitch?*'

He looks terrible. Hair a mess. Shirt askew. He stops a few feet from me, a tentative smile softening his handsome face. 'You wanted to speak to me?'

My heart literally slams into my chest and my mouth dries up like a peach stone left in the sun. And then I run at him. Ten steps and I'm in his arms.

'What are you doing here?' I cry. 'I thought you were in the middle of your tour.'

'I am.' He winces.

'So doesn't that mean you have another concert on in Singapore tonight?'

'Yeah,' he groans. 'At 7 pm. Do you want to come? I think I can arrange tickets for you and the kids – that's plane tickets, too.'

I blink. 'Are you kidding me?'

'I wish I were.' He rubs his eyes wearily. 'But I kind of have to leave for the airport again in a couple of hours. My fans will kill me if I don't show up tonight.'

'Wait.' My head is spinning as I try to get everything straight. 'You've come here from Singapore?'

'I left as soon as last night's concert finished. Five and half hours on the plane, three hours in the car. Five hundred metres on foot. I didn't want to drive right up to the house in case you had visitors or reporters lurking.'

No wonder he's a mess. 'That's insane,' my voice shakes. 'Especially if you have to get back again by tonight.'

'Well,' he shrugs. 'You called.'

There's a pause as I search his eyes.

He hesitates. 'I'm . . . er . . . hoping it was to say you forgive me.'

'Yes.' I grab his face and pull it down to mine. 'I do.' His lips connect and mould to mine. He hikes me up his body and I wrap my legs around him. I can't believe he's here, and I never want to let him go. We kiss and kiss and kiss.

'I love you,' I whisper when our mouths finally move apart for a second. 'I've missed you so much. I'm sorry I told you to leave.'

'I deserved it.' He shakes his head. 'I should have told you the whole truth, Grace.'

'Yes, you should have,' I agree with a sigh. 'But after experiencing fame for a few weeks, I understand why you didn't.'

He nods. 'It wasn't just that. I was scared I would lose you – that you wouldn't want to be part of all my craziness. So I stalled. And in the end I lost you anyway. It was dumb. So dumb.'

'Well, we can't be smart all the time.' I roll my eyes. 'Look at me, I'm the only person in Yallingup who didn't recognise you. So embarrassing. I've been getting crap from my sister since this whole debacle started. She's dying to meet you, by the way.'

He laughs and rubs his thumb across my cheek and down my jawline. 'I've missed you so much. And the kids, too. How are they?'

'Sleeping. No one's in the hospital, so I'd say they're great.' I smile through my tears at his tenderness.

'Don't cry.' He kisses the wetness on my cheeks.

'They're happy tears,' I say. 'Shocked, dumbfounded tears.'

'Why dumbfounded?'

'I just can't believe this is happening to me. How you could possibly want me?' I smack the side of his arm.

'Ow.' He rubs it. 'What was that for?'

'Well, it's unbelievable,' I protest. 'After all those perfect actresses and models you've dated? Then there's me. I have stretch marks, you know! Varicose veins and *freckles*!'

'Hello?' He tilts his chin. 'Have you seen my scar recently? You've got nothing on me, babe.'

I shake my head. 'But you're beautiful.'

'So are you.' He tucks a strand of hair gently behind my ear. 'Utterly gorgeous. Inside and out. I'm always going to love you, Grace.'

I grin ecstatically and fling my arms around his neck. 'And I'm always going to love you.'

'What about Singapore?' he asks. 'Do you think you and the kids and even your mum will fly back with me this afternoon?'

'Are you kidding me?' I throw back my head and laugh. 'Alfie will race you to the airport.'

'Great!' His arms tighten around me. 'Because I couldn't bear another stint of separation now. I only went on tour to take the heat off you, you know. Did it work?'

'Sure.' I grin. 'If you don't count the side effects of loneliness and jealousy. What's with that woman in New York?'

Mitch's brow furrows in confusion. 'What woman?'

I'm completely satisfied with his response and stand on tiptoe to kiss him again. 'Good answer. Should I go wake up the kids?' I ask. 'Tell my mum about Singapore? Start packing?'

He nuzzles my neck, immediately causing my calf muscles to liquefy. 'No, not yet. I want to enjoy you all to myself just a little longer.'

I pull back and take his hand. 'Then let me show you the new curtains I've just put up in my bedroom. They're *amazing*.'

'Really?' He raises his eyebrows.

'Yes.' I wink. 'You have to see them.'

'I thought you'd never ask.' He kisses me again before we walk hand-in-hand up the porch steps and into the house.

Chapter 38

Heavenly Love
Music and lyrics by Michel Beauchene
Copyright 2018

I believe everything happens for a reason
Including the way I met you.
I was on the verge of destruction
Because I didn't have a clue

You're the one who made me realise
We don't suffer just for the pain
It's given to make us grow stronger
And learn to believe again

You are my heavenly love
My saving Grace
The woman who showed me
Love's true face
A selfless heart
A generous soul

The missing half
That makes me whole

I want to hold you in my arms forever
And always be by your side
Wake up to you every morning
Be the one to kiss you goodnight

May I be your companion on this journey
This strange adventure we call life
I never want to let you go
Please say you'll be my wife

You are my heavenly love
My saving Grace
The woman who showed me
Love's true face
A selfless heart
A generous soul
The missing half
That makes me whole

Let's watch the kids grow up together
Let's argue till we're blue
Let's get older holding hands
Share the dreams we pursue

You give me more joy than I could imagine
My soul is bound to yours
And if there's stormy waters
This heavenly love endures

You are my heavenly love
My saving Grace
The woman who showed me

Love's true face
A selfless heart
A generous soul
The missing half
That makes me whole

Epilogue

Two years later

So I didn't get a job in Dunsborough or Yallingup. It's kind of hard when you're the wife of a pop star. For some reason employers believe you're more of a distraction than an asset to their business. Something to do with their female employees being more interested in probing you for details about your husband than balancing their clients' books.

Not that I'm disappointed about my career prospects being chopped off at the knees. My heart was never fully in accounting anyway. Instead, I took the opportunity to go into business with my mother and finally cashed that cheque she gave me – as part of our partnership agreement. We are now joint owners of the reopened, newly renovated and much-improved Gum Leaf Grove Bed and Breakfast. Not being the sole owner means that occasionally the kids and I can take off with Mitch if he's performing somewhere we really want to see.

In general, he's not too focused on being a performer these days, though. He lost his movie deal when he refused to get plastic surgery to cover up his scars. His exploration into other areas of music has also meant he's spending more time writing songs for other artists than singing them himself. Every now and then, however, he'll wow some crowd with his talent. I never tire of seeing my husband on stage, particularly when he performs the song he wrote for me, 'Heavenly Love'.

But when he's at home, he's at home, and is just as much a part of the business as me or my mum. We've had to get a little more security, and it took the townsfolk of Yallingup a little while to get used to having a celebrity as a local, but Eve and Bronwyn soon sorted them out.

When 'Memory Lane' shut down due to a surprising lack of business, we hired Doris to help out in the mornings with breakfast and keeping the rooms clean. I think she's finding the pace a lot faster. As was my desire, we have returned the sitting room to its former glory, sourcing the exact furniture, or as close as possible from around the country. Even the curtains, which were the hardest of all to find, have been replicated – bought second-hand and cut down to the correct size, because the fabric was no longer being manufactured. The room is a special space for me, my retreat when things get too hectic. When Carmen came to visit last year for the first time, she left us with a gorgeous photo of Alice and Jake when my ex-husband was just eight years old. This resides on the fireplace mantel. The boys like having their father in the room.

Business is definitely booming. We have a roaring trade and are nearly always fully booked – mainly due to tourists hoping to catch a glimpse of the reclusive pop star in the south-west, I think. Even my sister has to give us plenty of notice if she's coming down for a holiday. She's really making good on her word and taking advantage of having family in the Margaret River wine region.

As for Scott Hunter, I found out that his tip-off was the reason Mitch got sprung. Although his deal with Bob Fletcher fell through, he used the blood money to buy a real-estate business in Perth. I hear it's about to go under due to the economic downturn and lack of sales. If I ever get a chance,

I think I might introduce him to Carrie. Those two would be a match made in heaven.

Overall, I'm so happy it hurts. I am totally and utterly in love with a man who returns that love with fullness of heart. His feelings for me are unconditional, selfless and real. My boys have a father again. His firm and loving presence is a constant in their little lives. I never tire of watching their daily interactions. Just today, Alfie had yet another accident. He jumped from the swing Mitch hung off the tree in our backyard. He was standing and swinging, of course, and jumped in high flight, rolling onto the ground.

'Where does it hurt?' asked Mitch when Alfie came running into the house, wailing like a siren at the top of his lungs.

'Here,' cried Alfie, pointing to his head. 'And here.' He pointed at his legs. 'And here and here.' He indicated his shoulders and his arms. 'And here as well.' He showed us his bum.

'Wow,' Mitch said, catching his face in his hands and tilting it back, so he could have a good look in his eyes. Alfie's pupils weren't dilated and we could tell he was suffering from shock more than anything else. 'This is really serious.'

Alfie stopped crying and went still with fear. 'It is?'

'Yeah, we're gonna have to take you to hospital right away.'

'We are?' he sniffled.

'Uh-huh.' Mitch nodded. 'I think you're gonna need a body transplant.'

'Really?' Alfie eyes widened.

'Yep.'

'Okay. Let's go.' Alfie started to head towards the car and Mitch had to quickly reach out and grab him by the arm. 'Mate, I'm kidding.'

'Oh.'

We all started laughing, including Ryan, who is starting to get what he calls the 'adult jokes'.

As they both ran off to play again, I couldn't help reflecting that that's exactly what I've had in recent times.

A body transplant.
Who would have thought that this would be me?
Grace Middleton.
Mother of three.
Owner of a bed and breakfast.
Wife of a pop star.
I mean, *seriously*.

Acknowledgements

First of all, I would like to say that it is truly a miracle that this book even exists. As a mum of four kids, two with special needs, writing a book 'on the side' is always a high-stress endeavour with many moments of self-doubt. This year came with a fresh set of surprises, making the creation of this novel even more challenging.

I must give my warmest appreciation to my parents-in-law, Steve and Shirley Papadopoulos, who literally saved my bacon in the lead-up to deadline. I wrote nearly the last quarter of the book at their home in Yallingup while they occupied my husband and kids. I was only allowed out of the study for food and wine – more of the latter than the former – before I was thrown back in with orders to keep writing, and some very strange plot line suggestions. Some of these may appear in future books but I make no promises!

Thanks especially to Steve, who answered all my real estate questions. Any mistakes made in the novel are a result of my misinterpretation, not his knowledge.

I would also like to thank my amazing critique partners, Karina Coldrick and Nicola Sheridan, who provided so much support and encouragement along the way. Nicola, thank you for still travelling all the way to Perth to meet up with me every couple of months. Having breakfast with you and discussing our latest writing crises is something I always look forward to and have come to rely on for each and every book. Karina, you really came through for me this year and I know I was frustrating you. I want to thank you for saying, 'You are overcomplicating this!' until it finally sank in and for giving me such fast feedback even when you were working under pressure yourself. You're the best!

Much gratitude to our nanny, Elysha Howlett, who took care of our four children while I wrote until she left for London early this year. I wish her all the best for her future. I must also thank our new caregiver, Rochelle Parker, who provided extra babysitting in her place when the deadline was looming very close.

As for research, I must thank my experts. Firstly, Ben Gould, vineyard owner and winemaker for Blind Corner in Wilyabrup, Margaret River, for his advice on leasing vineyards. Sue Moultan, David Moultan and Frédérique Perrin Parker, for their help translating English into colloquial French. My book sounds so much more worldly for your help – it is much appreciated!

My gratitude to Penguin Random House for publishing yet another one of my books with as much enthusiasm as ever, especially to my publisher, Beverley Cousins, who is wonderful to work with. Thank you for your enduring patience (particularly with extending deadlines) and faith in my work. Thanks also to my publicist, Jess Malpass, and the rest of the publishing team for getting behind this book and making it great.

Thanks also to my agent, Clare Forster, who always checks up on me just when I need it. Your support and advice are always so appreciated, along with your many kind words that are such excellent confidence boosters.

My love to Jacenta, my sister and my support system. You, holding me up, was all I needed to keep going. You're an amazing woman.

Thank you Todd, for your patience during the writing of another novel and for taking our children off my hands in the lead-up to submission.

As for my little 'angels', Luke, James, Beth and Michael – thank you for 'helping' Mummy finish yet another book. You are my joy, my hope and my inspiration. I love you guys so much.

Finally, I must send up a prayer to heaven, thanking Blessed Mother, Blessed Lord, all the angels and the saints. For as I said in the beginning, this book would not exist but for divine intervention. Amen.

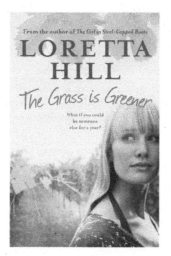

The grass always seems greener on the other side . . . until you get there.

For generations Bronwyn Eddings's family has thrived in the legal profession, and a position at their prestigious firm is hers by right. Only problem is: she does not want it.

Her best friend Claudia has always dreamed of being a lawyer, but tragedy struck and she took up the reins of her father's vineyard instead. It was supposed to be temporary . . . now there's no end in sight.

Bronwyn wants Claudia's life so badly. Claudia can't imagine anything better than Bronwyn's job. So the friends hatch a crazy plan to swap places.

Both are determined to be the person they always thought they could never be. But achieving your dreams isn't easy – and falling in love with men who oppose them is *not* a good idea . . .

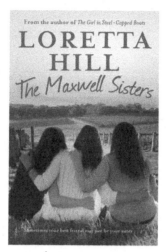

A heartwarming romantic comedy about three extraordinary women on a journey to find love and rediscover family.

All families have their problems. No more so than the Maxwells of Tawny Brooks Winery. Situated in the heart of the Margaret River wine region, this world-renowned winery was the childhood home to three sisters, Natasha, Eve and Phoebe.

Today all three women are enmeshed in their city lives and eager to forget their past – and their fractured sibling relationships. Until Phoebe decides to get married at home . . .

Now the sisters must all return to face a host of family obligations, vintage in full swing and interfering in-laws who just can't take a hint. As one romance blossoms and others fall apart, it seems they are all in need of some sisterly advice.

But old wounds cut deep. Somehow, the Maxwell sisters must find a way back to one another – or risk losing each other forever.

'Misunderstandings, secrets, revelations, romance, family drama and clever comedy ensue' *Sunshine Coast Daily*

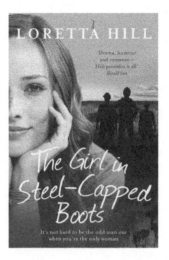

Loretta Hill's bestselling debut is a delectable story of red dust and romance, and of dreams discovered in the most unlikely places . . .

Lena Todd is a city girl who thrives on cocktails and cappuccinos. So when her boss announces he's sending her to the outback to join a construction team, her world is turned upside down.

Lena's new accommodation will be an aluminium box called a donga.

Her new social network: 350 men.

Her daily foot attire: steel-capped boots.

Unfortunately, Lena can't refuse. Mistakes in her past are choking her confidence. She needs to do something to right those wrongs and prove herself. Going into a remote community might just be the place to do that – if only tall, dark and obnoxious Dan didn't seem so determined to stand in her way . . .

'A funny, touching tale – let the escapism begin!' *Cleo*

'An A-plus debut novel' *Grazia*

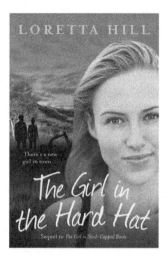

The sequel to *The Girl in Steel-Capped Boots* – another funny, deliciously romantic tale of a woman in a man's world.

To tame a bad boy you will need:
a) one hard hat
b) 350 sulky FIFO workers
c) a tropical cyclone.

Wendy Hopkins arrives in the Pilbara to search for the father who abandoned her at birth. So getting mixed up in construction site politics is not high on her to-do list.

But when she takes a job as the new safety manager at the iron ore wharf just out of town, she quickly becomes the most hated person in the area. Nicknamed 'The Sergeant', she is the butt of every joke and the prime target of notorious womaniser Gavin Jones.

Giving up is not an option, though.

For, as it turns out, only Wendy can save these workers from the coming storm, find a man who wants to stay hidden and put a bad boy firmly in his place.

'If you love a bit of rural Australian romance and drama, then this is the read for you' *New Idea*

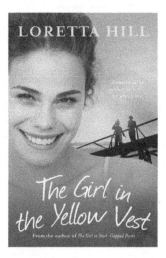

A scintillating romantic comedy, set on the beautiful Queensland coast, from the author of the bestselling *The Girl in Steel-Capped Boots* and *The Girl in the Hard Hat*.

'We can't choose who we fall in love with. It could be our best friend . . . or our worst enemy.'

Emily Woods counts cracks for a living. Concrete cracks. So when her long-term boyfriend dumps her, she decides it's time for a change of scenery. Her best friend, Will, suggests joining his construction team in Queensland. Working next door to the Great Barrier Reef seems like just the sort of adventure she needs to reboot her life . . . until she realises that Will is not the person she thought he was.

Charlotte Templeton is frustrated with the lack of respect FIFO workers have for her seaside resort. But picking a fight with their tyrannical project manager, Mark Crawford, seems to lead to more complications than resolutions. The man is too pompous, too rude, and too damned good looking.

As both women strive to protect their dreams and achieve their goals, they discover that secrets will come out, loyalty often hurts, and sometimes the perfect man is the *wrong* one.

'A real page-turner . . . Be careful though – this book is addictive and you may lose a day or two of your life' *West Australian*